john niven

straight
white male

WILLIAM HEINEMANN: LONDON

Published by William Heinemann 2013

2 4 6 8 10 9 7 5 3 1

First published in Great Britain in 2013 by
William Heinemann
Random House, 20 Vauxhall Bridge Road,
London SW1V 2SA

www.randomhouse.co.uk

Addresses for companies within The Random House Group Limited can be
found at: www.randomhouse.co.uk/offices.htm

The Random House Group Limited Reg. No. 954009

A CIP catalogue record for this book
is available from the British Library

ISBN 9780434022861 (Hardback)
ISBN 9780434022090 (Trade Paperback)

The Random House Group Limited supports the Forest Stewardship
Council® (FSC®), the leading international forest-certification organisation.
Our books carrying the FSC label are printed on FSC®-certified paper.
FSC is the only forest-certification scheme supported by the leading
environmental organisations, including Greenpeace.
Our paper procurement policy can be found
at www.randomhouse.co.uk/environment

Typeset in Perpetua by Palimpsest Book Production Limited,
Falkirk, Stirlingshire

Printed and bound in Great Britain by
Clays Ltd, St Ives PLC

For my brother, Gary Niven
(1968-2010)

If I could only be tough like him,
Then I could win,
My own, small, battle of the sexes.

                    XTC, 'Sgt. Rock (Is Going To
                                    Help Me)'

PART ONE

America

ONE

He recrossed his legs, comfortable in the club chair, and gazed out through the floor-to-ceiling windows, pretending to consider the question. From where he sat, nicely chilled by the AC, high in Century City (the shark tank of CAA just down the street), Kennedy Marr could look east and see downtown Los Angeles broiling in the July heat. 'Broiling'. *Ach – these Americans.* He'd been here eight years and he still didn't really know what 'broiling' was. Somewhere between frying and boiling? Wouldn't 'froiling' be better? Whatever – it was just after 11 a.m. and it was already *froiling.* This demented city, this insult to nature: a garden carved out of desert basin. Like maintaining a 20,000-hectare greenhouse in the Arctic. He became aware that Dr Brendle – one of this demented city's more demented creations, Kennedy thought – was looking at him expectantly, his pinched, serious face demanding an answer. Kennedy now realised he had completely forgotten what the question had been. *Not* a listener.

'Could you, ah, could you rephrase that please?' he said, smoothing down the leg of his linen suit, feeling the sluggish tug of the enormous screwdriver he'd guzzled at a bar off Santa Monica Boulevard on the way here, to fortify himself for this hellish, weekly appointment.

'Well, another way of putting it,' Brendle said, clicking his pen on and off, 'would be to ask why, as an intelligent man whose working life must involve a good degree of self-analysis, do you continue to indulge in behaviour that you know is hurtful to those around you?'

Kennedy pretended to think about this while he framed his response. What he *wanted* to say was 'Ach. Stick it up in your fucking hole.' He imagined saying it, his accent hardening, veering from the soft, southern Irish brogue he used for general American consumption – restaurants, women, chat shows – into the rougher-edged Limerick estate one he was born with. Finally Kennedy said, 'I don't see how my work is that relevant, Les. You know, "be not too hasty to trust the teachers of morality; they discourse like angels but they live like men", and all that bollocks.'

Brendle smiled. 'I see.' He made a note.

You see? You see what, you horrible fucking gobshite?

Brendle sighed, removed his glasses and rubbed his eyeballs. 'I'm perfectly aware you don't want to be here, Kennedy. I'm also aware that you, ah, preferred Dr Schlesinger.' The bastard, Kennedy noticed, even allowed himself a little smile here. 'And I'm also very conscious of Freud's maxim that there are no people more impervious to psychoanalysis than the Irish. However, as you have no choice, wouldn't it be an idea to try and obtain *something*

from the experience? To try and understand *why* you're
here? It seems to me . . .'

Kennedy drifted off. He had another meeting to go to
after this, at his manager's office. Two meetings in one day?
How on earth had he allowed this hell to be scheduled? He
looked at the wall behind Brendle, at the framed diplomas
and citations. Why *was* he here? He felt it was hard to answer
this more simply than with R. P. McMurphy's response to
the same question: *As near as I can figure out it's cause I fight
and fuck too much.*

A couple of months back, in the spring, happy hour in
the Powerhouse just off Hollywood Boulevard, a regular,
fertile hunting ground where Kennedy had been enjoying
his fifth or sixth Long Island iced tea of the evening, he'd
got talking to a woman at the bar – in her early thirties,
not unattractive, looked like she knew how to work a cock,
so to speak – and it turned out she'd vaguely heard of him.
She'd heard of one of his books and had certainly heard of
some of the movies he'd worked on.

As they tended to when you were writing a novel, one
sentence led to another and, pretty soon, Kennedy had his
hand jammed inside her blouse, her hands in his thick black
hair, in a booth in the back corner, near the pool table.
Low orange light, the Stooges on the jukebox, their teeth
mashing together and a nipple tautening pleasingly between
his thumb and index finger when he heard the words, 'HEY!
WHAT THE FUCK!' Quickly followed by 'Oh shit' from
the owner of the nipple.

And the guy – this BAW (Boyfriend, Asshole, Whatever) – wasn't bad, Kennedy had to admit later. He didn't
instantly swing a wild, badly aimed punch like so many

would have done. Or start the trash-talking, giving his opponent valuable seconds to get to their feet. No. He simply reached across the table, grabbed Kennedy by the lapels – the lapels of a very nice suit from Gieves & Hawkes of No. 1 Savile Row as a matter of fact – and tore him out of the booth. Which was when Kennedy realised exactly how very big the fellow was. He wore some sort of mechanic's outfit, with the name 'Todd' stitched above the breast pocket. This Todd held Kennedy up, Kennedy's feet cartoon bicycling in the air, and held him close to his empurpling face. And it was a useful face this, no question – latticed with acne, a broad, trenched forehead, bulbous nose dotted with broken blood vessels, but the eyes hard and clear. He started to say, *'What the fuck do you think you're . . .'* which was a mistake. Because it gave Kennedy a moment to think.

With pub fighting, as in all the creative arts, it was crucial to avoid cliché. You had to come at it from strange angles and oblique perspectives. Your opening had to be strong and unexpected. Then, scene by scene, you had to make your point quickly and get the fuck out of there. In this last respect pub fighting was very much like the bitch Kennedy had betrayed the novel for. It was like screenwriting, where economy was king. So, while Todd tore on into the words *'doing with my fucking girlfriend'*, Kennedy cast his opening sentence.

He clamped his hands around the back of the guy's head, lunged forward, and sank his teeth into the luscious strawberry of his nose.

Todd now tried to reverse his strategy – to get Kennedy the fuck off him. The two of them spun around the bar, smashing glasses, knocking into people, while the girlfriend screamed, Iggy howled '1969', and blood streamed into Kennedy's mouth. (Brief Aids fear.) Then, with a super-human roar, Todd tore Kennedy off his face and threw him across the room, sending him smashing down onto the pool table. Man, that hurt. Kennedy looked up to see – bad this, very bad – his opponent hurtling towards him, his face and shirt covered in blood. Just as Todd reached him, drawing his fist back, getting ready to pummel Kennedy into the red baize, Kennedy became aware of shapes and noises behind the guy – black outlines, the crackle and fizz of radios, and the clatter of nightsticks being drawn in a confined wooden space.

The LAPD.

'Thank you,' Kennedy said, straightening his tie, wiping blood from his mouth, as two of the cops piled onto his thrashing, screaming foe, driving him to the floor, fumbling for the plastic cuffs.

'You OK, buddy?' the third cop was asking Kennedy.

'I think so, officer,' Kennedy panted, wiping blood that the cop had clearly taken to be his own from his face.

'HEY! HEY!' from the cops on the floor as Todd bucked and kicked and raged, throwing one of them off. 'Shit. This guy. Here, get his—'

'Fuck this – CLEAR!' one of the cops shouted.

Kennedy picked up an abandoned whisky from a nearby table and drained it while he watched his opponent being tasered unconscious.

He really was, as his mother had often told him, born under a lucky star.

But not *that* lucky of course. Inevitably, boringly, there

7

were many witnesses to how the actual thing got started, to the fact that Kennedy had drunk half a dozen cocktails, that he'd been cleaning the guy's girlfriend's lungs with his tongue, that he'd nearly chewed the guy's hooter off. This being California and Kennedy being the only one in the bar with any real net worth, the lawsuits soon started flopping into the in-tray of the weary Bernie P. Wigram, Attorney-at-Law, Kennedy's lawyer.

Todd was suing Kennedy for the cost of a new nose. His girlfriend was suing Kennedy for sexual assault. Some woman was suing Kennedy for the trauma of having witnessed the fight. The fucking *bar* was suing Kennedy. He was only mildly surprised that Iggy Pop wasn't filing a suit for something like 'conducting an unlicensed fight to the soundtrack of his music'. Everyone settled in the end – the whole tab running into the low six figures – and Kennedy went to court only on the assault charge. As it was his third appearance on a public disorder indictment in less than two years (punching out a director by the pool at the London Hotel in West Hollywood, urinating in someone's garden on Fountain) the judge gave him a stark choice: court-mandated therapy or sixty days in jail. So here he was, gazing hatefully at Brendle and wishing for the umpteenth time that he'd taken the jail term. The forty-four-year-old author, the youngest writer ever to make the Booker shortlist: sitting in an office in Century City on a Monday morning listening to the wisdom and insight of a man with a lower-second-class degree from a state university.

And that crack about Dr Schlesinger . . .

Dr Nicole Schlesinger had been Brendle's predecessor

as Kennedy's court-appointed therapist. And she'd been far more agreeable. So agreeable in fact that after their third session Kennedy had taken her for drinks at the Chateau Marmont, where he'd introduced her to Brett Ratner, Angelina Jolie and the concept of double Martinis.

He hadn't even made it home that night. He fucked her in a bungalow out by the jungly pool at the Chateau.

Enter Dr Leslie Brendle. Who was now looking at him again, expecting an answer to something or other. God, he wanted a cigarette. 'Sorry?' Kennedy said.

Brendle sighed. 'Let's try something less contentious. Tell me about your weekend. What happened?'

'Oh, the usual. Nothing much.'

But stuff always happened.

Friday night had been the usual: dinner with the boys at some new restaurant a friend of a friend was opening, then on to Soho House for drinks and then home in the early hours with some actress girl who had once been in an ABC sitcom. Saturday he'd had a quiet night in. Ah, well, after a fashion . . .

Kennedy had been stretched out in bed with whisky, cigar and laptop, quietly enjoying some YouPorn footage – a lesbian duo with a brace of draught-excluder-sized dildos – when a Skype call burbled through from a girl called Megan he'd met in New York a few months back. He clicked on 'accept' and one thing led to another and pretty soon Megan was providing Kennedy with her own floor show, live from her Brooklyn apartment. He reduced the YouPorn window and was enjoying Megan's work very much – such brio! such determination! The enthusiasm of the amateur versus the slick professionalism going down next to her – when he felt his iPhone buzzing on the bed next to him: a text from PattyCakes2, Patricia, a red-headed live wire he'd met at a reading in San Francisco last year. She was replying to a message he'd sent her earlier asking 'How's tricks? What you up to?' Her reply took the form of an attached photo. Kennedy's eyes strayed from the laptop to the phone and saw that she seemed to be . . . was . . . was that an *aubergine*? He started typing an encouraging reply with his thumb, one eye still on Megan who was now – *Jesus* – and one hand languidly massaging the front of his boxer shorts. Suddenly a phone started ringing somewhere. He looked around the room, spilling whisky in the process, before he realised it was coming from the screen. Megan saying, 'Hang on, baby, I gotta take this,' and walking out of shot.

Well, fucking hell. Moving the cursor and re-enlarging the YouPorn window Kennedy found that, at some point in the last few minutes, his lesbians had been joined by a seven-foot ebony quarterback and that the business had reached a happy conclusion. Indeed it looked like someone had hosed the trio down with a water cannon directly connected to a mains supply of wallpaper paste.

Scrolling down the YouPorn menu Kennedy clicked on the words 'I'M KHLOE – PLAYING WITH MYSELF LIVE NOW!' and soon found himself having a chat with a twenty-something Midwestern girl wielding an atomic-pink vibrator.

'Hi, Jim,' she said, using the name Kennedy had given. 'What do you want me to do?'

'Well, just, I think, just use your best judgement, Khloe,' Kennedy said. And very soon, she was. *Oof.* Then his mobile was buzzing again – the 'FaceTime' app. Incoming. He clicked on it to discover that Patricia in San Fran had decided to go live. There she was – mashing two heavy breasts together, tugging on her nipples as though she were trying, urgently, to remove them and saying, 'I want you inside me.' Then another voice was saying, 'Sorry, baby, where were we?' And Kennedy realised Megan was back on Skype. He tapped the volume on the laptop down and shuttled his gaze between Khloe and Megan on the two open windows on the laptop and Patricia on the iPhone, like an air traffic controller working three screens, trying to head off impending disaster as the converging flight paths racked up above him. (He also became aware of something physical, a vaguely unpleasant sensation. It took him a moment to identify it. Rolling the pad of his thumb up and down over his erect penis he felt something, undoubtedly felt something beneath the skin. It was tiny but hard, like there was a grain of sand embedded just beneath the skin of his cock. This was new. By manoeuvring his thumb more up the side of the shaft rather than directly on top of it – almost like he was holding it while making a 'thumbs up' gesture – he found he was able to avoid direct contact with the area and continue wanking in satisfactory fashion.)

While juggling all of this Kennedy was also trying to drink and smoke a Cohiba, clearly giving the lie to the myth about the contemporary male's inability to multitask. Kennedy was multitasking like a surgeon in a busy field hospital who was studying for the Bar while talking down a fleet of hijacked 747s.

'Oh oh oh, Jesus Christ . . .' Patricia in San Francisco was moaning. (And just how long could an aubergine *take* that kind of punishment?) *'I want you to come in my fucking face,'* Megan in New York was screaming, one stockinged leg hooked over the headboard, middle and index fingers of her right hand moving like a hummingbird's wings over the tuft of her crotch.

'YOU WANT THIS TO BE YOUR COCK, DON'T YOU, JIM?' Khloe in Fuck-Knows-Where was yelling as, on all fours, she began pushing the pink monster into her rectum. (And who the fuck was Jim?)

Wearing two different headphones in each ear – one giving him Patricia from the iPhone, the other Khloe and Megan from the laptop – and responding only in generic sex-speak, avoiding using any real names, solved the problem of alerting the girls to one another's presence, but it did mean that, as matters advanced on all fronts, Kennedy was increasingly being treated to a deafening stereo barrage of what sounded like the inside of a delivery room during a fire. Panic. Confusion. Grunting and screaming. It was here, his legs juddering and shaking as the point of no return approached, that Kennedy made what would prove to be his cataclysmic mistake. Hurriedly reaching for the Kleenex he felt the headphone to the iPhone tugging loose from his right ear. Grabbing the phone and lifting it over up – he was very keen not to lose Patricia's feed at that particular moment, when she so close to proving his theory about the limited resilience of eggplant correct – he fumbled and dropped the device straight into the tumbler of iced Macallan and soda balanced on his chest. Leaping forward to try and whip it out he upended the whole glassful – sending it cascading all over the keyboard of the MacAir balanced on his stomach.

A few minutes later, as he sat there panting and blinking amid the soaked 500-thread-count sheets and the thousands of dollars' worth of ruined technology, Kennedy reflected – and he reflected ruefully. Yes, rue was definitely involved here – that he might just have avoided disaster, might just have been able to rectify the situation, had he not been ejaculating at the same time.

Man, the Internet.

In the olden days, back in wanking's Jurassic age (Kennedy often felt wanking was now at some zenith, some Renaissance peak. Technology was allowing self-abuse to enjoy its Elizabethan drama moment), grimly buck-toothed over the cracked, waxed copy of *Razzle*, of *Shaven Ravers* or *Spunk Sluts*, your only loss or damage might be the odd matted pair of pages or a written-off sock. Say what you like about having a turn at yourself back in the day, he thought – sipping philosophically on a fresh cocktail as he inspected the fizzing, sputtering ruin of the laptop, the corpse of the iPhone – it didn't set you back the sharp end of *three thousand fucking dollars*.

Why *did* he do this stuff to himself? Hormones, he supposed. The human body: why did its – frankly – limited repertoire of moves manage to fascinate him so endlessly? Like the number of symphonies you could wring from the same twelve notes. The degree to which people like Kennedy (and as a writer he had to believe people were like him. Boy, did he need to believe that) would willingly wreck their lives for a slightly different varietal of orgasm.

These were questions definitely worth pursuing.

'You're withholding,' Brendle said.

Maybe it *was* worth listening to the guy. He might be a

dull, second-rate intellect, but it was probably a very safe bet that the good doctor's evening hadn't ended with him sleeping in the spare room: his own bed, phone, laptop and dignity the smouldering victims of a hellish, continent-spanning four-way wank.

But how to tell Dr Brendle that it was not just the sexual act itself, but really just the very sharpest part of the act, the final stretch, the home run, when he was keening against himself, taut over some twenty-something with skin like a fresh page, when he could feel life itself hammering and boiling within his centre, desperate to be let loose and throw itself forward, when he was just on the verge of touching that third rail, of completion, if he could only stay there and ride the most urgent part of the thrill for as long as possible, until sweat beaded his face and his scrotum disappeared concave inside his body and his eyes narrowed and with his teeth bared and snarling, his face that of a speeding chipmunk with an overbite in a wind tunnel as he screamed unholy madness and cursed the gods and punched the headboard just to hang on, only in that part could he forget it all. Only there could he truly forget his dead and dying and the gravestone with his name being etched upon it. Only there could he forget the faces of his daughter, of his ex-wives, his mother, his sister, of those he had loved and betrayed and lost in his unquenchable desire to do just this very thing.

Saul Bellow spoke of the 'pain schedule' we must all tally towards the end of life, about that sad ledger where most of the debits are to do with love, to do with offences against love. And he had offended love. *Fuck him ragged* had Kennedy Marr offended love. He had sinned against it. He had caused pain and heartbreak and had bled trust from women, beautiful women who had once lain beneath him and looked at him with eyes that said, *'I lay it all before you. This is everything I am and I trust you with all of it.'*

Well, he had sprayed semen over all of that and gone looking for more. He thought of Millie and Robin, his ex-wife and daughter, back in England. Robin was sixteen now. He and Millie had split when she was only four – she didn't really have any concrete memories of them being together. He saw her half a dozen times a year – she'd come out for a week or two here and there. Usually a month in the summer holidays. They'd meet in London when he was over on business. They were pals. They swapped compilations over iTunes, Robin trying to get Kennedy into stuff she was listening to (what was that thing she sent the other week now? Something J? Jaysuss – the voice on that fella, curdle milk so it would) and Kennedy trying, usually with more success, to get her into the music of his youth. She played bass in a wee band. Was what they called an 'indie kid' nowadays. As he'd been himself back in the eighties. Though it wasn't routinely called that then. It was just called 'not being a dickhead'. Not being into Bon Jovi and wearing double denim. She was cute too, Robin. Super-cute. What was it Kennedy's grandfather had said, back in Limerick, all those years ago, about having daughters as opposed to sons? That was it – *'If ye have a son you only have one cock to worry about.'* You don't have to think about all the free-floating lust out there, all the other Kennedys. His daughter seemed to like him. But did she . . . was it . . . ach. *Get it away from me*, Kennedy thought. He'd do his thinking about all this when he usually did: at night, with the whisky bottle close to hand. You had to think about it – 'Existence was the job', as Bellow said.

How to tell Dr Brendle that he had mortally offended love and that he knew love would be there at the reckoning? That he would owe it the most when he needed it the most, when he had nothing left to offer? And love would not be denied its debit. So. You uncapped the whisky. You chopped the line or popped the Xanax or the Vicodin. You bent the girl over and you held on to the third rail as hard as you could for as long as you could and you did it *again and again and again.*

How to tell the good doctor all of this? Kennedy sighed. 'Ach,' he said. 'Stick it up in your fucking hole.'

TWO

'You'll have it soon, Eric. Very soon. I know we're running late on this but, as you know, Kennedy takes his responsibilities seriously. He takes every draft seriously. *Very* seriously. Even a polish. In fact, he hates the word "polish".'

Braden Childs, long-suffering manager to Kennedy Marr (and now might be a good time to clear this up: *anyone* involved with Kennedy Marr in a professional or personal capacity – from cleaners to agents to ex-wives – thoroughly deserved the prefix 'long-suffering'), listened hopefully into the silence on the other end of the receiver. Nowadays he rolled this speech out with the practised assurance of 'Hi, welcome to Burger King, may I please take your order?' Or of a seasoned escort listing her dos and don'ts. It used to *astonish* him how often he had to give it on Kennedy's behalf. Now he was just numb. Like a German soldier on retreat through the hinterlands of the Soviet Union in '44 – another day, another horror.

'He hates the word "polish", huh?' Finally. This was Eric

Joffe, producer (*Demonic Force*, *Unfaithful Memories*). 'Have you any idea how seriously fucking late we're running on this picture?'

'You're anxious, Eric,' Braden said. 'I can hear that.'

'Anxious? Braden, I passed anxious back in April. I'm into outta-my-fucking-mind now. I'm into search-and-destroy. The Writers Guild? I'm thinking about hit men. WE'RE SHOOTING IN SEPTEMBER AND THERE'S NO FUCKING SCRIPT!'

'Friday, Eric. I guarantee it.'

'Listen. If a UPS van does not roll up to my house on Friday with the script I am suing you and your client for breach. For the two-fifty I paid that Irish cocksucker on signature and for the costs and damages due to the delayed start of my shoot. You hear me? This is real. This is a real thing.'

'I hear you, Eric. Friday. I'll talk to you in the week.'

'*Friday!*'

Click.

Braden replaced the receiver and extended his middle finger to it. In truth Joffe didn't worry him too much. He was over the hill. A has-been who hadn't had a hit since forever and who was just about hanging on to a three-picture deal at Universal. He still did the whole Don Simpson/ Joel Silver shouting-swearing thing some of the old guys thought was a thing to do. He'd wanted some class lent to his piece-of-shit thriller and a polish from someone with Kennedy's reputation seemed just the ticket. He was paying half a million bucks just to have Kennedy's name somewhere on the marquee of a movie that, in all likelihood, wouldn't earn dollar one at the box office. However, eyes flicking down his call sheet for the afternoon now, Braden quickly alighted on a name that *did* worry him. Greatly.

Scott Spengler.

The last four movies Spengler had produced had grossed a combined 1.2 billion dollars *domestic*. He was smart, he was hip, he understood material and stars loved him. He didn't shout or scream. He'd just quietly make sure nothing he had any influence over ever came your way again. In a town that ran on influence – on the nod – this was power. Spengler had juice. Real juice.

'Danny,' Braden called out of the open door, 'can you get me Scott Spengler's office?' He looked at his watch. 'And find out where the fuck Kennedy is.' Outside, Danny – twenty-two, UCLA film grad – started working the phone.

Braden swung his feet up onto the desk (battered Adidas. Agents wore suits, managers wore jeans and sneakers) and started leafing through half a dozen stapled sheets of A4 paper. Kennedy's pipeline. By his elbow on the desk were some documents from the IRS and a report from Kennedy's accountant, Craig Baumgarten. (Baumgarten himself was, at that very moment, waiting in the conference room down the hall.) In Braden's head was a Rolodex of the producers, studios and publishing houses they were delinquent in delivering projects to.

The difference between a manager and an agent: managers guide and shape your whole career. Agents – in Kennedy's case Jimmy Warr over in the glass tower of ICT – simply try to generate as much work as they can. In addition to Childs & Dunn, Kennedy also had his British book agent, Connie Blatt, and Stropson & Myers, his British film and

TV agents. Add to this Craig Baumgarten at Baumgarten, Finch & Strunk (accountants) and Bernie Wigram (legal) and you had the team who guided and managed the career of Kennedy Marr. Everyone taking their piece.

'Jenny at Scott's office on two,' Danny shouted through the door. Lifting his eyes from an entry in Kennedy's pipeline for a novel called 'UNTITLED' (it nestled just below a novel called 'UNDELIVERED'), Childs picked up the phone and hit the flashing green light.

'Hi. Jenny?'

'Hi, Braden. I have Scott from Australia for you.'

'Oh, right. Sure.' The great man himself, straight on the line from the outback. He was on location, shooting a picture with Tom and Scarlett. (You soon learned this: the real players returned their calls. The wannabes fucked you around.)

'Braden.'

'Hey, Scott. Sorry I missed your call earlier. How's things going out there?'

'Fine. Look —' Another thing about true moguls: no small talk — 'Michael wants to meet with Kennedy.'

'Right.'

'He's a fan. Just wants to say hello.'

'Great.' Michael Curzon, the twenty-six-year-old lead actor in Spengler's new picture Kennedy had written. Curzon was hot. A comer. Not a true star yet.

'Jenny'll come back to you and schedule a dinner.'

'Sure. I'll check with Kennedy. I'm seeing him shortly.'

'Good. One other thing —' Crackle and static, the line cutting out for a moment. A pause. Childs could hear wind. He pictured Spengler walking around outside his undoubtedly vast trailer somewhere on the set. 'Julie signed her deal this morning.'

'I . . .' Shit. Holy fucking Christ.

'I wanted to tell you because it'll probably be in the trades by tomorrow.'

'That's . . . wow. Congratulations, Scott. That's . . . huge.'

'You can tell Kennedy. I'm sure she'll want to meet him in due course.'

'What's that mean for your budget?'

'North, pal. Hundred mil?'

Childs whistled respectfully.

'I'm figuring the studio will want to push principal photography up now. Kennedy's on schedule with the rewrite, yes?'

'Absolutely,' Childs lied.

'Good. Speak to you soon. Bye.'

'Bye, Sc—' Click.

Childs sat back and let the enormity wash over him.

Julie Teal, arguably the biggest female star under thirty, had committed to the picture. Budget, interest and expectations would all rise accordingly. The studio wanted to start shooting sooner in order to have the movie ready for the following Christmas. Where was Kennedy with the script? In fact – fuck the script, where the fuck was *Kennedy*? Another glance at his heavy IWC Chronometer – it was approaching 1 p.m. Kennedy would probably demand lunch the moment he arrived. Which would mean kissing the rest of the afternoon goodbye. 'Danny?' he called again and this time Danny appeared in the door. Slim, bearded. White shirt loose outside chinos. 'Is Craig here yet?'

'He's waiting in the conference room.'

'Thanks. Try Kennedy again.'

Childs took the pipeline statement and stacked it on top of the accountant's report and the IRS documentation. He added another pipeline statement – from Connie Blatt in London: projected European book royalties and advances for the coming year – to the pile and sat it on top of a fat file containing Kennedy's bank and credit card statements for the past twelve months.

These would form the tools of their intervention.

THREE

The interventionee stood sweltering on the corner of Robertson and Wilshire – savouring the last lungful of sweetly toxic Marlboro smoke before re-entering the building. As was his habit Kennedy had parked in the base-ment ('Sweet ride, man,' the Mexican valet kid had cooed at his growling DB9) and extinguished his cigarette before taking the elevator to the first floor, where he went out through the glass doors of reception to smoke another cigarette before resuming the elevator ride to the joyless, nicotine-less ninth-floor offices of Childs & Dunn. In retro-spect this gratuitous, deeply unnecessary cigarette (as opposed the other fifty-nine or so non-gratuitous, deeply necessary cigarettes he smoked during the course of an average day) was a mistake, because it allowed his phone to ring (his spare phone: when you drank like Kennedy did it was a good idea to always have a spare phone backed up and ready to roll) and him to answer it.

'Hello?'

'You've got to be kidding me with this, Kennedy.'

'Vicky. Hi.'

'I mean, without even telling me?'

'Ah, you'll have to be more specific, Vicky.'

Vicky Marr, formerly Lombardi, the soon-to-be second ex-Mrs Marr, twelve years his junior, a features writer who'd interviewed him, someone who'd loved him intensely, someone whom Kennedy had, in the most appalling way possible, turned into his enemy.

'You reduced the credit limit on my Amex without telling me? Have you any idea how embarrassing this is?'

'I, uh, I did what now?'

'I just had my card declined. I rang them and they told me the limit had been reduced.' The sorrow the current Mrs Marr managed to wring out of 'reduced' was impressive, Kennedy thought.

'Ah, Vicky, are you on meth or something? Think about this now. Me? Ringing American Express? Talking to some bastard, being put on hold, arranging something like this? Can't you see the *effort* that would all take?'

'Well, it did seem . . . out of character,' she allowed.

'Anyway, it's not like I *have* to let you have a card on my account. I said you could continue to use it while the divorce was finalised because –'

'Maybe because you're still feeling a little guilty about fucking my best friend *at our wedding*! Huh? Would that be it, Kennedy?'

A bad business. Yes. Unedifying.

Kennedy hadn't intended to be unfaithful at their wedding, just over two years back. Not that he'd ever *been* faithful to Vicky in any real sense anyway.

He dimly recalled a drunken grope-and-fumble session with a cloakroom girl on his first date with her, at some high-priced steakhouse on the Upper West Side. He'd left his cigarettes in his jacket, forgotten the ticket, and she'd let him into the cloakroom to look for it. She was reading English at Columbia, she was a fan, and pretty soon they were thrashing about in the sweet-smelling folds of expensive Manhattan overcoats while, sixty yards away, Vicky swilled a 200-dollar Barolo around a goldfish-bowl-sized balloon. He could still remember the texture, the firmness, of the cloakroom girl's rump through the thin cotton of her dress. Kennedy Marr would have taken two or three stabs to give you his daughter's birthday, but he could give you chapter and verse on the ass of a girl he felt up, what, three years ago? What was going on there? Maybe he needed to be in therapy. Then he remembered – he *was* in fucking therapy.

But the wedding. Simone at the wedding. In his defence (and Kennedy needed defending, oh Christ did he need that) it was very late in the day, he was fucking *punished* with booze and his own bride *had* just surprised him in their suite at the Beverly Hills Hotel with a *very* choice line of cocaine. Then stumbling along the corridor, making his way back to the Polo Lounge, and bumping into Simone who – and again the defence steps forward here, hiking its thumbs into its lapels – did look ridiculously hot that night, and they'd always had a little thing between them, and she was wrecked too, and the disabled toilet near the lobby was close to hand. A mad blur. A cord being pulled in the throes of passion. Very much the wrong cord. Then Kennedy was hearing screams and turning – light barking in his face – and there were the members of staff, expecting to find a distressed handicapped person, finding instead the author on tippy toes, his wife's friend splayed forward over the throne of the toilet, her hands clutching the extra assistance bars while Kennedy pounded her from behind. And Vicky right there in between the staff, still in her wedding dress, growling, fists balled, and the sensory realisation that it was quite something being punched in the face while your cock was still in someone's ass. The judge in the divorce case had laughed – actually laughed – when Vicky's lawyer read out the (mercifully sanitised) account of the events of their wedding night. They had been married less than nine hours. The divorce settlement was still rumbling on. Fucking California.

And Vicky was rumbling on too, the iPhone growing hot against his ear here on the sidewalk. 'And another thing – Murray will be in touch about the Warhol.' Murray Chalmers, attorney for the soon-to-be second ex-Mrs Marr.

'I bought the fucking Warhol!'

'You bought it FOR ME, KENNEDY!'

'For the house!'

'*Our* house.'

'Look, Vicky, I'm going into a meeting, OK? I'll talk to you later.'

'DON'T YOU DARE HA—'

Click. Then onto silent.

FOUR

From one circle of hell into another.

'It can't be as bad as this now,' Kennedy said, refusing to look properly at the satanic columns of figures. 'I mean, shit, are you guys fucking kidding me?'

He'd known something was up – that something had gone badly tits – when he saw the accountant guy (Craig something?) already sitting at the conference table as Braden ushered him into the room. (After the usual rituals had been adhered to, of course. After the staff had fussed over Kennedy, after someone had brought him his restorative lunchtime whisky and soda, after one of the new kids had told him he was 'like, just their *favourite* writer of all time' and so forth.)

Silence. Braden got up and said, 'Craig.'

'It is bad, yes. The IRS is very serious about these back taxes. Your spending is just, well . . . but there are things we can do. I've come up with a plan. Let me take you through it . . .' He slid a sheet of paper across the table to Kennedy. Who used it as a coaster. 'Now. Outgoings . . .'

Kennedy looked at the column of zeros, almost charging off the page, like the row of wheels on a rampaging loco-motive, while Baumgarten went through them. Maintenance payments for Vicky pending a final – and undoubtedly hefty – divorce settlement, alimony and child support for Millie and Robin back in England. (Oh, we'll get to Millie and Robin back in England soon enough. Not in daylight, mind. Later, in the Scotch-y amber of the Los Angeles twilight, when England was safely asleep. When Kennedy had a pint of liquor in him and he could almost face thinking about them.) The mortgage on the house up in the Hollywood Hills, the cars, the plane tickets, the insane restaurant tabs, the holidays, the health care, the utilities, the magazines and periodicals (he spent nearly three thousand dollars on maga-zines and periodicals in fiscal 2012? Really? Where were all the fucking things?), the charge accounts at Barney's and Saks, at Turner's liquor on Sunset, the concierge service he used, 'professional services' – the fees to lawyers, account-ants and PR people – the limo account, the maid, cleaners and gardeners, the pool guy, the fact that, on top of all this, he somehow still seemed to owe the Internal Revenue Service *ONE POINT FOUR MILLION DOLLARS*. Then, finally, Baumgarten was saying, 'And, that's about it.' It was enough. Enough? It was fucking *deranged*.

Kennedy went to speak. Braden held a finger up. Kennedy filled his mouth with Scotch instead. 'In terms of income due over the next twelve months . . .' Baumgarten began. There were several delivery fees due on the various outstanding polishes and rewrites he was working on, ranging from a couple of hundred thousand dollars to half a million when the Spengler picture commenced shooting. There was the steady, dependable flow of royalties from his six novels, similarly the trickle of residuals arriving biannually in their pale green WGA envelopes. It was a lot too. Enough every year to keep any sane man in comfort for a decade. (Was this the problem, Kennedy wondered – I'm not sane?) But clearly the debit column was outstripping the credit.

'We can't pay the IRS and have you live like you do, Kennedy. It just doesn't add up. You'll be broke by the end of the year.'

'OK,' Kennedy said, 'I'm Mr Micawber here. Right, I get it.'

'Good. I've already had Craig reduce the limits on all your ancillary cards.'

Ah. Vicky. Kennedy tried for incredulous – 'Without my fucking permission?'

'You wouldn't return my calls. This is very, very serious, Kennedy. Whichever way Craig and I slice this up we're coming up way short.'

Kennedy sighed. 'So what are you suggesting?'

'Two routes,' Braden said. The American pronunciation, rhyming with 'doubts'. 'One – we immediately make a down payment to the IRS of about two-fifty – which will just about clean out your reserve account, I'm afraid – and you follow the cuts Craig's suggesting here . . .'

Another sheet of A4 came sliding across the table. 'You sell the house, move into a condo and put the difference toward your tax bill. Should be six, seven hundred thou easy. You can cut back on your personal spending hugely.

Look at this.' He fished something, a receipt, out of a file. 'Eighteen hundred dollars for dinner at Dan Tana's? On a Tuesday night? What was the occasion?'

'It, uh. A Tuesday? Let me see . . .'

'Shit, Kennedy, there are things you can cut back on that you won't even *miss*. Here.' Another receipt came out. 'Nearly *four thousand dollars* on a pair of goddamn shoes? One of those *laces* –' Braden pointed to Kennedy's fine handmade brogues – 'probably cost more than the average pair of –'

'You want me to wear *average* shoes?' Kennedy said, flattening a hand on his chest in mock horror. Baumgarten shook his head, deeply upset to hear money being disrespected in this way.

'Do you really *need* to buy your shoes from –' Braden looked at the receipt again – 'John Lobb of Mayfair?'

'"O reason not the need",' Kennedy said. '"Our basest beggars are in the poorest thing superfluous. Allow not nature more than nature needs, Man's life is as cheap as beast's."'

'Great. Make with the Shakespeare. You'll be the best-read guy in tax jail.'

In his inside pocket Kennedy felt his phone vibrate against his heart. He ignored it. Probably Vicky. Kennedy felt like this might be an activity he would be doing much of today – ignoring his phone. He did owe his brother Patrick a call though. Would definitely have to get around to that one some time.

'Oh, lighten up,' Kennedy said. 'OK. Route one? The whole austerity thing? Not hugely feeling that. What's route two?'

'Finish the novel.'

'Ach. Fuck.'

Suddenly route one seemed hugely alluring. Kennedy saw himself staying home at nights, in his cosy little condo in, where? Silver Lake? Fucking Mount Olympus? Eating pizza from . . . Raffallo's? Sandwiches from Chick-fil-A? Driving a Hyundai. Shopping at Ralph's. (Did Ralph's do shoes?) Having 'staycations'. Deliver the novel? Contrary to what Braden – and Jimmy at ICT, and Connie in London, and every publisher they'd taken huge commencement advances from, and every interviewer he'd spoken to in the last five years – thought, Kennedy hadn't even *started* the novel. He hadn't written a word of fiction in five years. He'd been too busy making too much money as a script doctor.

An interesting and misleading term this, Kennedy thought. 'Script doctor' was used in Hollywood to mean someone brought in to fix sick, dying screenplays. In reality you often had more in common with Nazi doctors, for the process frequently involved performing unnecessary surgery on perfectly healthy patients purely to assuage the fears of panicking executives, producers or stars who all believed that one more pass, one more draft, might be the thing that put the movie 'over the line'. Who gave a fuck about paying someone like Kennedy a few hundred grand when the budget was over eighty million dollars? Other times the patient was so far gone that the term 'doctor' was woefully inadequate. 'Script executioner', 'script under-taker' would have been nearer the mark. Why had Kennedy succeeded 'out here', at this dark art, where so many novelists before him had failed? Fitzgerald, Faulkner,

Chandler had all crapped out in Hollywood. Possibly because, as Billy Wilder noted, none of them had taken it *seriously*. A small part of him was always aware of the primacy of the novel, but Kennedy took the screenplay seriously enough to keep the cheques flowing, to keep busy.

Busy inserting meaningful speeches into blockbusters for starlets who moved their lips when they read. Busy fixing the third-act problems of people who could barely write (and remember – the problems of the third act are the problems of the first). Busy jumping from rewrite to polish to dialogue pass because, of course, all this was easier (and much more remunerative) than *spreading his intestines across the page for two fucking years writing a novel*. Because the only things he wanted to write about he couldn't. He wasn't blocked so much as . . . finished. The novel? That was a man's business. He was done with it. Not that anyone knew that yet of course.

'And route three?' Kennedy said, swishing the ice in his empty glass.

'Seriously, Kennedy,' Braden said. 'Talk to Connie. There's been a huge gap. People are desperate for a new novel from you. The various delivery advances owing around the world?' He consulted another sheet of paper. 'UK, US, Germany . . . there's several hundred thousand due when you turn the book in. Delivering this one also fulfils your contract so Connie can go out and negotiate a new two-book deal. Granted the market's not what it was ten, even five, years ago, but she thinks she'd still be looking at maybe half a mil on signature.'

'Of course,' Baumgarten cut in, tapping at his calculator, 'even if you did all that, less tax and commission . . . you'd end up with about 700k in dollars.' 'Thou'. 'Grand'. 'K'. 'Bucks'. 'Benjamins'. Kennedy thought of the Eskimo, with all their words for snow. 'Which isn't going to completely solve the problem, but we'd be getting there. You'd keep your flow healthy at least.'

'Can't we, you know . . . let's just go out and get some more work?' Kennedy said hopefully. 'A few nice rewrites, a couple of dialogue polishes . . .'

'Are you kidding me?' Braden said. 'We are delinquent on about half a dozen projects right now. I had Eric Joffe on the phone earlier threatening to kill me.'

Kennedy's brow knotted. 'Who the fuck is Eric Joffe?'

'*Maximum Velocity*? *The rewrite you're doing for him?*'

'Oh yeah. Nearly there. Lick of paint. Terrible fucking title.'

'It's a small town, Kennedy. Word gets around. I cannot in good conscience go out and get you more work when we have studios and producers screaming for delivery on overdue projects.'

'"*In good conscience*"?' Kennedy repeated. 'Who the fuck have you been talking to? The Agent Santa?'

'Ha. You know, you don't have a reputation for being easy.'

'When am I not nice?'

'Don Rainer questioned a character motivation issue. You asked him what it was like living with brain cancer.'

'Well, he was —'

'You told Tony Scott, God rest his soul, to stick his notes up in his fucking hole.'

'Oh, they were completely —'

'Finish the novel, Kennedy.'

Kennedy looked at these men – these bloodsucking animals suggesting that he tear his insides apart and rearrange them on paper over the course of many hellish months, years, just for the health of his 'flow' – and made his longest speech of the meeting.

'I really need to be taken to lunch. Braden? Lunch. *Right now.*' He held his bone-dry glass upside down.

Braden Childs sighed. He sighed as he saw the rest of his day vaporising in a cloud of spirits, being borne away on the gilded wings of aperitifs, good wine and strong digestifs. The goddamned Irish. He looked at his client, sitting there in his good suit and his 4,000-dollar brogues, holding his empty glass, making a sad face. It was like Fellini presents *Angela's* fucking *Ashes*.

FIVE

Professor David Bell looked around the long conference table at the other members of the committee. There were only five of them and the meeting could easily have been held somewhere smaller. But the grand tradition of the F. W. Bingham Award demanded that things be done in a certain way. So here they were, in the grandest meeting room at Shelton's, one of the grandest, oldest gentlemen's clubs in Mayfair. Light, summery London rain patterned on the high Georgian windows behind Bell as he cleared his throat.

It had been a very long and, occasionally, very heated day. Empty bottles of mineral water and dirty coffee cups littered the table. Dozens of books were stacked high, scraps of paper and Post-it notes sticking from their pages, marking the places where champions of one writer or another had taken to quoting from their candidate's work to bolster their case. Everyone in the room had been required to read the entire oeuvre of every novelist on the longlist: some two hundred books spread across twenty-odd writers. This had been whittled down to a shortlist of five. They had come here at 9 a.m. to choose one name from that five. Now, more than thirteen hours later, with the clock hands moving past 10 p.m., they had finally accomplished their task.

Bell looked around at their tired faces, three of them smiling, two of them most definitely not smiling.

Among the smiling faces were those of Petronella Fuente, the poet and feminist critic, Marcus Finn, the noted cultural commentator, and Professor Dominic Lyons, Dean of Deeping University, the former alma mater of the late, great F. W. Bingham himself. The two unsmiling faces: Amanda Costello, the novelist and columnist, and Gregor Trencher, the academic. Bell, Lyons and Trencher had formed the core of this committee for over two decades, and they had gone through this selection process four times previously, the award only being offered every five years. The remaining three committee positions were rotated every time around, the idea being to bring in fresh blood and new perspectives.

'Well,' Professor Bell said, 'so we're all agreed then?'

Costello tutted and folded her arms tightly across her chest.

'Miss Costello,' Bell said gently, 'we have heard your views and in the end the majority has decided. I must now ask that you abide by the tradition of the committee and publicly support our statement that the decision was unanimous.'

'Yes, yes,' Amanda Costello snapped, glowering at Petronella. 'I just can't believe that you would vote for a . . . a man like that.'

'We're judging the work, surely,' Fuente replied. 'Not someone's personal life. And the novels, in my view, are magnificent.'

'May I remind you all of the terms of the award?' Trencher cut in. '*Who will be also be likely to enrich the life of the university.*' He looked around. 'As Miss Costello points out, is this man likely to do that?'

'I believe so, yes,' said Professor Lyons. 'Speaking as the only person here who will have to deal with the recipient after the award has been made I can only say that in my view he undoubtedly will. His name will be hugely appealing to both students and prospective students.'

'Ha!' Costello said. 'Enriching your funding stream and enriching the cultural and intellectual life of your university are not the same thing.'

'We cannot have one without the other.'

'His "name"?' said Trencher. 'The value of his notoriety? Why not elect some sordid little thriller writer then? Why not Stephen bloody King? As you say, this is supposed to be about the work, not someone's level of celebrity.'

'One is a direct result of the other, surely?' Fuente countered.

'Not nec—'

'Enough.' Professor Bell rapped a pen against his water glass. 'Please, ladies and gentlemen, we've heard all the arguments, we've voted, and the decision has been made. I must thank you all for the incredible hard work and dedication you've shown in doing such a thorough job. Now, if you'll excuse me, I must go and inform the recipient-elect's representatives.' He looked at his watch. 'Oh dear.' Standing up now, Bell added, 'I must also ask that everyone here maintains total secrecy as to the identity of the winner until we have definite confirmation that they will be accepting it.' He looked from face to face, lingering a little longer on Trencher and Costello. 'Now I would normally ask you all to stay for a drink; however, given the lateness of the hour, I'm sure we're all keen to get off. So thank you once again.' He went round and shook everyone's hand, happy. He felt sure it was the right decision. It wouldn't be completely straightforward, what with the fellow's ex-wife situation and all that. Still, most people were remarkably civilised about all that stuff these days, weren't they?

The moment he left the room the argument resumed.

S I X

They went to Le Orpheus in Beverly Hills, where Kennedy – a known tipper of preposterous magnitude – was greeted by the maître d' in very much the manner of a priest welcoming Christ himself to a Sunday-morning service. And the comparison was apt – for lunch was the closest thing Kenendy Marr had to church: a sacred institution, with its own arcane rituals that had to be observed.

First, Braden knew, he liked to have the initial aperitif at the bar where, holding the Martini glass (gin, dry as tinder, two olives) tenderly by the stem or rim, so as not to warm its precious quicksilver by even a degree, he could survey the congregation, the swishing asses and crackling thighs of rich women walking in clinging garments. The trip to the bar was essential, Kennedy felt, because it lent an extra layer to the performance, it gave it its opening act.

In act two, and Kennedy knew this as much as anyone, the hero had to choose to walk into a new and unfamiliar world. Luke had to *choose* to get on the *Millennium Falcon*. So, towards the end of that first bracingly strong Martini, by which point Braden would already be feeling dots of sweat beading his forehead, his brain shimmering, Kennedy would raise a finger to the waiter and they would be shown to their table. Arriving at the table it was important that Kennedy place himself at the chair that offered the best field of fire upon the room. Maximum defilade. Braden had often watched his client performing complex calculations in his head, doing proper *A Beautiful Mind* stuff, diagrams and equations seeming to appear in the air around him as they crossed the floors of busy restaurants, his pace quickening as he calculated approach routes and vectors, Kennedy slipping past waiters and around chairs like a greased quarterback in order to slink successfully into his desired seat. One time he'd seen Kennedy almost come to blows with a major movie star as they both performed the same manoeuvre, coming round the circular table at the same time, each of them simultaneously descending the right and left buttock respectively towards the alpha chair.

Once successfully seated, the gospel of the menu in one hand, his head devoutly inclined as he listened to the waiter perform the incantation of the specials, Kennedy would receive the second Martini he had ordered as they left the bar, to be sipped during the trying process of selection and ordering. Always three courses. Different wines with appetiser and entrée. Dessert wine with pudding. Then cognac – or grappa, or amaretto or whatever – with the chain of dark, bitter espressos.

Braden's corporate Amex panged like a cirrhotic liver every time a lunch with Kennedy loomed.

Here today, beneath the high, frescoed ceiling, amid the ping and scrape of crystal and steel, Kennedy ordered razor clams to start followed by the calf's liver medium rare. A bottle of Chablis would accompany the shellfish and a Pinot to go with the main. Braden went with the soup and the chopped salad – standard Hollywood executive fare. He ate like this every day and hit the gym four times a week. Kennedy, needless to say, did not. It astonished Braden that the man never seemed to gain a pound.

Kennedy flattened a thick linen napkin across his thighs and leaned back with his Martini, sighing happily as he gazed across the restaurant. 'Mary mother of God riding a dildo,' he said. 'Would you look at that over there?'

'Christ, Kennedy,' Braden said. 'For a man with a million-dollar-plus tax bill you don't look worried.'

'Ach. It'll all work out. I mean, would you look over there for Chrissakes? What's the matter with you? What an ass. *What a fucking ass*, Braden.'

Braden sighed. 'Anyway, I do have some good news. I couldn't tell you in front of Craig. I spoke with Scott Spengler this morning.' Braden paused dramatically, clasping his hands together on the tablecloth. 'Julie Teal signed her deal.'

Kennedy made a face. 'Horrible rhyme that, pal. Far too on the nose. It'd work for a limerick, or a nursery rhyme like enough: "*Julie Teal, signed her deal, her hole was filled with dough. But the result was poor, this worthless whoor, blew the whole lot on blow.*"'

'This is good news. Julie's huge. You could use your name on a hit. No way they won't greenlight the picture now.

And that's unfair – she's been through rehab. She's over the whole coke thing.'

'So pert. What are you thinking on the nipples? With that complexion? I'd imagine dark, chocolatey.' Kennedy was still enraptured, gazing across the restaurant.

'Oh, and we're scheduling a dinner with you and Michael Curzon.'

That did it. Kennedy's head swivelled round. 'Eh?'

'Apparently he's a fan. Wants to meet you.'

'Get fucked. Are you kidding me?' Kennedy felt his phone buzz against his heart again.

'Kennedy, they are paying you nearly a million dollars to write this screenplay. The lead actor wants to break bread. This is a must-do, buddy.'

'I don't want to live this life,' Kennedy said.

'Ninety-eight per cent of the population would kill to have your fucking life,' Braden said.

'I'm in hell.'

'For Christ's sake. It's just dinner.'

'"*Just dinner*"? Oh, you're a one, aren't you? You blood-sucking fuck. "Just dinner"? It'll be two hours of listening to some – how old is this cunt?'

'He's twenty-six.'

'Jesus. Oh Jesus fuck. Oh fuck me. Two hours of listening to some twenty-six-year-old spunker talking about how they "see" the character? About "motivation" and "back-story"? I'd sooner suck off a fucking pig.'

'Apparently he's quite bright.'

'Really? "Quite bright"? Wow. You know, Braden, it's always been my goal, my aim in life you might say, to one day, if I work hard enough, read enough books and make enough money, to maybe, one day, attain the lofty position of being able to sit down to dinner with "quite bright" twenty-six-year-old actors on a regular basis. That's the Algonquin I was always shooting for. "Quite bright" no less. I fucking hated quite bright twenty-six-year-olds when I *was* one.'

When Kennedy Marr was twenty-six, nearly two decades ago, John Major running the country and Tony Blair on the rise, while he wrote what would eventually become his debut novel *Unthinkable* in a tiny two-room attic flat in Maida Vale, with Millie padding around, getting broody, happy. Still working. Still supporting them both.

'Look,' Braden said, 'don't fuck this up, huh? Just make nice like I know you can. Make with the anecdotes and the Irish charm.'

'I. Don't. Want. To. Live. This. Life,' Kennedy said, tapping the table with the blade of his knife on each word.

But his face was already brightening at the approaching squad of waiters, at the words, 'Your clams, sir.' At the sight of the bottle of Chablis being held out for his approval just as he drained the last of his Martini, iced water from the bucket beading and loosening the label. At the sight of the almost pornographically beautiful girl holding the bottle. 'Great service here,' Kennedy said, leaning forward to Braden, grinning wolfishly as he tucked his napkin in. 'Great fucking service.' The phone began buzzing against his heart again. He ignored it, started running a fork down the pearly inside of the first long, thin razor clam. How did you turn off the vibrate thing? It occurred to him that if he did that he might as well turn the bloody thing off altogether. But that could mean missing a genuinely

interesting call, maybe from Monica out at Venice Beach.
Or Katrina over in the Valley. Or Pam up on Coldwater
Canyon.

Kennedy's disdainful crack about the pat obviousness of
the 'Teal/Deal' rhyme had been from the heart. For
Kennedy Marr had once written poetry. He knew the
seductiveness of the late-night couplet, wrought in whisky
by a cold windowpane overlooking wet streets. He had
felt – rarely, but distinctly – the pleasure of a finely tuned
stanza, a latent universe in a few lines, its DNA tightly
coiled and encoded, waiting to be unpicked so that meaning
could multiply to infinity. He still dabbled here and there
but he . . . he just didn't have the balls for it any more.
He wasn't hard enough. To write poetry now, today? In the
midst of the Internet and pay-per-view and the runway
expansions at Heathrow and LAX and the shock jocks and
the reality shows and the rollover jackpot? To write *poetry*
in the middle of all that? You had to be fucking hard to do
that. Kennedy wasn't even hard enough to take on the novel
any more, where a different kind of hardness was required.
You had to be a punchbag: tough enough to take whatever
the bastard threw at you for months and years. Stamina.
You had to go into the ring and still be standing at the end
of the last round. You didn't ever knock the novel out.
You won on points – if you were lucky. And here was
Kennedy – the arteries of his talent furred and ragged from
a decade-plus of chateaubriand and Pinot, from talk shows
(*'Yes, Jane/Mike, it is very different from the last book . . .'*), and
seven-figure advances and book tours (*'Yes, guy from Kiel/
Turin/Idaho, it is very different from the last book . . .'*), from
the thousands of hours spent in conference rooms,

restaurants and offices listening to *arse*. Listening to – 'I think he needs to be more likeable.'

Listening to – 'We need more of an arc here.'

To – 'Where's the conflict?'

To – 'Steven's availability looks good.'

There was nothing quite like Hollywood. If you wanted a new car designed the chances were you'd go out and find a guy who'd built a few decent cars in his time and leave him to it. What you probably wouldn't do was get him to design the car and then have his blueprints critiqued and torn to pieces for many months by a bunch of people who had never built or designed a car in their lives. Who barely knew how to *drive* a car.

You might as well, Kennedy often reflected in these endless meetings, have a team of eunuchs design a fucking dildo.

SEVEN

Giving up on the phone for now, Patrick Marr finished typing a brief email to his elder brother, hit 'Send', and looked out the window of his tiny office – a glorified cupboard under the stairs really, he'd had to give up the office upstairs when their third child was born two years back – at the wind and rain blowing across the garden. Had it been daylight the Irish Sea would have been visible in the distance, maybe the speck of a ferry churning towards Dublin, just north of here. He'd have seen his garden littered with toys: a tattered football net, a red-and-yellow plastic slide, the half-inflated paddling pool optimistically put out when they had a couple of fine days back in late May. Now, of course, filled with rainwater. The Irish summer. He heard a door closing down the hallway and went towards it.

Dr Bourke was coming up the hall, out of what used to be the dining room and was now a temporary bedroom, a sickroom. 'And how is she, Doctor?' Patrick asked.

'Let's talk in the kitchen now, Patrick,' Bourke said.

A few minutes later Patrick was waving goodbye to the doctor's car as his wife Anne came down the stairs with a basket of washing. He closed the door and turned to her.

'Looks like we'll be getting our dining room back soon enough,' he said.

'Oh, darling,' Anne said. She put the basket down and embraced her husband. 'Did you get hold of Kennedy yet?' She felt him shake his head against her neck. 'Oh, that bloody eejit,' Anne said.

'I just sent him an email,' Patrick said. 'I'm sure we'll hear from him in the morning.'

'Aye, and he'll be pissed no doubt,' Anne said. Not Kennedy's biggest fan. (The wives of his friends and family were rarely huge fans of Kennedy's. Unless he was having an affair with them of course.)

'No doubt,' Patrick said, managing a smile. In the living room behind him was a photograph of his brother. He was with the actor Sean Penn. They were both pissed.

From the former dining room came the sound of a bell ringing. The wee hand-held school bell he'd picked up for her at that car boot sale down in Wicklow the other month. 'Coming, Ma,' Patrick sighed, heading towards the noise at the end of the hall. *Don't tell her any more than you have to*, Bourke had said. *No need to frighten her.*

Anne watched her husband walking away and thought, as she often did: *You're too good, Patrick Marr. You're just too good so you are.*

EIGHT

A few crumbs of tarte au citron on the plate and a twenty-three-dollar glass of Sauternes in his hand, the liquid heavy as cough syrup, the author feeling expansive now in the four-o'clock sunlight slanting across the restaurant, the place having taken on the underwater tint of afternoon drinking. It was a submarine, a diving bell. Kennedy sat alone at the table. Braden was outside taking a call – his phone had started going crazy towards the end of the meal. As had Kennedy's, which remained staunchly ignored in the inside pocket of his suit. But then a two-hour lunch was SOP for the author. For a Hollywood manager it constituted an unauthorised vacation. Kennedy raised his glass to nobody and murmured, 'To absent friends. Fuck them.' He drained it. Called for brandy. *Sure and it's far from how you were raised*, as his mother would have said.

Limerick in the seventies and eighties. A rough old time and place. The town was far enough south to be considered countrified, rural, but it was still a hard part of the world, with enough knackers, enough desperate people. Way before the 'Celtic Tiger' and all of that bollocks. Kennedy had been desperate too right enough, not desperate enough to sell drugs or run into the Credit Union with a shotgun, or drive a car through the windows of the petrol station, like many of his school friends had, but desperate enough to read enough books to get him out of there. Not up to Dublin, to Trinity, the obvious choice. Kennedy needed to put water between him and his family, his mammy, da, Patrick and Geraldine. (Wee Gerry – the middle child. Already doomed.) He loved them, but by the time he was eighteen they felt like manacles made of human flesh. Like a . . . a what, a something of personal albatrosses clustered around the TV every night. (*Must look up the collective noun for albatrosses*, he thought.) He needed to feel a different land mass beneath his feet.

'*I will not serve that in which I no longer believe, whether it calls itself my home, my fatherland, or my church: and I will try to express myself in some mode of life or art as freely as I can, and as wholly as I can, using for my defence the only arms I allow myself to use – silence, exile, and cunning.*'

Well, it hadn't been as grand as all that of course, as old James J. It just felt wrong where he was. It had as far back as he could remember. His bedroom in the grim pebble-dashed house, the orange street light that burned outside its window. Someone had fucked up. He wasn't meant to be here. It all felt wrong. Perhaps somewhere else would feel right. So, across the Irish Sea to Glasgow, to read English in the Gothic quads of the university, in the city's leafy West End. It was 1987.

A woman – attractive, mid-thirties – sashayed by and smiled at Kennedy. He smiled back and sang to himself – *'Yes, I feel the pull, but a major part of me is unavailable, what I had I gave, resist the urge to save me, I will not be saved.'*

He looked across the room to see Braden coming back to the table, cradling his cellphone. 'It's *Variety*,' he whispered, one hand covering the mouthpiece. 'Word's out about Julie, they want a quote.'

'Oh for fuck's sake . . .'

'Spengler's office says it's fine, but, Kennedy, keep it simple and bland, huh? Just "what an honour it is be working with her, what a fine talent she is" kind of thing, OK?'

'"Simple and bland." You know me well,' Kennedy said, taking the BlackBerry. 'Hello?'

'Kennedy? Hi. Nathan Castle at *Variety*. So. Wow. Julie Teal. How's it feel to have her on board?'

'It's grand, Nathan. She's a fine, fine actor.' Kennedy mimed putting a gun under his chin to Braden. 'I'm really looking forward to, ah, to seeing what she does with the role.' He mimed pulling the trigger, throwing his head back, as the waiter arrived with the Hennessy XO.

'Have you guys actually met yet?'

'Not yet, no. But I've only heard good things about Julie.' *I've only heard she's a coke-addled whoor with the IQ of a teacup who, on her way up, would have gang-banged a dumpster full of tramps to get a non-speaking walk-on in a tampon commercial.*

'With talent like Julie and Michael on board the budget on the movie must be getting high. Are you feeling a lot of pressure?'

'Ach, I don't get into all that, Nathan. It's not really my concern whether the budget's five million or a hundred million. The job's the same every time out – to deliver the actors and director the best script you possibly can.' Braden nodded, pleased, thumb up as he stirred his coffee. Kennedy mimed sucking off a huge cock.

'Great. Great,' Castle said. 'You're known as a writer who is very, ah, protective of their work.'

'Mmmm,' sipping that cognac now.

'Protective' no less. Kennedy felt that when someone with twenty-odd years of experience of crafting narratives spent months redrafting and finessing a script, then the result *might just* be preferable to whatever mad bunch of balls a twenty-something actor who had barely finished high school came up with on the spot. That got you labelled 'protective'. This town. This fucking town.

'Given Julie's recent, ah, controversial comments about the actor's role in the creative process,' Castle went on, 'do you anticipate a lot of rewriting to accommodate her thoughts?'

'Ah, what did she say?'

'Hang on.' Ruffling of paper on the other end. Kennedy pictured Castle in his cubbyhole over at the *Variety* offices on Wilshire. 'She said . . . ah, right, "*Obviously I think writers are really important, but actors often don't get the credit they deserve in bringing a character to life. Whoever's written the screenplay, I always end up writing a lot of my own dialogue.*"'

Kennedy felt his hand tightening around the glass. 'She fucking sai—' Red alert from Braden: shaking his head, miming slicing his throat, hanging up. Kennedy held the phone away from him, downed the whole glass in one. 'Well,' Kennedy said, and it cost him a lot, 'I don't think there's a writer I know who wouldn't welcome whatever . . . whatever help a talented actor can bring to their work.' *This fucking talentless slut.*

'OK. Great. Well, good luck. Scott Spengler, Julie Teal, Michael Curzon, Kennedy Marr . . . it looks like the fates are really aligning for this one, huh?'

'Ach – I don't believe in fate, Nathan. But let's just say we've certainly got a lot of talent clustering on this picture. Myself excepted of course,' he laughed.

'Great. Thanks, Kennedy. Thanks for your time.'

'Oh, it's grand. No problem.' Click. Kennedy thumbed the BlackBerry off, tossed it onto the table.

'Well done,' Braden said.

'Clustering?' Kennedy said. 'Cluster fuck more like. That wee cow . . .'

Braden smiled and laid his corporate American Express card on top of the check, the paleness of its green reminding Kennedy of the shallow bays of the Irish Sea in summer. 'Talent is as talent does, Kennedy.'

'Ach, fuck. Anyway – thanks for lunch.'

'My pleasure. But listen, the whole IRS thing? They're not gonna go away. The budgeting? Delivering the novel? It's all real. This is a real thing. You need to think about it. Seriously.'

'Yeah, yeah.'

Finally, out on the sidewalk, capping off his lunch with deep draughts of Marlboro while they waited for the valets to bring their cars around, he slipped his phone out. Five missed calls: two from Connie in London, one from someone called 'Saskia' (who?) and two from his brother Patrick in Dublin. Connie's was probably just an agent call (*'Hi, darling, just checking in. Everything well?'* Just checking in? Kennedy often thought. I'm not a fucking hotel), but Patrick? He thought for a moment and then checked the date on the crystal bubble of his Rolex. The 1st. Oh yeah. There you go. That meant he'd have to speak to his mum too. He'd call them later. Kennedy had to be *really* drunk to talk to his family, properly Scotch-for-blood drunk. Italicised drunk. Not this comedy white-wine drunk, this drunk lite.

NINE

While Kennedy Marr had been going about resolutely not believing in fate in a restaurant in Beverly Hills, three thousand miles away it had been nearly midnight in southwest London, when fate busily made a telephone ring.

'Oh for fuck's sake,' said Connie Blatt, who had only just let the manuscript she'd been reading in bed fall onto her chest as she drifted off into a light doze. Her iPhone trilled and buzzed from the dresser by the window. She thought she'd turned it off. Connie scowled in its direction. However, once you had teenage children and elderly parents, ignoring a late-night call was impossible. So Connie flounced out of bed and across the large cold room. (A product of the English upper classes – of grand country houses and boarding schools – Connie very much believed in keeping rooms unseasonably cold all year round.) Outside the windows of the Victorian villa a wet summer wind slapped at the trees on Clapham Common. Connie snatched up the ringing phone and her heart rate spiked ever so slightly at the words 'NUMBER BLOCKED' on the screen. The police? An A&E department? She slid the bar across the screen and said, 'Hello?'

'Miss Blatt?'

'Yes?'

'I do apologise for the lateness of the hour. This is Professor David Bell. I believe we met once before. A party at the RSA?' The voice was English, upper class, moneyed. Very much like Connie's own. He sounded old though, this fellow.

'I . . . yes. Sorry, what time is it?'

'It's almost midnight. I really do apologise. It's just . . . it was important to let you know as soon as the committee had reached their decision.'

What committee? What decision? *Who the fuck was this man?* 'I see,' Connie said, not seeing anything.

'It's just, these days, with the Internet, the "Twittersphere" and all that –' Connie could hear the air quotes from here – 'these things do tend to leak out rather fast and it's important for us to let the recipient know before they hear about it somewhere else.'

'Yes, I'm not quite sure I –'

'Also, as chairman, it's important for me to ascertain if the recipient is going to, well, accept the award.'

'I'm terribly sorry, Professor Bell, but –'

'As you know the award is only granted every five years and this year was as, ah, closely fought a contest as we've ever had. I really do think the right decision was made in the end, howev—'

Right. Enough. Who was this mad old buffer?

'Professor, forgive me, but I'm going to have to come right out and ask it – what award are you talking about?'

A pause. 'I'm sorry, I thought I'd said. Why, my dear, the F. W. Bingham Award. I'm chairman of the judging panel.'

'Oh,' Connie said. 'I see.' The F.W. Bingham Aw— was that the one where . . . ? *Holy shit.*

Six minutes later, four of which Connie had spent profusely thanking Professor Bell, everyone he worked with and the estate and the very mouldering bones of F. W. Bingham himself, Connie was dialling Kennedy's number and trying to work out the time difference between London and LA.

TEN

Drink-driving in Hollywood. If you were white, and drove a reasonably nice car, there was really only one rule: avoid Sunset Strip at night between Friday and Sunday. Otherwise – fill your boots. Kennedy knew an excellent route that took him home from the Chateau Marmont: round the back of the hotel, along some side streets and out onto Franklin avoiding Sunset. It being just after 4 p.m. on a Monday, however, he steered the Aston Martin with boozy languidness straight down Sunset, heading east, passing the white towers of the Chateau on his left. He stopped at the lights at the junction with Laurel and, taking a restorative sip from a miniature of whisky he'd discovered in the door jamb, regarded his fellow humans: a couple in an open-topped Bentley beside him. A man in a BMW in front of him, barking into his hands-free. A girl in a Mazda behind him, applying lip gloss in her rear-view. Just up ahead, a busload of sweltering Mexicans. (On the side of the bus:

Julie Teal's huge perfect face smiling at him, each tooth the size of a hardback. Some comedy she'd been in a few months back. A hit.) Bentley, Beamer, Mazda, bus and, finally, completing the downward trajectory, coming windmilling up Sunset, a pedestrian. An *outdoorsman*.

It was a phrase Kennedy loved. Only in LA would a tramp earn such a dignified sobriquet, as though they had chosen the life of sleeping on sidewalks in urine-soaked pants in eighty-degree heat above all the other possibilities life had to offer. *'Yeah, I was enrolled in pre-law at Harvard but I just felt the life of the outdoorsman was a better fit for me.'*

This particular outdoorsman was a beauty too. Black, maybe in his forties, around Kennedy's age, he wore what at a distance looked like a reasonably respectable suit and a bow tie. On closer inspection the suit was shredded, worn through to the knees. The shirt a fantastic patchwork of stains. He was a talker too, this fellow, jabbering at the air, bitching and cursing the fates, or business partners, or ex-wives, or whatever had led to him to be here, crazy, in LA. A lot of talkers among the bums of Los Angeles, Kennedy had observed. In London these guys just made with the cardboard sign and looked at you forlornly. Over here they were all bellowing their life stories up and down Sunset, from Silver Lake to Santa Monica, from dawn till dusk. The incredible need to share. To build a narrative. Maybe they were all fucking screenwriters. Speaking of which, over on the other side of the road, Kennedy could see a bunch of future outdoorsmen tapping away at their MacBooks in Peet's Coffee & Tea, pounding out buddy movies, thrillers, horrors and romcoms that had one connective strand: they would never be sold. The bow-tied outdoorsman passed near the car and Kennedy held a cocked twenty out of the window. The guy saw it and veered towards him. He took the note without making eye contact, without acknowledgement, and without breaking off his monologue for a second. Impressive, Kennedy thought. He always gave money to bums, staggeringly large bills sometimes. 'You know why you do that?' one of his ex-partners had said to him once. Millie or Vicky? He couldn't remember. Most likely Vicky, he'd been poorer much of the time he and Millie were together. 'Why do I do it?' Kennedy had asked dutifully. 'As a kind of insurance. A pension plan,' she'd said. 'An investment in human kindness. Because you think that's where you'll end up one day.' Thinking about it now, that sounded more like Millie actually.

Did he fear winding up a tramp? Did he fear it more after the events of this morning? ('This is real. It's a real thing.') It was true – Kennedy was never last to the bar. He never said, 'Let's fly economy.' He'd rather just pick the whole check up than get into the whole 'who didn't have rice?' thing. Pick the check up? He'd sooner chop his cock off and throw it on the table than get into that. Nah. Everything would be fine. Braden loved to panic. He looked around him, at the sunshine. The palm fronds. The traffic. He loved it here. This was where he was meant to have been all along. He looked again at the couple in the Bentley. The girl in the passenger seat was thirtyish, attractive, in tight sweats, cleavage bulging, fresh from the gym, or the yoga class. The driver, needless to say, was very much her senior. Fifty-something: a frazzled old rogue with thinning silver mane and the gold Rolex heavy on his wrist.

Kennedy saw them around in the Hollywood Hills, these men. Solid of paunch, greying of hair, a light sheen of sweat on their high foreheads as they lumbered from house to carport and slid behind the wheels of their heavy Fusillades, their vintage Sturmbuckers or Carrions. He saw them picking up steak in Bristol Farms on Sunset or mournfully walking the humidor at Ivan's. More often than not there would be the twenty-six-year-old chick in cut-offs and T-shirt teetering primly ahead of them, filling the cart with endive and lettuce. With radicchio and bean sprouts and champagne.

Kennedy mixed with them on the plane to Hawaii during the holidays. His people. One of them. The girls happy and excited, high on rum and first class. (And why wouldn't you be – at twenty-six? With so little in the debit column? With the pain schedule just a scribbled-on napkin? Not the crammed ledger it would become later. The Russian novel.) The men? Less so. Frowning into their *GQ*s, into their screens and bulky thrillers. The girls were still at the start of the roller coaster: excited as the track clacks thickly beneath you, as the crest approaches, your tummy rising, the blue all around you heady and intoxicating. The men, these scoundrels of middle age, they were thundering towards the end, rattling towards the final bend. And what do you do then?

You *scream.*

They had all offended love, these men. Had all sinned against it and now they were paying. In expensive hotel suites they had roared expletives and the name of Christ into the glossy shoulder blades of the prototypes of the girls they now walked the produce aisles with. The photographs of their wives and children had borne silent witness from the screens of muted iPhones and BlackBerries as they performed untold violations on rented sheets. They had talked to their wives of meetings and schedules while these girls dozed beside them, a patina of semen drying on their bronzed flanks. On flights home, wallowing in business and first, watching the stewardess's legs, they had deleted messages and emails and call histories and straightened their stories and their hair.

And love had found them out. They had broken the hearts of those who had trusted them and now they woke in the night, sweating and screaming from bad dreams, to find their voices reverberating off empty wood-framed houses. No wife drew them to her and whispered, *'Shhh, it's just a dream. Go back to sleep.'* Now the only words they heard from that voice, the voice that once soothed them so sweetly, was talk of figures, of money due and the dates it was due on. Of schedules of childcare and handovers. Money talk. Hate talk. The opposite of love.

And finally, when the night was finished doing what it had to do to them (*Oh these nights!* Kennedy thought. *These fucking nights!*), no children came scampering to their beds in the milky dawn light. (The pain endemic to the middle-aged divorcee who does not see his children daily. When you could not get their faces out of your head. What were you meant to do with such thoughts? *'There's nothing you can do with thoughts like that.'* Kingsley saying this, to

Martin. '*You can only hope to coexist with them. They never go away. They're always with you.*') They woke with no hot tiny limbs across their chests. Just pressure. The pressure brought by the knowledge that all of this was drawing closer to being over, that the pain schedule was being drawn up and there were many, many zeros in the debit column. They had sinned against love, these old bastards, with the twenty-six-year-olds. What did they think love was going to do? *Stand for it?* Just lean back, chew gum and say, 'Go ahead. You're fine, pal.' Like fuck. So love came at them in the night and unmanned them. It made them dream of Christmases past as they thrashed on those high-thread-count sheets. It woke them on the verge of tears. They got up from the damp bed and stumbled bearishly downstairs where the only sound they heard was the welcoming drip of the automated coffee pot. Perhaps, on certain days, there would be the vacuum and the distant '*Hola*' of the maid. They braved the sprinkler systems for the mail and news-papers and, behind them in the big houses, their things stayed resolutely in the sad piles where they had left them the night before. The lonely ribbon of the single black sock coiled on the bedroom floor. The stale water glass.

Kennedy looked at the couple in the Bentley and thought –

Come, lover.
Feast upon the edge of the abyss.
Gorge oblivious. While, black leagues below,
Sightless birds turn slowly in awful circles.

Already quietly happy with the use of 'gorge', with its gentle double role as verb and noun, as the lights changed and they pulled off, Kennedy noticed for the first time that the girl was wearing glasses. He was pleased by the extra resonance British readers would have found in the last line of the verse.

ELEVEN

Dr Dennis Drummond (PhD dissertation — *Vectors of Power: The Romantic Poets as Political Construct*, Manchester University, 1989), head of the Department of English at Deeping University and senior lecturer in Marxist critical theory, snatched up the ringing bedside phone, letting the student essay he'd been marking fall to the floor. (Marking viciously down. This kid clearly had a lot to learn. Was still mired in quaint nineteenth-century ideas about the value of narrative.) Drummond was forty-seven and what little hair remained on his head was wispy and frail, as thin as an undergraduate's thesis. Beside him in bed his wife slept the fitful, nervy sleep of someone who has not been fucked in a very long time.

'Hello?'

'Dennis, hi. It's Amanda.'

'Amanda. Thank you for calling.'

'You said no matter how late.'

'No, please.' They had known each other since around

the millennium, when they had been on a conference panel together at Loughborough University: 'Intra-textual Fascism: Defoe, Dickens, Lawrence and the Maintenance of Cultural Hegemony 1720–1930'. By the end of the afternoon they had declared all of these writers bankrupt, imperialist rapists and walked off well pleased to a spartan vegan lunch. Amanda Costello was the sort of writer who began every piece with something like *'Writing as a hetero-sexual CIS whose middle-class lifestyle is susceptible to be influenced by factors well without the experience of minorities engaged in the struggle . . .'* Drummond enjoyed her prose very much. If 'enjoyed' is quite the word we want here. Rather, he found she addressed all troublesome political issues thoroughly at the outset, rather than patronising the reader with anything as Empire and demotic as an interesting or arresting sentence. She was clear and hardline. Her privilege always thoroughly checked. 'Please go on,' Drummond said.

She told him. Drummond felt sick. Faint.

They shared mutual outrage for a few minutes. Many a 'disgraceful' and an 'appalling' and an 'unbelievable' were exchanged.

'Your boss, Lyons,' Costello said, 'he was very keen.'

'Oh, that fossil,' Drummond said. 'That fucking old fool.'

'Academia today.' Costello sighed. 'They might as well have chosen someone off . . . I don't know. That thing. In the jungle.'

'Well. Thank you for letting me know.' *Jungle? What jungle thing? Was she referring to the recent, newly unearthed Lévi-Strauss essays?* 'Forewarned and all that.'

'Poor you. That awful, misogynistic throwback in your department for a year.'

'Mmm. We'll see,' Drummond said. 'Thanks again. Goodnight, Amanda.'

He hung up and turned the light out. Lying back, looking up in the dark at the bedroom ceiling of this small house that his family had long outgrown, Drummond felt his heartstrings tautening. Of all the people. Anyone, literally *anyone*, would have been preferable to that . . . that capitalist *thug*.

TWELVE

Making a left to head north on La Brea, across Hollywood Boulevard, past Ivan's where he bought his cigarettes and cigars (so cheap to smoke yourself titless here: a carton of Marlboro Lights at fifty dollars? That was just over three quid a pack. Nine quid now in London. Boringly difficult to get Cuban cigars though. He made do with Faux-hibans, Con-durans), a right to head east on Franklin and then, finally, another left that took Kennedy winding up Hillcrest into the Hills themselves.

He parked in the off-street bay and went in through the front garden gate to find – as he had hoped – the day's activity winding down: Raoul packing up his chemicals and telescopic net by the edge of the green-tiled infinity pool; Hector the gardener using a hand-held leaf blower to get the last of the leaves and twigs off the patio; Maria and Selina, the cleaners, lugging the trash bags up the garden towards him, their last task of the day.

'Hi, guys,' Kennedy said.

'*Hola*, Mr Kennedy,' the quartet chorused.

'Mr 'Ennedy?' It was Raoul, with his softly spoken war against consonants. Kennedy slipped his Clubmasters off, loosened his tie, and joined him beside the pool. 'I pu' some new 'emicals in the jacuzzi. 'Leaned the filter out. Should be goo' now, but I'd wait a couple hours before you use it . . .' The eight-person hot tub was at the far end of the swimming pool, slightly elevated above it. Behind it, far below them, you could see downtown rippling in the smog. Kennedy walked along the edge of the pool and looked down into the tub. The water was bubbling and foaming and did look much clearer than when he'd left that morning. 'Thanks, Raoul,' Kennedy said.

'I 'hink wha' thee prollem was . . .' Raoul began.

And Kennedy did what he always did when someone began explaining something like this to him. He went away to his happy place. When a plumber started explaining the cause of the blockage, or an electrician the solution to a problem, or a mechanic, or anyone who had to explain mankind's dealings with the physical world, he simply stopped listening. The words became a gentle burble, waves lapping at Kennedy's ear as he said things like 'Ah ha. Mmmm. Yes. I see' until the person shut up or went away. What was it with these physical-world wranglers? These masters of reality, with their insistence on explaining the workings of things to him, their eulogies to the broken fridge seal, the manifold and fuel pump, their diatribes about guttering and roof tiles?

When he thought of the countless hours wasted listening to these speeches . . . couldn't they just leave him alone?

It was like when Millie – and then later Vicky and now,

more recently, one of the Samanthas or Christines or Lauras who hung around for more than a day or two – had wanted to tell him about her day, usually around six o'clock when Kennedy was in the kitchen, embarking upon the sacred ritual with gin, ice, vermouth, olive and frosted stemmed glass. The monologue about who said what to whom would begin and, after a few sentences, Kennedy would hear that white noise, those gentle waves lapping at the shore of his brain. *Why are you telling me this?* Imagine it, Kennedy would think. Imagine feeling the need to tell someone about your day? Still, life had its conventions. 'Hmmm' and 'Yes' and 'I see', he would say.

'You see?' Raoul was saying, now, here by the poolside, in the early-evening sun, and Kennedy realised some response was required of him. Silence now too. Hector had turned off the leaf blower and was packing his stuff up.

'Yeah,' he nodded. 'Got you. Good. Well, thanks, Raoul. See you next week, huh?'

Raoul nodded, pleased, picked up his toolbox and headed for the gate with Hector. A metallic 'snick' somewhere behind him and Kennedy was finally alone in the garden, quiet save for the gulping water in the hot tub and the distant buzz of a traffic helicopter above the 101.

He went into the house, through the front door that gave directly into the huge living area. Down a few steps would take him into the sunken conversation pit – two long, deep sofas facing each other across a glass-topped coffee table. Books lined the shelves of the pit, a fifty-inch plasma screen on a multi-positional wall mount above the fireplace overlooked it. Kennedy skirted the pit, walking around the hardwood floor and through an archway into the kitchen – another big room split in half by the central island that incorporated a professional Viking range. Copper pots and pans and heavy Le Creuset cookware hung above it. Serious cooking kit, even though, naturally, Kennedy's culinary skills lay elsewhere: with depressing the lever of the burnished Dualit toaster. With the speed dial. With the impossible-to-get reservation. With the crisp twenty or fifty folded into the head waiter's palm, or slipped into the breast pocket of a favoured maître d'. With the strong, healthy credit card pressed firmly on top of the long, intricate check.

Dropping his car keys on the counter Kennedy continued on out of the kitchen, through another archway and down a hallway. A door to his left opened into another lounge, with a pool table with golden baize and a bar at the far end, the walls bearing glass-framed posters for his novels and for the movies he had written. To his right a door opened onto the dining room, the long oak table that could seat fourteen. Kennedy walked on down the hall and went up the staircase at the end.

Up one flight and you were into the part of the house Kennedy really lived in – a three-room complex: his study and bedroom sharing an interconnecting bathroom. Into his study – where the cleaners were forbidden to enter. (Too many moved notes, too many napkins and envelopes and matchbooks bearing Kennedy's cramped illegible scrawl had been lost.) It was a large room – maybe twenty feet long and fifteen feet wide – with French windows that opened out onto a balcony that overlooked the pool and garden.

At the far end a sofa faced two armchairs. There were two desks in the room: a long, wide one faced the rear wall in the middle of the room. Kennedy's working area. His iMac sat in the middle, huge and dominating. The hard drive, the research books, the piles of screenplays and the novels they were based on lay heaped and scattered around the twenty-eight-inch screen. A pinboard on the wall to the left of the desk was covered with Post-it notes and index cards: outlines, scene structures. A clear plastic bag containing some loose change was tacked to the bottom left-hand corner of the board. A smaller desk at the other end of the room was basically chaos: a mountain of opened and unopened mail. Letters and books from junior editors soliciting quotes. Invitations to parties, launches, readings, seminars, symposiums, retreats and conventions. Royalty statements from his agents. Hanging on the wall above the desk was a huge glass frame containing fifteen A4 letters in three rows of five: all rejection letters for *Unthinkable*, all dated around the winter of 1995. *HarperCollins*, *Jonathan Cape*, *Faber*, *Penguin*, *John Murray*, *Canongate*, *Picador*, *Fourth Estate* . . . and so on and so on. The other motivational device Kennedy employed was a single sentence, printed out in Courier Bold – the font he always typed in – on a strip of paper and taped to the bottom of his iMac, over the Apple logo. It was a quote from James Joyce and, long before this, in the undergraduate hellhole in Glasgow, in his workspace in the corner of the teeny bedroom in Maida Vale, it had been taped first to his portable Olivetti, then to his grey, plasticky Amstrad. It said:

WRITE IT, DAMN YOU. WHAT ELSE ARE YOU GOOD FOR?

He knew others favoured different quotes. Some writers liked Iris Murdoch's 'Every book is the wreck of a great idea'. It was good and true – the published novel's bleached bones the skeleton of some colossal monster whose true identity was known only to one person. And, even then, glimpsed by them only intermittently as it disappeared in the jungly foliage through which it was hunted – but Kennedy felt it lacked the motivational oomph of his countryman's harsh exhortation.

He wandered through to his bedroom where, thankfully, all signs of Saturday night's atrocity had been erased by the cleaners. Women – they lived on their own and you had, what? Full fridges. Cleanliness. Paid bills. Fresh clothes neatly folded and stacked in drawers. Men? Unless you did what Kennedy did and threw money and staff at the situation you had chaos. Squalor. The rafts of T-shirts and pyjama bottoms stuffed down the back of the bed, gradually transitioning from bedwear to spunk rags to science experiments. Final demands and a radioactive carton of Chinese food sharing shelf space with a jar of mustard. If only, he reflected, and not for the first time, he could hire cleaners for his mind. That's what his mind needed. Staff.

Stripping his shirt off (why did he wear white shirts? Why not just a vest of food-attracting Velcro?), he walked back through to the office, over to his work desk, ran a hand across the keyboard, took a deep breath and tapped on the red-and-white 'Diary' icon on the bar at the bottom. The Week in View: a traditional, dreaded Monday ritual.

The diary and the telephone: one-way instruments of pain and torture. When you were a struggling writer, as all writers once were (gleaming behind glass in front of him now: '. . . *while* UNTHINKABLE *showed much promise we feel that in the current marketplace* . . .'), you'd stare at your, well, Kennedy hadn't had a diary back then, if he had it would have been a blank sheet with maybe the words 'laundry' or 'call Mum' scribbled here and there, but you'd stare at the telephone, willing it into life: a commission, a job, *any fucking thing*. Kennedy had once danced a whoop-la of joy around the 8 x 6 kitchen in Maida Vale because the editor of *Time Out* had asked him to submit a hundred-word review of the movie *Die Hard 3*. He could still remember – maybe two months after that call – his ravenous fingers tearing open the envelope that contained the cheque for that review. Eighteen of your English pounds. His memory kept trying to invent a nice thing he'd done for Millie with the money. In reality it had vanished into the punishing stream of his overdraft like a pebble tossed over Niagara Falls. Now, when the telephone rang (speaking of which, he could – again – hear the distant trilling of his iPhone from the bedroom), it instantly prompted the words 'What fresh hell is this?' (Similarly, he reflected, with enough success other individuals and organisations in your life gradually morphed: the bank manager moved from being a figure of dread and terror into a . . . a nothing. A non-entity. His role, however, was swiftly assumed by the Inland Revenue. Life, ensuring you were never without a nemesis.)

He looked at the digitised diary page writ obscenely large across the huge screen of the iMac. Kennedy's diary was currently maintained by Stephanie at Braden's office, a cute film graduate whom Kennedy often delighted by singing 'Stephanie Says' by the Velvet Underground whenever he saw her. He had also reduced her to tears on several occasions. Mainly because, troublingly, Stephanie insisted on clinging to the frankly Edwardian view that if you agreed to do something you would actually turn up to do it.

Ominous, this screen. Lots of blue text signifying business meetings. A similarly worrying amount of orange text signifying social events, the colours having been picked arbitrarily by Stephanie's predecessor Nancy. (Nancy? Yes. Yes he had.) His eye flitted over the screen, picking out random, awful, harrowing words: *Screening. General. Drinks. Pitch. Dinner. Interview. Warner Bros. Charlie Birthday Dinner.* (Who in the terrible name of Satan's swollen nutbag was Charlie?) *Lunch. General. Fox. Breakfast.* ('Breakfast'? Yeah, right. Kennedy allowed himself a mirthless bark of laughter at that one. He must have been fucking *flying* when he agreed to that.) *Pitch. Drinks. General.*

A 'General' meeting. Studio-speak for talking about nothing, nothing that would never happen. You went in and they said, 'Hi, I'm Steve Prick, Vice President of Arse, and this is Barbara Balls, Head of Nonsense, and we love your stuff. Tell us – what are you working on?' And you told them and they said, 'Oh wow. Incredible. We need to do something together.' And, most likely, you never heard from Mr Prick and Miss Balls again. A 'Pitch' meeting. You went in and they said, 'Hi, I'm Helen Asshole, Head of Baloney, and this is Kevin Fist, senior VP of Astrology. Please, tell us about your idea,' and you went through every single moment of the film you were thinking about writing beat by beat, from FADE IN to FADE OUT, and they said, 'Wow. Sounds great. We'll get back to you on this,' and, most likely, you never heard from Miss Asshole or Mr Fist again. Although, in Kennedy's case, you heard back often enough to keep the cheques and meetings flowing.

Why? Why were all these appalling things happening to him? Because Kennedy hated doing *anything.* Well, not quite. What Kennedy liked to do was work and eat and drink with people he knew very well at bars and restaurants within a fifteen-minute drive of his house. Yet here he was, traversing Greater Los Angeles to break bread – or sashimi, or filet mignon, or pan-fried fucking ostrich tits in blowfish cum – with . . . with some cunt called Charlie? Oh, a bad business. Yes. Very bad.

Paramount. General. HBO. Pitch.

Then his eyes alighted on something truly horrifying:

7.30. Saskia Kram: Poetry Reading, Downtown.

Who the fuck was Saskia Kram? It was tomorrow night. This simply could not be happening. The centre would not hold. Hear the falconer? The falcon had stuck its iPod on and cranked some drum and bass up as far as it would fucking well go. *Poetry reading?* Kennedy enjoyed poetry in the way that any sane adult enjoyed poetry – in the house, alone, late at night, jackknifed over the whisky bottle, the Yeats or the Larkin tear-stained on your lap as you wept over the ruination of your life. To go to a poetry *reading?* To sit in a room drinkless, soberish, and listen to . . . to Saskia Kram (and again – who the fuck?) declaiming her schtick in a roomful of crazed bastards? You'd simply have to be insane to do this. It would be like going to the theatre. It was unimaginable. *Unthinkable.* Kennedy hit 'speaker-phone' and stabbed the speed dial.

'Hi, Childs and –'

'Stephanie, Kennedy.'

'Oh, hi! I was just about to call y—'

'What in the cunting name of fuck is this fucking poetry reading thing?'

'Ah, I'm sorr—'

'Saskia Kram? Who the fu—'

'Oh, she's *great*. Hold on, I'm just getting your diary up –'

'Cancel. Cancel. *Cancel*.'

'Oh, right. Yeah. Ah, Kennedy? *You* asked me to put that in. Ages ago.'

'I must have been coked up. Meth. Cancel.' He sang the last word in a fruity soprano.

'You're down to introduce her. It's at Barnstaples bookstore downtown.'

'C.A.N.C.E.L.'

'If you just –'

'Negative.'

'Kennedy, if –'

'Fuck her and the stanza she rode in on.'

'Kennedy, if you just Google her photo, I think you'll –'

Kennedy was already typing the words into the box.

'She just published this collection called *Trees*, they're all poems obliquely about –'

And there she was – huge on Kennedy's screen. And the moment her face appeared Kennedy remembered. Because Saskia Kram . . . she was . . . poets didn't . . . they didn't look like *this*. Looking at the sandy-blonde hair cascading down cheekbones, cheekbones like, well, like razor clams, looking into the blue of her eyes, the inch-long kohl-embossed lashes, her coy expression, the lips slightly parted, Kennedy remembered: the dinner party that night, at his American paperback editor's house in Pacific Palisades. Saskia Kram sat next to him. How she was a huge fan. Talk of the launch of her new collection of poems, here in LA, in a couple of months. How honoured she'd be if he introduced her. The cheerful – frankly paralytic – bonhomie with which he'd accepted. (All this remembrance accompanied by twin tugs of dread: 1) he *must* have made a pass at her that night. What happened? And 2) her publisher had undoubtedly sent a copy of her book to him. He looked across the room – to the teetering skyscraper of opened, unopened and half-opened manuscripts and bound proofs.)

Stephanie was still going. '. . . *New York Times* said "redefines the notion of feminism, indeed what it means to be a women at this juncture in history".' Christ, a feminist poet. Millie would probably know her stuff all right. Millie, the academic.

'Yeah. I remember. Sorry, Steph. I'll be there.'

'You're looking at her now, right?' He could hear her smile. He ignored it.

'Are they sending a car?'

'Kennedy – it's a *poetry* reading at an independent bookstore. I'll book a car from your service if you like.'

'Yeah. Fine. Lincoln Town Car please? The idiots sent a stretch last time. Fucking hen-night mobile.' *Sure and it's far from how you were raised.* 'Sorry about all the cunts and fucks and stuff earlier.'

'No problem. Right, while I've got you, dinner with Michael Curzon. Is this Thursday good for you?'

'Oh Christ.'

'Braden said –'

'Yeah, yeah. I know. It's a must-do. Can't we make it drinks?'

'Movie star want dinner with charming Irish writer.'

'Ach feck. OK. Christ.'

'He wants to go to the Chav. Off Hollywood.'

'Oh no. Can't we go to Animal?'

'Movie star vegetarian.'

'These bastards. The Chateau then.'

'Movie star want Chav. Chav hip.'

'Yeah, fine. Fuck.'

'It's in. Thursday at eight. Have fun.'

'I'm in hell, Stephanie. I live in hell.'

'Oh, buck up, Kennedy. Big kiss. Bye. Oh – and good luck with Saskia tomorrow night.'

'Ach. Stick it up in your fucken hole,' Kennedy said, but not without affection. Then – 'Oh, oh, Steph?'

'Mmmm?'

'I need a new laptop.'

'Again?'

'Yeah, I . . . I dropped a drink on the fucking thing.'

A theatrical sigh. 'You go through laptops like most writers use paper, Kennedy.'

'Yeah, yeah.'

He hung up and gazed reverently at the face of Saskia Kram for a moment (making a mental note to search Google images later for more masturbation-orientated photographs of the renowned feminist poet) before – rashly – clicking on his email account. Horror: the final reel of a horror film. Just blood and viscera and screaming: a wall of stark, black text, an entire screen of unopened emails. Kennedy had a policy – someone had to email him three times before he considered the matter urgent enough for him to respond. It used to be twice. Among the most recent and frequent incoming were one from his brother (subject header: 'Mum') and three from Connie Blatt (*three* times in last twenty-four hours, the subject headers, progressively: 'Call me', 'Call Me!' and 'CALL ME!'). He went into voicemail on his phone, deleting two fresh ones from Vicky (the Warhol, the card limit), and listened to the last message Connie had left. It began, as did all of Connie's messages, with a few seconds of silence. Static. The rumblings of a pocket call, then –

'Ahhhhh, oh,' while Connie searched to remember who she had called, 'ummmm, yes . . . hi there . . . Kennedy darling! It's Connie. Listen, ummmm . . .' A pause while she covered the mouthpiece and talked to someone else, a dog, an assistant. 'Something rather, ah, rather interesting's come up which, ahhhh, I do need to speak to you about. Fear not – it's very good news. Potentially. So . . .' more 'ahhh' and 'ummm' and 'errr' before, 'do please give me a call when you get this message, darling. Lots of love. Byeeee.' Kennedy hung up and checked the time. Getting on for six o'clock. Two in the morning over there. Fuck it – these all sounded like tomorrow problems anyway.

No glasses on his desk. He took a pull of Macallan straight from the bottle in his top drawer, lit a Marlboro, and wandered out onto the balcony, into the coming dusk: sirens in the distance, the rhythmic thud of rotors from the choppers over the 101. Feeling the burn of the fine malt whisky, the sooty perfume of the nicotine, Kennedy Marr extrapolated —

'*At our backs, the arid winds*
Of the force of choices we have made
That have led us here,
To this last banquet.'

Downtown was just beginning to twinkle to the south. The squeak and squawk of tyres and horns on Franklin. A nimbus moon already hung in the darkening sky, 'as pale as a Sex Pistol'. Amis, that. Not bad. It wasn't bad.

Spread out below him, the city's ripped backsides.

THIRTEEN

'Could you repeat that please, Connie?' Braden stood on the balcony of his condo in Brentwood, looking north-east across the midnight town, towards the blackness of the Hollywood Hills, in Kennedy's direction. He pictured Kennedy passed out across the bed. Or, worse, still propping up the bar somewhere. Connie repeated the figure, this time adding, 'Tax-free.' Connie standing in the bright kitchen in Clapham with her toast, her tea and John Humphrys burbling gentle yet strident on Radio 4. She'd given up trying Kennedy. She'd thought she'd prob-ably get more sense – and enthusiasm – out of Braden. She was right.

'*Tax-free?*' he repeated, the words sounding as sweet as 'world peace' to his American business ears. As sweet as anything possibly could, apart from maybe 'gross points'.

'Indeed, darling.'

'Sterling, right?' Braden asked again, the word ancient, archaic on his Yankee tongue.

'Yes, dear. Good old English pounds.'

'Shit.'

'Quite. If only he'd answer his bloody phone.'

'Well, we had a pretty long lunch earlier. I had a feeling he was gonna carry on.' Braden leaned back against the railings and surveyed his living room through the open sliding door: an expanse of oatmeal and glass, the car keys and Evian bottle on the coffee table the only sign that this was not a show home. 'I gotta say, this would solve a hell of a lot of problems.'

'It certainly would. Not that it doesn't raise quite a few too, mind you. Namely Millie and Robin. Could you juggle all his movie stuff?' The word 'movie' as odd and alien in Connie's mouth as 'sterling' had been in Braden's.

'That's what I'm trying to figure. When would he need to be there?'

'Term starts in October, but they'd want him here mid-September to get organised.'

'Christ. He'd have to work his balls off to deliver a few things. We might have to pay a couple of the smaller guys back, walk off the projects. The only real issue is Scott Spengler. Technically he owes another draft on that, although now Julie Teal's on board, in terms of further rewrites, who knows?'

'Julie Teal? Is she the one who was in that thing with what's-his-face? All cowboys and stuff? Oooh, I like her.'

'The terms of this thing, the whaddyacallit?'

'The F. W. Bingham Award.'

'Yeah. They're pretty inflexible, huh?'

'I fear so. An academic year.'

'Like full semesters?'

'"Terms" we say here, darling. And of course the other problem is Kennedy.'

'How so? I mean apart from the obvious.'

'Well, will he want to do it?'

'He's *got* to do it.'

A girlish squeak of delight popped out of Connie. 'Ha! "Got to" and our Kennedy have ever been but slender acquaintances, Braden.'

'I think you should come out. He listens to you.'

'Well, having already anticipated this to be a battle worth fighting, I'm already packed.' She looked at her suitcase in the hall. Somewhere above her two teenage boys persisted in the sleep that would occupy them for hours to come. All that accumulated energy and what did they do with it? Wanking and drinking. 'I'm on the four o'clock out of Heathrow. I'll be in your lovely city tomorrow.'

'Oh, that's great, Connie. Thank you. You need a car?'

'I'll get a taxi, dear. I'm at the Chateau. But remember – mum's the word. They're having kittens about word of the offer getting out in case he declines it.'

'Sure. Call me when you're settled at the hotel. I'll check his schedule, see where we can pin him down.'

'Perfect. I must say – I'm rather looking forward to it. I do enjoy an ambush.'

FOURTEEN

Shortly after this call concluded – at 9.03 a.m. BST, precisely three minutes after she had walked into her office in the English Department of Deeping University in Warwickshire – another of the women in the life of Kennedy Marr was also very unexpectedly discussing the F. W. Bingham Award.

'Are you fu— ah, I'm sorry?' Dr Millie Dyer (formerly Marr, lecturer in medieval literature, Deeping University) said, her fists balled on her hips, her incredulity lent extra drama by the fact that she was slightly out of breath. In her late forties now Millie was growing into middle age very nicely – she could still get into the same jeans she wore when she met Kennedy over twenty years ago. Her face was untroubled by cracks and lines. The face of someone who was usually in bed by 10 p.m. having drunk no more than a single glass of wine. She stood there, getting her breath back.

Dennis Drummond, the head of the department, had

rung her at her desk at 9.01 and it taken her two minutes to walk the long corridor and then climb the three flights of stairs to his office. She looked from Drummond to the two professors flanking his desk. Professor Dominic Lyons she knew very well. He was the head of the university. Professor David Bell she knew only by reputation. Both professors were beaming. Dr Drummond – less so.

'Yes,' said Bell. 'A very exciting appointment, I'm sure you'll agree, Dr Dyer. Even, given your, ah, personal history.'

'A real marquee name,' Lyons added. 'Should be a tremendous help with publicity and applications.'

She looked at Drummond. He was now looking at his desk while bending a ballpoint pen. The pen looked to be close to breaking point and the desk was neat. There was a little holder for paper clips and rubber bands. There were no paper clips in the rubber-band compartment and vice versa.

'I can't believe he wouldn't tell me himself,' Millie said.

'Well, he hasn't accepted yet,' Bell said. 'I'm not sure he even *knows* yet. He's in Hollywood, you see, and –'

'Yes, I'm perfectly aware my ex-husband lives in Los Angeles.'

'Oh, of course, excuse me. The committee only reached their decision late last night. I've spoken to his agent, Miss Blatt.' Connie. Millie always liked Connie. 'And she assures us of a prompt response. Although now, well, it must be . . .' He looked at his watch. Millie was surprised to see a stainless-steel wristwatch rather than a half-hunter. 'Let's see, eight hours, is it?'

'It's 1 a.m. over there,' Millie said.

'Yes. I fear he must be asleep.' Millie allowed herself a smile at that one, picturing Kennedy sliding along the wet mahogany, moving in on some poor twenty-something, raising a cocked fifty at the barman. 'Which is why I must ask for this conversation to be treated in the strictest confidence. I only felt it appropriate to tell you, given your, the unique . . . circumstances of, as I say, your, ah, relationship to the recipient-elect.'

He picked up his raincoat from the back of a chair. 'We're drafting a press release now. All being well we'll have his answer – and I'm sure we all hope, for the good of the university, that it's a "yes" – by tomorrow and announce it to the media before the end of the week. Professor Lyons.' They shook, Lyons standing. 'Dr Drummond.' Drummond offered his hand from behind his desk, with only the slightest lean forward to indicate he might have been thinking about standing up. 'Nice to have met you, Dr Dyer.' Millie took his hand, like parchment, the soft brown of the liver spots.

'Yes,' Millie said. 'Well, thanks for letting me know.'

Bell smiled and closed the door behind him. There was the appropriate pause between the three colleagues, to allow Bell to make it down the corridor to minimum safe distance. Lyons got as far as holding up his palms and saying 'Now look', before Drummond cut in with 'You've got to be fucking kidding me.'

'Dennis –'

'Services to Literature? Kennedy Marr? He hasn't written a novel in years. And those he has, well, if they qualify as "literature" now, then –'

'And Kennedy, *teaching*?' Millie cut in. Had she been

more theatrically inclined she might well have shuddered here.

'He's spent the best part of the last decade whoring himself out to the highest bidder,' Drummond said. 'Cranking out "buddy movies" and "romcoms" and Christ knows what.'

'Look –' Lyons tried again.

'Services to Kennedy Marr would be more –' Millie began.

'This is good news for the university,' Lyons said.

It'll be good news for the local pubs, restaurants and drug dealers, Millie thought.

'When there were so many other worthy candidates,' Drummond lamented.

'Right,' Lyons said, standing up, feeling it was time to pull rank. 'Both of you, that's quite enough. Firstly, Dr Drummond, you are well aware of this institution's relationship with the F. W. Bingham Award, an award that I personally have no influence over. It is decided by an independent committee.'

'You're *on* the committee!'

'I am but one voice. And besides, the vote was unanimous.'

Drummond held his gaze. *Your boss Lyons – he was very keen.* 'So you approve, Professor?' Drummond asked. 'Given that –'

'As a matter of fact I do,' Lyons said. 'The reality is that universities must now function as commercial entities in a competitive marketplace. Mr Marr is a best-selling author who has also worked on many very important, commercially successful films and whose presence on campus will, I believe, generate a lot of media interest that will in turn impact on applications – applications to *your department*, Dennis – which creates revenue.'

Lyons crossed the room and looked out of the window at the white modern buildings, the leafy campus, a few students – those engaged in resits and research – scurrying across in the light summer rain, holding umbrellas and textbooks above their heads. Behind his back Drummond and Millie exchanged a look. 'And, yes, his personal history may be . . . colourful, as I'm sure no one knows as well as Dr Dyer here, and, yes, we could argue from now until the start of term about exactly what constitutes literature, the fact remains, however – he is a *name*. Now –' he turned to face them – 'while I am perfectly happy to entertain your reservations and misgivings in private I must insist that publicly we are united in seeing this as a positive for the university.'

Silence. Then, huffily, from Drummond, folding his arms and pushing himself away from his desk, 'Well, as head of the department, I must insist on seeing his proposed syllabus as soon as possible. Reading lists and so forth.'

'Of course.'

And here, as she registered these words – 'proposed syllabus', 'reading lists' – Millie's face brightened. She tried to picture Kennedy compiling a reading list, composing a lecture, reading a student's work, or diligently marking up an essay.

'Good. Well, I had best get on. Heads down, bully and shove and all that. Drummond. Dr Dyer.'

The moment the door closed behind him Millie said

to Drummond, 'You know what? All of this is literally academic.'

'How so?'

'Because once he hears what's involved there is no way on earth Kennedy is going to accept the award.'

'Hope springs,' Drummond said.

FIFTEEN

'The . . . how, *you fucking what?*'

Braden and Connie were both wearing fixed, idiotic grins. Kennedy didn't even have a drink in his hand yet. He was being asked to absorb all this *cold*.

He'd been surprised enough to see Connie in the first place. Squinting into the sunlight as he emerged from the darkened lobby of the Chateau (having gone through the ritual exchange of pleasantries with the staff on the way. Despite a few . . . transgressions Kennedy was much loved here), down the steps into the courtyard garden, and there she was – sitting with Braden at one of the tables beneath the arches along the wall, tired but radiant in a summer print frock and straw hat, her glass of white wine and fat novel on the table across from Braden's mineral water and BlackBerry. (The English and American agenting worlds neatly juxtaposed there, Kennedy thought.) They'd no sooner embraced and he'd asked 'What the hell are you doing here? Why didn't you tell me you were in town?'

than Connie had taken his hand, lowered him into the wicker seat, and was saying, 'Now, darling, something *marvellous* has come up back home . . .'

It took her a minute or two to get it all out, during which time Kennedy had managed to hail a waitress and order the Martini that was now being prepared over at the bar.

Connie finished and laughed, regarding his dumbstruck face.

'I mean – who the fuck is F. W. Bingham?' Kennedy asked.

Connie explained. Francis Weldon Bingham had been a professor of literature at Deeping University, back in the 1930s, when it had just been a tiny college. A boozy old fruit who liked to party, one of his favourite things had been arranging guest lecturers. 'Basically, darling,' Connie said, 'he was a star-fucker. He'd pay the great and good of the day an enormous stipend to come and talk to the students so that he'd have interesting company to go out on the piss with.' H. G. Wells, Scott and Zelda Fitzgerald, Huxley, Dorothy Parker, Hemingway and many others had all given guest lectures during Bingham's tenure. He had also been an extraordinarily rich old fruit (the family fortune built, some said, upon slavery in the late eighteenth century) who, upon his death, had bequeathed an enormous chunk of his estate to set up an award to allow his good work to continue.

Kennedy's drink arrived. As he took it from the tray he ordered the next one. Connie paused to allow him to, very gratefully, sink half the icy gin in one gulp and then continued.

The deal, it appeared, was this: the award was bestowed every five years to 'a writer of extraordinary and celebrated merit, one of the foremost practioners of their craft'. The recipient was expected to spend one academic year (September to May) at Deeping lecturing to the students in 'any aspect of literature, but with a focus on its composition' and to 'enrich the life of the university' while they were there.

A frown crossed Kennedy's face. Well, this wasn't strictly true; he'd been frowning from the start. Better to say his frown increased in intensity at this point. Connie watched him, not surprised that it had taken him this long to put two and two together. Kennedy and other people's lives were but slender acquaintances. 'Hang on. Deeping?' he said. 'That's . . . isn't that where Millie . . .?' Connie nodded. 'Yes, what are the odds, eh?'

'Christ.'

Recipients were expected to hold tutorials and to read and critique students' work. The university would arrange for all the recipient's travel ('First class of course, darling') and find them suitable accommodation. In return the recipient received an honorarium of five hundred thousand pounds.

Tax-free.

Braden shook his head slowly in wonderment.

Kennedy drained the Martini and felt the tautening swell of his bladder. 'Let me see if I've got this straight. They want me to give me half a million quid to go and live in fucking *Warwickshire* –' Kennedy had been there a couple of times, visiting Robin on trips back to London. A couple of hours up the M40 as he recalled. Kennedy didn't really do outside W1 – 'for a year, on the same campus as my *ex-wife*, and teach *creative writing* –' Kennedy did a good job of making this sound like 'infant sodomy' – 'to some bunch of bastards?'

'Well, yes, darling,' Connie said. 'That rather is about the size of it.' She giggled and yawned at the same time. She was *tired*. She'd actually got in the evening before. Jet-lagged, unable to sleep, she'd come out here, to the patio bar, where a nightcap had turned into a chat with some producer fellow that had turned into another nightcap in her room that had turned into a fairly athletic sex session that finished when Connie kicked him out just before dawn. Sweet young thing he'd been too. 'It's an odd one, definitely,' she added through the yawn.

'Odd? Odd? It's just . . . *deranged*,' Kennedy said. 'I mean, thank them, obviously, but there's just, there's no way. I've got my hands full here. We've got, what, Braden, three, four movies in pre-production? A bunch of other stuff in development –'

'Actually,' Braden said, 'I think I can square most of the projects. Scott will be a problem, no doubt, but –'

'Hang on.' Kennedy took his second Martini from the tray. Connie ordered another glass of wine. 'Hang on a fucking minute, you *want* me to go?'

Braden sighed. 'Kennedy, you don't seem to be listening to me. If we don't give the IRS a million dollars before the end of the year they are going to come around and take the shirt off your fucking back. This goddamned award is *half a million sterling*. At spot market rate today that's around . . .' Braden tapped at a calculator he'd magically produced from somewhere while Kennedy turned a

,gin-soaked olive around in his mouth. 'Getting on for three-quarters of a million dollars. *Tax. Free.* Also, because you'll be out of the US for so long, we can substantially reduce your tax liabilities here for the coming year.'

Braden's eyes glittering and dancing as he said these hallowed phrases. Fucking Americans and their attitude to taxes. Many a dinner-party conversation on this topic had descended into near violence for Kennedy. The Yanks seemed to think that the idea that you should pay a single solitary cent in taxes was laughable and communistic in nature. When some producer, or some studio boss, leaned in to him over dessert, and said something like, 'Hey, you should check this out. My guy got me into it. The money goes to the Caymans, then . . .' Kennedy's standard response was, 'You like robbing poor people? Why don't we go out now and mug a couple of bums? Set a few dumpsters on fire? You fucking *animal.*' But, out here, even the poor hated the idea of paying taxes. Parts of places like Kentucky, areas with the largest percentage of people on food stamps that were also solidly Republican. Like the corpulent poor, the right-wing poor were a curious modern phenomenon.

Kennedy felt it had to do with the Horatio Alger myth, the rags to riches crap most Americans still believed. The happy resolution to the third act, where they all became millionaires. They didn't like the idea of paying taxes because, even if they were sleeping on the sidewalk and eating turds, they felt they were just one deal away from the big time. Kennedy was a firm believer in 'from each according to his means, to each according to his needs'. How had he landed up with over a million bucks in back taxes? Well, as much as he loved the fair redistribution of wealth, Kennedy Marr really loved spending money on cars, suits and champagne. He tuned back into Braden.

'Ultimately, I'd have to go out and get you a cheque for 1.5 million bucks to leave you 750 after tax and commission and, buddy, that just ain't happening right now.'

Kennedy thought for a moment. 'Then I'll finish all the outstanding stuff. The delivery advances —'

'Still won't cover what you owe the IRS and keep you turning over for the next year.'

'Christ, it's all just about money, isn't it?'

'Oh, grow up,' Braden said.

Connie added, 'It's a Get Out of Jail Free card, darling.'

'It's a deportation order. Forced fucking repatriation is what it is.'

Kennedy sighed and turned away from this pair arraigned against his liberty. He looked around the leafy courtyard garden of the Chateau Marmont. The early-evening sunlight was coming slanting through the trees, the traffic noise from Sunset just audible behind the high, hedged walls that kept the real world at bay. A redhead in a clinging black dress crossed her long legs, the incredible sheen of her thighs. A waiter poured champagne. A man cut into his perfectly rare brioche burger, the stack of thin fries wobbling beside it. A brunette a few tables away smiled at him. Late thirties. If those tits were real then this chick ought to be on TV, she really should. For a moment, looking up into the LA sun, Kennedy felt deep and profound love for everything connected with the city. For the traffic. For the outdoorsmen. For every ludicrous and unnecessary meeting he had ever been forced to have. He even felt love for all the agents who wore their little Bluetooth headsets all the time and who tape-recorded all your meetings.

Then he pictured all of it, all of the obverse, with perfect clarity for a moment – the dismal office, wind rattling the window, reading a short story set in, fuck knows, in interwar Poland? Rural French Canada in the 1900s? Then the knock at the door, some acne-ridden twenty-year-old talent vacuum coming in and telling you about what they'd been 'trying to say'. The pubs and 'restaurants' of rural Warwickshire: overcooked steaks and the utter absence of any kind of valet parking. Standing in some . . . 'staffroom'? Listening to a conversation about what? About deconstruction? Marxist critical theory? Derrida and Lacan? Did they still go on about stuff like that in universities? Robin and Millie. Patrick and Ma. The shuttle he'd no doubt be obliged to take to Dublin every few weeks. Sitting on the tarmac at rain-lashed Heathrow at 7 p.m. on a winter Friday. And then the interminable cab ride to Patrick's place, through those fucking housing estates. Millie and Robin. Christ.

'No. Negative. Not doing it.'

'Fine,' said Braden. 'Then it's hello condo. I'll start making plans to put the house on the market. Severely restrict your personal spending. If we really grit our teeth for the next couple of years we might just get through it.'

'Oh, don't be so melodramatic,' Kennedy said, checking his watch. 'Look, I need to make a move.'

'Or finish the new novel by Christmas,' Connie said.

Kennedy clamped his head between his hands and made a low-pitched growling noise. He really needed to pee very badly.

'There must be something else we can do,' Kennedy said. 'TV. Let's pitch a show. Get a pilot.'

'OK. What's the idea?' Braden said.

'Oh, fuck knows,' Kennedy said. 'Who cares? A couple of skanks share an apartment. No, wait. One's a prude and the other's a skank. Skank talks prude into becoming a skank.'

'Wow,' Braden said flatly. 'Got a title?'

'*Skanks?*' Kennedy said hopefully.

'Jesus,' Braden said.

'Come on. Would it really be so bad?' Connie asked. 'It's only nine months. You'd be so much nearer your family. Millie and Robin. Your mother hasn't been —'

'Connie? Enough,' Kennedy said.

'Or, well,' Connie ploughed on, 'wouldn't it be nice to, you know —' there really was no other way to say it she realised — 'to "give something back"?'

Now it was Kennedy's turn to say it. 'Oh, grow up,' he said.

SIXTEEN

Late, always late, sweating and in extreme distress, Kennedy pushed his way through the throng packed into the bookstore. A throng that appeared, he noticed, to be composed almost entirely of women. Why did one accept the offers to do these things, these readings, speeches, panels and talks? The usual reasons, as Kingsley Amis said, 'a mixture of curiosity and vanity'. And, in Kennedy's case, it had to be said, lust. The object of his lust, the poet herself, was now smiling and waving hello to him from the side of the makeshift stage, where she was huddled with the organisers, a hearty-looking pair of bull diesels in their late fifties who both appeared to be wearing hessian dungarees topped and tailed by buzz cuts and biker boots. Kennedy was wearing a black, two-button Paul Smith suit. Chosen after some deliberation.

The Suits of Kennedy Marr . . .

Earlier that day, sipping a restorative rum and Coke, the ice clanging like bells in the heavy crystal tumbler, Kennedy

Marr surveyed his walk-in closet, preparing for the feminist poetry reading. What to wear? Saskia Kram's slim volume of poems lay unregarded on the bed.

He surveyed the rack of suits before him – hung men. All guilty. This fellow here, the bespoke houndstooth, he'd been a willing accomplice to the cocaine-assisted cunnilingus performed on a script supervisor at a wrap party no more than thirty yards from where the girl's boyfriend stood chatting with the director. Ah, this lad further along, the dark grey pinstripe, he'd been party to the whisky-fuelled brawl on the sidewalk outside the Plaza, after that awards ceremony in New York, with the critic, what's-his-face, who'd jokingly coughed 'shouldn't have won' behind Kennedy's back as he left. Well, Kennedy had wheeled round and caught the fucker square in the eyeball, the cigarette he'd been holding in his balled fist exploding like a tiny firework off the guy's face, scattering pinpricks of burning ash across Kennedy's chest. A tiny burn mark was still visible just above the breast pocket. And now, moving on down, who was this? Of course – the navy single-button Lesley & Roberts. Loyal servant. He'd ridden shotgun the night of the party Connie threw at her house years back, to celebrate his making the Booker shortlist. He'd been there when Kennedy popped out to get more cigarettes, that girl tagging along, a publicist at somewhere or other. Millie calling out for him to get her some Nurofen please. The Lesley & Roberts suit went along with Kennedy's hurried coupling with the publicist, in those bushes on Clapham Common, the branch that snagged at his knee, the repair almost invisible. The tiny stains, the burn marks, the tears and mends. All admissible. All hard evidence.

Yes, all guilty men.

His hand had stopped on the rack and pulled out the perfect partner. The Paul Smith two-button with narrow lapels. Black. Many advantages to the black suit – the slimming effect, its suitability for such a wide range of functions and, most of all, its ability to absorb all manner of sin into its dark soul. Kennedy matched it with a dark grey shirt and black tie, drained his glass – and a goodly half-pint of rum and Coke it had been – and hurried downstairs to the Town Car waiting to take him to the Chateau, remembering to tuck the copy of *Trees* by Saskia Kram into his inside pocket on the way.

The copy of *Trees* that now lay unregarded on the seat beside him as he frantically crossed and recrossed his legs. It had been an eventful ride downtown. Kennedy had chosen a third Martini – and a brief chat with that thirty-something brunette – over his window for a bathroom visit. Already quite urgent when he got into the car, by the time they were on Olympic cutting downtown Kennedy's need to urinate was into Defcon 2. He had the chauffeur pull into a Burger King where he waited, hopping from one foot to the other, for the toilet to vacate. Nearly ten minutes later, and fearing some bloated monster inside was now passing kidneys, heart and spleen into the bowl, he hailed a member of staff. 'Busted,' the lazy-eyed black kid told him.

'Sorry?' Kennedy said.

'S'busted,' the kid shrugged.

Kennedy ran back to the car, a torrent of swear words flying behind him.

Now, here in this sweltering bookstore, his bladder felt like someone had taken an American football and pumped it full of water, distending it to twice its natural size – to the size of a basketball, a medicine ball, a pulsing spacehopper.

'Hi, Saskia,' Kennedy said, coming through the ropes, extending his hand.

'Kennedy! You made it! Thanks so much for doing this.' She embraced him, the light pressure of her stomach against his almost forcing the very piss out of him. She was slender, those sharp, perfect white teeth, that tumbling blonde hair. She smelt of the beach – surf and sandalwood – and he remembered that she lived out by Malibu, at Point Dume. 'This is Janet and Willow, the organisers,' Saskia gestured to the diesels in turn, who were already glaring at Kennedy. Because he was late? Because of his books? Simply because of the terrible prick and balls swinging between his legs like a butcher knife and a pair of hand grenades? Who knew? 'Hi there,' Kennedy said.

'Right,' Janet said gruffly, 'let's get going.'

'Ah, if I could just use the bathroom first,' Kennedy said.

'Uh, use the bathroom?' Willow said, doing a very good job of making it sound like Kennedy had actually asked to defecate in her mouth.

'It's way out back,' Janet said. 'Through the storeroom. We're running very late, you know.' She gestured to the chattering crowd of perhaps two hundred people. 'Surely you can –'

'Look, I . . .' He thought for a second. It *was* just an introduction. *'She's been called blah blah, I think her poetry is blah blah, please welcome . . .'* On and off in two minutes, run to the bathroom, slip out the back door to that bar he'd spotted across the street, pound a few, then slip back in time for the wine and mingle at the end. Offer Saskia a ride back uptown, suggest dinner on the way, Dan Tana's would squeeze them in, back to his place and boom, bash, bosh. Job done. 'Sure, OK,' Kennedy said.

As he and Saskia followed Janet's ass up the steps onto the stage (and this was quite an ass. It looked like someone had strapped the flanks of two cows together) and into the bright lights, the terrible enormity hit Kennedy.

A desk.

Two chairs.

Two microphones.

Oh Jesus. Was he expected to . . . ?

'Ah, excuse me.' He turned and tried to whisper to Willow (fucking *Willow*? Really?) behind him. 'Do you want me to –'

'Shhhhh,' she said fiercely, pressing a finger to her lips. Because Janet was talking, saying his name, and then, applause ringing out, he was being ushered into the glare.

'Good evening, ladies and gentlemen,' Kennedy said, taking his seat, the compression on his bladder feeling like it was about to push the piss out of the pores in his fucking skull. 'It is my great pleasure . . .'

Theoretically he'd had worse times. But not many, and not lately. After his (brief) introduction he'd tried to creep offstage – to be confronted by Janet and Willow, arms folded grimly, their very faces telling him of the magnitude of the insult this would represent. He'd eased himself into his seat only to hear Saskia say the dread words, 'This is quite a long poem . . .'

And his short introduction had been off the mark. Way

off the mark. *'Ladies and gentlemen'*? If there were any gentlemen here they were in heavy drag. Because it was basically a sea, an ocean, of lesbians.

The ones in the front few rows made Janet and Willow look like the oiled, thonged and stilettoed stars of a TV show called *Real Prostitutes of the San Fernando Valley*. Some of them seemed to be wearing potato sacks and barbed wire. It wouldn't have surprised Kennedy to see twinned canisters of Mace dangling as earrings. Several of them were dressed identically: work jeans, boots, severe wedge haircuts and the kind of shawls favoured by Afghan rebels. Kennedy wondered if they had that moment when they all met at a gathering like this where they looked at each other and thought: Holy shit, *I'm a clone*. (Then again, we all had our uniforms, he reflected: Kennedy and his friends, braying on the balcony at Soho House in their white shirts, jeans, suit jackets, brogues and Rolexes.) Many of the audience were openly drooling at Saskia as – standing, her breasts firm against a thin, white cotton blouse – she purred her way into what felt like the seventeenth stanza, the tenth canto. When Kennedy caught the eye of one of the women the level of dislike that radiated back was so intense that he might as well have been wearing a name tag that said 'Hello, my name is MR RAPIST'.

Here was an angry, politicised world, the kind of world stamped out in acronyms, whose business was seeking offence, the world of NW (Non-White), WoC (Women of Colour), TERF (Trans Exclusionary Radical Feminists) and BME (Black and Minority Ethnic), a world of people who minted neologisms like banknotes in the Weimar Republic, who wrote rage-spattered essays and blogs and poetry for no money whatsoever. It didn't look like much fun from where he was sitting, high on the stage in his expensive suit and white skin, festooned with functioning limbs, his income in seven figures, his torso unencumbered by tits or the mad ram's horns of a uterus and fallopian tubes, his mind untroubled by the lust for his own sex or the urge to have his prick chopped off. An apex predator.

Kennedy checked his privilege and found it to be good.

But, dear God, what was happening inside of him? It felt like his bladder, having long since expanded to annex his stomach, was now making powerful advances into his lungs, sternum and throat. He almost feared to open his mouth in case a torrent of urine cascaded out. He felt like he was simply a tautening bag of piss. His feet thrummed gently on the floor and, now and then, a tiny squeak or moan escaped from him.

Finally the audience was noisily applauding and cheering and Kennedy joined in, grateful for the chance to move around, to growl and roar in fury. He started to get to his feet, just as he heard Saskia saying, 'I wrote this next poem three years ago when I was . . .'

He lowered himself slowly back into the chair, the very action nudging the urine into the actual shaft of his penis. Incredible scrunching of the testicles and urethra was now the only thing standing between him and Defcon 1. Spots of light danced in his vision. Beads of sweat broke out on his forehead. Kennedy leaned forward on the desk and put his head in his hands, doing a good job of making it look like he was concentrating very hard on the poem Saskia was reading — 'Tear me *apart I asked him, and he tore, he tore, he tore . . .'* – when, in reality, she could have stripped naked and been doing herself on the table with a two-foot joy boy for all Kennedy knew. His eyes were closed and he was repeating the mantra of *'Suckthepissbackupsuckthepissbackupsuck . . .'* over and over to himself. He began to see strange, clear visions dancing behind his eyes: him eating bread on the kitchen floor in the tiny house, a toddler at his mother's ankles. Then he was on a bike, eight or nine years old, and wheeling through the streets of Limerick. Gazing at Joanna Mulreany in English, in fourth year. Hunkered down in the circular Reading Room at Glasgow University, preparing for his finals. Cuddling Millie and Robin in bed when Robin was tiny.

Kennedy realised he was seeing his life flashing before his eyes.

Then, finally, somehow, it was all over and the audience was applauding, rising to their feet, as was Kennedy for the third time, when he felt a hand on his shoulder and Willow – or Janet – was actually pushing him back into his place, reaching around him and taking the microphone and saying, 'Thank you, Saskia. Now does anyone have any questions?'

Defcon 1.

As a forest of hands shot up Kennedy thought something like, 'Ach, fuck it.' Relief unbounded. The warmth, the release. It was almost better than the sweetest orgasm. He felt it flooding down his left thigh, flowing under his arse, down his legs, draining into his shoes. Still it went on. It felt like two or three litres of the stuff. Kennedy Marr sat there – a beatific grin on his face.

There were indeed many advantages to the black Paul Smith suit, he reflected a few moments later as he slunk towards the back entrance of the bookstore. (*No, no, I'm fine. Just my stomach. Please excuse me.*) Not least its ability to allow a man to piss himself in public and pass relatively unnoticed.

SEVENTEEN

A quarter past five in the morning, the weakly glowing arms of her wee alarm clock were telling her. Ach – any thing after five counted as a full night's sleep for Kathleen Marr these days. She'd never been a great sleeper, unlike her Rory – dead these twenty years now. Kennedy took after her. Up till all hours so he was. Patrick was more like his dad. Geraldine had been too. She sat up in bed, wincing a little – her back, never the same after Gerry, she just hadn't wanted to come out, that girl – and turned the bedside light on. The sideboard over there, now used as a kind of chest of drawers for her. An odd kind of bedroom Patrick's dining room had been the past few months. Oh well, her last morning waking up in here. Her suitcase stood packed by the sideboard, a carrier bag next to it with the new toothbrush, slippers and toiletries that Patrick had bought for her. Such a good boy. Had always taken care of her. Unlike some. Kathleen thought this without bitterness. Children were all different. They had different talents. Her

Patrick was a carer – look at his job now. Some of the stuff he had to go through with these poor demented kids.

She looked at the clutter of photographs on her bedside table, the ones she'd brought from her place. One of the whole family, taken down at the harbour in Kilrush, back in the mid-1980s. A sunny day, but Kennedy all in black already, maybe sixteen or seventeen? Geraldine fourteen or fifteen. Scowling in her tracksuit. A row about something or other no doubt. Wee Patrick would be ten or eleven. Just a wee boy still. Grinning from ear to ear. Always the easiest of the lot. Her and Rory sat behind them on the low stone wall in front of the Atlantic Ocean. Next to it another photo of Kennedy, taken just a few years back, on the red carpet at some premiere he was at. He was laughing, pointing at someone, his arm around that Vicky, his second wife. Beautiful girl so she was now. Kathleen had only met her the once, at lunch in Dublin, at that hotel your boys from U2 owned. The Clarence was it? Kennedy had been staying there. The lunch had probably lasted longer than the bloody marriage. He should have stayed with Millie – she'd always liked Millie. There were photos of her grandchildren: Robin when she was three or four, up on Kennedy's shoulders on a beach somewhere, the two of them wearing sunglasses; Patrick's three – unwrapping their presents last Christmas. There at the front was a photo of Gerry on her own, laughing. Taken at some party. She'd found it among her things. After. Kathleen didn't know whose party it was, or what had been going on, but she liked it because it was the only photograph she had of her daughter where she was smiling. She was holding a can of cider and you could see the cuts and bruises on her hand. Oh, Gerry. Ten years now. She'd have been forty-two this week. Rory would have been seventy-nine. It was hard to imagine.

Kathleen Marr lay there for a while, communing with her dead in her makeshift bedroom as dawn crept westwards outside, making its way across the sea from England. She wondered if Patrick had spoken to Kennedy yet. She'd like to see him. She needed to see him. He was a bugger right enough, but she knew how busy he was, how hard he had to work, how expensive flights were. Sure he'd be over soon enough.

Upstairs she heard a toilet flushing. Six o'clock now. Patrick getting up. Getting ready to help deal with the kids before he got the Dart into Dublin for work. He'd be knocking softly on that door soon. Bringing her a wee cup of tea. Asking if she wanted a piece of toast. She never did. Not these days. But Patrick always asked. Such a good boy. How different they all were, children. She rolled over on her side – so light now she barely made an impression on the mattress – and drifted back off to sleep, looking at Kennedy, beaming on the red carpet in front of that Chinese theatre where they have all the fancy premieres.

EIGHTEEN

Dining with a movie star. The tedious rituals that had to observed, even with someone like Michael Curzon who, while not A-list stellar, was still enough of a name to create grief. The day after the bookstore incident Curzon's office rang Spengler's office who rang Braden's office who rang Kennedy *three* times in connection with the meal: once to switch the location of the dinner (because word had got out on the Internet that Michael was going to be eating there and he feared a scrum of fans outside), a second time to cancel the meal entirely (Michael was going on a friend's private jet to Vegas at the last minute and could he please reschedule? Nothing would have given Kennedy greater pleasure), and a third time to say the dinner was still on at the original location.

So here was Kennedy – at the bar in the Chav (that fucking name. Didn't the clowns realise how insulting it was? They just thought it was funny and 'English'. They might as well have called it the Toothless White Trash) just off Hollywood Boulevard, drinking a double vodka/rocks/ twist and scanning the crowd while he observed another sacrosanct ritual of the movie star: the lateness of their arrival.

It had not been an uneventful day for him either. First thing he'd rung Saskia Kram to apologise for his running out without properly saying goodbye the night before, and for his contributions to her talk having been largely restricted to barks, grunts and yelps. While Kennedy talked to her, from where he lay splayed and hung-over on the bed, he could see the bathtub in his en suite, with the black suit floating in it like a corpse.

Then – while he tried to work on the Spengler script – he fielded calls from Connie and Braden, both alternating tag-team style, applying the pressure for his accepting this idiotic fucking award. And then, worst of all, oh very bad indeed, there was no way it should have happened, so few people had the number, the time difference with back home was such that he never thought for a second that . . . oh well, whatever, around six o'clock, just as he was getting dressed, fixing a drink, dropping ice into a highball glass, he snatched up the ringing home phone and got his brother.

'Jesus Christ, Kennedy.'

'Patrick. Wow. How's tricks?'

'Oh, I'm grand, Kennedy. It's you I'm worried about. I've been trying to get hold of you for two fucking days.'

'I . . . really? My phone must –'

'Don't you check your email?'

'Oh, right, they must have gone into my . . . junk mail?'

Kennedy heard his younger brother sighing down the line. He pictured the sigh running down a cable stretching along the floor of the Atlantic, all the way from Ireland. 'Anyway,' Kennedy said, trying to recover, looking at his watch, doing the math, 'what's up? What time is it back there?'

'It's two o'clock in the morning.'

'What are you doing up at this time? Wait, you didn't have another baby?'

'No, Kennedy, I stayed up until this time because I figured I might have a better chance of getting hold of you.'

'Come on, I'm kidding. Look, I'm just getting ready to go out here so I haven't really got long. Maybe we –'

'She's really not well, Kennedy.'

'Ach, come on. Sure and we've heard that before.' Kennedy's accent – thickening within a few moments of talking to his brother.

'I'm not fucking around here.'

'I'll call her. Tomorrow. I promise. It's just been . . . crazy here lately.'

'You need to come and see Mam.'

'I will. I will. The next few months are nuts.'

'Look, I know you can't deal with this. That's fine. I'll deal with it for both us. I'll do the hospital runs. I'll do her shopping and go round every other night and what have you. But you need to *come and see her.*'

'I hear you, Patrick. It's . . . I'm right in the middle of pre-production on this fucking picture and –'

'Kennedy, she –'

'– I'll get sued for fucking breach if I don't deliver –'

'Kennedy?'

'– by the middle of –'

'KENNEDY!'

'Jesus! What?'

'She weighs six stone.'

Silence. He'd been out here so long he had to do the math. Convert it. Six times, what? Fourteen pounds to the stone? Around eighty pounds? Could that be . . .

'Oh Jesus. Jesus fuck.'

'She didn't want me telling you because, get this,' Patrick laughed, a short bark, 'because "your work is so important".'

Six stone? When had he last seen her? About a year ago? On a trip back to see Robin, was it?

'Anyway. Now you know.'

'OK. Right. I . . . I'll call her in the morning.'

'She's been a bit down this week. You know. With . . .'

'Yeah.' With Gerry's birthday. 'I know. I'm sorry, Patrick. I should have called. I . . . I'm a dick.'

'Well. This we know.'

'Look, Patrick, there's some stuff afoot just now, I'm not quite sure yet, but it looks like I might be back in England for a while. At the end of the summer. I'll be around. I'll come out and spend some time with her. I mean, she's not going to . . .'

'I don't think so. She's a right old battler.'

'And I'll call her.'

'OK. Fair enough. Are you well now?'

'Ach, I'm fine.'

'Where you running off to?'

'Huh?'

'You said you were off out.' His brother, actually listening to what other people said. He really was a remarkable person.

'Oh, I've got this stupid fecking dinner. With an actor fella. Michael Curzon.'

'Is that right? Is that your man that was in that thing with the time machine and whatnot?'

'The very same.'

'Fair play to you.'

'I'm sorry, Patrick.'

'*Absolvo te*. Take care of yourself now, Kennedy.'

'You too. Love to Anne and the kids.'

Kennedy had hung up and sat on the edge of the bed for a while, in his unbuttoned shirt and boxers, with the glass full of ice in his right hand. Patrick. The youngest of them. Not yet forty and married to the same woman for nearly fifteen years. Three kids. In the same job for just as long. He lived in a tiny cottage just outside Dublin and rode the Dart into the city every day then got on the bus to his office. (Yeah, a bus. A fucking *bus*. Kennedy tried to picture it.) Appropriately, when it came to dealing with Kennedy, Patrick was a social worker, mainly dealing with kids in their late teens from the roughest parts of Dublin. He tried to help them with their housing issues. Their drug and alcohol and sexual abuse issues. Their benefit claims. Their unmet educational needs. On a daily basis Patrick had to listen to the very worst that humanity could do to itself. The kids who'd been abused and beaten and thrown out of their homes. The girls with two or three kids by the age of eighteen who couldn't read or write. The wee boys with both parents in prison. Patrick did this uncomplainingly day in and day out year after year for very long hours for very little money. (Kennedy could probably have pitched *Skanks* in forty-five minutes and walked off the lot with a cheque for far in excess of what his brother earned in a year.) Kennedy threw a shit fit if the gin wasn't cold enough. He whined more during the course of the average meal than Patrick had in his lifetime.

Because your work is so important.

Well, like Patrick, Kennedy had managed a laugh at that as he poured vodka from the bedroom fridge, listening to the pleasing splintering of the ice.

The real reason he was putting off going to see his mother was impossible for an atheistic man like Kennedy to voice. Because he didn't believe in all that crap. Nonetheless he knew the strange thought was running through him. *'Dying to see you.'* This was, in a sense, absolutely correct.

Ma had to see him before she died.

If he did not go she could not die.

It really was this simple.

'Excuse me, Mr Marr?'

Kennedy looked up from his glass. 'Yeah?'

The waiter who'd greeted his arrival at the Chav – young, incredibly good-looking, camp, most likely an actor – leaned in and lowered his voice in a ludicrously dramatic fashion as he said, clearly impressed, 'Your other party is here. Please let me show you to your table.'

Through to the back dining room, returning a few nods and hellos as he went, across the room to the back wall and there, in the very back banquette, alone at a table that would have seated four, even though the restaurant was packed, was Michael Curzon, standing now to greet him, Kennedy trying to force his features into something resembling a civil, benevolent grin. Curzon was defiantly dressed down, wearing a grey fleece with the hood pulled up. He lowered it now as Kennedy extended his hand.

'Michael. Hi.'

'Kennedy. It's a pleasure.'

Curzon's face, a face Kennedy knew from the screen, was idiotically, obscenely handsome. Everything – cheekbones, lips, jawline, nose, stubble – looked like it had come straight off a blueprint called 'MOVIE STAR 200010877'. The eyes were green as a liqueur, like Midori, like absinthe.

The hand-shaking done, heads turning subtly towards them while it happened, Curzon flopped back down into the semi-darkness of the booth. He had the standard apparatus on the table in front of him: Marlboro Lights, mineral water, BlackBerry. The waiter handed them menus. He was nervy, well aware of the star wattage at the table. 'And can I get you anything from the bar?'

'Vodka, rocks, twist,' Kennedy said.

Curzon smiled slightly and shook his head at the waiter. The gesture said, 'Nothing for me thank you and, boy, this guy likes to party, huh?' Fucking LA, where a cocktail might as well have been freebase. Kennedy changed his mind. 'Make it a double,' he said. Fuck this guy. *Fuck him.*

The waiter scribbled it down. 'And let me tell you about our specials this evening . . .' All these waiters in LA, rattling off long lists of 'specials'. Actors, showing you they could memorise dialogue, trying to inject drama, pathos and humour into phrases like 'on a bed of', 'pan-fried', 'line-caught', 'grass-fed' and 'free-range'. As Kennedy listened to the waiter he realised that, until relatively recently, Curzon had probably been one of these guys. Until the crazed digit of fame had pointed his way, he had been working his tight buns in waiter pants, filling water glasses and reeling off the specials. Curzon heard the waiter out and ordered a chopped salad. Kennedy went for the baked sea bream and told the guy to bring a bottle of Sancerre with the food. 'Ah, I'm not drinking?' Curzon said, phrasing it very much as a question. He might as well have said 'Hello?' first.

'Excellent,' Kennedy said. The waiter looked at them both, from one to the other, confused. Curzon shrugged in a 'your funeral' way and the guy went off to get Kennedy's vodka.

'I'd just like to say, Kennedy,' Curzon began, 'I'm a huge fan of, well, not just *Unthinkable*, obviously, but all your work. The other books, the movies . . .'

'Thank you. I've really enjoyed your work too.' Kennedy shot his cuffs and leaned across the table. 'So, Michael, what's on your mind?'

'Right to it, huh?' Curzon said, laughing.

'Please.'

'OK. I heard you were, uh, direct. I think in the script, which is brilliant by the way, but I think the relationship between my character and Julie's could use a little extra . . . heat. Chemistry. Whatever you want to call it.'

'Heat?'

'Yeah.'

'Chemistry?'

'Mmmm.'

'Right,' Kennedy said, thinking. Or rather, pretending to think.

'It just feels to me,' Curzon went on, 'that we could add another layer. That . . .' Kennedy felt his spine stiffening.

'Add another layer', a phrase much beloved of actors, producers, directors and studio executives, who thought that it meant something. What it usually meant was 'we're going to drive you insane writing yet another draft of this perfectly fine script before we go back to what you had in the first place'. 'That these two incredibly passionate people,' Curzon continued, 'that, uh, given the tension that exists between them on the page, that in, umm, in a dramatic sense, it would be more convincing – like cathartic? – if they somehow . . .'

Kennedy stopped listening and just watched the kid trying to talk. He tried to remember being twenty-six. Had he ever been this inarticulate? This uncomfortable in the realm of ideas? Somewhere during Curzon's mumbling, halting monologue, filled with crap about 'arcs' and 'journeys' and 'transformation', a big glass of vodka had appeared at Kennedy's elbow. He drank about half of it in one gulp and held a finger up, stopping Curzon mid-flow just as he was saying '. . . if that tension was to be, somehow, released –'

'You want to fuck Julie, right?' Kennedy said

'Excuse me?'

'In the script. In the movie. You want your character – Will – to fuck Gillian, Julie's character.'

'I, well . . .'

'OK,' Kennedy said. 'Let me see if I can make that happen.'

Curzon looked at him, his finely wrought HD eyebrows going up a notch. Clearly he'd been expecting more of a fight. Why fight? Kennedy thought. Just tell this mutant fuckstick handpump exactly what he wanted to hear and then go ahead and ignore it. He doubted Curzon had the juice to have him replaced. Julie Teal . . . now that would be a whole other kettle of Strindberg bullshit.

'I just think, in a purely dramatic sense, it would heighten everything. In terms of the message of the film . . .' Curzon said as their food arrived.

The sea bream came wrapped in the tinfoil it had been baked in, the crimped edges around the top slightly blackened, charred from the oven. He opened it – a cloud of fragrant steam and the whole fish, with chilies, garlic and tiny cherry tomatoes, red and yellow, perfectly cooked until almost bursting.

That tinfoil.

He'd taken her for lunch that day, Geraldine. He'd driven to her tiny council flat in Limerick in the Mercedes he'd rented at Dublin airport and they'd gone out to lunch. How long ago was it now? Nine years? Ten? He'd have been thirty-four, still, just, flushed with youth and success. Still, just, bruised from the divorce from Millie. Gerry would have been two years younger. Mam had been worried – Gerry'd been losing a lot of weight. Never answered her phone, or came to the door sometimes, even though Mam knew she was in there. She'd opened the door cautiously, the chain on. 'Kennedy?' she'd said. 'It's yourself. For fuck's sake – you scared me.' She'd forgotten the arrangement. He noticed how jumpy she seemed to be about an unexpected knock. He noticed the scuffs on her front door. (Kick marks?) Her red eyes and hacking cough.

She'd gone to get herself ready, telling him to help himself to the joint of pungent skunk weed smouldering in the overflowing ashtray, the packet of twenty Benson & Hedges beside it. (Kennedy reflected that the only people who smoked in their houses nowadays were pretty much the aristocracy and the long-term unemployed. Smoking in your home, like having any number of children without consequence, had ceased to be for the middle classes. It was now the sole provenance of the top and bottom ends of the social scale.) He'd opened a window and taken a jolt from the silver hip flask instead and settled on the faux leather sofa. It was a room that, say, Truman Capote would have described well. The thin faux-wood laminate flooring that creaked and cracked when you walked upon it. The cheap, imitation-leather sofa. The dated glass-and-chrome coffee table that Kennedy seemed to remember had come from some aunt or uncle or cousin. The little circular dining table in the corner, covered in dirty dishes. The artwork on the walls, a cheaply framed market trader movie poster: Al Pacino in *Scarface*. The photographs on the mantelpiece in generic faux pewter frames inscribed with captions designed to stress the themes contained in the pictures within – 'HAPPY TIMES', 'LOVE' – a recent shot of his daughter Robin (Robin six and wildly happy, cradling her first acoustic guitar) and Rowan and Eamonn, Patrick's toddlers. Her library sat on a low shelf – his own three published novels at that time, a copy of *Mr Nice* and a couple of *Harry Potters*. Smack in the middle of the room, the only thing of any value in the flat, the huge fifty-inch flat-screen television with the Xbox nestled below it. The whole place was straight out of the pages of *Lifestyles of the Minor League Drug Dealer*.

Walking through to the kitchen he'd looked down the short hallway and noticed that her bedroom door was closed. The kitchen was just a box room really, about enough room to fully extend your arms. The window looked out onto the back gardens of the neighbouring flats: wheelie bins and aluminium whirly gigs and bits of rubbish chasing each other in circles. The calendar on the wall: still on March (it was May). He flipped a few pages. All empty save for the odd sole entry in one or other month in Gerry's girlish hand – 'Mam Birthday', 'Doctor', 'Benefit Interview'. (A strange pang here – after a few years of success Kennedy had begun to long for his own diary to be this bereft. It was becoming an instrument of torture: *8.55 Heathrow. 12th: Waterstone's Manchester. Dinner: Connie. Lunch: ICM. Meeting: Curtis Brown. LA. Berlin. Dublin. Awards.*) He opened the little fridge: a rind of cheese, a bottle of ketchup and a two-litre bottle of White Lightning cider. The freezer compartment was a solid block of white ice with a slit in the middle that might just have accommodated a thin-crust pizza. He opened a drawer – a letter, black type, a box edged in red. 'If payment is not received by . . .' There were many more beneath it. He opened the cupboard above – the stale, musty smell. Two cans of mushroom soup, a can of beans and a cluster of small brown medicine bottles: 'Lorazepam', 'Diazepam', 'Codeine'. He stepped on the pedal and opened the bin: a broken-up pizza box covered in burned, charred squares of tinfoil.

Hell. Everywhere you looked, tiny circles of hell.

Kennedy reviewed all the adjectives. What would Capote have on that list? *Thin, little, cheap, faux.* If you removed the television and the Xbox the entire contents of the flat might have fetched a couple of hundred euro.

When Gerry reappeared she was happier. Her eyes shining as she slipped her coat on and they went out together into the biting spring wind. She'd been impressed by the car. Was full of questions about what he'd been up to and who he'd met and how much she'd liked his books, and sometimes, here and there, when she laughed or said 'Is that right now?' in amazement, Kennedy could see little glimpses of the baby sister he remembered. Then her phone rang and she answered it. She listened for a moment before exploding. *'You listen to me, you stupid fucking eejit, I'll come round there, I'll come round there with Billy fucking Williams and we'll cut your fucking throat, you fucking prick, you. Friday meant Friday. Not tomorrow. Not next week. Fucking Friday. Yeah, yeah. See and you do, you fucking eejit fucking prick, you.'* She went on, seemingly oblivious to him there in the driver's seat. *'Disrespect.'* *'The wee thing with the silencer that goes "pfft pfft bye bye".'* *'A fecking bodybag.'*

By the time Gerry had finished Kennedy had pulled over and was staring at her in astonishment, not recognising her. 'What the fuck, Gerry?' he asked her.

'What?'

'Who was that?'

'Ach – just some eejit trying it on. Bit of business. You don't want to know.'

'Why were you talking like that?'

'Like what?'

'Like some idiotic gangster.'

'Hey – you don't know what it's like round here,' she said, irritated, gesturing vaguely through the windscreen at Limerick, at a bus shelter, an old lady making her way across the road, pulling her wee shopping trolley. The wind. 'You've got to talk the fucking talk sometimes.'

They'd gone to a country pub, off the road towards

Shannon. She'd eaten nothing. A spoonful of soup. Maybe a forkful of mash. She'd sipped at a pint of lager while Kennedy made his way alone through a decent bottle of claret. He had watched his sister while she spoke to him: the heavy sovereign ring glinting on her right hand. The chunky gold chain around her neck. The tattooed cherries on her wrist. The way she'd suspiciously scan the room whenever anyone came near them. How deeply uncomfortable she was in these circumstances: with the glasses and the silverware and the service.

Finally he'd asked it. 'Gerry,' he'd said, coming across the table, leaning close to her, 'what are you going to do?'

'Eh?'

'With the rest of your life. What are you going to do?'

'How do you mean?'

'Well, whatever you're doing now, it doesn't look like it's going that great. When you were little what did you see yourself doing? Like, what would your ideal job be?'

She looked at him like he'd gone completely fucking insane.

'Fuck off,' she said, laughing. Was he taking the piss?

'Seriously,' Kennedy said.

'Job? Fuck. I don't know. I sometimes think I'd quite like to have been a nurse.' She said this apologetically, Kennedy thought. As though it were fantastical. As though she might as well have been talking about becoming chairman of ICI. Chancellor. An astronaut. 'But, fuck, you need exams and that. Your kind of stuff.' She swirled flat lager.

'That's not impossible. You're only thirty-two. Night school. Go back and do your —'

'Aye. I suppose,' Gerry said, bored, uninterested now. 'I'd help you.'

'Is that right?'

'Sure.'

'Listen, right, if you want to help me, this thing went on recently. That stuff in the car was, well, it wasn't my fault but . . .'

Kennedy listened. He nodded, gradually realising that Gerry had her ideal job. It was lying on a pleather sofa, smoking skunk and heroin and playing Xbox. He listened to her telling him the kind of story she had been telling him for over a decade now: basically all a variant on a movie called *The Sure Thing Goes Wrong*. He nodded. He wrote her a cheque on his Irish account for two thousand euros. She hugged him, tears of gratitude in her eyes.

It was dark when he dropped her back at the flat. As she went to get out of the car, on impulse, he put a hand on her shoulder. 'Hang on. Here.' He handed her all the cash from his wallet, a couple of hundred. She kissed him on the cheek as she folded the notes in her hand. 'I'm just a fuck-up, Kennedy,' she said. 'You're as well not bothering with me.'

He watched her go through the door and vanish down the communal hallway, towards the stairs, up towards the miserable flat. *Bye, bye. Bye-bye, Kenny.* The way she used to wave to him from the window as he went off to school. Him five or six, her three or four, a toddler in her fluffy yellow romper suit. The wave, her wee fingers just flexing at the joints – *Bye-bye, Gerry. Bye-bye.*

Kennedy wiped his mouth, dropped his napkin on top of the sea bream carcass, and looked at Curzon, who was still crapping on about the 'message' of the film.

Kennedy leaned across and interrupted. 'The *message* of the film? The fucking . . . Michael, tell me, do you know what drama is? What art is? What it does? Or should do, rather.'

'Hey,' Curzon said, 'obviously I'm not a writer, but –'

'Just –' Kennedy held up a hand – 'define this "message of the film" for me.'

Curzon sat there for a moment, looking flummoxed, like he'd been called out in class. Actually looking like he was getting angry. Kennedy pictured the tower of scripts by Curzon's bed. The odd self-help book. A few unread novels. 'Look –' Curzon said.

Kennedy cut him off. 'The purpose of art is to *delight*. Not to enlighten. Not to teach. *Certain men and women –*' Kennedy looked past the kid, into the mirror behind him on the wall, into his own, tired, lined, middle-aged face, and continued quoting Mamet to the letter – '*certain men and women whose art can delight us have been given dispensation from going out and fetching water and carrying wood.*' He leaned forward again, elbows on the table, closer to the actor's face. '*Artists do not wonder "what is it good for?" They aren't driven to "help people" or to "make money". They are driven to lessen the burden of the unbearable disparity between their conscious and unconscious minds and so to achieve peace.*'

That yellow romper suit. Her skin, later.

Kennedy leaned back and drained his wine glass.

'Man,' Curzon said, 'that's really beautiful. Did you say that?'

'Yeah,' Kennedy said, his twinned index and middle fingers raised, signalling for the check. 'I fucking did.'

Across the restaurant a girl – early twenties, surely a

model – caught his eye, held his gaze, and smiled, completely ignoring her date. Yes, Kennedy had to admit, smiling back, they were limited, but there were definitely upsides to dining with movie stars. Their waiter came over. 'Was everything OK for you?'

'Yeah, just the check thanks.' Kennedy said.

The waiter nodded and signalled for a busboy to come and clear their plates. Just then, and it was brief, the slightest of glances, a look passed between the waiter and Curzon. A shy, glancing grin.

Ah, Kennedy thought, realising why the guy wanted to fuck Julie in the film so badly.

NINETEEN

Dr Dennis Drummond, working late in his office beneath the warmth of the anglepoise. Square in the middle of his desk sat the telephone-book-sized press pack Kennedy's UK publisher had provided him with. Sixteen years' worth: the articles beginning back in 1997 with the publication of *Unthinkable*, and carrying on right up until his arrest in a bar-room brawl in Los Angeles earlier this year.

Drummond's own media pack would, it had to be said, have made scanter reading. A short story or pamphlet next to the *Moby-Dick* of press spread out in front of him now. He was the author of three novels: *A Circular Defence* (Picador, 1991), *On Beaten Wings* (Cronulla Independent Press, 1993) and *Nefarious* (Unpublished, 1997). (Well, three and a half. Forty-odd thousand words of an as yet untitled work lurked in the bowels of an old Dell PC that was hidden under a pile of lecture notes in a corner of his office at home.) His reviews totalled five: four around the time of his major publisher debut and one – in the

Bookseller – for his sophomore effort. Two of the reviews pinpointed exactly what went wrong in Drummond's novels: nothing actually happened. Here was a man who had taken Raymond Chandler's maxim 'when in doubt, have a man come through the door with a gun in his hand' and replaced it with 'when in doubt, go into a thousand-word description of the texture of a Formica tabletop. Or have a character go off on a five-page interior monologue recalling a minor incident from childhood.' The bald facts (and here Drummond inched his shining bald head further under the lamp to better read the publisher's blurb, his fingertips brushing back gently through the thin layer of silvery stubble on his head) were that Kennedy Marr's collected body of work – six novels and a collection of short stories – had shifted over five million copies, nearly half of that on *Unthinkable*, which was now in its fifth or sixth edition. His books had been translated into twenty-eight languages. Dennis Drummond's two published novels – both long out of print – had sold a combined 700 units. He was in two languages: English and Latvian. (The Latvian sale a mad oddity – his agent knew someone who knew someone who was working at a government-funded press over there – that had netted him a 300-pound advance. He would have seen 150 pounds of this, had his novel recouped the tiny advance he had been paid. Needless to say – it had not.)

He flipped on through the pages of the media pack, looking for that half-remembered quote from an interview he wanted to add to the collection of Kennedy Marr quotes in his notebook.

An unenviable position for the writer like Dr Drummond.

He had been given his shot. Out of the millions of unsoli-
cited manuscripts that circled the globe every year his had
been selected by a major publishing house. He had experienced the flushed joy of taking the hardback edition of his
own novel out of the Jiffy bag and tenderly running a hand
over its jacket. (The very same copy that sat somewhere
on the bookshelves behind him, positioned around eye level
for someone sitting opposite him.) He had once had an
agent. What he had written, his angle on the world, his
idea of how we talk, think and interact with one another,
had been taken to market. And the people at the market,
the public, had resoundingly said, 'No thank you. We're
good.' Meanwhile, over at the Kennedy Marr stall, they
were fifteen-deep. They were waving money over their
heads and screaming out their orders. People were fighting
over the last few copies while fainting women were carried
clear by overworked paramedics. At the Kennedy Marr stall
it was forever Christmas Eve on Oxford Street, the first
day of the January sales. Meanwhile here was Drummond,
with a mountain of sweaters to sell in July. It seemed like
the final insult that *Unthinkable* had been published in 1997:
the very year that Drummond's third – and so far final –
novel had failed to find a publisher. Reading through the
press pack another terrible symmetry struck him: Kennedy
had probably been informed of his being the youngest ever
novelist to make the Booker shortlist around the same time
that Drummond's agent had taken him for that awful pint
of beer in the Pillars of Hercules on Greek Street, where
he told him the dread words about his third novel's attempts
to find a home: 'I think we've done all we can with this
one.' (Meanwhile, a few steps away on Dean Street,

Kennedy: in the Groucho Club, up to his armpits in tits and Bollinger.)

Finally he found it, there in an interview in *The Times*, from five years ago, around the publication of his last novel. The quote began, *'I don't see how it can be taught, really.'* Drummond began copying it into his notebook, aware that another thing cut him deeply too. As he had turned the pages, as the mid-nineties turned into the new millennium, as the new millennium moved into its second decade, Kennedy Marr's face looked out from the photocopied newsprint: still topped with the same thick, black head of hair it had been nearly twenty years ago.

The light of the anglepoise – still warm on Drummond's naked head as he wrote. Warwickshire rain on the window.

TWENTY

Conference call with Scott Spengler. They were in Braden's office, gathered around the matt-black, pyramid-shaped speakerphone: Connie, Braden, Kennedy and Danny the assistant, taking notes. On the low table: a silver jug of coffee, a pitcher of orange juice, and a basket of freshly baked croissants, with only Kennedy's hand venturing now and then into the venomous den of carbs. A slight, low-level anxiety flickered through the room, as was usual when people were waiting to be connected with one of the giants of the business. (Remember – Scott Spengler's films had grossed a combined 1.5 billion dollars at the box office.) While an assistant put them on hold yet again, while satellite connections hummed and buzzed between here and the outback, Connie had another pop.

'I've been here three days, Kennedy. I can't stall them forever.'

'You don't have to stall them. Tell them "no".'

Braden pushed a piece of paper across the glass-topped coffee table towards him. Kennedy had already seen it. Twice. It said 'IRS' at the top. A lot of red type. Seven figures. Kennedy pushed it back.

Suddenly an assistant's voice burst clear out of the speaker. 'I have Scott for you.' Then, the great man himself, 'Hi there. Who am I talking to?'

'Hi, Scott. It's Braden and you've got Kennedy and also Connie, Kennedy's English agent.'

'Morning, everyone.'

'Morning,' the four of them chorused.

'Right. We are officially green-lit.'

Braden led the customary whooping and cheering. Connie and Danny joining in enthusiastically, Kennedy, as was his wont, less so.

'The studio definitely want the picture for next Christmas, so we're being fast-tracked into production. We're going to start shooting some interiors on the lot in Burbank in six weeks' time. Kennedy, I heard you met with Michael. Thanks for that and Michael loves you by the way.'

'No problem,' Kennedy said. 'Nice kid.'

'Julie also has some thoughts so you'll need to meet with her too in due course. Now there's a few exciting developments in terms of financing and locations that will impact on the script too. I get back tonight. I've set up a breakfast with me, you and Kevin at my place tomorrow morning.' Kevin McConnell, the director.

'Developments? Do –' Kennedy began, but Spengler was set to 'output'.

'Now, we'll be at Burbank for two months then we're going to England end of October.'

'England?' Braden said, his head snapping up, looking directly at Kennedy. Connie looking at him too.

'Yeah. Pinewood. Pain in the ass for everyone but it's the only place with a soundstage big enough that fits with our schedule. We'll be there through to Christmas when we wrap.' Kennedy covered his face. This couldn't be happening. He could feel the smiles of Connie and Braden burning through the backs of his hands. 'Hey, Kennedy,' Spengler said, 'how about that? Back to the old countree, huh?'

'Yeah, great,' Kennedy said. Connie was actually laughing now.

'Good work so far, everyone. Let's keep it up. Gonna be a great picture. See you tomorrow, Kennedy.'

'Bye,' everyone chorused. A digitised 'beep' and the producer was gone.

Kennedy sat there looking at them.

'Well,' Connie said.

'Oh, you're loving this, aren't you? You pair of fucking bastards,' Kennedy said.

Braden was already tapping at his calculator. 'With your principal photography cheque on this and the Bingham money you are free and clear, buddy. We can pay the IRS off and you can live high on the hog for the foreseeable future.'

'Face it, darling,' Connie said. 'The die is cast. The fates want you to go home.'

'But, what . . . what . . .' Kennedy flailed around, looking for a last card to play. 'What about my appointments with Dr Brendle? The court order?'

'If you have to leave the country for work I'm sure we

can come to an arrangement there,' Braden said. 'Either resume when you come back or arrange something in England.'

Kennedy tilted the chair all the way back, looking up at the ceiling, lying almost flat. He looked very much like a boxer who had been holding onto the ropes, fighting against all the odds, somehow managing to stay upright until that final, killer blow had sent him sprawling to the canvas. He sighed. 'I better call Millie.'

'Yayyyy!' Connie said, clapping her hands together girlishly. 'I'll call the F. W. Bingham people.'

'Danny?' Braden said. 'Could you go get us a bottle of champagne and some glasses please? In fact, get the Cristal from Bob's office.' He hefted the pitcher of orange juice into the middle of the table. 'I think we'll make these mimosas.'

Kennedy moaned and slumped forward onto the table. In his despair he could see only one tiny upside. No more Brendle.

TWENTY-ONE

The big cottage nestled in the countryside outside Deeping, a little too far north to be considered truly in the Cotswolds. It dated from the late sixteenth century, though it had been added to since: a large, modern glass-walled kitchen jutting out of the back. (Courtesy of Kennedy: a three-week uncredited dialogue polish on an Angelina Jolie vehicle that never saw the light of day.)

Millie negotiated the narrow, uneven Tudor staircase and knocked on her daughter's bedroom door. Music was very faintly audible from inside, something hard and atonal. She knocked again, louder, and entered.

Robin Marr was stretched out on her bed in jeans, T-shirt (the Breeders) and headphones, her eyes closed, a plectrum clamped between her teeth as she used her fingers to play along with whatever she was listening to on her unplugged bass. (A vintage Fender Mustang, a gift from her father.) Millie shook her bare foot and Robin jumped up. 'Mum! You sacred the shi—'

'We need to talk.'

Robin slipped the headphones off and sat up, the music shrill through the tiny speakers before she hit 'Pause' on her iPod. 'You're going to damage your ears,' Millie heard herself saying, not fully recognising herself in the process. She sat on the end of her daughter's bed and took in the clothes strewn everywhere, the open textbooks and folders scattered here and there, the dirty plates, mugs and glasses, the posters – Hole, Manic Street Preachers, Sonic Youth – and the laptop open: Facebook and Twitter both up. Robin plucked a couple of notes on the bass. 'Please, Robin,' Millie said. Robin sighed and set the instrument down. She blew her fringe out of her eyes, her hair bobbed, thick and black, her father's hair. At sixteen the very beautiful woman Robin was going to become was really starting to come through the puppy fat she was shedding every day. 'I just got off the phone with your dad. He's going to call you in a bit.'

'Is something wrong?'

'Not wrong, exactly. Just . . . odd. I knew he'd been offered this thing but I hadn't mentioned it because I thought he'd never . . . Anyway, he's won this award, a fellowship, and, well, one of the terms of it is that he has to come and spend an academic year here, at Deeping.'

'Really? Doing what?'

Millie felt herself fighting a grin. 'Teaching.'

'Dad? *Teaching?*'

Mother and daughter both cracked up. 'Jesus Christ,' Robin said after a moment.

'I know,' Millie said.

'Hang on, he's going to come and live *here*?' Robin pointed at the bed, the floor.

'Oh God no. The university will rent him a house off campus somewhere. But he'll be around a fair bit. He'll be up and down to Pinewood. Some film he's written is shooting over here later in the year. That girl's in it apparently. The one you like. Thingy. Ooh, you know . . .'

Robin made the gesture, both hands rotating gently at the wrists – *comeoncomeoncomeon*. Something she'd picked up from Kennedy. 'Oh bloody hell! He just told me.' Nothing made Millie feel older than moments like these. 'She was in that thing, where they go on the roadtrip. The one with the brown hair and the little mole. She did that funny dance.'

'Julie Teal?'

'Yes!'

'Wow.'

This was a rare wow from Robin – one offered with no sarcasm or irony. She had been to movie sets often with her father, on holiday trips to LA. Private tours of the studio lots too. But it had only been relatively recently that she had she begun to find anything he did remotely impressive. Last year, when she and her friend Gwen had flown over for a fortnight in the summer holidays, they'd gone to some restaurant where the head waiter guy had led them past the waiting crush at the bar and straight to a good booth in the front. Kevin Spacey had stopped on his way past the table to say hi and shake Kennedy's hand. 'Your dad's *cool*,' Gwen had whispered to Robin, behind the huge menu, while Dad had talked to the waiter, giving a complicated drinks order. (*'Just wash the ice with it . . .'*) And it had struck Robin like a mild epiphany – yeah, I guess he is.

'Will he get a lot of money for this thing?'

'Half a million bloody quid.'

'Jesus. Will we –'

'Oh yes, we'll get our bit.

'But Dad. Teaching,' Robin repeated.

'God help them. Anyway. There it is. They'll be announcing it and it'll probably be in the papers tomorrow and everything. How do you feel about it?'

'About Dad being here? Well, he's not teaching *me*.'

When Robin was seven, just before Kennedy moved to LA, she'd been asked to write a description of her parents for a school essay. She'd written that her father had the patience of 'a very hungry great white shark'. Kennedy had been mightily impressed by the metaphor, at age seven and all. 'It might be nice. Having him around more,' Robin finally decided, picking the bass back up.

'Mmmm,' Millie said as enthusiastically as she could manage. Robin fretted a note high up and slapped the string with her thumb, running the note down the neck comically. *B-Doinnnngggg.*

TWENTY-TWO

To Scott Spengler's house for the breakfast-cum-script conference. ('Some exciting developments.' Ominous. Always ominous.) Kennedy took Sunset, passing Soho House ('The' Soho House as everyone out here insisted on saying) on his left, and suddenly the greenery of Beverly Hills was all around him. (What would you have if all the time all the screenwriters in LA spent in their cars going to script meetings could be converted into writing time? Kennedy wondered. You'd have a lot more scripts: many of them probably no worse than if all the meetings had never taken place. But, as Woody Allen said, people in Hollywood *liked* the meetings. They *wanted* to have the dinners and lunches and breakfasts and conference calls because that was why they got into the job: for the social aspect. Writers just wanted to sit in a room and have the phone not ring.) He'd made all the calls: Millie, Robin, Patrick. His mum. She was delighted he was coming home for a while, but went to some length to assure him she was fine and not to be interrupting his work to come and see her. ('With how busy you are and how dear flights are and all that.') Braden and Connie were dealing with all the practicalities: plane tickets, houses, money. A deportation order. He could see it no other way – a fucking deport-ation order.

He made a right just after the Beverly Hills Hotel and after a few hundred yards the satnav was chirruping, *'You have arrived at your destination.'* He looked up at the imposing gate, a discreet brushed-aluminium panel set in the wall beside it. Before he could speak a voice said, 'Can I help you?'

'Kennedy Marr. I'm here to see Scott.'

A crackle, a pause, then, 'Good morning, Mr Marr. Park in front please.'

The gates slowly parted and he drove into Scott Spengler's private kingdom.

An acre of mature gardens separated the gate from the house. He threaded the gravel drive through them, taking in rose bushes, pergolas, an enormous copper fountain and, up ahead, directly opposite the colonnaded entrance, what looked very much like a Henry Moore. No, *two* Henry Moores. The house itself was what realtors called 'French chateau' style. The sheer acreage of glass stretching away on either side. The square footage, what, thirty, forty thou-sand? The forecourt he was parking on – next to a Prius and a Bentley – could have held a couple of dozen cars. And all of this just a few hundred yards from Sunset? Kennedy guessed at a price tag in the thirty- to forty-million-dollar region. The gardeners, maids, cleaners and contractors required to keep the wheels on this wagon . . .

As they often did when confronted with insane, titanic

displays of wealth like this Kennedy's thoughts tended towards – *how can you be arsed?*

A grinning Latino houseboy showed him through a marble entrance hall the size of a decent public library and down a passageway – taking in a Matisse, a Whistler and a Rothko as he went – and out onto a back patio. More acreage, a tiered lawn stretching away towards tennis courts and pool(s), and there, at a shaded wrought-iron table, beaker of orange juice in hand, was Spengler – blue jeans, white shirt – and a bearded bear in his early thirties – all in black, frowning into the *New York Times*. Kevin McConnell, the director. 'Kennedy,' Spengler said, rising to greet him, grinning, showing no sign of having just flown in from Australia, looking far younger than his fifty-one years.

'Hey,' Kennedy said. 'Nice place.' It felt like about the most superfluous thing you could say. Like saying 'Nice bod' if, say, Julie Teal unrobed in front of you.

'Thanks, you wanna buy it? We're moving.'

'How come?'

'Ah, wife wants a change. A fucking project. What do I know? I just work here. Kennedy, this is Kevin.'

The director looked up, nonchalant. 'Hey, man,' he extended a hand lazily. 'Good to finally meet you.'

'You want some food?' Spengler asked, gesturing towards an adjacent table on which the contents of a good-sized delicatessen had been spread out: pitchers of orange, peach and grapefruit juice, dishes of cantaloupe, grapes, orange segments, cereal, oatmeal, bagels, bacon, sausage, ham, scrambled eggs. Of course, no one was eating anything. 'You should try this melon and prosciutto. I have it flown in from Italy. It's the best.'

'No, I'm fine, thanks. Just some coffee.'

'Consuela?' Spengler said. A hovering maid poured Kennedy some coffee.

'I have to say, Kennedy,' Kevin cut in, 'I love the script. Great work. Really great.'

'Well, thank you.'

'We're loath to change a word of it, Kennedy, seriously,' Spengler said.

Loath to? The first gentle alarm bells clanging in Kennedy's mind.

'But here's the thing,' Spengler went on. 'We need to relocate the entire thing to Europe.'

'Ah, how do you mean? You're gonna shoot some exteriors over there?'

'No. We want to set the movie in Europe now.'

'So . . . the lead characters, they're going to be European? But Julie and Michael, they —'

'No, they're still American.'

'But . . .' Kennedy said, the enormity dawning on him. 'Why are they living in Europe? What are they doing there? They . . . they go stay with one of their mothers at one point. What's *she* doing in Europe?'

'Hey, that's why you're on the payroll, buddy,' Spengler said. 'You're the writer. You figure it out.'

Kennedy stirred his coffee and asked, 'And *why* are we suddenly doing this? The studio bought and green-lit a movie set on the eastern seaboard of the United States.'

'It's complicated,' Spengler said. 'But if we can use four or five European locations there's a tax situation we can make come about that's gonna work out great for everyone.'

'Four or five locations?' Kennedy said. 'How . . . I mean, what language will they be speaking in this film?'

'Just, you know . . .' McConnell and Spengler looked at each other. 'Non-specific European,' Spengler concluded.

Kennedy looked at them both. Was this a fucking joke? Was there a camera somewhere?

'At the moment it's looking like we'll do Romania, Montenegro, Serbia and one other and then finish up with six weeks at Pinewood doing interiors. Wrap by January and into post.' Spengler leaned back and clasped his hands behind his head, pleased.

'Listen, dude, basically,' Kevin said, 'over there, with the crew and location situations so much cheaper, I can make our hundred-million-dollar budget look like two hundred million dollars on the screen.'

Kennedy looked at the guy. Fucking directors. Somewhere along the line Hollywood decreed that the guy who knew best about everything was the director. Their crews called them 'gaffer' and 'guvnor'. Half of them came from advertising or music videos. So you could tie a pair of tights around a lens or make a bullet go in slow motion. Big fucking deal. It was unquestionably a tough physical job on location: twenty-hour days with all manner of bastards throwing two hundred problems a minute at you. Is this the right kind of car for the neighbour to drive? Should that vase be in shot or out of shot? The female lead won't come out of her trailer. The male lead's doing blow again. The camel trainer has to leave by five so we need to get the camel shot done by then. We're losing the light. The lab's scratched the negative. Like someone said, you'd need to pay a member of the public a million bucks to get them to direct a movie. That's why actual directors get five to ten million – they know what's involved. But *intellectually* difficult? Compared to staring at a blank page and dreaming an entire world into being? Give me a fucking break, Kennedy thought. He took a long, hot draught of coffee before replying. 'Yeah, Kevin, I hear you, *dude*. But, uh, the thing is, it doesn't matter if it looks like a billion dollars – if the movie doesn't actually *make any sense* people are gonna be throwing handfuls of their own shit at the screen.'

McConnell looked from Kennedy to Spengler and back again. 'Well, I don't think that's very constructive,' he said.

'You're making a colossal – and idiotic – artistic decision for purely commercial reasons,' Kennedy said. 'You're asking me to damage a decent piece of work.'

'The essential elements of the story will remain the same,' Spengler said. 'Characterisation. Everything. Rather than a road movie, a chase, set here, it becomes a pan-European version of that.'

'"Non-specific European",' Kennedy corrected.

'You know,' Spengler said, spreading his hands out, gesturing at everything around them, 'some people might say I know a little bit about making movies.'

I'm in hell, Kennedy thought. *I am living in the bowels of hell surrounded by maniacs*. 'Ach,' he said finally, draining his coffee cup, standing up and buttoning his suit. 'Stick it up in your fucking holes.'

TWENTY-THREE

He drove out to Malibu, reckless on the PCH1, Ray-Bans on, the top down and a headful of steam as he accelerated hard with that vinyl station he liked loud on the radio, AC/DC doing 'You Shook Me All Night Long'. He looked over to his left, at the foaming breakers of the ocean, the palm trees bending slightly in the breeze, the sun a lemon disc high above the water. *Was this not the life, though? Was this not the sheer and utter life, you fucking cunts?*

Kennedy had lived not too far from the sea, back home, when he was a kid. In summers his family would follow the Shannon down from Limerick to the south-west coast, to Kilrush, or further on to Kilkee, hard up against the Atlantic. Six of them in a caravan. Him and Patrick and Geraldine's glee at the big bed that the three of them shared, that folded down out of the living-room wall. Granny in the other bed – in the kitchen area. Ma and Da in the tiny bedroom at the back. The fights with Gerry sometimes.

'Start a fight in an empty house, that girl,' Da always said. Granny too – what had she said to Gerry that time? Something bad. Something really bad. Six of them in that caravan. Now there were three of them, soon there would be just him and Patr— *six stone . . .*

He turned the radio up as AC/DC segued neatly into the Cult's 'Love Removal Machine' – *'BABYBABY BABYBABYBABY I FELL FROM THE SKY!'* And the roads, the traffic, in rural Ireland in the 1970s: a freak show of single lanes, potholes, cattle and tractors. Three or four hours to travel a hundred miles. In the rain, with the air full of manure and silage. When he was about fifteen, the mid-1980s, he'd stayed up late with his da one night and they'd watched the film *Foul Play* on the telly. Chevy Chase, Dudley Moore and Goldie Hawn. It opened with a drive along this very road, the PCH1, between San Francisco and LA, and Kennedy could remember thinking, nearly thirty years ago, *'Now that's a fucking coastline.'* Da laughing at the film. Laughing and coughing. The spotted hanky. *Like the crimson mottling on a trout . . . six fucking stone.*

He nudged the accelerator, pointing the grey Aston Martin north, trying to power away from his dead and dying, on along to Zuma Beach.

Kennedy walked on the sand. Surfers. Dog walkers. An exercise class of some kind going on. A fair wind whipping in from the Pacific too.

Gulls.

It had been weeks after Geraldine's death that he'd got the call from the police station in Brighton. (*Oh, Gerry – what now?*) It hadn't occurred to him – her things. The clothes she'd been wearing when she'd done it. He'd driven down, leaving his packing for Los Angeles, and parked in the NCP near the Grand. Appropriately it had been a cold, grey day in early March. Wind slapping along the seafront, across the deserted pier, the rusted hulk of the old pier crumpled in the water like the broken skeleton of some prehistoric beast. Gerry had always wanted to live by the sea.

The sergeant at the desk had been all business, forms and identification. No words of sorrow or comfort, just another piece of paperwork to be put straight. He went off and Kennedy sat on a hard bench waiting for what seemed like a very time, looking at the posters – pickpocketing, burglary, car theft – before the guy came back hefting a large, clear plastic bag with the words 'Sussex Police' stamped on it in blue. He'd carried it back to the car over his shoulder, the cold air slowly numbing his hand.

The indescribable sadness of the gulls' cries carrying on the wind.

Back in London, in the flat in Maida Vale he was renting close to Millie and Robin, he'd spread the contents of the bag out across the floor of his study, among the packing crates ready for storage. Her parka with fur-lined collar. Her Armani jeans and tiny trainers. Her bra and underwear. There was her sweater with, horribly, a matted sheen of saliva stained across the front, white and crusted. There was her tobacco tin containing some loose tobacco, Rizlas and a cheap plastic lighter. Then, finally, at the bottom of the sack, the saddest object of all: a small, clear plastic evidence bag. It had the words 'Police Evidence' stamped all the way around the sides. On the front the words 'NO WET CLOTHING. NO

UNPROTECTED SHARP OBJECTS. ALL SECTIONS OF LABEL TO BE COMPLETED.' Inside the bag were three one-pound coins, a single twenty-pence piece, four five-pence pieces, a two-pence piece and two pennies. Her only bank account was dead – long overdrawn and deactivated. Her rented flat was in arrears and she was close to eviction. There had been no other cash or bank books in the flat when they cleared it out. So – that three pounds and forty-four pence.

Gerry's net worth at the time of her death.

What she had to show for thirty-two years on the planet.

He'd fingered the money for a long time, moving it around his desk, the dates on the various coins making him think of what had been happening that particular year for both of them. 1987: first year at university for Kennedy. For the sixteen-year-old Gerry: leaving school with nothing. 1997: publication and the Booker shortlist for him. Gerry's first trip to rehab. 2001: Divorcing Millie. Gerry's first trip to prison.

Kennedy had tacked the evidence bag up on the cork pinboard in his office and looked at it every day.

Oh, Gerry. What have you done now?

Nothing now. Nothing ever again.

He stared out to sea, out to where the dolphins who frequented this point of the California coastline were frolicking, a couple of hundred yards offshore, blowing crystal spume as they rose, dived and basked. A few lines came to him.

Diving deep into uncharted waters
Lungs bursting,
Temples of wood and ice pulsing,
There to stare, amazed
Into the jewelled eyes of fathomless creatures

His phone rang. Braden. Here we go. He slid the bar across. Instantly – 'Are you out of your fucking mind?'

'Hi, Braden.'

'You tell Scott Spengler, *Scott Spengler*, to go fuck himself?'

'That's not quite what I said.'

'Spare me the semantics. You know, contractually, you still owe him another pass, right?'

'What he's suggesting is idiotic and unworkable and damaging to the script.' Kennedy lit a cigarette, turning his back to the wind.

'So fuck? Deliver the draft and let's get paid and get the fuck outta Dodge.'

'I quit. The notes are unreasonable.'

'Unreasonable? Really? Do you want to get into a legal definition of that? A protracted legal battle with Scott Spengler? He'll tort you into the fucking poorhouse just for fun.'

'Fuck him.'

A sigh. 'You know, you Irish bastard, it's unbelievable. He *likes* you.'

'Huh?'

'Spengler. He likes you. Kevin too. They "admire your passion and honesty". They're sending over their notes and they still want you on the picture.'

'I want *off* the picture. It's gonna be a train wreck. Have you heard what they want to do?'

'It can't be that bad.'

He told him. Braden said, 'Well, yeah, it sounds like a cluster fuck, but you've been around the block. This is the game. This is why you get the big bucks. Got to suck it up. Or they'll just replace you and get someone in to fuck it up even more. If you stay on you can at least try to protect your wor—'

'Yeah, yeah,' Kennedy said. 'Protect my work.'

'Kennedy, you need to get your head around this. The picture's happening, we're taking this award thing, you're going to England for a while and it'll all be happy days, OK?'

Kennedy sighed. 'Yeah. Look, have them send the notes over. I . . . I'll talk to you later.'

He hung up and stared along the beach. A child nearby – a boy of around three – was tagging after his parents, eating a hot dog. Something about the way he struggled with it, the way it was too big and unwieldy . . . no, it was the fact that he was eating it on his own, something he had probably only been capable of very recently. Seeing little children feeding themselves, that first sign of independence, of being able to do something for themselves, always moved him. Because then they're on the way to the point where they won't need you. Where they'll be gone. *And you were never really there anyway.*

Unhappy ghost!

Kennedy flicked the butt into the breeze and walked tiredly back towards the car. He had only recently figured out why your forties were so tiring – you were carrying all these corpses around with you.

All these ghosts, strapped to your back.

TWENTY-FOUR

'I love the way you guys just call it a "line", you know? All the implications of stasis? We call it a "queue", because the notion is that a queue occasionally *moves*.' Kennedy smiled pleasantly. The security guard – black, heavyset, in his thirties, the same guy who had told Kennedy fifteen minutes earlier that he appreciated that he was travelling first class and that he had fast-track clearance but the fast-track lane was closed – just stared back and said, 'Please remain in line, sir.' The guy moved off, to check the rest of the line was still not moving. Kennedy murmured 'You fucking *handpump*' at the serge blue slab of his departing back, gun swinging lazily at his hip.

The remainder of the summer had passed in a tsunami of deadlines and writing. He woke up around six every morning with a gun in his mouth and was hunched over the iMac with steaming coffee cup by six thirty seven days a week typing 'INT. OFFICE – DAY' or 'EXT. LA STREET – NIGHT' or 'PULL BACK TO REVEAL'. He went from one Final Draft document to another like a man at an orgy stumbling from one warm half-remembered body to another. In truth, it was mostly shitwork: cutting redundant scenes, sharpening dialogue, killing clichés, smoothing transitions. Good screenwriting, Bill Goldman argued, was very much like shitwork. Like housework. Do it properly and no one notices. Do it badly, however. The husband did not come home and say, 'Wow, honey. The windows really sparkle! And look at this floor!' But if it wasn't done he might well come home and say, 'Hey, what am I breaking my balls for? To come home to a goddamn zoo?'

He exchanged emails with the people at Deeping every few days. Mostly with a woman called Angela. Some houses for his consideration. Could he let them know of his proposed syllabus? There had been so many applications for the twenty tutorial places on his course – could he suggest a way of eliminating candidates? He observed his three-emails-before-it-was-urgent-enough-to-reply-to rule. And then fired back the most brief, perfunctory answers possible. He let Connie's office deal with the house renting and furniture stuff. He trusted Connie's taste. His only specification was that they rent him a DB9 for the duration of his stay. (Millie emailed telling him of the howl of outrage that went around the faculty at this. *Fuck them*, Kennedy thought. It's a fucking repatriation order, I'm going to have a few creature comforts. And, once you'd driven an Aston for a while, everything else was pretty much like sitting on a roller skate powered by an elastic band.) Robin sent him a playlist titled 'DAD'S ENGLISH ADVENTURE'. He wished he had time to listen to it.

Production started out on the lot at Burbank and Kennedy

drove up the 101 to finally have his meeting with Julie Teal.
They had lunch in the commissary.

Even in sweatwear, with no make-up, waiting to get into
costume, Teal was something: one of those miracle biology
deals, the body, the face, the features all cherries (those
cherries on Geraldine's forearm), all bells or lemons.
Jackpot. Shorter than he'd imagined, as they always were,
and with an enormous head: Easter Island atop a Barbie
doll. Her face was completely . . . malleable. A blank canvas.
She was, apparently, twenty-seven. She could play anything
from twenty-one to thirty-five. She'd eaten nothing from
the counter of course. An assistant brought her a flask of
green tea and a plastic box prepared by her personal chef
containing a jumble of bean sprouts, seaweed and tofu.
'Mmmm,' she'd cooed, tucking into this atrocity. Kennedy
was sucking on a Life Saver to mask vodka fumes. The one
diktat Spengler's office had given him: no drinking in front
of Julie, still raw from rehab.

'So, Julie,' Kennedy asked, uncapping his pen, taking out
his notebook, 'what's on your mind with the script?'

'I love the script.'

'Really? I was under the impression that –'

'No. Honestly. You're an amazing writer, Kennedy.'

'Well, thank you.' Recapping his pen.

'The only thing I'd say . . .'

Uncapping that pen again.

'. . . is that sometimes, during rehearsal, performance,
as you get to know the character better, peel the layers
back . . .' *Fuck me.* '. . . other possibilities do start to suggest
themselves in terms of how you play it. Where you want
it to go. But you're going to be around in England, right?'

'I am indeed.'

'Great. So if there's any teensy rewriting then I'm sure we can work on it together.'

'Grand.'

'God, I love your accent! It's adorable.'

So reasonable. So pleasant. So ominous . . .

Kennedy knew well never to completely relax around movie stars. What they loved in a script could change overnight following a close textual analysis from, say, their hairdresser. Or their shrink. Or the opening of a big movie starring a friend or rival whose character had certain traits they coveted. There was of course another possible reason for Teal's lack of critique: she hadn't actually read the fucking script yet.

Somehow, between all of this, July bled, or broiled, or froiled, into August then into September and now here he was – at LAX. Staring at the non-moving line. He tried again to catch the eye of the security guard, hoping, praying, for him to somehow say, 'OK. You're clearly a big shot. Come this way.' But the jobsworth just stared back at him, sleepy-eyed. Kennedy had never had a job (*'Oh, because I've never wanted one'*) and it could be said that, on occasion, he found it difficult to sympathise with those who did.

He'd left university at twenty-two and Millie, already teaching, had supported them for two years while he wrote his novel. She supported them for another year when he threw it in the bin and began outlining what would become *Unthinkable*. And for another year after that while he wrote it. And then one more year while all those rejection letters poured in.

Five. Fucking. Years.

Towards the end of this period Millie already had her PhD and a junior lectureship. She wanted a baby. Kennedy was twenty-seven. She was nearly thirty.

'If I'm not published by the time I'm thirty,' Kennedy remembered saying into her tear-stained face one night, both of them lying on the mattress on the floor in the tiny attic flat, 'I'll become a lawyer.' Well, that had cheered her up. She'd fucking well *pissed* herself at that one.

He looked along the line, at the poor, tired, huddled mass of America moving – or rather *not* moving – towards the security scanners. He'd joined this line because it had been moving quickly. The reason it had been moving quickly, of course, is that there had been a platoon of specialist al-Qaeda operatives, Muslim SEALS if you will, being hauled out of it ahead of him. All of whom were now, presumably, being tasered, stripped, tagged and bagged while everyone behind them – including the three-year-old girl with cheeks like milk and apples now having her pink rucksack torn apart – was assumed to have been an accomplice. Here it was, fundamentalist terrorism's true contribution to world culture: boredom.

Kennedy tried to remember when he'd last experienced boredom on a par with the non-moving line, when he'd felt the utter mind-numbing restriction of having to remain somewhere where you had nothing to contribute, nothing to do. Where you just had to suffer. Certain development meetings certainly, but they could always be enlivened with a choice sarcastic remark. (Try that at LAX these days. You'd wind up pants down in a mirrored room with some brick shithouse up to his bicep in your fucking coalhole. And then the tedious coach-class flight to Guantánamo.)

No, when had he last been in a mind-numbing situation controlled by morons where a certain level of docile cooperation and sincerity was absolutely required of you? It came to him.

Couples therapy.

Towards the end with Millie, the last-ditch attempt to salvage things. Once a week for a couple of months they had gone to the cheerless office in Kentish Town where a succession of cheerless women with 2:2s from regional polytechnics had tried to understand his infidelities. They had tried to understand it through the prism of Millie's accounts of course, because Kennedy had remained largely silent. It had astonished him how much she'd had to say, how much she'd needed to cry. Could the human body possibly contain this reservoir of tears? he'd wonder as she made a fresh attack on the ever-present box of Kleenex. She talked of narcissism, of her father, of Kennedy's ego. About the emails she'd found, about the text messages. Later, in the truly terminal stages, she talked of the triangulation she'd made between text messages, emails and restaurant receipts from his wallet. He was asked how this made him feel. Why did he think he did these things? The therapist talked about the 'bank account' of trust. About how it took a very long time to build up a credit balance in this account and how very quickly it could be wiped out by one massive withdrawal. (Kennedy had managed a bleak inner laugh at the terminology there.) Millie called him a 'fucking bastard'. She said she wished she'd never met him.

And all the time Kennedy would nod sombrely and pretend to be thinking about a response and look at the gently sweeping second hand on the clock and think to himself – *Closer. This, like everything else, is all getting closer to being over.* He'd murmur, 'I see.' Or, 'Really?' Or, on occasion, at one of the therapist's greater banalities, 'Wow.' He'd even tried to pretend to cry a couple of times, trying for what actors called 'an emotional memory'. (It only struck Kennedy after the fact how truly odd it was to be having to reach for an emotional memory when the emotional reality was pretty fucking strong, i.e. having this person who had loved you – who had borne your child, who had supported you for half a decade while you tried to throw whatever you had to say at the world – sitting two feet away with their heart breaking. Some months later, in his notebook from this period, he'd found the phrase *'the pastel-green poster with seagulls, an attempt to lull tranquillity?'* and realised he'd jotted down a few observations about the interior of the therapist's office, in case he might need it in a novel some day. Graham Greene's 'chip of ice in the heart'.)

The need for 'honesty' was stressed many times in that room. Kennedy felt that the honesty needed in relationships was very much like the honesty people said they wanted when they asked you to read their unpublished manuscripts or unproduced screenplays. Meaning: not so much. They wanted to hear, 'Wow. There's some terrific stuff here, but you might want to . . .' Or, 'You definitely have some raw talent. You just need to . . .' Or whatever. What they definitely *didn't* want was honesty. Because honesty, ninety-nine times out of a hundred, was 'Please never put pen to paper again'. It was 'You have no talent whatsoever. Go off and make model airplanes, take a cookery class, build Eiffel Towers out of matchsticks or some fucking thing.' These people, at the dinner parties, at the book launches and the lunches and the weddings, with their treatments and their outlines and their novels, they didn't want honesty. They had sat down and tried to describe reality, or to catch the way people really speak to one another, or to comment on some aspect of the human condition, and they had come up horrifyingly short. They had been found wanting. Their take *didn't matter*. (And we think here of Dr Drummond's lonely hardback of *A Circular Defence* – Picador, 1991 – gathering dust on a shelf.) And who wants to be told that? They want to be told *'Good try. Keep going.'* They want to be told *'I didn't mean it. She didn't mean anything. I made a terrible mistake.'*

Honesty would have been – *'Trust is a bank account? Is it? Is it really, you terrible retarded dyke? And here was me thinking it was just a ludicrous middle-class guilt trip. Because who cares? Existentially speaking – who fucking cares? Fuck someone else, don't fuck someone else, the planet's still going to turn and everyone in this room will be powder in sixty years. I watched my daddy die, pissing his pants with blood on his lips. But by all means let's continue about me getting my dick sucked that one time on the roof terrace at Soho House by some girl from Penguin. Let's get into that for half an hour. And, you know what, every time you unsnap a bra and feel a pair of strange new breasts tumbling out warm against you, you feel immortal. It's like writing a book. It's like kissing the face of fucking god. Nipples, what's with that? The variety, the incredible variety, brown, pink, small, big, it's just insane. How can it go on? There are so many pairs of tits in this world I am never going to experience it makes me want to blow my fucking head off.'*

Honesty would have been – *'I really like fucking and she won't fuck me quite enough.'* That would have about covered it, there in that drab room with the dim therapist and the crying wife.

'And what do you want from all of this, Kennedy?' The therapist had asked him, after Millie had finished her own tearful monologue on the subject, with much use of words like 'honesty' and 'truth'. *What did men want?* Again, worthy of a paper, this subject, he thought.

All Kennedy wanted – all he'd ever wanted – was to do exactly as he pleased all the time in an utterly consequence-free environment. Was this so much to ask for?

Finally the line started moving and soon enough he was being respectfully ushered into the soft blue light of first class.

TWENTY-FIVE

Glancing back briefly to enjoy the spectacle of his fellow man being led towards the fluorescent-tube Hades of economy, he magnanimously accepted a beaded glass of champagne as he sank into the sofa-sized chair. He looked around to check out his fellow winners here in the swollen bulb of the jumbo, the very helmet of the plane, those bastards to whom life had thrown sevens, dealt trumps and royal flushes.

A florid middle-aged tycoon across the aisle from him was scrolling through his BlackBerry, looking at the device with a steady hostility while his Grisham lay unregarded on his lap. A kid on the far side across from the tycoon was talking quietly on his phone. He was wearing a hoodie and looked to be about twenty-five. You saw this more and more these days: the Internet titans. Two years out of college and holed up in first. Then – oh most upsetting! – he saw the rich middle-aged couple up ahead in the A seats, standing talking in the aisle, holding hands, wedding bands glittering as they laughed over their drinks. They looked to be in their mid-forties, around Kennedy's age, and appeared to have waltzed straight out of a Ralph Lauren advertisement, glowing with health and money and love. She giggled and tucked her head into his cashmere armpit while he smoothed her hair. Casting around the cabin the man caught Kennedy's eye and raised his glass. Kennedy returned the gesture while wishing a good deal of misfortune on the fucker.

These guys – how did they do it? These supermen – how did they tough it out? Married to the same woman for twenty or thirty years. Lived in the same house. He thought of the last twenty years – the mad blur of property and sex, of packing crates and removal men and postcodes and limbs and anuses and cunt lips pressed hard against his face and women whose names he could not remember screaming his name in hotel rooms and flats. Yeah, he got the fact that you didn't have to go out every seven years or so and find a woman who basically hated you and *buy her a fucking house.* But, even so, what did these guys do? Was it that they never had the opportunity? Did Sandra at the office never tug that tie towards the stationery cupboard at the Christmas party, or whatever they did at those things? Did that redhead at the bar at the conference never say 'What room are you in?' Did the girl at that drink after work never smile just a bit too long? Or did all this and more go on and they all said, 'I'm sorry, I'd love to, but I'm married.' Did they just stop looking?

But they didn't, in his experience. By forty they all sat in the bar – at the reunion, on the fishing trip, on the stag night – and said, 'Christ, the arse/the tits/the mouth on that?' Desire was there all right, but the will was gone. Was the will gone because of the statistically high chances of rejection? Or because of the fear of reprisals – the house, the alimony, the kids and all that? Or was it – and Kennedy came at this odd, alien thought carefully – because of *the genuine love of the loved one*?

Monogamy – like poetry, that was a man's business. Oh yes. A real hard man's business that.

In the air, seat belts off, he accepted a refill from the stewardess – basically a catwalk model crammed into livery – and looked out of the window as the plane banked right, following the coastline north towards San Francisco before making its turn inland to cross the great, demented belly of America.

He took a hearty swig and fell to examining the menu: *cheese mousse with asparagus and lemon . . . roast guinea fowl with broad beans, sweet potato mash and port jus . . . megrim sole with crayfish tails and lemon and caper brown butter . . .*

Millie had been cooking fish that night, right at the end, some kind of stew, or tagine, while they argued in the kitchen. She hadn't been crying then. That reservoir was drained. She had simply been very, very angry as she brought all the powers of reason and analysis she'd used obtaining that doctorate to bear on him. What was it she'd said? The true and awful thing? He'd been leaning back against the fridge, drunk, brimming balloon of Rioja or something in hand, and saying something like 'But I need you . . .'

That's right. She'd said: *'Kennedy – you don't need anyone.'* She'd been prodding a knife into the fish, checking if it was done, not looking at him. *'You don't need a wife, or a lover, or a partner. You just need a decent PA. You just need the fucking*

*trains to run on time so you can disappear to your study and be
somewhere else all the time.'* She'd motioned with the knife,
one of the Sabatier ones with the black handles, tiny bits
of white cod flecked on the point, a sliver of black olive
or something too (*Why? In the name of Christ, why?* You'd
have to cock a pistol at his temple to get him to remember
the date of his wedding anniversary. Waterboarding might
be required for him to recall his only brother's birthday,
but Kennedy Marr could describe to you in infinite detail
the detritus on the blade of a knife his ex-wife was holding
during an argument twelve years ago), as she'd gestured
around at the house, at the water and power that flowed
from pipes and sockets, at the food that filled the vast
brushed-aluminium fridge, at the cars that were taxed and
insured and maintained. At all the stuff she did. Kennedy
remembered her complaining about a water bill one time.
He'd looked up from his novel or script, frowning, and
asked, 'You mean water isn't free?' She'd rolled her beautiful
eyes to the heavens.

'But . . .' he'd said, coming towards her, going for that
hug, being rebuffed.

'You don't give a shit about me, or about Robin. You
just want to go and stick your fucking cock in some girl,
don't you?'

Urrr – get it away from me, he thought – summoning the
stewardess now, upgrading from champagne to a Bloody
Mary for his pre-lunch cocktail – *I like not these thoughts.
Bring me some other thoughts.*

He turned to his book, a slim volume of collected Yeats.
His countryman. Old WB. There he'd been at fifty: the
shock of white hair, the stern rimmed glasses, but wired

right into young Georgie, a girl half his age. And still laying a *ton* of pipe on the side. Still laying pipe in Paris aged seventy – Margot, Ethel and more. But even all the fucking couldn't save him. You sweated and strained and roared as you came and still it bore down upon you, insect wings beating at your back. All the writing and the fucking couldn't save you. The story was still only ending one way: dead and buried in Paris. Body dug up and reinterred in Sligo. The lines on the gravestone: *'Cast a cold Eye, On Life, on Death. Horseman, pass by!'* Fucking *Sligo*. Jesus.

The businessman across from him sighed, loudly, music-ally, as he laid his BlackBerry down. Kennedy turned and saw the guy was shaking his head, looking to start a conver-sation. Unusual this, in first class, in Kennedy's experience. Normally the rich just ignored each other. In stark contrast to the communal sing-songs and group therapy of economy. What the hell, Kennedy thought. He was about drunk enough. He smiled at the guy, raised his glass slightly.

'Hi there,' the big, warm palm was already floating across the aisle to meet him, 'Peter. Peter Arthur.'

PART TWO

England

TWENTY-SIX

'And sign here please.' Kennedy did so and was rewarded with a ziplock evidence bag (*three pounds and forty-four pence*) containing his wallet, watch, phone and belt. His shoes sat next to it on the counter. 'You'll be notified about the court date.'

'Right, OK. Thank you, officer.'

No stranger to the cell Kennedy Marr.

There had been the local police station in Limerick. (Teenager, affray.) There had been the harsh concrete bench in some Victorian jail on the south side of Glasgow. (Student, drunk and disorderly.) Or the slightly more salubrious 1960s cop shop somewhere near Cheltenham. (Drunk-driving, celebrating a successful appearance at the literature festival.) He'd even known the rarified atmosphere of the holding tank at the Beverly Hills police station on Santa Monica Boulevard, after that ruck outside Dan Tana's.

But Heathrow was a first. He'd never been in an airport police cell before. The cell itself hadn't been bad, but it definitely ran the sofas and showers of the Concorde lounge a distant second in terms of the ideal decompression zone after an eleven-hour flight. He slipped his Rolex on and checked the time – 8.12 a.m. Nearly twelve hours after he'd landed. 'And here.' The desk sergeant indicated another space for his signature. He was a tall, bearded man about Kennedy's age. As he watched him sign he said, 'Bit old to be behaving like this, aren't we, sir?'

'Yeah.' It was true. Kennedy, a meticulous editor when it came to his work, struggled with the edit function in life sometimes.

The introductions had gone how they often went up there in the clouds.

'Kennedy Marr,' shaking hands.

'Is that an Irish accent I hear there?' Peter Arthur's accent was plain old Virginian.

'It is, yes.'

'Oh, my wife would love you. Yes, sir.'

It turned out the guy had very vaguely heard of him. 'Think the wife was reading one a while back. I haven't read any of your books myself.'

Kennedy sighed.

You heard this line surprisingly often. It was generally offered apropos of nothing: Kennedy had never in his life said to anyone 'Have you actually read any of my books?' (well, the odd German interviewer perhaps) and yet a certain type of handpump frequently felt the need to say, on being introduced to him, 'Sorry, I haven't read any of your books.' It was usually offered this way, as an apology ('I'm sorry', or 'I'm afraid'), when, of course, it was nothing of the sort, it was quite the opposite. It was a taunt. Provocation. In effect what it said was: 'You might reckon you're a big-shot writer, Mr Big-Shot Writer, but you know what? Down here in the real world there's people like me who don't give a shit about your books. Read your piss? I've got better things to do with my time. Go and get fucked.' Depending on how drunk he was, Kennedy had a range of stock responses to the statement, ranging from the brief – 'Don't apologise. I'm surprised you can read' – to the more hyperbolic – 'Oh, you haven't read any of my books? Well, to be honest I've never . . . sorry, what is it you do? Because I've no idea who you are. Anyway, whatever you do, rest assured I've never come to see you do it. Manage the bank, juggle hedge funds, fix cars, review restaurants, bait badgers or whatever the fuck it is you do. In fact, keep on not reading my books and I'll keep on not knowing or giving a shit about what you do. Deal?'

But pleasant, amiable Kennedy Marr just breathed deeply and said. 'Ach well. No problem.'

Then Peter Arthur had three Drambuies, lowered his voice and – clearly having mistaken Kennedy for a fellow traveller by this point – said conspiratorially, 'That Obama. He's piece of work, huh?'

Ah.

He went on for a bit. The usual stuff – 'He's a socialist, he's a communist, he's a Jedi . . .' Whatever. 'Obamacare this' and 'the taxpayer that'. Kennedy had two choices: 1) do the good liberal schtick – 'Mmmm. But don't you think . . . ? Yes. I see. But, on the other hand . . .' Or 2) see how far he could get the guy to go. Drunk himself, and with a long flight in prospect, he decided to go with option two, strategically chiming in with stuff like 'Fuckin' A', 'You're right, friend' and 'That comminazi'.

'I mean, I said to people during the election,' Peter Arthur said, leaning across the aisle to Kennedy, 'if he gets in again, if he somehow rigs it, we should march on Washington and tear him outta the White House before he wrecks the country forever.'

'Fuckin' A.'

'You know what's next, don't you? People he's packing the Supreme Court with? It's going to be as easy to get an abortion as a case of beer.'

'You're right, friend.'

Peter shook his florid jowls sorrowfully. 'A holocaust of the unborn. Paid for with your own tax dollar.'

'Goddamn comminazi.'

'I mean, there was a time, and I'm not talking all that long ago, when there was an emphasis on the *family*. Husbands worked and wives raised the children. These days – all the single parents and the whole if-you-don't-hire-so-many-women-you're-in-breach-of-whatever.' Jesus, you didn't meet people like this in West Hollywood, you really didn't. 'I mean, don't misunderstand me, I'm not *against* women having a career of course. Does your wife work, Kennedy?'

'Oh yeah.'

'What does she do?'

'She's an abortionist,' Kennedy said, sipping his fifth or seventh drink.

'How's that?'

'You know – she performs abortions. Listen, *friend*, where I come from people tend to avoid accosting strangers about politics. Because there was a time you'd wind up out back of the pub with a fucking pistol at your kneecap that way. But while we're on it, abortion shouldn't just be legal in your country, it should be fucking *mandatory* in several states. "As easy to get as a case of beer"? How about a Magnum? A SIG Sauer? A fucking Glock? They're easier to get than an abortion in some places, you fat retarded fuck.' Actually, counting the first-class lounge, it might have been Kennedy's *eighth* cocktail. He was properly drunk now, Limerick lock-in drunk. 'Of course I can see how the concept of paying a few cents in the dollar to help people with literally fucking nothing might be abhorrent to you. God forbid you and your family of bloated bastards should go a single day without stuffing your holes with bison. And another thing, while we're on it, Peter Arthur? Was one feckin' Christian name not enough for your bastard parents?'

'You listen now,' Peter Arthur said, straining towards him, neck veins bulging. 'You bring my family into this there's gonna be trouble. You understand me?' Fucking Americans, with their sanctity-of-the-family crap. Kennedy cleared his throat. He leaned across and spoke very slowly and clearly.

'Take your tax dollars and stick them up in your wife's fat, rotten hole.'

Peter Arthur launched himself across the aisle, springing with surprising speed and venom for one so large. But Kennedy was ready. He headbutted the guy in the face and the tycoon's nose bust like an overripe tomato. The other passengers screaming, them rolling on the floor swinging and gouging and then the steward's knee in his back.

Needless to say the rest of the boozeless flight was not pleasant for Kennedy.

He turned his phone on and it started beeping and buzzing away. Thirty-eight missed calls. Twenty-five new text messages. His Twitter account simply seemed to have exploded.

The doors opened and, for a split second, he thought he'd gone through some kind of wormhole and come out at a film premiere instead of international arrivals: flash-bulbs popping, people shouting his name, thrusting micro-phones at him, TV crews. Head down. Sunglasses on.

'Kennedy!'

'Mr Marr!'

'What happened?'

'Have you been charged?'

'Kennedy!'

'How's the head?'

'Were you drunk?'

'Mr Marr?'

This last one had a slightly different quality to it, almost a hint of concern. He looked up and saw a guy in his early thirties – overweight, something of the nightclub bouncer about him – standing there with a piece of paper with his name scrawled on it. 'I'm your driver.'

'Thank Christ,' Kennedy said, having to raise his voice above the din of the reporters. 'Where's the car?'

A few minutes later – having been pursued through the terminal and all the way across to Short Stay parking by the mob, despite his repeated mantra of 'fuckofffuck-offfuckoff' – Kennedy was sprawled flat across the back seat of a big Mercedes, exhausted and hung-over, as it threaded its way out of Heathrow. 'Oh Jaysuss,' he groaned.

'Quite an arrival then,' the guy said from the wheel. 'I've had some wait times, but twelve hours . . .'

'Yeah. Sorry about that.'

'All goes on the account, mate. Here, there's some pain-killers and water back there. I took the liberty. You might wanna look at all this too . . .'

A flop, something heavy hitting Kennedy's legs. He looked down: a doorstep of the morning papers. He lifted his sunglasses and began to leaf through. *Oh Jaysuss* . . .

At around that moment, in the kitchen in Warwickshire, about a hundred miles north of him, Millie was making coffee and checking her Twitter feed. She saw a prominent Kennedy hashtag. Clicked on it. Then another, then a link to the BBC news site and: 'Author Arrested at Heathrow' with a photograph of Kennedy, head down, handcuffed. 'Oh Christ,' Millie said. Upstairs she could hear Robin's feet, padding from bathroom to bedroom. 'Oh, you fucking idiot.'

Over in Clapham, turning on her trusty Roberts and reaching for the bread bin, Connie Blatt heard the words 'the author, who was the youngest ever novelist to be shortlisted for the Booker Prize for his debut *Unthinkable* in 1997 . . .' Connie's face, brightening, 'was arrested at Heathrow airport last night following a fracas on a British Airways flight.' Connie's face, falling. She hurried to the mat to retrieve her *Guardian*. Yes, there he was, page 5.

In Hampstead Professor David Bell stared at the front page of his *Telegraph*, where Kennedy had made a sidebar: 'DOA: Drunk On Arrival.' 'Oh dear,' he said, turning to the story. 'Oh dear, oh dear, oh dear.' He became aware that the phone was ringing, then his wife was in the doorway saying, 'It's someone from the press.'

Kennedy let the *Independent* (*'who arrived back in the UK to take up a one-year teaching position at Deeping University, Warwickshire, part of the conditions of the prestigious F. W. Bingham award . . .'*) fall to the floor of the car and sat up. 'What's your name?'

'Keith.' The guy reached back and Kennedy shook his hand.

'Thanks, Keith. Now, how long do you reckon this drive is?'

'M40 the way it's looking? Two hours at least.'

'Right.' Kennedy swallowed four Nurofen and two Valium with a glug from the Evian bottle. He balled his suit jacket up for use as a pillow. 'Wake me up when we get there.'

TWENTY-SEVEN

The Dean took *The Times*. 'Good Lord,' he said as he read the page 3 news item over again. The telephone on his desk rang.

'Dr Drummond is here to see you.'

'Oh Chr— very well. Send him in please.'

The briefest of pauses, a sharp knock, and Dennis Drummond was striding in, a fat wedge of newspapers tucked under his arm. He dropped them on the Dean's desk. 'Have you –'

'Yes, Dennis. I just heard.'

Drummond opened the *Mail* and read, '"A notorious drinker . . . the recipient of a half-a-million-pound literary award earlier this year is said to have physically attacked another passenger following an argument. The writer, 44, *who will be teaching at Deeping University, Warwickshire . . ."'* Drummond let the paper drop. 'I mean, the university's name is all over half of these articles.'

'Yes, it's not the greatest start admittedly. However, I –'

'*"Not the greatest start"?*'

'I feel we must give Mr Marr the chance to present his side of the story. You know the way the press can distort these things.'

'This is gross misconduct, surely you —'

'Well, he is a public figure. So sometimes things that might slip under the radar get picked up on.'

'I warned you about this. It's no secret the kind of person he is.'

'Dennis, we've been over this and your reservations have been noted.'

'I do not want that man in my department.'

'What exactly are you saying, Dr Drummond?' The Dean, leaning back in his chair, interlocking his fingers, becoming formal.

Drummond looked at him. Were they really on the verge of he-goes-or-I-go territory? Something told Drummond not to have his bluff called on this. 'I . . . just. I'm very unhappy about his presence here. I think he has no interest in teaching and I believe he will damage the reputation of the department and the university.'

'OK. Duly noted. However, Dennis, and again, we've been through this, Mr Marr is going to be here for a while and during his stay I expect you treat him with professional courtesy. I don't think that's unreasonable.'

Drummond snorted. 'Unreasonable, eh?'

He smacked a final, open newspaper in front of the Dean, turned on his heel and left.

The Dean looked at it. Something called the *Star*. He was unfamiliar with it. It didn't look like the *Morning Star*, the one John Pilger and George Orwell had written for.

There was a two-page spread on Kennedy and a photograph of a young woman with, good Lord, with her breasts out. A photo of Kennedy on the red carpet with some actors the Dean didn't recognise. A smaller, inset US police department photo showed Kennedy at the time of an arrest in LA a few years ago, looking very much the worse for wear. (*'Was arrested for drunk-driving in West Hollywood . . . possession of cocaine . . . drunk and disorderly . . .'*) The caption beneath the photograph of the young woman said. *'The boozy woman-ising writer, 44, is working at Pinewood Studios with the Sex-Sational Julie Teal on her new film.'* The photograph was a still from one of Teal's early films.

His phone rang again. 'Hello?'

'Sorry to disturb you, I have Miss Welles from the Admissions office for you. Some interesting news apparently.'

'Thank you, Camilla, put her through.'

The Dean listened. A few moments later he was saying, 'Oh really? Well, well. That is interesting news. *Very* interesting news.'

TWENTY-EIGHT

Now this, this was a bit more fucking like it, Kennedy thought as he padded along the corridor. A pleasant surprise this, which made a change from all those other kinds of surprises he'd been getting lately.

A beautiful Georgian manor house of pale Cotswold stone, with nearly four acres surrounding it. ('Bloody hell, all right for some, eh?' Keith had said as they pulled up the long gravel drive. He'd been even more impressed when he saw the pale blue rented Aston Martin hunkered down on its fat tyres to the side of the house. 'Fucking hell, guv. DB9? This yours an' all?' He'd walked all around the car, respectfully, taking in every angle and curve, like someone at the Met or the Guggenheim confronted with a rare sculpture. 'Someone's dinged it a little here, mate,' he'd said, pointing to an invisible chip or scratch. Refreshed, having slept all the way, Kennedy had tipped him heftily and taken his business card. Someone like Keith was likely to be of much use to someone like Kennedy in a rural location:

where you couldn't really do anything without driving. Kennedy, obviously, couldn't do much without drinking.) There had been welcoming hampers in the vast kitchen from the F. W. Bingham committee, Connie and the Dean of Deeping, and it was from these that he had gleaned the ingredients required to make the soothing lunchtime cocktail he was now sipping, a Bloody Mimosa: champagne and tomato juice. Heading on through the house he saw a comfortable-looking study off to his right, a drawing room, some kind of futility room (washers, dryers, ironing board, etc.), and a dining room painted deep red, with refectory table set for twelve (sudden, brief flash of fear – would they be expecting him to entertain?). He came down three steps into the main sitting room and whistled: a long, broad, oak-panelled space. The far end was a wall of glass overlooking the grounds. The furniture was good: two big sofas of worn caramel leather faced each other across a low teak table. You could just about stand a man up in the fireplace. Two armchairs faced each other across a chessboard further up. Bookshelves all along one wall. A baby grand piano at the far end near the windows and an Eames chair with footstool positioned to allow one to wallow with a book and enjoy the view. Which was something: not another building in his eyeline. Just a gently sloping lawn bordered by fields on his left and woodland on the right, with a massive oak right in the middle and poplars lining the very end of the property.

Passing back through the kitchen in order to recharge his glass he moved on up the grand staircase and along the upstairs hallway. Bedrooms and bathrooms off on either side, paintings lining the walls, mostly oils, mostly portraits of glowering men – doubtless the old bastards whose cruelty and acumen had been responsible for this becoming the family seat of someone or other – until he got to the end and entered what was clearly the master suite. It was enormous: just about on a par with the sitting room somewhere below. There were windows on two sides, including three huge, almost floor-to-ceiling ones on the wall opposite the bed. The room was done in pale yellow arts and crafts wallpaper, the furnishings all looking to be from the 1930s at the latest. The only signs of modernity were the new oatmeal carpet, thick and soft beneath his bare feet, and the great black slab of the flat-screen TV on the wall facing the bed. He pushed open a door and found himself in a large, sunny bathroom, clearly a smaller adjoining bedroom that had been converted. The old Victorian bath was positioned directly in front of the picture window, to let you gaze contentedly across your Empire while you soaked. He sat on the edge of the tub, looking out of the window, sipping the mimosa and reflecting on how agreeable all of this might actually be if it weren't for the fact that he had to leave it and travel to the campus almost every day – 'just ten minutes down the road' Keith had told him – to listen to teenagers talking about their attempts at fiction. Just as he had this thought he heard a distant knocking somewhere, what sounded like a thudding at the heavy front door. He sighed and drained his glass. What fresh hell was this?

'Good afternoon,' the smiling middle-aged lady on the doorstep said. 'I'm Angela Marcus. I – are you OK?'

'Huh?'

'Your face, it –'

Kennedy turned and looked in the big mirror above the

fireplace in the hall. The tomato juice. It looked like he'd been going down on a menstruating sea lion. 'Shit, sorry, just tomato juice, come, come in. Just give me a second.'

He dived into a small bathroom, rinsing and wiping his face, and came out mopping himself with a towel. 'Sorry, you were saying?'

'Yes, Angela Marcus?' She extended her hand and they shook. Something about the question mark in her voice — she expected Kennedy to know who she was. He raised an eyebrow, making a 'thinking' face. 'We did exchange emails some time ago?'

'Ahhh . . .'

'I'm your secretary, Mr Marr.'

'Oh! Grand. Right. Sorry. Shit! Yes — come on through. Sorry, I'm a wee bit . . . jet-lagged.'

They went into the great sitting room. 'Lovely room, isn't it?' Angela said.

'Yeah, it's something. Drink?'

She looked at her watch. 'Well, perhaps a small sherry would be nice. Yes. Lovely. Thank you.' Kennedy — immediately warming to the woman. She looked to be a little older than him, late forties, with straight, sandy-blonde hair cut in a bob and a great mouthful of huge, healthy teeth, big as wardrobes the front ones. Wearing a grey suit with a black polo neck, a sizeable chest lurking under there too.

'Sherry, right. Sorry, I'm not sure where anything is. There's some champagne in the fri—'

'The cocktail cabinet's in the middle of that bookcase,' she pointed. 'I think you'll find it's quite well stocked.'

Kennedy found the panel and folded it down. He

whistled – a skyline of bottles, decanters, glasses, mixers. 'Wow. Did you do all this?' Kennedy asked, over his shoulder, finding the sherry and cracking it open.

'Preparing the house for your arrival was one of my tasks, yes, Mr Marr.'

'Bang-up job, Angela. And please, Kennedy.' He came back over with two glasses of Manzanilla.

'Thank you.' She took the sherry and sipped it. 'I suppose, in the circumstances, Kennedy, I've no need to ask if you had a pleasant flight?'

Kennedy laughed. 'I suppose there's a bit of a shitstorm going on about all this?'

'You could say that, yes. There was due to be a reception party for you tonight but, given events, we've moved it to Monday to give you a chance to . . . acclimatise better. Oh, Millie, your wife, sorry! ex-wife, told me to remind you that she and Robin would be over tomorrow, Saturday, to say hello and that the three of you were going to have lunch together.'

'Oh yeah. Grand.' Obviously Kennedy had no recollection of making this arrangement either.

'So I thought it would be a good idea if I popped over today and went through the week in view. And I'm sure you've got a few questions of your own.' She set her glass down and produced a notebook.

'Fire away,' Kennedy said, warmed by the sherry, feeling the sleepy tug of jet lag coursing through him.

'Now, apart from your family tomorrow the weekend is clear. You've got lunch with the Dean on Monday at one.'

'What's he like?'

'Professor Lyons? Lovely man. Now, that's in his office

and will probably last an hour minimum. Then you have to meet with Dr Drummond, the head of the English Department. He's a writer too. Well, was a writer.'

'Is that so?' Kennedy said.

'He'll show you round your office in the afternoon, let you get settled in a bit, then there's the drinks reception at seven and then dinner, again with the Dean and Professor Bell, chairman of the F. W. Bingham committee.'

'Fu—' He stopped. 'Full. Pretty full day.'

'I'm afraid so. Now, Tuesday . . .'

Kennedy recrossed to the bar and brought the bottle back with him. He topped his glass up; Angela smiled but held a flattened palm over hers. 'I must keep sharp while we're working.'

'Oh, do you mind if I . . . ?'

'Please, by all means. I'm a complete lightweight, you see.' Yes, liking this old girl more and more. 'Tuesday you'll need to start reviewing all of the submissions for places on your course. We're only two weeks away from the students coming back so you'll need to make some decisions on that front soon, I'm afraid.'

'Decisions?'

'Yes. Your course is incredibly oversubscribed. I think we've had over two hundred applications for the twenty-odd places.'

'About these "submissions" . . .'

'Yes, as you said in your email, just the opening chapter or first few pages of whatever novel or screenplay or short story they're working on. No more than one thousand words.' Why did people keep insisting on remembering things Kennedy had said? Bringing up stuff he'd agreed to do? 'I'll arrange to have them delivered in the morning. You can make a start over the weekend.'

'What . . . what are you telling me here, Angela?'

'You'll need, you know, to read them.'

He looked at her, his expression slackening into one of sheer horror. 'Two hundred of them?'

'Ish.' She took a sip of her sherry.

'Are you saying that, in the next two weeks, I have to read *two hundred thousand words* of undergraduate prose?'

It was Angela's turn to stare at him. 'Well, yes. This is teaching, I'm afraid.'

Kennedy sprawled back in the chair, covering his face with his hands, letting out a low, rising moan. 'Whose fucking idea was this?'

'Well, yours.'

He sighed and drained his glass. 'You're learning a very important lesson at the outset here, Angela. Never, ever, listen to a fucking word I say.'

A short while later, after some more practical questions had been gone over – the housekeeper, Mrs Baird would be arriving tomorrow, she'd cook any meals he wanted, keep the place shipshape etc. – Kennedy showed her out.

'You know,' Angela said, back on the doorstep, 'I think it's quite sweet.'

'What's sweet?'

'Well, that someone like you – lauded, successful, admired and all that – should be so nervous about teaching undergraduates.'

'I'm not . . . nervous.'

'Hmmm. OK then. See you tomorrow.'

She left and Kennedy decided to have a wank and go to sleep.

Somewhere into the wank something started troubling him. It wasn't the images being beamed onto the laptop – solidly extreme and troubling though they were. It wasn't the fact that here he was, in the middle of the afternoon, the working day, a professional, some would say eminent, man in his forties, stretched out on the floor of his office and dementedly pounding his pudding as if his very life depended upon it. No. It was that grain of sand just below the skin, under his thumb, down near the root, the one he'd noticed in LA a few months back. It felt marginally bigger, more like a grain of rice now. Moments later, lying there panting and mopping, he explored again, squeezing and pressing around where he had felt it. Nothing. It seemed to have vanished with his erection.

His mobile trilled into life. 'Hello?'

'A grand entrance right enough. You even made the papers over here.'

'Patrick. I . . .'

'How's things?'

Kennedy looked down at the matted disgrace of his own stomach. 'Ah, fine. Just . . . tired. Did Ma see any of it?'

'No. You're good there, brother.'

'Wasn't my fault by the way.'

'Sure and I've heard that before. Anyway, I won't keep you long. Just, now you're back, I wondered if you'd given any thought to coming over to see Ma?'

'Yeah, lemme just, check the diary . . . ah, how about . . .' He lay there, thinking. Just pick a date, not too soon, not too far away. 'I've got a lot of reading to do before term

starts . . . first week the students are here will probably
be crazy . . .'

'Mmmm.'

'How about . . . three weeks from today?'

'Friday 18th of October?

'Yeah.'

'If that's as soon as you can manage, fine. I'll tell her.'

'Thanks, Patrick. How is she?'

'Ach, in herself she's fine. Loving it at the hospital, having
a bit more life about her. It's just . . . not eating.'

'Right. Fuck.'

'Anyway. I'll let you get some rest. See you on the 18th.'

'Bye, Patrick.'

He drifted off to sleep in a square of sunshine on the
carpet, his trousers around his ankles and a matted wad of
Kleenex stuck to his stomach like a half-melted snowball.

TWENTY-NINE

'Bloody hell, Dad! It's massive!' Robin said. 'And that car is *ridic* by the way.' She disappeared down the passage ahead of them, poking her head into various rooms, Millie and Kennedy following a few yards behind. 'Mmm,' Millie said. 'Don't think this place hasn't been the cause of a few comments from the mere mortals.'

'Yeah?'

'Have you any idea how much it's costing to rent this till next May? It would have paid for two new PhDs.'

'Ah, but does the world really need a couple more post-graduate theses like "The Internal Dissonance of the Venerable Bede"? And would your PhDs have seen an "80 per cent rise in the number of applications to the English Department"? Would they have generated an "unprece-dented volume of media interest"?'

'Oh yeah – "drunk on arrival",' Millie said, doing some quoting of her own, '"author is charged over air rage incident".' You really started enhancing the image of Deeping the minute you got off the plane, didn't you?'

'Ach, you don't read 'em. Just weigh 'em, Millie.'

They stopped outside the open door to his study and looked in. There they were: his dread Twin Towers of pain, all 200,000-plus words, delivered first thing by Angela and now arranged in two fat stacks in the middle of the desk. Read it? Christ, Kennedy could hardly even fucking look at it.

'Got your work cut out then?' Millie said, smiling.

'What can I say?' Kennedy said, forcing levity. 'Men want to be him, women want to be with him.'

'I still can't quite believe you're actually doing this.'

'Of all the English lit departments in all the world.'

'You. Dealing with students.'

'Hey – bitch gotta make rent.'

From down the hall, 'Shit, Mum – come and see the size of this!'

'Robin! Stop swearing!' They could hear her playing a few chords on the sitting-room piano, what sounded like the intro of 'Talk Show Host' by Radiohead. Millie wandered off along the hallway towards the sound. Kennedy lingered in the study doorway for a moment then walked towards the Towers. The top piece of work on the closest one, the South Tower, was entitled 'SERENADE', by someone called Carl Millar. He lifted the title page and saw a densely packed block of prose. He read the first sentence – '*The alarm went off with an urgent drone*' – and hurriedly slapped the page back down. Jesus. Jesus fucking Christ. Could he actually get through this? Really – you're opening with *the alarm clock going off*? Way to go, Carl. Way to come at your story from an oblique and unexpected angle. And 'an urgent drone'? A fucking *urgent* drone? What the fuck was that when it was at home? What was its counterpoint? A relaxed siren? Christ, was this worth a half a million quid?

Kennedy backed away from the Towers, almost with palms extended towards them – as though they were an armed intruder, or a nuclear device – and headed for the sitting room.

When he entered, what he saw made him stop, made him conscious of his breathing and the blood in his veins. At the far end of the room Millie and Robin were at the piano, Robin sitting on the stool shaping chords – studiously, biting her bottom lip the way she did when she was concentrating – while Millie stood over her turning the pages of the sheet music. It was something classical now, something Kennedy didn't recognise. (He kept meaning to get around to classical music but it was like learning that second language, or making sure you ate your five-a-day.) Mother and daughter were beautifully lit, framed in the weak peach-coloured light coming through the wall of glass behind them. Something about walking into the room on a Saturday morning with his mind on something else and then suddenly seeing them like that . . .

Unbidden, the fantasy flashed through him: he imagined that they had all not long got out of bed, that they had stayed up late the night before watching a movie, just the three of them, he and Millie cuddling on one of the deep sofas, Robin at their feet on a beanbag or something, Millie eating a rare bar of chocolate, Kennedy sober. Perhaps wearing a cardigan. Soon they would all share a late breakfast and then potter, hang around the house, or maybe go shopping, or for a walk (here, admittedly, Kennedy stretched his own credulity), before returning to this big, lovely country house for the autumnal stew that Millie had put in the bottom of the Aga when she got up, whose smells of garlic and thyme and sweet root vegetables now filled the house. The home. The family home. Yes, for a fraction of a second, gazing at his ex-wife and daughter, Kennedy Marr inhabited the life he had never had. The life he had passed on. Yes, they were always with you, these things. They never went away. *You could only hope to somehow coexist with them.*

The music stopped and he realised they were both looking at him. 'Dad?' Robin said.

'Kennedy, are you –'

'Yeah,' he said, his voice thicker than he had expected it to be. He cleared his throat, manned up. 'Shall we go to the pub? Come on – let's go to lunch. Where's good to drink in this godforsaken county?'

'Haven't you got a couple of hundred short stories to get through?' Millie asked.

'Ach, bollocks. What was that place you took me to before, when I was over a couple of years ago? I think it's near here.'

THIRTY

The Falcon's Rest was a little over a mile down the road,
pretty much equidistant between the house and campus.
The moment he walked in, Kennedy – a veteran of public
houses, an authority on bars and inns – knew this would
be his local.

Reassuringly busy without being crowded, a strong smell
of woodsmoke from the log fire burning in the grate, no
music playing, what looked to be a phenomenal selection
of local ales on draught, a decent if unspectacular range of
malts behind the bar, a restaurant through the back, the
day's menu listed on a chalkboard above the fire (a couple
of pies, steak, chops, fish, solid unpretentious stuff), and,
importantly, what looked and sounded to be a broad mix
of ages and social types at the bar: from ruddy-faced, tweedy
retired judges, to plumbers and plasterers, to a couple of
well-heeled, well-kept middle-aged women hunched over
a bottle of Malbec. Kennedy got the round in (a pint of
Kingsland Pale Ale and a large Laphroiag chaser for him,

a gin and tonic for Millie and a half lager shandy for Robin. He told the barmaid – a very doable tattooed Australian girl – to keep the change from the twenty) and they found a table in the corner in a window bay.

'Chee—,' Kennedy began, raising his frothing pint.

'Oh, there's Clarissa!' Robin said, getting up and disappearing across the bar, to where a blonde girl about her age was at the dartboard with a boy a little older.

'Fucking, *Clarissa*, is it?' Kennedy said sourly. 'The parents big Richardson fans, are they? Don't they know how it ended for that slag?'

'Clarissa Drummond. They go to school together. Her dad's head of the English Department.'

'Oh yeah, Dennis Drummond the writer.'

'Well,' Millie said

'Cheers.' Kennedy knocked the dimpled mug against her G&T. 'So, what's happening? What's new? God, you look well, Millie, did I say that already? How's your love life?'

'None of your bloody business.'

'Fair enough.'

'Have you rung Patrick yet?'

'Yes! Fucking hell, I just got in yesterday. I need to –'

'You need to go and see your mum, Kennedy, that's what you need to be doing.'

'I know, I know. I'm on it. I'm going to get Angela to look into flights and hotels and whatnot on Monday.'

'Angela? I . . . she's your *academic* assistant, Kennedy. She's not some Hollywood dogsbody who's going to be picking up your dry-cleaning, shopping for your Christmas gifts and booking your bloody travel.'

'I'm sure we can come to an arrangement. What can she earn anyway?'

'Jesus.'

'I'm kidding. I'm perfectly capable of booking a fucking flight, you know.'

Millie snorted. 'Oh yeah – the man who thought water was free. Who thought the government just sent you a tax disc for the car as part of paying your income tax. Who –'

'OK, OK. Anyway, come on and fill me in now. Who are the good guys? At the university, I mean.'

'I think, given the manner of your arrival, you'll be struggling to find any fans.'

'It wasn't my fault!'

'It never is, Kennedy. You know, when we were together, going out with you for the night, I'd start holding my breath when I was in the shower. Doing my make-up. The whole evening, always spent waiting for the other shoe to drop.'

'Come on – you loved it. It's why you've never remarried.'

She laughed. 'Your narcissism is truly bottomless, isn't it? The reason I never remarried is because I'm responsible about who I let into my daughter's life. You, on the other hand, you'd fuck mud.'

'You know, you're still a really good-looking woman Millie. Though clearly sexually frustrated.'

'And you –' she sucked on her rind of lemon, speaking pleasantly, taking her time – 'are a philandering, self-regarding fantasist with anger-management issues who has clearly spent most of his adult life struggling with a deeply denied sense of homosexual panic.'

'Sure and I'm very good on structure though,' Kennedy

said, finishing the whisky, gathering the glasses. 'Here, I'll get some menus. You fancy another?'

'I'm driving.'

'Fuck off, you're in the country.' He stood up, catching sight of the small TV through an archway, in the lounge, and noticing they had the rugby on. Looked like Wales v England. Nasty-looking scrum on the Welsh line. *Come on, you Taffs, get those colonial bastards out* – 'Mum?' He heard Robin's voice behind him. 'After lunch, can I go over to Clarissa's?'

Kennedy turned. Robin said, 'Clarissa, this is my dad,'

'Hi, Clarissa.' He extended his hand.

'Hi! Wow, I'm, like, really excited to meet you.'

'You mean you *are* excited to meet me or it's *like* you're excited to meet me?'

'*Dad*,' Robin said.

'My friend Donnie,' this Clarissa went on, shaking his hand childishly, hardly holding it, 'has literally read all of your books.'

'As opposed to metaphorically read them?'

The girl looked confused. Robin sighed.

'I mean,' Kennedy went on, 'did he –'

'Oh, do shut up, Kennedy,' Millie said, then, to Robin, 'Sure.'

His parenting done, Kennedy turned back to the TV. *No, no, you eejits, don't let the fecker get down the line there.* Behind him he heard, 'Oh, hi, Dennis. Karen.'

Punt it up. Just fucking punt it –

'Kennedy?'

That's it, come on now, don't –

'Kennedy!'

He turned. 'What?'

'This is Dennis and Karen.'

They shook hands.

A thin, beakish man in Barbour, brogues *and* flat cap. The full deck – a look that in Kennedy's experience said 'I live in west London'. He might as well have called the ensemble 'Country Pub Visit'. Most likely bald too, Kennedy thought, from the silvery stubble running into the cap. 'Oh, grand. Hi there. Pleased to meet you.'

They shook hands. Drummond taking Kennedy in, finding him taller, altogether burlier than he'd expected from the photographs. Kennedy, in his turn, took in Karen. Useful rack. Pleasant smile.

'Yes. We're scheduled to meet tomorrow, I think.'

'Is that right now? Can I get you a drink, Dennis?'

'Oh no, thank you. We're just getting off in a minute. I hope –' Shouting and groaning from the little crowd next door gathered around the TV. Kennedy turned back – fucking English bastards had it right back on the line now. *Oh Jesus, come on!* More talking behind him. 'Sorry?'

'I said, I hope you're OK. After all that business on your flight.' Behind the guy, Millie was talking to the wife. Robin to the daughter.

'Oh yeah. Grand, grand. Just a wee misunderstanding.'

A roar went up. Kennedy wheeled back round to see the English scrum half bouncing the ball off the turf, raising his arms in triumph. *Bastard.* More talking aimed at the back of his head. 'Sorry?'

'Rugby fan, I see?' It was instantly apparent that this Drummond had zero interest in sports, which rendered him only fractionally alive in Kennedy's book.

'Well, yeah. Where I come from.' He turned back to get a look at the scoreline – 28–12. Five minutes left. All over now. Kennedy turned back to Drummond. 'Excuse me a sec,' he said, shouldering his way off through the crush.

Outside he smoked and scrolled through some emails on his phone. The usual: Braden, Spengler, Connie, Vicky (who wanted to have her bathroom remodelled and would be sending him the bill). Angela with a revised schedule. A few interview requests from various newspapers wanting his side of the story on the whole air rage thing. Kennedy heard feet scrunching on the gravel nearby and looked up to see the family Drummond leaving the pub, heading towards the car park. Kennedy smiled and made a vague wave with his cigarette. Drummond nodded back, the faintest trace of a smile, a sneer rather, playing on his lips. *Oh yeah?* Kennedy thought. *Fuck you.*

Back into the warmth and woodsmoke of the pub, he pressed his way to the bar with a cocked twenty and made with the 'Same again please'.

As the drinks arrived, he found himself gazing idly through the window to see Drummond's Prius edging past his Aston and on out of the car park. Kennedy emitted a sort of a low growl as he stared at the departing vehicle. The Aussie barmaid followed his line of vision and said, 'Oh, Dennis. Friend of yours?'

'Christ no.'

'D'you know something?' The girl leaned in across the bar. 'In all the time I've worked here I've served that guy heaps of times and never had –'

'So much as a tip off him?'

'How d'ya know that?'

'I just spent thirty seconds with him.'

Kennedy did indeed have a great talent for sniffing out the joyless, the tight-fisted, the last-to-the-bar, we-didn't-have-a-starter merchants. 'I'm Kennedy, by the way,' he said, extending his hand through the pumps.

'Nicky. And we've all heard about you, mate,' she said, smiling.

'Is that right?' Kennedy said, smiling too.

THIRTY-ONE

Lunch with the Dean had been exceedingly pleasant. Local pheasant and then apple crumble. He'd even broken out a bottle of '73 Palmer.

His offices were in the old part of the university: a Victorian cod-Gothic jumble on the northern slope of the campus, a few wings and a tower grouped around two quads lined with copper beeches. Through the Dean's windows, over behind the tower and down the slope, you could just see the white facade and brown-smoked glass of the library and the newer buildings – mostly 1960s horror shows – grouped around it.

During the pheasant he'd brushed off the air rage stuff ('Oh, these things happen. The chap in question sounds quite odious I have to say'), and by the time they were both chasing the last sweet pieces of crumble through the custard, Kennedy felt they had truly come to understand one another: Kennedy's name attached to the university was giving them a shot of glamour and an uptake in applications. 'A remarkable spike in our website traffic and in phone calls to the switchboard,' as Miss Welles from Admissions had told the Dean following Kennedy's press blitz after the flight kerfuffle.

'Funding is king today, Mr Marr. Every one of those overseas students is a little shot of gold in the arm.'

In return Kennedy was clearly going to do the absolute minimum amount of work he could get away with.

They moved to a pair of comfortable armchairs over beside the window. Stirring their coffee the Dean turned to one final matter. 'There is one slightly delicate thing I wanted to touch upon, Mr –'

'Please, Kennedy.'

'Kennedy. You have, how to put it, something of a reputation as a ladies' man.'

'I do?'

'Well, one reads things. And, of course, this is all no business of mine. What's the Johnson phrase? "They discourse like angels but they live like men"?'

Kennedy smiled. 'I know it well.'

'It's just, especially with some of the younger students, relations that might prove . . .' The Dean was fairly twisting his coffee spoon now.

'Professor Lyons –'

'Please, Dominic.'

'Dominic, there's nothing to worry you on that score. I have a daughter nearly the same age as some of these girls.'

'Of course. Quite so. I'm sorry to bring it up, I just felt I should . . . you know.'

A knock at the door and the Dean's secretary's head

appeared. 'Sorry to interrupt but Dr Drummond is outside. You said —'

'Ah yes. Dr Drummond. Head of the English Department. I thought you two should meet seeing as, technically speaking, you'll be in his department. Show him in, thank you.'

'We met at the weekend actually. In the pub. Millie introduced us.'

'Millie? Ah yes — Dr Dyer! Your ex-wife, of course. I believe Dennis wrote a few novels too. Not quite in the same bracket as yourself, but I'm told his stuff's very . . . ah, interesting.' Then, standing, 'Ah, Dennis, come in, come in. I understand you two have met already?'

Kennedy stood, smiling, extending his hand as Drummond entered. 'We did indeed. Hi there. Nice to see you again.'

'Kennedy.'

'Have a seat, Dennis.' The Dean gestured to a hardbacked chair nearby. 'Coffee?'

'No, thank you.' Drummond took in the little dining table set at the back of the room, the dirty plates and empty decanter. Needless to say, in seven years here, he had never been invited to lunch in the Dean's office. 'I have a ton of work to get through. Speaking of which, Kennedy, I was hoping I'd have receiv—'

'I have to say, Dennis,' Kennedy said, cutting him off, 'I very much enjoyed *A Circular Defence*.'

This had the welcome effect of silencing Drummond.

When had he last heard these hallowed words? Nearly two decades ago? That woman, the one who wanted her book signed that time? The one who made up 50 per cent of the audience for his talk at the Barsford Literary Festival in 1994? The one who it later turned out thought he was someone else? 'Really brave novel,' Kennedy continued. 'Loved it.' Saying that he 'loved it' might have been pushing the envelope a bit. Indeed, from the few scraps of information Kennedy had gleaned about the book from googling Drummond's name the previous evening he suspected that were he ever to be made to read *A Circular Defence* – if, say, he found himself in a situation where home intruders were offering him the stark choice of reading the novel or taking a front-row seat for the rape and torture of his immediate family, basically if he ever found himself in the final reel of *Cape Fear*, confronted by a psychotic Drummond fan, some kind of bookish Max Cady – he might well find himself not loving it. He suspected that he might find himself impervious to its charms. That he might, indeed, find himself gripped by murderous rage. But it was always pleasurable to wrong-foot a handpump. When novelists meet . . . what was the quote? *'On the way up, the aspirant sees literary eminence as an ocean liner, with a champagne reception awaiting him in first class. Once there, he encounters a kind of Medusa's raft, littered with snarling skeletons.'*

'I . . . well. Thank you. Your work, of course, is –'

'Ach.' Kennedy waved away whatever insincere, backhanded compliment was heading his way. 'And what are you working on at the moment?'

'Well, it's difficult. I have such a heavy teaching load these days. But I'm outlining a new book.'

'Grand.'

'Yes, early days. But, on the subject of teaching, I wanted –'

'Funnily enough, I don't really do that myself.'

'You don't . . . *outline?*' Drummond said these three words as though Kennedy had just said 'I don't wear condoms while I'm fucking kids'.

'Well, I know who the characters are going to be, what the world is. The general "What if?" Then you just let them go, don't you? It's a bit like driving from London to Edinburgh in the 1940s. You know the first part of the road well enough and you know when you're getting there. But in the middle – you're just winging it, don't you find? Hoping the ice holds below your feet.'

'I . . . here on the creative writing course we try to emphasise the importance of a detailed outline. As I suspect most authors would.'

'Stephen King doesn't. He said, "If I don't know what's going to happen next then there's a good chance the reader won't be able to guess."'

'Well, I hardly think Stephen King qualifies as litera—'

'I love Stephen King.'

'Really?'

'Sure. And I think if we're looking at your respective methodologies in terms of productivity . . .' Kennedy grinned and spread his hands, the gesture saying simply, 'Between 1993, the year of your last published work, and today, Stephen King has produced about twenty-three novels to your zero. Take your outline, grease it, and insert it into your anus.'

'Well, I'm sure we could have a long and interesting "quality versus quantity" chat.'

'Oh indeed,' Kennedy said, still somehow managing to smile.

'But what I was trying to say was – I don't seem to have

received the proposed reading list for your course yet. We need to have these copied and available for when the students return.'

'Oh, fine. I'll drop that into you later. Been giving it a lot of thought.'

'Yes. Thank you. And how have you been getting on with your writing samples? An unprecedented number by the way.'

'Oh, grand.' Kennedy thought of the Twin Towers of pain, listing untouched on the desk at home. 'Some very talented kids in there.'

'Have you chosen the lucky twenty?'

'Getting there,' Kennedy said.

'Because term starts in two weeks.'

'Of course.'

The two men, smiling pure loathing at one another now.

'Well then,' the Dean cut in, looking at his watch, 'I'll let Dr Drummond show you to your quarters. I'll see you both at the welcome reception later.'

'Grand,' Kennedy said. 'And thanks again for lunch.'

THIRTY—TWO

They set off down the corridor, Drummond striding ahead, stiff, jerky and fast. An unfucked kind of walk. Kennedy sauntered behind, hands in his pockets, taking in bits of architecture – a flying buttress here, a chipped Ionic column there. Really he was forcing Drummond to slow down, to lose his rhythm, much as you would try and force your tempo upon an opponent in a tight tennis match. Drummond stopped, gently patting the palms of his hands together, waiting for him to catch up as they exited into the late-September sunlight of the quad. Obviously the instant they found themselves outdoors Kennedy lit a cigarette, this being Kennedy's automatic, Pavlovian response to stepping outdoors. Drummond immediately did a ridiculous hand-fanning gesture. Even looked like he might say something for a second. Kennedy wouldn't have minded that. Kennedy *wanted* him to say something. 'So,' Drummond said, 'I understand we're to lose you for a few days here and there this term. Some film or other you're working on.' This last tossed off ultra dismissively.

'Ach – hopefully not too much. They're doing a lot of the interiors, the heavy dialogue scenes, at Pinewood. Just down the M40. You know how actors can be . . .'

'Mmmm,' Drummond said, clueless. 'Must be a terrible distraction.'

'From what?'

'From the fiction. It's been, what, four years since your last book?' Drummond, almost managing to sound concerned here.

'Five actually.' This prick.

'It's been the downfall of many novelists of course, Hollywood. Faulkner, Fitzgerald.' They followed the path around the Administration buildings towards the white blocks of the English Department.

'Yeah, the thing is, Dennis, there just aren't too many publishers willing to pay you half a million bucks to write a 120-page novel that mostly consists of dialogue.'

'Art versus commerce, eh?' Drummond said loftily. His most recent fee for a commercial work had been a cheque some months ago for £129 from the *Critical Quarterly*, for his 3,000-word Marxist deconstruction of *Middlemarch*, a piece he'd delivered nearly three years back.

'Well, like the great man said,' Kennedy said, 'we have no obligation to make art. We have no obligation to make history. Or to make a statement. Our obligation is to make money. And to make money it may be necessary to make art, to make history, to make a statement.'

'Hemingway?' Drummond said, holding the door open for him.

'Don Simpson,' Kennedy said, flicking his glowing, half-smoked Marlboro Light into a flower bed, enjoying the look of distaste on Drummond's face.

They went up the stairs and onto a long corridor, Drummond already fishing excitedly in his pocket for the key. At the far end, some distance away, workmen were coming and going with crates and furniture. Drummond, relishing the moment, reached for the handle to the first door on his left, slipped the key into the lock and pushed it open with a flourish, to reveal –

A monastic cell, about eight feet by ten, with one tiny slit window looking out onto a brick wall. It was painted the colour of old nurses' tights, the very same colour it had originally been painted in 1983. A wilting aspidistra in a terracotta pot stood on the windowsill, an Orwellian touch Drummond hoped would not be lost on the cell's new occupant. 'I do apologise,' Drummond began saying, just as he'd rehearsed. 'I'm sure this isn't quite what you're used to, but space is very lim— ' He turned round. Kennedy was still walking, like he hadn't heard him. 'Ah, Mr Marr? Kennedy?' Kennedy turned back. 'In here?' Drummond was pointing to the open doorway he stood in front of.

'Oh,' Kennedy said, 'didn't you hear? Come on . . .' He gestured with his head down the corridor and resumed his stately pace, disappearing into a room on the other side, the one the workman were coming and going from. Drummond followed, confused, noticing now that furniture was piled up outside. He entered and found he had briefly lost the power of speech.

The room they were standing in was the old common room: with two large arched windows overlooking the

campus and woodland beyond. It was almost the size of
the Dean's offices. Far bigger than Drummond's own. Men
in overalls were removing the last of the old furniture while
their colleagues entered by another door carrying new
furniture, the packing crates labelled 'HEAL'S OF
LONDON'. A deep, plush new sofa was already installed
at the far end. An enormous Edwardian partner's desk had
been deposited at the end they stood at, basically a twenty-
square-foot slab of walnut with a hand-tooled leather inlay.
A man was up a stepladder putting the finishing touches
to a new coat of paint, a fresh dove-grey colour, the cans
of Farrow & Ball paint clustered around the bottom of the
ladder. Kennedy stood in the middle, casually flipping
through crates of books.

'This . . .' Drummond tried to begin, his voice a stran-
gulated whisper.

'Where's the bar going then, guvnor?' a voice behind
Drummond asked. He turned and saw two more men in
the doorway, both holding, in fact *struggling* to hold, heavy
crates marked 'MAJESTIC WINE'.

'Oh, grand, grand, lads,' Kennedy said, coming towards
them. 'Up at the end there, by the wee fridge.'

Fridge?

Kennedy reached into one of the crates as the men passed
and pulled out a bottle of Four Roses bourbon. 'Drink?'

'This room,' Drummond began again, trying to control
himself, 'has been assigned to *three* PhD students who are
starting next term.'

'Ach, sure and it's all sorted, Dennis. Angela spoke with
the Dean's office. They're going to put two of your boys
in the wee one you were just looking at down the hall and

one of them upstairs. They've just finished their under-graduate degrees, these lads, they'll be pigs in shit just having their own room. When you get to our time of life though, sure and you need your creature comforts a bit more. They can have this one back next May when I leave. Seemed a waste to leave it empty for a whole term, you know? Now, where did they put those lemons?'

'This . . . the furniture.' Drummond's right eyelid appeared to be vibrating as he stepped in close to Kennedy, lowering his voice. 'This is *my* department. How *dare* you go to the Dean behind my back to make arrangements that directly affect the management and resources of –'

'Oh, I paid for all this myself of course.' Kennedy gestured to the furniture, to the workmen, more of whom, incred-ibly, were now coming in carrying a chaise longue. 'Well, my agent Connie did the actual shopping. I'm donating it all to the university when I leave. Be some comfy bums for them PhD fellas of yours and no mistaking, eh?' He clapped Drummond playfully on the arm. 'Now, I'm making whiskey sours. You sure I can't twist your arm?'

'Where's this going, mate?' Two more men in the doorway, each of them holding one end of a cardboard packing crate boldly stencilled with the words 'PANASONIC 47" 3D READY'.

'I think on the wall between the two windows there,' Kennedy said. 'What do you reckon? Yeah, I think so, work away, lads.'

Drummond turned on his heel and left.

Cracking the seal on the Four Roses, Kennedy turned

back to the packed, industrious room and raised his voice above the hubbub of work. 'OK, fellas, we need the cocktail shaker, the lemons and the Gomme syrup. Come on now . . .'

THIRTY-THREE

Term time landed the second week of October, the students arriving as the first leaves started to fall. Flooding the campus, filling up the bars and refectory and libraries. You saw parents dropping off the first years outside the halls of residence, the freshers unloading their scant possessions from the boots of people carriers and estate cars: computers, stereos, boxes of books and crockery.

Watching them from his office window as his first tutorial group took their seats behind him, Kennedy remembered his mother – crying on the windy autumnal street off University Avenue as his da unloaded the last of his stuff from the car. They were heading straight back down the motorway to Holyhead and a night at a Travelodge before catching the first ferry back in the morning. (His mother crying all the way home his da told him later. *'Jaysuss, woman, you'd think he was away to the other side of the bloody world now.'*) Geraldine – just turned sixteen – had been left in charge of Patrick and the house for the night, a decision that would, of course, prove to have appalling consequences: the party, the front windows put in, the living-room door off its hinges, the reek of vomit in every room, Geraldine with two black eyes and wee twelve-year-old Patrick traumatised. The terrible fist fight his da and Geraldine got into, the hateful things that were said, things Gerry could never get rid of later, after he died. And worse – the things unsaid between them. Things she couldn't get out of her head no matter how much she inhaled, imbibed, injected.

And the gift his ma had given him as they left him waving goodbye outside the dirty sandstone tenement – a tea towel embroidered with butterflies and the aphorism *'The first thing we give our children is roots, the last is wings'*. Well, he'd pissed himself at that at the time of course. And what had happened to that tea towel? He felt vaguely certain it had been pressed into service as a makeshift spunk-rag, ending its days stiffly crystallised and stuffed down the side of the single bed in another rented Hillhead flat. How he wished he had it now. Another possession given away, like all the ones he had given to his characters over the years, to lessen the burden of the riches he carried.

In the end, on the last possible evening before he absolutely had to provide the names of the twenty students who were going to be in his three tutorial groups, he came up with an unusual solution to the seemingly irresolvable problem of the Twin Towers of doom. He drank half a bottle of whisky, marched into the study screaming 'RIGHT!' and launched a karate kick at the North Tower. While its pages were still twirling down, with a second scream of 'BASTARDS!' he drove a fist into the midriff of its southern

neighbour and their pages joined in the air – pretty confetti
floating gently. Then, in much the manner of a fireman
searching through the wreckage for survivors, he tiptoed
through the carnage picking out twenty manuscripts at
random. He divided these into two piles of seven and one
of six and bingo – his three tutorial groups. What was all
the fuss about?

He turned back from the window and faced the first
seven hopefuls, gathered in a cluster of chairs around his
desk, most of them looking pretty impressed with the
sumptuousness of his office, which now, thanks to the
blank cheque he'd given Connie to go to Heal's with,
looked like a well-appointed Hampstead sitting room. Part
two of his plan had involved actually reading the twenty
manuscripts he'd selected. Sadly this too had fallen by the
wayside when, on the evening he'd allocated for the task,
a text message had arrived from Aussie Nicky at the
Falcon's, saying simply 'Hey babes wot u up 2?' This had
ended with them paralytic and locked in a sweating knot
on the living-room floor around 4 a.m., wiping out much
of his allotted reading time.

What he had managed to do, however, was scribble down
the names of the twenty students with the titles of their
pieces on a sheet of A4 paper. In brackets after the title
he'd written 'short story' or 'novel' or 'screenplay',
depending on the format they'd attempted. With the aid
of this crib sheet and a gentle skimming of the text while
he got them to read a passage aloud he was confident he
could get by.

'So, ah, Tim, is it?' He indicated a bepimpled undergraduate, a sweating spore of books and wanking, on the

far left. 'Why don't we start with you? Just tell . . . tell us a bit about yourself. Where you come from, why you want to take this course.'

'Uh, why?'

'You know. Why you feel, ah, driven to be a writer.'

'Gosh. Right. Uh, I suppose . . .' The guy started banging on about how he discovered books and Kennedy took the opportunity to scan the room.

Seven undergraduate faces: four guys and three girls. (Yeah, he really should have thought this through.) Besides this Tim now speaking there was another pimpled late-teens bumboy who was staring at Kennedy like he was the burning bush and an older mature-student-type guy, in his mid-thirties Kennedy guessed, sitting with arms folded in 'impress me' manner. Among the women there was another mature student, around his own age with a savage wedge of hair and a sizeable butt encased in enough loose denim to carpet the room, a studious-looking girl of about twenty already frantically taking notes, and finally, at the back . . . hello.

She looked to be in her early twenties, with shoulder-length red hair and very little make-up apart from a bold slash of red across the lips. And these were some lips, high-end stuff, full and glossy, a faint trace of a smile playing across them now as she listened to Ted or Tom or Tim or whoever mumbling on about 'human truth'. She was wearing a grey roll-neck sweater and had a check scarf wrapped around her shoulders, but even these couldn't fully disguise the fact that she had one of those ridiculous body deals – slim with a tiny waist and giant rack. A shortish denim skirt and black tights completed the look. And the legs, by Christ these were useful legs which she was recrossing now. Topping it all off were the glasses, thick-rimmed black NHS jobs that only served to accentuate her huge, clear green eyes. She yawned and stretched and those incredible globes strained against the grey wool of her . . .

He became aware of the silence. Tony or Theo or whatever had finished talking and now everyone was looking at Kennedy expectantly.

'Right. Excellent. Thank you, Ted.'

'Ah, Tim.'

'Right, Tim. Sorry. Ah –' He indicated the mature-student guy next to Tim.

'Brian.'

'OK, Brian. How about you?'

Brian started his ramble and Kennedy nodded along while managing to steal some sideways glances at the beauty. She reached down into her bag for something and out of the corner of his eye he saw the skirt ride up a few inches and did he, was that . . . a glimpse of white flesh at the top of the thigh? At the hemline of the skirt? Was she . . . fuck. *Those were no tights.*

Finally, after much excruciating waffling and banging on and some frankly incredible balls about what literature did and was and how it was made and consumed, it came to her. 'And you are?' Kennedy said.

'Paige Patterson,' she said, looking right at him, confident, the double plosive of the name bursting very enjoyably from that mouth, the little half-smile still playing across her lips, her accent Home Counties, almost nondescript.

'Ah,' Kennedy said, scanning his list, 'Paige Patterson . . .

yes. Your screenplay was . . . *Bone Collectors*? She nodded.
'So, go on.'

'Ah, why am I here?' she said, pushing the glasses a little
further up the bridge of her nose.

Kennedy nodded. 'Why are you here? Why, say, the
screenplay rather than the novel?'

'Well, to be honest, I just want to make a lot of money.'

A couple of laughs. Her classmates turning to look at
her, Brian the Mature Student shaking his head slowly.

'Surely, for the serious writer,' one or other of the
pimplers said, 'making money should be a byproduct of
creating art?'

Paige ignored the guy, still looking at Kennedy.

'No one but a blockhead ever wrote but for money,'
Kennedy said.

By the time they'd all finished their little speeches and
Kennedy had waffled on about what they'd be covering
over the term, the hour was up and they were filing out,
all clutching a copy of the reading list he'd distributed.
(The reading list he'd scribbled on the back of an envelope
in the Falcon's the night before and given to Angela to
type up that morning.) Being at the back she was last out
of the room. 'Hey,' he said, 'I appreciated your candour.
It's . . . refreshing.'

She shrugged, pulling on her coat. 'Life's too short. See
you next week.'

He watched from the window as the seven of them
emerged from the stairwell and started breaking off in
different directions across the quad. The two pimplers
together, heading towards the refectory, the mature
students gathered together, discussing something, and

Paige – disappearing alone into the thronging students emerging now from other classes, her black-stockinged legs teetering on heels. He turned back to his desk and rooted through the pile of folders Angela had delivered earlier that day: one for each of his students. He found it about halfway down: 'PATTERSON, P.'

She was twenty-three and came from Hampshire. State comprehensive. Decent, if unspectacular, grades. She'd done the first two years of her BA from age nineteen to twenty-one. Then she'd dropped out for two years, returning this term to complete the last year, changing her course from American Lit to Creative Writing in the process. Twenty-three. He was forty-four. When he turned fifty she'd still be (just) in her twenties. When he was sixty she'd be, what? Thirty-nine? When . . .

'Oh stop it,' he said out loud to himself, his voice sounding strange and disembodied alone there in his office.

He poured himself a whisky. Dusk falling outside his two great arched windows. England in October – clocks go back soon. Dark at four o'clock. Icy mist, scraping frost off the windscreen. What time would it be in LA? 8 a.m. The sun rising up over the mountains behind Silver Lake, getting ready to make its way across town to drop into the ocean at the end of the day. Warm bars of it falling through the eastern windows of his bedroom, landing slanted across the bed. The vanilla ice-cream scent of the bougainvillea on his balcony . . .

'Oh look – you're here for a while and that's that, OK?'

This habit of talking to himself, definitely worsening in the past few years. Eccentricity hardening into actual madness he supposed. He picked up the first ten pages of *Bone Collectors* by Paige Patterson and stretched out on the sofa.

Half an hour later he finished reading it for the second time and let the pages fall to the floor as he sipped his second whisky, puzzled.

The story was a screwball romantic comedy, a two-hander in the *Romancing the Stone* ballpark, but set in the frontier land of the late 1800s. It featured a woman, Jenna, and a guy, Parker. They were both kind of adventurer palaeontologists, tracking down dinosaur bones in the Wild MidWest, big business in those days, as a clunking expositional speech on page 3 assured us. They were clearly not going to get on very well for a while and then they were going to get on big time. There were some of the usual technical howlers of course – detailed camera angles, that kind of stuff – but the funny thing was . . . at least it had a sense of place. And you got to page 10 and you wouldn't have chosen a bullet in the brain over finding out what happened next.

Some of the other efforts he made himself look at . . . in the holy name of God.

One was a novel set in some kind of future dystopia that was seemingly narrated by an escaped lab rat. Fair enough and novels had been fashioned from stranger premises and go where the muse takes you and all that, but the rat spoke, or interior-monologued rather, only in a kind of cod Shakespearean that (and this was unclear) it seemed to have learned from being forced, *Clockwork Orange* style, to watch videotapes (*videotapes*? in 3000 and whatever?) showing mankind's past achievements.

219

Two of the screenplays featured scenes of male rape in the first ten pages, one of them almost certainly paedophiliac in nature. And he very much hoped, looking again now at the title page, that mature student Brian Healy had been placed on some sort of register somewhere. One screenplay opened with a full page of description that had the camera beginning on a 'cloud-filled sky', moving on to a 'windswept' landscape, then on to a 'barren' highway, then on to . . . Christ knows. Christina Kemp clearly hadn't heard Hitchcock's aphorism: that you can maybe do this sort of thing in European cinema but that in commercial cinema, that is to say American cinema, if you open on a shot of cloud then the next shot had better be a plane, and if the plane hadn't at least fucking exploded by the third shot then your test-screening cards in Pasadena were really going to stink.

Mainly, though, they all failed in the most common way – they failed *tonally*. They attempted what all works of fiction attempted to do: to create a new world, an anterior to this one. And they came up short. If you don't buy the tone of the thing, you're dead. And reading some of the dialogue . . . he wondered if some of the authors had ever had a conversation with another human being in their lives. He thought of Wordsworth's definition of poetry – *emotion recollected in tranquillity*. This lot . . . it was tedium recollected in banality. A bright 'PING' from his computer, alerting him to an incoming email. Wearily he pushed himself up and walked to the desk. It was from Braden. The subject in the box: URGENT: FW FROM SCOTT SPENGLER'S OFFICE. He clicked on it.

Hi Professor

Hope you're settling in OK. As you know the production arrives in England next week. As anticipated it looks like there will be some rewriting as a result of things that have come up on location. Can you please be available for a script conference with me, Kevin and Julie at Pinewood, next Friday (Oct. 18th)? We're on the 007 stage. Passes will be at the gate for you. 2 p.m.

Best,
Scott

The 18th. Why did that ring a bell? Fuck.

Ireland. Patrick and Ma. He'd have to cancel. He could already hear the gentle resignation in Ma's voice. The incredulity in Patrick's. Oh well.

He checked his watch. Just gone six. Six o'clock on a Friday night. What did these fuckers do for R&R around here at six on a Friday?

Jacket over his shoulder he wandered down the hallway, peeking into empty office after empty office. There was a light on in Dennis Drummond's and he carefully tiptoed past that. Finally, down at the bottom, he heard the clacking of a keyboard and peered into the open door of Melissa Gently, Romantic Poetry. They'd been introduced at his meet-and-greet thing. 'Hey, Melissa.'

'JESUS!' She almost hit the ceiling. 'Oh, Kennedy, oh God. Sorry – you scared me!'

'Christ, sorry about that. What's up?'

'Oh, this bloody paper I'm writing.' Her full-moon spectacles glaring straight at him.

'What's it on?'

'Coleridge's use of the impersonal pronoun.'

'Wow. That's . . . hey, do you fancy a drink in the staff club? My treat.'

'Oh, how kind. That would be . . . but, ah, I'd better . . .' She pointed to the glowing computer screen with a trembling finger. 'You know.'

'Sure. Well, see you . . .'

'Monday?'

'Yeah. Monday. Night.'

Out into the car park, empty save for his rented Aston, Melissa's alfalfa-coloured 2CV and Drummond's Prius. Turning into the wind he looked across campus to where light and, faintly, noise were coming from the Student Union. An amusing pint with the undergraduates? And what did they call these boozers now old Mandela and Biko were no longer centre stage? The Julian Assange bar? Surely not, given all the rapey stuff. No, he thought. Best not. Wandering in there alone among the freshers, hanging with the eighteen- and nineteen-year-olds on a Friday night, reeking of Eau de Sex Offender. Turning on the ignition he looked at the car clock, 6.24. Jesus Christ. In LA on a Friday night he'd have been in Soho House about now. Out on the smoking terrace with the guys and girls, bitching about the prospects for the weekend's grosses, looking north at dusk falling on the Hollywood Hills, a Martini that could blind a fucking dwarf clamped in his great wanking paddle. (The Hands of Kennedy Marr: they'd gotten him into so much trouble, so many situations. The pudding fingers that had made so many disgraceful calls, punched out all those unreasonable texts and emails, curled their way around wine glass and brandy balloon. Slid gracefully up the spines of women in the banquettes of fine restaurants or jammed themselves hurriedly between thighs and into blouses in the back of taxis. Dread instruments, awful appendages!)

An idea: go and see Robin. Take her out to dinner. Father and daughter heading out to eat on a Friday evening – what could be more normal? Regular people probably did stuff like that all the time, didn't they? In fact, if they hurried they could probably bomb it down the M40 to Le Manoir by eight. Henri would fit him in.

THIRTY-FOUR

'Oh, no can do, Pop. People to go, places to see. Where is . . .' He was standing in the doorway to Robin's bedroom. She was on the floor, sifting through the mess, reaching under the bed.

'What places, what people? You're sixteen – what can you possibly have going on that's more appealing than your *own father* taking you to a *Michelin-starred* restaurant for the evening?'

'Ha!' She pulled a Doc Marten boot out from under the bed and started lacing it up, sitting on the floor. 'It's so funny that you always used to think that was a good time.'

'What did I think was a good time? And, by the way, the state of this bloody bedroom.'

'Oh, don't you start. Taking me to fancy restaurants when I was little. I'd rather have had a McDonald's and gone to the park.'

'The park? Jesus Christ, Robin, who goes to the park? Pensioners and paedophiles go to parks.'

She laughed, standing up and pulling on her pea coat now. 'And kids, Dad, that's why the paedos go, no? We can go out next week. It's Friday night. Ollie's picking me up.'

'Ollie? Who the fuck is Ollie?'

'A mate.'

'Don't say "mate". Jesus, what is this, a building site?'

'Christ. Bye, Dad.' She pecked him on the cheek, smelling of lemons and youth, and hurried past him and down the stairs. Kennedy followed.

'And where are you going?'

She laughed. 'A party.'

'And will there, will there be . . .' Christ, what did you say? He was no good at this stuff. What did normal people give a shit about? 'Drinking and drugs and stuff at this party?'

'God, I hope so,' Robin said, giving her lipstick a last check in the hall mirror. Good answer.

'Very funny.'

'Bye, Dad,' she said again, then, shouting in the direction of the living room, 'BYE, MUM!' A muffled reply from Millie.

'OK,' Kennedy said. 'So, next weekend. Sunday. How about we go out for Sunday lunch?'

'Sure,' Robin said. 'It's a date.' She pecked him on the cheek again and was out the door into the night.

He watched her run crunching down the drive, towards a blue Vauxhall Polo, music thumping from within it, the passenger door open and the interior light on, revealing the cheerful, grinning rapist at the wheel. (*If you have a son you only have one cock to worry about.*) The kid, this fucking

Ollie, waved to Kennedy, who stared straight back, hands in his pockets.

For a second he thought about pelting after her, rugby-tackling her onto the stinging gravel and wrestling her back inside.

A memory came, unbidden, from what, over a decade ago? Yes, pre-LA, post-break-up, Robin would have been maybe five. He'd been round visiting. When he'd gone to leave she'd wrapped herself around his leg. *'Stay. Daddy, stay.'* He'd turned it into a game, untangling her and trying to get away while she ran after him, giggling, wrapping herself around his leg again and again. But, finally, he really did have to go and she realised it was no game. He was leaving. (A reservation. Tanya? Tara?) 'When are you coming back?' Robin asked, lip trembling. 'The day after this day?' The day after this day – Robin's kiddie phrase for tomorrow. 'No, Robs.' He'd looked back as he reached the car – her face pressed against the window, tiny palm spread on the glass, tears streaming down her face as Millie loomed in the background to comfort her. *I have broken love*, Kennedy thought, a few minutes later, in the lay-by where he was doing his own weeping.

What were you meant to do with these thoughts? Where did you put them? Why did the years not dim their power to cripple and unman you? Their half-life was incredibly strong: more than ten years on and the image of that flattened palm, that pale tiny starfish, was still capable of moving him to ring a dealer. Of making him uncap the whisky at six o'clock on the nose.

Literature helped. It was all there on the page, the work of men who had broken love. The Dead White Males had it all down cold: Nabokov's Pnin sobbing at the kitchen table – '*I haf nofing. Nofing.*' Bellow's Herzog furiously annotating his loneliness in train, plane and cab, trying to paper over the cuts with text. Updike's Harry Angstrom sadly watching the litter blow along the Brewer highway, blowing away like his youth and love.

Sighing, coexisting with it, he walked into the living room. Millie was curled up in an armchair near the back, frowning into a fat manuscript on her lap with a glass of wine at her side. She looked impossibly grown up. How did they do it, these adults? The splash of Pinot sipped for half an hour, the good book and early bed. A bit of Radio 4. How did they learn it? Kennedy always thought that growing up would be like DIY, you'd just come to it by osmosis as you got older. But here he was, at the end of the second act, scratching his befuddled head over the wonky shelf as he upended the Scotch bottle into his mouth.

'I mean,' Kennedy said, 'what is all this? All this "It's Friday night, Dad" shit? When did she get so fucking busy? "Ollie" no less. Who is this sex case? I mean – what do we *know* about him?'

Millie turned her page, not looking up. 'What can I tell you, Kennedy? She's nearly seventeen. You missed it. You missed it all.'

Yes, well. Perhaps he had prioritised other things.

He'd prioritised, for instance, sitting hunched over the glowing laptop at the top of the house, a strong drink in his hand and important thoughts in his head, over the toddler that could have been nestled warm against his side two floors below, following the bedtime story in wonderment. (*'Players and painted stage took all my love, and not those things that they were emblems of.*') He'd prioritised waking hung-over in five-star hotel suites with some girl he barely knew over having that downy five-year-old climbing into his bed for a cuddle and a lie-in. He'd prioritised guzzling champagne and cocktails with relative strangers in fashionable restaurants and private members' clubs over putting his head round the door and checking on Robin's splayed, sleeping eight-year-old form, the chest gently rising and falling in the soft glow of her night light. He'd prioritised bending a variety of flexible twenty-somethings into astonishingly intricate positions in apartments, in cars, in the toilets of nightclubs over . . . over whatever. Over flying that kite. Having that picnic. Making those pancakes. Watching that DVD together on the sofa on a rainy afternoon. Yes, priorities.

On occasion it was possible for the stupidity of the choices Kennedy had made to hit him with the blood-freezing force of a baseball bat.

'I'm having a drink, do you want a drink?' Kennedy crossed the room, reaching for the malt.

'I've got one. And I'm going out in a bit.' A silence, filled with the crack and rasp of Kennedy breaking the seal. Then, still not looking up, Millie said, 'Kennedy?'

'Mmmm?'

'What are you doing?'

'Huh?' Pouring. Pouring big. 'Making myself a drink.'

'I mean – why are you here? At seven on a Friday night? Haven't *you* got places to go? People to see?'

'I, yeah. Of course. I just fancied . . . I don't know. Whatever.' He tossed the drink back, letting it burn, looking out the French windows across the garden, onto the fields, his eyes tearing with the fumes. Yes, with the fumes. Millie watched him for a moment, stood there at her windows. She'd always thought of Kennedy as youthful compared to most of the men she knew his age. A bit of a belly starting, yes, but no glasses. A thick head of dark hair, no signs of baldness, no receding. Not even a hint of grey. But right now, caught there by the lamplight, looking out sadly at the damp, black night, he suddenly looked very old indeed. 'Poor Kennedy,' she said. He shrugged. Reached for the bottle again. On pure instinct, force of habit wrought from spending twelve years with him, Millie felt herself going to say, 'Darling, do you *really* need another drink?' But she didn't. She just said, 'Poor, poor Kennedy.'

Quite a place to be, that. When there's no one to tell you not to have another drink.

THIRTY-FIVE

The circus hit town. The papers were full of it. 'STAR PARTIES TILL 5AM!' screamed the *Mirror*, with a photograph of Michael Curzon stumbling out of some nightclub with a cigarette dangling from his mouth and a blonde on each arm. (*Yeah, right*, Kennedy thought.) The *Sun* ran with a 'THE TEAL THING!' headline above a feature outlining the outrageous demands the actress had been making of the production and the Mandarin Oriental hotel in Knightsbridge: including the specific types of containers she demanded her Diet Coke and Evian water be served in, the 'lighting concepts' that were acceptable for rooms she was expected to inhabit for more than two minutes, and all the usual stuff about members of staff, indeed any human below the level of director, producer or co-star, not being allowed to make direct eye contact with her. Meanwhile the *Telegraph* had a story about outraged neighbours in the sleepy Buckinghamshire village where Scott Spengler had sequestered himself for the two or so months the movie was at Pinewood. Apparently the mansion he'd rented was unacceptable to basic LA standards and, prior to the great man's arrival, workmen had been tearing up lawns and putting in tennis courts and jacuzzis and the like. (It was a curious facet of cultural difference, Kennedy thought. Very rich British people, if they were staying somewhere in the short-to-medium term, would pretty much manage to rub along with whatever was there. The super-rich American would bring all their wealth to bear on having everything exactly as they were used to having it. Why was this? Well, Kennedy supposed, the maniacs built a fucking *country* out of nothing, didn't they? Fashioned it from scratch out of scrub weed and blood. They weren't going to leave an en suite bathroom to chance, were they?)

Kennedy arrived at Pinewood feeling . . . grand. Just grand. Eventually, grudgingly, the security guard was convinced by both his passport and his driving licence that he was who he said he was. He issued them passes and directed Keith's Mercedes towards the 007 stage.

Predictably enough the drive down the M40 had been enlivened by the bottle of Macallan Kennedy brought, *Exile on Main Street* at top volume, and the several high-quality, tightly packed joints Keith had pre-rolled and, with pleasing regularity, passed back to Kennedy. Knowing there was no way he was getting through this ordeal sober, he'd rung and booked Keith for the round trip. ('Sure thing guv. Call it a ton and a half, yeah?') The Aston nestled safely in the drive at home.

His ma had, of course, been absolutely fine about the delay of his visit. 'Really, son? God now, you go to your meeting. Sure and that's more important. Ach – I'm fine.

You know our Patrick, one of nature's worriers. You work away, son, and I'll see you soon. Work away. Sure and you've got to take the work when they're giving it to you Kennedy . . .'

Kennedy's mam's understanding of what he did was . . . limited. She'd been to a couple of awards dinners and a movie premiere with him. Visited him on the set once or twice. She had a fat photo album full of clippings: reviews, interviews, news stories. (Kennedy being one of the few living writers who made it onto the news pages. Not usually in a good way.) She'd seen him on TV frequently. Yet, even after over a decade of all this, she still seemed to think he lived in the very dangerous world of not having a 'proper' job. That his work was touch-and-go and could end at any moment. He often sensed that Ma would have been happier, more relaxed at any rate, if Kennedy had been, say, the owner of a prosperous local garage. Or something senior at the bank. They had only directly discussed money on one occasion. Maybe five years ago, was it? On a phone call home from LA? He'd been complaining about a trip he'd had to make to New York, to meet with the director of a movie he was doing a polish on. 'Ach, is it worth it now, son?' his ma had said.

'How do you mean, Ma?'

'Is it worth going all that way? I mean with the money and everything, the flights and hotels.'

'The studio pays for all that, Ma.'

'But are you earning enough out of it to make it worth your while, son?'

'How much do you think I get paid, Ma?'

'Sure and I've no idea son.'

He told her – a dollar number in the mid six figures.

A long pause, just sub-Atlantic crackle down the line, and then his ma saying, 'In the name of the Lord . . .'

But still he sensed that, to his mother, for all her pride, it was just snake oil. Smoke and mirrors. Kidology, as his father would have said. She feared that the rug might be pulled from under his feet at any minute. That someone might just walk in and announce that the jig was finally up. (In this, his ma's fears were similar to those of many writers.)

Patrick's reaction to the delayed visit had been, typically, more robust. 'Are you fucking joking me?'

Kennedy had protested – the enormity of the budget. Scott Spengler. Julie Teal. How he wanted to make sure he had a few clear days to spend with him and Ma, not some rushed afternoon. Patrick had to understand – the pressures of film-making, of shooting a movie . . .

'*The pressures of film-making?*' Patrick had repeated slowly, quietly.

'I'm sorry, Patrick.'

'No, you're grand now. My best to you, brother. I hope you hold up under the "pressures of film-making".'

'Patrick, I really am sorry. I'll be out next weekend. Shit, no I can't. I've got lunch with Robin that Sunday.'

'Jesus, Kennedy – you'll have been back over a *month* by then.'

'I know, I know, I know. Tell you what, I'll have lunch with Robin and get a flight out late afternoon, early evening. Take the Monday off and stay the night.'

A sigh. 'OK, Kennedy. Let's just say we'll see you when we see you. You know where we are.'

Click. The rare sound of Patrick putting the phone down

on him without saying goodbye. Fuck. He'd get him something nice. A watch. A new suit or something. Rich in cash,
poor in spirit.

If I do not go, she will not die.

'Christ, would ya look at this?' Keith was saying, as he
pulled into the parking space they'd been allocated next to
the hangar. Inside the doorway – a doorway that would
have about allowed a 747 to pass through – powerful lights
cut through layers of dry ice that floated over a gigantic
tank of water several hundred feet square. 'All this cos of
some stuff you wrote, guv?'

'Aye, Keith,' Kennedy said, getting out the car. 'Sure and
it's a headfuck right enough.'

You typed a scene in your office in LA.

EXT. OCEAN, NIGHT

Shivering, Gillian and Will cling onto a piece of
driftwood while searchlights rake the misty water.

A year or so later dozens of carpenters and electricians are
scratching their heads over blueprints while someone pumps
500,000 gallons of water into a fucking tank in the south-east
of England.

They were walking towards the hangar door when
another security guard cut them off, arms extended, a
walkie-talkie in one hand. 'Excuse me,' American this one,
'this is a closed set.' They produced their passes and the
guy got on his radio. 'Yeah, Kennedy Marr. The writer . . .
OK? Sure. Apologies, gentlemen, come right this way,' and
into the enormity of the 007 hangar itself where they just
had another two sets of security to pass through before

Kennedy was pointing Keith in the direction of the craft services table ('Fucking starving, guv') and then Scott Spengler was walking towards him, arms spread. Spengler. Madman. Creator and Master of this temporary universe. They embraced in the middle of the 59,000-square-foot stage, in front of the 240-foot-wide green screen that backed the tank, onto which the image of a burning tanker would later be added in post. Kennedy had originally set the scene in the morning in a motel room in Kansas. Now, for international financing reasons, it was happening in the Baltic Sea at night. (Had other artists ever had to deal with this kind of thing? The guy looking up in the Sistine Chapel and saying, 'Yeah, looking pretty good. But some new money just came in. Can you repaint the background to look like Australia?') Over near the tank Kennedy could see Kevin doing the director thing – gesturing, pointing. Fucking handpump.

'How we doing then?' Kennedy asked.

'You don't wanna know. I'm trying to figure out how we're a week behind on the first day. Julie's in her trailer. Just down there. Go on in there and work that old Irish charm now.'

Another security guard right outside Teal's trailer – this fucker making all the others look like they'd just escaped from particularly stringent Gulags – frowned and scowled and shone his flashlight over Kennedy's pass for a good while before popping his head inside the door and conducting a muttered conversation with someone within and then, miraculously, he was being ushered in.

'Trailer' obviously wouldn't cover it. 'Trailer' was like using B&B to describe the Savoy. Through some wizardry of extensions and fold-outs the place was easily fifty feet long, swelling to twenty wide down at the back, where Teal was stretched out on a sofa, on the phone, surrounded by people. A muscular flunky was reading *Variety*, a girl tapped at a laptop in the corner, a make-up artist was rooting through a flight case of brushes and bottles and tubs. Music played softly as Kennedy entered the inner sanctum. He went to say hello and she held up a finger to him as she continued her conversation, as though he were room service waiting for a tip.

This, like everything else, is getting closer to being over, Kennedy thought.

'No way,' Teal said. 'I can get there by the fifth. Tell him . . .' Everyone else ignored him while she talked on. Why not? – he was just the writer. He might as well have come to fix the air conditioning.

Finally, with a 'Ciao', she hung up, stood up and extended a hand, 'Sorry about that. Hi there. Nice to see you again. Do you want something? Some food? Something to drink?'

She seemed . . . different from the last time they met, in the commissary in Burbank, back at the beginning of September. More animated. Something in the eyes. A certain twitch to the mouth. She blew her nose. 'Sorry. I have a cold.'

'I'll take a wee malt whisky if you have it.'

Teal looked at him blankly. She turned to her assistant and gave her the same look. 'Uh, we don't have any liquor in here.' The word 'liquor' made to sound like 'kiddie porn'. 'I'll go and see what catering have.'

'Thanks, Mel,' Teal said, sitting down, picking up a script.

'Here, have a seat, Kennedy. Juan, get your ass outta here, I'm meeting with my writer.'

The bodybuilder grudgingly got up and shuffled off down the hallway. Kennedy sat down, doing his best not to bristle at her use of the possessive. Yes, 'my writer'. We were well into production now. Full movie-star mode, the placid chumminess of pre-production long gone.

'So, I understand you have some notes, Julie?' Taking out that notebook, uncapping that pen.

'Yeah, it's . . . some things have come up as we've gotten into the process. Just some things I think can play a little smarter . . .'

Play a little smarter. Kennedy had written six novels (one of them an international best-seller) and over a dozen screenplays (two of them huge box-office hits) yet he found he had to listen to this line surprisingly frequently. Usually from actors, directors and producers who had never written anything longer than an email or a Tweet in their lives. Why not just come out and say 'what you've written here is fucking dumb'? he wondered.

She turned to a page. Kennedy noticed a *lot* of notes scribbled in the margin in childish hand. 'Ah, here, for instance, in this scene we're shooting today. When Gillian says, "You don't need a lover, or a partner, or a wife. You just need a decent assistant. You just need the fucking trains to run on time, Will."'

'Yeah?'

'I don't think my character would say that.'

Kennedy looked at the girl. She really was so good looking it was an insult to the rest of humanity. Her features – lips, teeth, eyes – were all just ever so slightly exaggerated, like the perfect vegetables you found in American supermarkets. It was hard to say exactly what did it. The overheated trailer, the fact that his ma lay dying in a Dublin hospital while he was sitting here being forced to listen to this, or maybe he was simply getting too old and too rich to be listening to shit like this now. Maybe just the fact that he was dying for a drink and a fag and there was no whisky in this smoke-free environment. Whatever the reason, something inside of him snapped and, instead of saying, 'Mmmm, interesting, do tell me more about how you see the character,' he said, 'May I?' She held the script out and Kennedy took it. He looked at the offending dialogue.

GILLIAN

You don't need a lover, or a partner, or a wife. You just need a decent assistant. You just need the fucking trains to run on time, Will.

'Yeah, the thing is,' Kennedy said, 'she does say it.'
'Uh, how do you mean?' Teal asked.
'Oh, she says it all right.' He nodded at the page.
'What do you mean?'
'I mean, she says it *right here*. You see here?' He pointed to the script. 'Here where the name "GILLIAN" appears centred and then there is a block of indented text beneath her name? That indicates dialogue. That means that's what she says at that moment in the script. That means you *say those fucking words.*'
'Excuse me?' Teal looking at him with real interest now.
'I mean, can this really be happening? You're talking to me about characterisation and motivation? I can't believe

238

you can lift a fucking spoon. If I had an ounce of self-respect left in me I'd kill you then myself.'

A full two seconds while she took this in. How long had it been since anyone had spoken to her this way? Kennedy found he had time to wonder before Teal exploded.

'*I AM TALKING ABOUT MY INTERPRETATION OF THE CHARACTER!*'

The make-up girl jumped. The bodybuilder reappeared menacingly in the doorway. The returning assistant stood frozen behind him, holding a bottle of J&B.

'Your *interpretation*? Listen, you feckin eejit – while you were waiting tables in the Valley, sucking exec producers' dicks and waiting for that call back on *Anal Monsters Volume Five*, I was doing a lot on interpretation. While you were still trying to write your feckin name in shite from your diaper on the bathroom floor I was walking out of university with a double first in Literature and Language. Twenty-five years of my life went into the words on that page. That's about as long as you've been alive. I've got fucking *ties* older than you. So, you know what, why not just shut your hole and play the character as written?'

She looked at him. Her mouth a tiny circle. A polo mint. When the words finally came they were whispered, steely and careful.

'You. Are. So. Off. This. Picture.'

'Grand. See you around.' Kennedy got up. 'You, Juan, bumboy, get out the fucking way. Go make yourself a protein shake or some fucking thing.' He pushed past the idiot and snatched the bottle of J&B out of the assistant's hands. 'This isn't malt by the way,' he said as he shouldered the door open, hearing Teal bursting into tears behind him.

Kennedy passed Spengler and Kevin on his way back to the car, screwing the cap off the bottle.

'Hey, how'd it go?' Spengler asked.

'Grand. She's thinking it over.'

THIRTY-SIX

'Hi, sorry I'm a bit –'

'No, no, that's fine. Come in. Come in.'

Kennedy ushered her into his office and directed her to the sitting area up at the end. Outside, the orange lamps that lined the path across the quad were flickering on. A tutorial right at the end of the working day had, of course, been part of his plan. Other details had not been neglected either.

There was the huge framed movie poster for the hit thriller he'd scripted. It wasn't on the wall obviously – how vulgar – but had been tucked down the side of the sofa opposite the one he was directing Paige to sit on, the bottom just visible with the magic, boxed words 'SCREENPLAY BY KENNEDY MARR'. Further behind this, on the bookshelves, just sitting at eye level, he'd carefully (yet casually, haphazardly) strewn a stack of foreign translations of his books – Italian, French, German, Norwegian, fucking *Turkish* – the different colours and scripts of their spines effectively spelling out P.L.A.Y.E.R. High up on the bookcase, pushed back from the edge, dusty and barely – yet very – visible, was his BAFTA for the *Unthinkable* screenplay. He'd left a cardboard box of unpacked stuff just behind the sofa Paige was sitting on. If her eye drifted in that direction – as it surely would when she had to talk to him as he stood at the bar – she'd see a bunch of framed photographs: location shots, studio shots. Kennedy with Ryan Gosling and Nicole Kidman. With Jack Nicholson even. ('Oh, these? Tacky, aren't they?')

She slipped her coat off and her smell hit him. Clean soap-and-water, not too perfumed. She dipped her head as she sat down, pulling a folder from her bag, and, through the gunsight of the twin dangling bangs of red hair, he got a pleasing shot of her cleavage: brown, freckled, the breasts firm, contained in a tightly cupping navy bra, as yet un-troubled by gravity.

'Drink?' he said, as casually as possible, trying to make it sound completely normal and reasonable, the kind of thing any civilised lecturer would offer a student at five o'clock before they discussed their work. He was trying very hard not to make it sound like 'Rohypnol?' Or 'Chloroform?' Or just 'Cock?'

'Sorry?' She looked up to face him.

'I was going to make myself a drink. Would you like one?'

'One what?'

'How about a Negroni?' He gestured towards the shelf of liquor that would have shamed some of London's better cocktail bars.

'Uh, what's in that?'

'Gin, vermouth and Campari.'

She looked at him for a moment. 'Uh, OK then.'

Kennedy got busy with the ice and the oranges, his back to her.

'So what were you up to?' Kennedy asked.

'Up to?'

'I saw you took two years out of your degree after the end of second year.' Pouring gin over ice and a twist of orange peel.

'Oh. I went to London. Got a job. Wrote.'

'Where were you working?' A splash of vermouth now.

'Here and there. Waitressing. That kind of thing.'

'And why did you come back?'

'I'd had enough.'

'Enough of what?' Finishing off with a long slug of Campari.

'Experience.'

'Ah.' He brought the drinks over and handed hers to her. 'Cheers.' He raised his glass and feasted on the cocktail as he sat down opposite, the last of the daylight from the windows behind him falling on her.

'Mmmm,' she said, sipping.

'So, I read the opening ten pages of your screenplay,' Kennedy said. She looked at him. No 'Oh really?' Or 'What did you think?' Or 'Oh God.' She just held his gaze, waiting for him to say whatever he was going to say. Confident. Unnerving. 'It's . . . a good idea. The expression needs some work though.'

'That's why I'm here. So – where am I going wrong?'

A faint burr, a crackle, as she crossed her long legs. Bronze, almost gold, tights today, the skirt cut to the mid-thigh. She pointed her toes upwards, letting the heel slip off the foot that was suspended in mid-air, settling further back into the folds of her leopard-print coat, spread out beneath and around her. Kennedy took a long pull on his drink, the ice creaking and cracking. 'Where do you think you're going wrong?'

'Well,' she said, 'in terms of overall structure . . .'

When he was her age, two decades ago, sitting in rooms like these, opposite men you thought held the key to all mythologies. Except . . . she didn't act like that at all. The faint smile playing around her lips, as though she sensed how inherently ridiculous he was. How knotted by lust and hopelessness. It was true – it didn't help at all. Success, approbation, the kind of minor celebrity a writer like Kennedy was afforded. None of it helped. It didn't make anything easier. Not even the first five minutes when you walked into a party and didn't know anyone there. 'Well,' Paige said, 'around the climax of act two, is there enough energy to launch us into the third act? I think . . .'

The fallout from his script conference with Teal had been immediate, dramatic and, frankly, bizarre. Keith had barely steered the car out of the Pinewood gates when his phone started ringing. He let it go to voicemail all the way up the M40, drinking steadily, then listened through.

Spengler first, stunned, disbelieving: 'Oh Christ. What the fuck have you done here? What did you *say*?'

Then Kevin, simply very angry: 'You fucking asshole. Thanks to you I now have a star who won't come out of her trailer while I have a crew and the biggest set in Europe sitting here doing nothing except costing *about a million bucks a day*.'

Then Teal. Just abuse: 'Fuck you . . . dare speak to me like that . . . never work in this town again . . .'

Then Braden: 'Well, you've really done it this time. I get woken up at 6 a.m. over here with Scott Spengler going fucking *bananas* . . .'

Then, later, Spengler again: 'Listen, Kennedy, can you call Julie? Just . . . give her a call.'

Then Kevin again: 'Well, I don't know quite what's happened here, but, whatever you've done, it seems to have done some good. I just wanted to say "sorry" about earlier. Heat of the moment and all that. See you soon, yeah?'

Eh? Then, shortly after that, a quiet, placid-sounding Teal. 'Hi, Kennedy? It's Julie. Can you please call me back? I wanted to . . . if you could just call me. I'm on . . .'

He dialled the number from the kitchen in Deeping, where he was eating cold stew the housekeeper had left out and drinking Barolo.

'Kennedy, hi.'

'Hi, Julie?'

'I wanted to say sorry for earlier. I . . . no one's spoken to me like that in a while. I just . . . I wanted to thank you.'

'Thank me?'

'It's, when you get to where I am, so many directors, writers, they just do whatever you want them to. Because you can open the picture. It's so rare in this business to meet someone who actually cares as much as you do about what they do.' This was news to Kennedy. He tried to imagine caring about something. Found it couldn't be done. 'I hope we can continue working together on this.'

'Sure, Julie. And I'm sorry too. Heat of the moment and all that.'

'Hey, we're passionate about what we do, right?'

'Sure.'

'Come by the set again soon, OK?'

'Will do. Goodnight now.'

Then Braden, cheerful this time: 'You Irish bastard, I don't know what you did but you're golden . . .'

Then finally Spengler again: 'Listen, I thought I knew everything when it comes to handling prima donna movie stars, but I clearly need to learn a few tricks from you, pal. Impressive. Right – we're having dinner next weekend. Friday or Saturday. Just you and me. I'll have the office arrange it.'

Fucking movie business: the world's biggest shithouse filled with its craziest rats.

He tuned back into Paige's voice, soft here in his office as rain brushed at the windows, then Kennedy cutting in – *'Look, Paige, how about we just go to a hotel and fuck each other's brains out?'*

Her face: going from bewilderment, to disbelief, to rage, as she brought the flat of her hand towards his cheek, tossing the drink in his face. (And no stranger to the hurled cocktail, Kennedy Marr. Familiar indeed he was with the blood-shocking splash of cold champagne in the face. He knew what it was like to watch a vanishing back storm out the door while you licked at tears of Chenin Blanc or Chablis.)

No, Kennedy thought, best not say anything like that.

'I just can't seem to get much past page 70,' Paige said.

'Third-act problems?' Kennedy said. *Oh, baby*, he wanted to say. *I'm having third-act problems of my own. You wouldn't believe how difficult the third act gets.* 'The problems of the final act are the problems of the first,' he said. 'The principles of drama are very simple – the action proceeds from an event that we witness at the beginning and builds through a series of conflicts to a satisfying conclusion. The rigorous application of these principles is, however, very difficult.'

She smiled at him. His glass was empty. Hers virtually untouched, resting on her thigh. 'David Mamet.' she said.

'That's right,' he nodded, the wind prowling at the glass now too, driving rain across the panes. 'Ten points for you.' Very quiet in here until Kennedy said, 'Would you like to have dinner with me tonight?'

She leaned forward and set the still-brimming glass down on the coffee table.

'I can't tonight.'

'Whyever not?'

She cocked her head to one side, that faint smile playing over her lips, and regarded him in the way you saw people looking at paintings in museums, taking in angles and details, regarding him whole, not just his eyes. She folded her arms, the effect being to push her breasts slightly together, the crease between them deepening, accentuating. 'Ask me again sometime.'

Later, when she'd gone, he sat in the armchair drinking her drink and thinking – *The problems of the third act are the problems of the first.*

What had gone so tits for him in the first act that he was still behaving like this now? What was he thinking asking girls twenty years younger than him out on dates? Had he no sense how Humbert he looked? Here he was at the beginning of the third act, the final one, and any number of red herrings and McGuffins were still striding about, plotless, themeless. Where there should have been clarity, a sense of strands drawing together, intertwining, heading for a resolution, there was just . . . chaos. He'd been behaving exactly this way, unaltered, for over twenty-five years now. What terrible event or chromosomal blip had done this? His friends, nearly all of them, had made a choice and run with it. Into the ennui and boredom of middle age admittedly but at least there was a story there. Some kind of conventional narrative structure. Meanwhile, here was Kennedy – disjointed. Episodic. A sketch show. A Japanese TV commercial. 'Random,' as Robin said.

He held her glass up to the light of the anglepoise on the desk behind him: her pink lipstick, frosted around the rim. He placed his mouth over the imprint left by hers and tasted waxy perfume as he drained the glass. It reminded him of Vicky, who'd gone in for make-up far more than Millie ever had.

Vicky – she'd really loved him. He remembered when she'd first said it, lying in bed in the Hills, some song on the radio and him sort of half singing along to it as he lay there reading, becoming aware that she was on her side, staring at him. 'What?' he'd said turning. 'I love you,' she'd said. And he'd done her friend at their wedding. What in the name of fuck? Why? Hormones, he supposed. She'd been bright and young and funny and beautiful and all the rest of that and it . . . it hadn't quite been enough, had it? *What had?* What did you do when everything wasn't quite enough? The whole Judy Garland thing: wanting to take the world and snort it and how did you know it was enough until it was too much?

You know what, Kennedy thought, she could have her new bathroom, and her trip to the islands, and the Warhol. Christ, she'd earned them.

THIRTY-SEVEN

'Oh, it's a bunch of bullshit,' Spengler said, referring to his much-publicised troubles with the villagers of Iver Heath, Buckinghamshire, a finger raised casually to summon the wine waiter. They were in Dabbous, off Goodge Street, where normal humans had a six-month wait for a table. Spengler (or rather, an underling within the Spengler organisation) had rung that morning and here they were, at a good corner table on a Saturday night. Why Dabbous? It was hot. You were Scott fucking Spengler. That was what you did. It wouldn't have mattered if they only served baked roadkill in a reduction of dung, if it was impossible to get a table that's where they would have been. 'We're miles from anyone. So we put a tennis court in. Fuck them. Anyway, I'll donate something to the village when I leave. A hall or something.' He still had that finger in the air. 'This place,' he sighed. 'You should swing by the house sometime for a drink or dinner. It's real close to the studio. I'll message you the address.' Finally the sommelier appeared. Spengler did not speak to him, simply adjusted the angle of his index finger downwards from 'summoning' position to pointing at Kennedy's empty glass. The guy hurriedly plucked the Dom Perignon from the silver bucket, the ice making a pleasant shucking noise as it released the bottle. The preposterously cheerful fizz of the pour and then the guy retreating again. Spengler – drinking only tap water. Kennedy was being careful too: didn't want to be too hung-over for his lunch with Robin tomorrow. Then, Christ, the flight to Dublin.

'So,' Kennedy said, 'how was Serbia?' The production had just spent a week over there, mostly shooting second unit stuff, part of their funding obligation.

'Jesus Christ, those people are fucking insane. Hiring local crew out there . . . The women though, Kennedy, the fucking women. I'm talking about a pair of nineteen-year-old twin supermodels performing a tonsillectomy on themselves with your johnson, all night long, for the price of a haircut. You know in the orgy scene?'

'Yeah.'

'Well, we hired in a bunch of –'

'Hang on, no. Orgy scene? There isn't an orgy scene.'

'The whaddya call it . . .'

'There's a short scene where a guy and two girls –'

'Yeah, that was it. Kevin felt we could ramp that up, to take advantage of the location. Visually. We had this ballroom – Julie and Michael weren't around, oh, a lot of their improv stuff is great by the way – so we –'

'*Improv* stuff?'

'Got a few dozen extras in and –'

Jesus Christ.

Kennedy listened as Spengler talked on about how art had bled into life and how the orgy scene had wound up being *very* real indeed in some places. Why was there an orgy scene in the fucking picture? He made a mental note to put a call into the WGA, get a sounding about taking his name off this thing.

In a way Kennedy wished his students were here. This would have been a truly educational experience. You crafted a political thriller, alone at the desk, every comma a point of art, every stage direction carefully chosen, nuance and subtext woven through the piece. Eighteen months later you sat there drinking champagne and eating an eight quid boiled egg ('Hen's egg' it said blood-boilingly on the menu. 'Are the cock's eggs off tonight?' Kennedy had asked the waiter) while a madman told you about how a couple of actors who'd barely finished high school were making fast and loose with your dialogue and, yeah, they'd slapped a gang bang in there too. Because, you know, they had a day free in the schedule and a big room the director wanted to use.

'Sorry?' Spengler had asked him something.

'How's the teaching thing going? At that place?'

'Oh fuck. It's . . . they're young. You know?'

'I bet they are – you animal.'

'No, I mean –'

'Any good screenwriters? Anyone I should be hiring?'

'There's this . . . no. Probably not.'

Suddenly there was a commotion somewhere behind them, over by the door. Hubbub and flashbulbs popping near the entrance. Kennedy and Spengler both turned to see Julie Teal entering with her entourage. Diners gawping openly. The maître d' hurrying her party to a dark banquette.

'Shit,' Kennedy said.

'I love it,' Spengler said. 'We'll go over and say hi in a minute. Let me just fill you in on why I wanted us to have dinner first . . .'

The real reason for the dinner turned out to be that all this improvisation on location in Serbia had thrown up some 'interesting' possibilities, some 'fresh perspectives' on the characters. Julie, Kevin and Michael had some 'strong' thoughts on new scenes, new backstory 'elements' they'd like to see introduced. It was all very 'exciting' and had really 'opened up' the story.

Kennedy listened and nodded over dessert then thirty quid balloons of Calvados. But really none of the adjectives being freely thrown around – 'interesting . . . exciting . . . fresh' – seemed right. 'Nightmare.' 'Shitshow.' 'Atrocity.' These were the terms he felt himself reaching for.

But Hollywood was a crapshoot. You threw the fucking dice and ran for the hills. You put together a cast like Kevin Kline, Susan Sarandon, Harvey Keitel, Alan Rickman, Danny Aiello and Rod Steiger, an Oscar-winning screenwriter and a thirty-year veteran like Norman Jewison producing and you got *The January Man*: an abortion that takes 4 mil at the box office before just becoming a blot on everyone's IMDb profile. Alternatively you put a rookie director together with a B-list cast and you go into production with no shooting script, making it up as you go along, and you got fucking *Jaws*. The unhappiest productions sometimes spat out gold and the most joyful, harmonious sets often produced dreck. And, ultimately, no one said to their wife or girlfriend, 'Hey baby, let's go see Movie X tonight. I hear the screenwriter's original vision was left largely untouched and it came in on time and on budget.' No one gave a fuck. If it was a turkey you carried the can as the dumbest son of a bitch who ever opened a laptop on Sunset Boulevard. If it was a smash everyone thought the director was a genius and who the fuck were you? One of Kennedy's favourite Hollywood stories: the writer goes to the premiere of his movie and can't get into the VIP section of the after-party. Finally a producer takes pity and gets him in there. A blonde is standing there. 'Hey,' the writer says, 'what did you do on the picture?'

'I'm the dog trainer,' she says. 'What did you do?'

'I wrote it.'

'Oh,' the girl says, 'it's so nice they invited you!'

'We'll send you Kevin's notes. He's been putting some material together with a script editor but, you know, we'll need your magic touch.'

'Mmmm,' Kennedy said as neutrally possible.

'Attaboy. OK, come on, let's go touch the hem.'

'Oh God, really?'

'Showbusiness, baby,' Spengler said, getting up. 'Come on, she loves you.'

'BOYS!' Teal squealed as she saw them approaching. She was surrounded by four other girls – all in their twenties, all models, actresses, whatever the fuck – and her minder, old Juan. A couple of them were dressed in a manner that bordered on fancy dress. A nod to Halloween or high-end couture? Who knew? 'What are you two doing here? We just decided to come at the last minute. Come, join us. Kennedy – you will sit next to me. Girls, Kennedy is just the best writer and, ohmigod, wait till you hear his accent.' Kennedy was surprised to see a glass of champagne in Teal's hand.

'Ach bollocks,' Kennedy said, triggering a fresh peal of screams. Extra chairs were produced, a bottle of Cristal was called for (obviously no one was eating) and, somewhere into the melee, Spengler disappeared, off into his chauffeur-driven Maybach for the ride out to Buckinghamshire, and Julie Teal nuzzled into Kennedy and whispered 'Hey – you wanna do some blow?'

Kennedy was only mildly surprised to hear the word 'Sure' coming out of his mouth.

THIRTY-EIGHT

Kennedy woke up. Or came to at any rate. He went to sit up and quickly decided that this ranked among the worst ideas he had ever, ever had. His head – *Jaysuss*. It felt like his blood and flesh had been replaced, respectively, with sawdust and flaking parchment. His mouth was the under-side of a Bedouin sandal after a fifty-mile desert hike. He fumbled for the Evian on the bedside table and upended it all over the floor. He managed to sluice the last remaining drops around his gums and blinked into the semi-darkness, trying desperately to work out where the fuck he was. A sheet of notepaper by the bed provided the general answer: the Mandarin Oriental hotel. Turning over and looking to his left provided the specific – in the sleeping form of Julie Teal.

Oh fuck. Fucking fuck.

The evening came back to him in fragmentary screen-grabs: the restaurant, Soho House (the Club: a curious institution. When you were young you ran with a gang. In your twenties no one had children, no one had much in the way of responsibilities, and the grave was a fantasy, a dirty rumour, something that happened to other people. So you went out all the time, and you bumped into other people all the time, because they were all out at the same places too. Then life happened – families, kids, careers – and for a good while no one went out any more. And then here comes middle age: with divorce, and the kids older, living their own lives, and there is boredom to be thwarted and adultery to be had and the grave is *right fucking there* and suddenly these places were packed with people you knew again. All these grinning cadavers, lined and rumpled and fat, and clutching flutes and highballs and saying *'Join us!'* and *'What are you having?'* and where everybody knows your name and all that. And, yes, Kennedy liked it. He was a clubbable man. But, at the same time, he felt the desperate edge beneath the party, something flickering behind those rictus grins, manifesting itself when someone laughed a little too hard, or held your eye for too long, and you saw it there, sliding behind their gaze, like a dark, terrible fish rising but not quite breaking the surface. You saw the fear), then some nightclub, another nightclub. Back here. And, at every turn, flashes of blinding white, like sheet lightning breaking out, people running down the street beside them, ahead of them, running backwards. Laughter, tears, champagne, shouting, cocaine and more and more cocaine. And, finally, the act itself . . .

'Ohhh – fuck me, fuck me, fuck me,' her spiked heels digging into his thighs at one point as he ran his hands up her creamy rump, along her back, and unhooked her bra, feeling tension being released, something heavy falling gratefully forward.

Sliding his hands around to her front and leaning forward, rubbing and pinching the nipples, her moaning and the urgency of her thrusts increasing, Kennedy stopping his thrusts and just kneeling there, on this bed, arms behind his back, letting her push herself slowly back onto him and then, even more slowly, forward again. In and out. In and out. He recalled his mind flipping to what it always flipped to when he was trying to ward off ejaculation: bad reviews. Kennedy couldn't really give you a line from a good review he'd had (those fools, what did they know?) but, fifteen years on, he could give you chapter and verse on his stinkers (all written by perceptive geniuses of course).

'Kennedy Marr's prose is a turgid jumble which has fooled itself into thinking it is important and original.'

'Cold and sterile. Not a single character you care about.'

'This charmless blockbuster, with a dire script from the celebrated novelist Mr Kennedy Marr . . .'

And then she'd been turning over. A long leg shooting straight in the air, a flash of white stomach, his glistening, erect prick, waiting, paused, and then – *ohhhhh, that felt nice* – she'd been guiding him back in, saying, 'Ohhhh fuuuckk!'

'While the director must take some responsibility the bulk of the blame surely falls on the shoulders of screenwriter Kennedy Marr . . .'

'Fuck me, fuck me, fuck me.' Her free hand, busily working the tuft of hair above her . . .

'Lacks the resonance and authority of his debut . . .'

'Oh Jesus Christ,' she'd panted. 'I'm so close.'

'An attitude in search of a story, the novel meanders along waiting for –'

'*KENNEDY – I'M COMING!*'

'KENNEDY MARR IS A SIGNIFICANT NEW WRITER WHOSE WORK WILL BE READ A HUNDRED YEARS FROM NOW FOR THE SHEER PLEASURE OF THE LANGUAUGE!'

Ahhhhh.

And, somewhere in all this, something bad, something he didn't want to fully remember. Teal, on her knees, blowing him, looking up as she (very professionally) worked his shaft with her hand and saying something, something, something about his cock?

Looking around the gloom of the vast suite, searching for his shoes, trousers, his mind, it came to him that there was something else very bad about all of this. Something worse than fucking the star of the movie. Worse than whatever it was she'd said to him. He looked at the green digital numbers on the bedside clock: 1.43 p.m. What day was it? Sunday. Wasn't there something he was meant to be –

Christ.

He found his mobile in the tangled mess of his suit and went next door to the sitting room. Robin answered on the third ring. As soon as she heard his voice, his cracked, broken whisper, she said, 'Shit. Are you OK, Dad?'

'Yeah, really sorry. Just . . . I think I'm coming down with something. Flu or something. There's a lot of it on the set. Sorry, darling, can we do lunch another time? Later in the week?'

'Sure. I hope you feel better.'

He hung up and lay staring at himself in a huge mirror above the fireplace, the face of a man who had just lied to his only child. As though reading his mind his phone chirruped at that exact moment – a text from Millie that simply read, 'Flu, eh?'

Could he face the flight to Dublin at five o'clock? He ran a check on his body, his mind. At his age? This was going to be a three-day hangover. A festival. Not the matinee hangovers of his youth – over by 3 p.m. The flight to Dublin? Then the dread hospital? He felt like he should be *in* hospital, not visiting one. He steeled himself and set about making the exact same call to Patrick he had just made to Robin.

Patrick laughed. He actually laughed.

THIRTY-NINE

'We're a joke. A laughing stock.'

'Well, I think that's putting it a bit strongly, Dennis.' This was all the Dean needed first thing on a Monday morning, Dr Dennis Drummond, once again in full ire. He'd just been finishing his second cup of Darjeeling, the tea darkening up nicely in the pot, when Drummond marched straight in – sans appointment and with a fat stack of that morning's tabloids wedged menacingly under his arm. He proceeded to lay them out on the Dean's desk in 'Exhibit A' fashion.

The *Mirror*: 'TEAL'S BOOZY ROMP WITH WRITER!' and a photograph of her and Kennedy staggering out of the Groucho with their arms wrapped around each other. Inset, smaller, was a photograph of her vast suite at the Mandarin Oriental with the caption 'LOVE NEST!'

The *Sun*: 'DRUGGY STAR'S FOUL MOUTHED TIRADE!' accompanied by a photograph of the insanely drunk Teal mid-rant as they arrived at the hotel, giving the finger to the camera, Kennedy in the background, an insanely drunken grin on his face.

The *Star*: a badly grabbed still from one of Julie Teal's early films, showing her with her tits out and the headline 'THEY'RE TEAL ALRIGHT!' A smaller picture of her with Kennedy was inset.

Even *The Times* had a small box on the third page with the headline: 'HOLLYWOOD STARLET'S NIGHT WITH F. W. BINGHAM RECIPIENT'.

All the articles said much the same thing about Kennedy. *'The notoriously hard-living Irish author . . . nearly twenty years her senior . . . writer on Teal's new thriller currently filming in London . . . is back in Britain lecturing at Deeping University in Warwickshire . . . controversially given the half-million-pound award earlier this year . . . has a 16-year-old daughter from a previous marriage . . .'*

The Dean tut-tutted as he turned the pages, holding the newsprint as though it were smeared in excrement. 'I mean really, who reads these things? Who *writes* them? Look! There's a split infinitive here! In the opening paragraph!'

Drummond looked at him incredulously. 'A split infinitive? The name of the university is mentioned in all of these articles. Right alongside "cocaine" and "marathon sex session" and Christ knows what. Enough is enough surely.'

'How do you mean? Tea?'

'No. I mean – surely you don't want this man to remain here?'

The Dean sighed as he poured his third cup. 'What exactly would you have me do?'

'Subject him to the same level of discipline that any of the rest of us would be. Are you telling me that if I'd been involved in a drunken brawl on an aeroplane and been arrested, was on the cover of every newspaper linked to drug-taking and all the rest of it, are you telling me I wouldn't be in breach of my contract?'

The Dean tried for a moment to imagine Dennis Drummond being quite that interesting. He found that it couldn't be done. 'Dennis, you forget, it's not quite the same thing. *I can't* fire him. Only the F. W. Bingham committee can do that, if they somehow decided to rescind the award for whatever reason.'

'You're on the committee.'

'I'm just one voice.'

'But you'd certainly vote against him.'

'Weellll . . .'

'I don't believe this.'

'We're into questions of probity here, aren't we? A man is entitled to a private life.'

'Private!' Drummond yelled, gesturing at the acreage of newsprint.

The Dean blew on his tea as he finally looked up at Drummond and said, quietly, 'Are you shouting at me, Dennis?'

'I . . . no. I certainly didn't mean to. It's just, this whole thing, his behaviour, it . . . sorry.'

'Apology accepted. I'll have a word with him.'

'Yes. Well, I don't know if that'll quite be enough.'

'You can leave these with me,' the Dean indicated the newspapers.

'Gladly.' Drummond closed the door firmly behind him, marching off, holding on to the single thought: *'If they somehow decided to rescind the award for whatever reason.'*

The Dean sipped his tea and turned a few pages. Good Lord, look at that. With her bits out and everything. The lot. Right there in a family newspaper. Extraordinary. Absolutely extraordinary.

While the Dean acquainted himself with tabloid news-paper culture, over in the English Department, Kennedy was coming up the stairs, heading for his office where he intended to pull the blinds and nap until he had to deal with that afternoon's tutorial group. He rounded a corner and ran slap bang into his ex-wife. They regarded each other for a second, Millie taking in how awful he still looked. You really couldn't be doing this shit, at his age. You really had to want it badly to keep it up in your forties. 'Millie –' Kennedy began.

'Well, congratulations. No, really, good going. I mean even by your standards this is a new low. Jesus Christ – lying to your own daughter and then she wakes up and has to read all this . . . this fucking shit.' Yes, she had a copy of *The Sun* under her arm.

Monday – horrible to the touch. Fuck knew what had happened to most of Sunday. He dimly remembered the train from Marylebone to Banbury or somewhere. Good old Keith picking him up. (*'Bloody hell, boss. Been getting stuck in, have we?'*)

Millie was as angry as he'd ever seen her. He stood there, dry-mouthed, head pounding, just taking it. Seven missed calls on his mobile from Scott Spengler's office this morning too. 'I don't really give a shit who you fuck, Kennedy, but couldn't it be someone that isn't going to end up in the papers?'

The tabloids had been unforgiving. Must have paid off one of the staff.

The actress — 27 — spent a steamy night of passion with the writer who is nearly 20 years her senior.

'Ach, it's a shitshow right enough.'

'A shitshow? Is that all you have —'

She stopped as a group of students passed them, mostly lads. On seeing Kennedy an immediate cheer went up, a couple of them even doing the time-honoured clenched-fist-resting-in-crook-of-elbow-pumping motion. Kennedy sighed. 'Look, let's go to my office, this is ridiculous.'

The moment the door shut behind them he regretted the decision to allow Millie full vent in a private space. 'You call your own fucking daughter up and blow her out for lunch at the last minute because you've "got flu" when all the while you've been in some hotel suite in London off your fucking face with some little actress?'

'I wasn't "off my face".'

But she was already rifling through the newspaper, looking for the spread. ' *"The pair crashed into the £3,500 a night suite in the early hours of the morning clearly inebriated"?*'

'They have to put it like that!'

'I knew it was a bad idea you coming back here. I fucking knew it. You know, you've been behaving like this for nearly twenty years now. When are you going to fucking grow up?'

'What did Robin say?'

'She kind of laughed. Said "Holy shit, Dad." But deep down how do you think she feels?'

'I . . . I'll make it up to her.'

'Kennedy — there's nothing to make up. You're just a kind of fun stranger to her. A comedy figure.'

'Oh, don't say that. Don't . . .'

Kennedy sat down on the sofa. Christ, he didn't feel too clever. There had been other pictures of Teal in the papers today too: taken yesterday afternoon, her giving out the whole 'no comment' and the 'we're just good friends' line while on her way to play tennis. *Tennis?* Just saying the fucking word made him want to pass out. Cocaine – definitely a young man's game.

On the drinks cabinet a bottle of Stoli winked at him, a bottle of Big Tom in the glass-fronted fridge below it. There *might* be celery in the refectory. All the makings of a decent Bloody Mary. Might just get him through this fucking tutorial. 'I . . . I'll give her a call in a bit.'

'You've been back here nearly two months now. You still haven't been to see your mother, you treat your daughter like this. Has it ever occurred to you that's it's possible to say no to sex? To say no to that last drink? I . . . I used to think you might be a half-decent person if you ever grew up but this is it, isn't it? This is all you're ever going to be: a drunken, narcissistic . . . yob.'

'A *yob?*'

Was this really happening? Now? Yes, it was, she was going for it. The full deck. People who didn't really drink – they could be incredibly insensitive when it came to the schedule of the drinking person: the hours when you were drunk and had no interest in anything they had to say. The hours, days now at his age, when you were tired and hung-over and, again, couldn't bear to listen to what they had to say. They just went about their sober business: telling you a few home truths. Pitching in with their 'And another thing'. With their 'Oh, and by the way'. With their 'Well, there's never a good time to talk to you so we're just going to talk about it now'. Had these people no mercy? No decency?

'Yes, Kennedy – a fucking yob. Oh, you think you're not because you can shut the world out for a few hours every day and put together something that makes people want to turn the page, or watch the next scene. Because you have some kind of facility for narrative you think the rest of humanity is just scenery, a necessary backdrop for your glorious adventures. Well, shall I tell you what you really are?'

'NO!' Oh God please no. Don't do that. Kennedy tried to stuff his fists in his ears as she bore down on him.

'You're a sad, middle-aged alcoholic who is going to die alone and who will only dimly realise at the very end how much he threw awa—'

'WILL YOU PLEASE SHUT THE FUCK UP?!' he screamed as the phone started ringing. He picked it up. 'Yeah? Oh, hi, Angela. Mmmm. Fuck. OK. Tell him I'll be along in a minute. Oh, if you're going to the refectory could you see if they have any cel—' He looked at Millie standing there, humming with righteousness, arms folded with the newspaper still clutched in one fist. 'Never mind. Thanks.' He put the phone down. 'The Dean wants a word.'

'I'm sure he's keen to congratulate you on all of this fine publicity you're bringing the university.'

'Look, Millie, I'm really sorry.' He winced as he sank slowly, gingerly, back down onto the sofa, looking very much like an octogenarian with arthritis in every possible joint lowering himself into an exceedingly hot bath. 'I'll call Robin later and apologise. I'll make it up to her.'

'Oh, go and fuck yourself, Kennedy.'

She threw the newspaper at him and headed for the door. Before she got there he said, weakly, 'Millie?'

She turned, hand on the doorknob. 'What?'

He spoke softly with a hand over his brow, his eyes closed. 'Do you think it's possible, just possible mind, that the reason you're so angry about all this has nothing to do with Robin but it's because, secretly, you long for me to change because you still want us to be together?'

She looked at him for several seconds before saying, 'I think it's possible that, very publicly, you're finally going completely insane.'

A sharp report as she slammed the door behind her. Simultaneously his mobile started ringing. Spengler's office. Again. Jesus. He threw the phone into the waste-paper basket, where it continued ringing, metallically amplified.

On paper, he thought, for the umpteenth time, this should all be good. This should all work. Plenty of money, interesting, many would say glamorous, work, desirable women attracted to him. Yet he appeared to be in a very convincing facsimile of hell. He seemed to have a keen interest, almost a zealot's mission, to make his life as difficult as possible. *Has it ever occurred you to that it's possible to say no to sex?* Kennedy gave this question some attention. Had he, indeed, ever turned down a fuck? Surely there must have been occasions? Yeah, that time . . . no, turning one down because you felt there was the possibility of an upgrade to another fuck probably didn't count.

The desk phone started ringing, Angela's line again. He picked this one up. 'I'm just coming!'

'No, no. Sorry. He knows. The Dean wants to know if

you're free for a dinner party at his house, first week of December. The Monday I think.'

'I . . . a Monday night? I suppose so. Who'll be there?'
'TBC.'

'Mmm.' He eyed that headline on the floor. 'Yeah, OK. Tell him I'll come.'

Sometimes it did cross his mind that one might be happier, that things might be altogether easier, if the whole issue was removed altogether. Didn't Kingsley say that finally losing his sex drive was something of a relief, as it had been like being 'shackled to a madman for fifty years'? Or there was James Lees-Milne, having his balls removed at the age of seventy-five, as a precaution against prostate cancer. What had he confided to his diary? Something to the effect that his castration had altered his character in unexpected, beneficial ways, making him judge things more objectively, uncoloured by lust and desire. And Oscar Wilde – who knew a thing or two about demonic beasting – said that virtue was simply the 'absence of temptation'.

The hours, the surely uncountable hours, spent drinking and talking and drugging when he could have been reading, thinking, *working*. And all because of some demented rumblings between his legs. Even if you just thought in terms of the self-abuse . . .

Kennedy did some arithmetic in his head: say five minutes on average, yes some were knocked out in barely a minute, but there had also been plenty of spectacular epics, some ten- to fifteen-minute jobs. Then say at least ten times a week. Again, yes, there had been the odd day of abstinence (big date coming up, influenza) but, as against that, there were the days of two, three or four. Christ — there had been days (teenagerdom, severe hangovers) of five or six times. Ten a week probably covered a decent average. Ten times five minutes = fifty minutes. Fifty times four gave you a monthly total of two hundred minutes, or just over three hours. Three hours times twelve for the annual average of thirty-six hours. This had been going on since the age of fourteen: thirty fucking years. Taking his iPhone from the bin now, clicking on the calculator function, with trembling fingers he tapped it in.

Thirty times thirty-six gave you the lifetime career stat of . . .

One thousand and eighty hours of pure onanism.

To write a draft of a novel took him (well, used to take him) about six months of working five mornings a week, roughly from breakfast till lunch. Say four solid hours a day without interruptions or distractions. Twenty hours a week. Eighty hours a month for six months = 480 hours. He tapped at the calculator again, dividing 1080 hours by 480, and gazed upon the sickening figure with horror.

Wanking alone had cost him 2.25 books.

Forget the days and weeks lost because of hangovers caused from staying up till four in the morning trying to close the deal. Just with the self-abuse, there it was: two novels and a short novella that could have been gracing the library shelves of the world, exchanged for over a thousand hours of furiously thrumming buck-toothed on his back, or buckled and hunched in bathrooms or even, on a couple of occasions, while driving a car. Some quarter of a million words of prose exchanged for what? For a couple of pints of semen pumped into socks, tissues, towels and underpants whose varying design aesthetics spanned four decades.

Oh, bad business! Yes, very bad.

Yeah, maybe that was the answer. That might do it. Perhaps Kingsley and Lees-Milne were right on the money – here was the way forward. He probably only had twenty years writing left in him. He didn't have the *time*. Just stroll into that private clinic, write the eye-watering cheque, and say, 'Right, let's be clear. I want the lot off, OK? Just leave me something to piss with. Because, honestly, you know what, lads? It's been nothing but fucking *grief*.'

FORTY

Kennedy watched Paige Patterson lift a forkful of salad to her mouth, the emerald-green leaves shining with olive oil. And, yes, it'd been nothing but grief and all that, but there it was, still there between his legs, still dictating the plays, so here they sat, in the restaurant of a place called the Bear, a kind of upmarket gastro-toilet, chosen by Kennedy for its distance from the campus and the consequent absence of any colleagues or students. Indeed, there were only two other diners in the whole place. Christ, the restaurants in rural England. Anchovy-less Caesar salads and piss-poor Sauvignon. Kennedy pined for the octopus at Moonshadows and a decent Martini, but contented himself with picking at an overcooked trout, sustained by frequent draughts of the least offensive white they had on the wine list. Paige had surprised him by accepting a glass without any urging. (How he'd rehearsed his arguments to her abstinence, finally deciding that mock overbearing would work best, *'Oh for God's sake just shut up and have a drink.'*) 'Mmmm,' she said now, sipping the comedy wine, her full, perfect lips now glossed by olive oil. (She'd declined dressing and asked the waiter to bring her some extra virgin and half a lemon on the side. She'd do well in LA, Kennedy thought.)

After the Teal disgrace, November seemed to be passing sensibly, half of it gone without incident. He'd cracked on with the rewrites on the film, now firmly into the territory of destroying his own work and not caring, and the students came and went every week. He nodded and listened and gave them all Cs. He'd rescheduled the visit to Dublin for a fortnight's time. The first week of December. If he moved it again he had a very strong sense that Patrick would be strapping Ma's bed onto the roof of the car and bringing her to him.

Dipping her head down towards the salad bowl again, Paige looked up at him with those huge eyes, tucking a strand of hair behind her ear, the lobe pink and nibbleable, and said, 'So what did the Dean say?'

'Oh, he was fine. Fine.'

And the Dean had been fine, bless him. 'We're in a spot here, eh? Ho-ho-ho. Bloody gutter press. You'd think with all there was going on in the world, no? Some of the trustees, indeed some of the staff, aren't too happy.' That utter penis Drummond, no doubt. 'But I think we can weather the storm. Heads down, bully and shove and all that.'

'"Heads down, bully and shove"?' Paige repeated, brow furrowing.

'It's an Old Etonian thing. Some game there. Some buggery festival no doubt.'

Paige sat back in the banquette and wiped her mouth. 'So?' she said.

'About *Bone Collectors?*' Kennedy asked. The full outline of her screenplay, the reason for this 'working' lunch, this 'tutorial in a convivial setting' as he'd billed it.

'No, silly. So what was she like? Julie Teal?'

'Julie? She's . . . you know, she's an actress. She's fucking Tonto. Nuts. She's a star – she wants every character she plays to be a cross between a nuclear physicist, a ninja, the World's Best Mom, and a five-grand-a-night hooker. You should come to the set sometime and meet her.'

'No no no.' Paige leaned forward, shaking her head, elbows on the table, closer. 'I mean – what was she like *in bed?*'

Fuck. 'In be— Oh, come on, Paige,' Kennedy trying for a little 'Ho-ho-ho' of his own, 'you can't believe everything you read in the papers.'

'Fuck off,' she said simply with no malice, smiling, holding his gaze. This girl, Jesus Christ.

'We're just working together!' he said feebly. 'She . . .' Kennedy, going for 'sexual modesty' here and finding it was like trying to form sentences in a language he could not speak.

'Really fuck off,' Paige said.

Kennedy laughed. 'Ach. She's . . .' He took a long swallow of wine. What had she been like in bed?

Slick, polished. *Empty, Paige, empty*, he wanted to say. *Another set of sensations to throw in the face of the abyss. Another distraction to enjoy while we caper in this brief crack of light between two eternities of darkness. Another –*

'She's got a great arse.'

'Ah, well, there is that, yeah.'

'And those tits. Fucking hell. You must have thought it was Christmas. Were they real?'

A sexual product of the 1980s, of a more genteel era, Kennedy sometimes forgot how girls were nowadays, that they talked like this. Sure and there had always been some mad whoor, some crazy or town bike, who would make with the filth back in the day, but now? They were all at it. When had it got this way? Sometime around the millennium he figured. Before that only porn stars and the insane talked like this. When he was at university – it was the 4 a.m. scramble to get past woolly tights, a forest of CND badges, Doc Martens covered in barbed wire and a pair of underpants that would have supplied enough material to fashion a convincing big top. Nowadays? They were all thongs and stockings. Swallowing swords with a butt-plug up them and their bushes shaved into Hitler moustaches. The late eighties looked like a Hovis ad, or a Merchant–Ivory production. Ron fucking Jeremy was directing the present. Was Robin like this in private? Was she going to be? Jesus wept.

'Yeah, I'm pretty sure they were,' Kennedy said, in a voice that sounded like a slightly higher-pitched impression of his own. They were inches apart now, in the dark booth.

'Tell me about the nipples, Kennedy,' she said.

'No, shurrup, c'mere . . .' His hand on the small of her back as he pulled her towards him. Her lips – softer than he'd ever imagined and slick with oil, the faint tang of that lemon. Their tongues met on the way into one another's mouths, eager shoppers trying to barge past each other in a doorway, his going up and exploring the ridged rooftop, hers going down, flicking and probing at the marshy floor of his mouth. Christ, *this* was a kiss. All that other stuff he'd been doing – that was for your auntie. Meeting the

Queen. An Amish birthday party. It felt like she was trying to extract a shred of spinach from his back molar using only the tip of her tongue now. Meanwhile, down in the Bomb Bay, they were loading up Little Boy. Fatman. The fucking Doomsday device . . . it felt like fluids were rushing to his balls from new and wholly unexpected parts of his body, making the long pilgrimage from his fingertips, his toes, his fucking *scalp*.

'Phew!' She broke off and pulled back, smiling at him, her hand clamped around the back of his neck. 'I'm just going to go to the toilet.'

Kennedy Marr worked fast. In very short succession he finished the wine, called for and settled the bill with a sheaf of twenties (no dicking around with the credit card machine), got their coats and did a quick Google search on his phone for the closest hotel. He was in luck: a reasonable-looking four-star gaff just a couple of miles down the road. He looked up from the screen and over towards the two other diners – a woman and her daughter. The daughter was around Paige's age, maybe a little younger, and very cute, but definitely not in the same league as the sexual master-piece now primping herself in the toilet. The woman was jowly, middle-aged, wearing thick glasses and a baggy sweater with some kind of brooch pinned to it. The kind of person you did see in restaurants over here – in West Hollywood she'd have looked like a cross between a bag lady and a hung-over Methuselah on a bad hair day. Kennedy became aware of the mother staring at him with a gaze that could not be described as . . . uncritical. It dawned on him: he was probably the same age as her. No more than a few years younger. Yet, in his mind, this woman didn't really exist for him. Her daughter was pretty real. He could imagine drinking with her. Laughing. Lifting her up in the air and lowering her onto his face like a muzzle. The woman? Just a mad old harridan. A nonentity. What on earth was wrong with him? What quirk of wiring made him unable to recognise his own kind? To recognise middle age even as he ploughed through it? *Ah, Dr Brendle. Perhaps there were things you could have told me.* Ach — fuck it. He smiled and nodded at the hag and she looked away, suddenly entranced by the dessert menu. He buttoned his jacket, suddenly conscious of the pain of the monumental erection straining at the waistband of his trousers, like a dog snuffling at the crack at the top of the window in a too-hot car.

He walked outside, lit a cigarette, and was standing by the car, keys jangling impatiently, by the time Paige came sauntering towards him. 'Hey there,' he smiled, pretending to be absorbed by his phone as he casually remote-unlocked the Aston, its lights flashing obligingly behind him.

'Ready to rock?' Paige said.

'Born ready, baby.'

'Good. I've got to be back by four.'

Eh? He looked at his watch. It was three fifteen. 'Four? But it's —'

'Yeah. Medieval English. Professor Wallace.'

'You're kidding?'

'Would that I were.' She was stepping around him now, opening the door.

'Oh fuck off. You can catch up. Get someone's notes or whatever. There's a hotel —'

'No can do, I'm afraid. Important one. I'm really keen to see how the Venerable Bede gets on this week.'

'But we . . . we didn't even discuss your outline yet.'

'Ha! As if. Look, I really can't today, Kennedy. But tell you what, what you were saying earlier? About visiting the set sometime? I'd like that. Maybe you could take me. We could make a day of it. Spend the night in London?'

Her fine eyebrows arched, comically searching for her hairline, before she kissed him on the check and lowered herself into the bucket seat, lifting a firm, finely toned calf in last. Kennedy sighed. 'Hang on a second. I'm just going to run to the loo.'

A very short while later Kennedy sighed again, melodically this time, as he ejaculated into the never-unwilling mouth of the bowl. He looked at his watch: a minute and twenty-three seconds. *There it goes*, he thought. A couple of sentences, maybe a paragraph, literally flushed down the toilet. On the way back out the woman looked up from her Death by Chocolate or whatever the fuck it was and shot him another look. *Yeah, yeah. Stick it up in your fookin' hole . . .*

He pounded a whisky, picked up the phone and, with fingers as nervous as those with which he'd called Karen McGill in fourth year, after he'd been told she thought he was 'nice' (this was before girls said 'fit' or 'well hung' or whatever else they said these days), dialled her mobile. Three trills and – 'Dad?'

'Hey, Robin, how's tricks?'

'OK. Just back from school.'

'Listen, about the other day, lunch on Sunday, I'm sorry, I . . . y'know, I bullshitted you.'

'"The flu",' she quoted, flatly, but not without some humour in her voice.

'Uh, yeah. Sorry about that.'

'Seems like you had a . . . fun night?'

'Oh, the whole thing got exaggerated. Just had a few drinks and slept in really.'

'Everyone was talking about it at school.'

'Christ.'

'No, they all think you rule.'

'Ha. Is that the view your mum's taking?'

'Mmm. Not so much.'

'Anyway. Let's rearrange. What do you fancy? Are you busy this Friday night? Dinner? Maybe a movie or something?'

'Friiidayyy . . .' She drew the word out, as though scanning the pages in an appointment diary. 'Yeah, Friday's OK.'

'Great. I'll come pick you up about seven.'

'OK, Dad, bye.'

'Oh – and tell your mum we're going out. Tell her, you know, tell her I rang.'

'OK.'

'Bye.'

FORTY-ONE

'OK! CUT! CUT! Right, people – CLEAR THE SET! CLEAR THE SET! WETDOWN! I NEED WETDOWN HERE!'

The enormous stage in the 007 hangar was immediately swamped with technicians, scrambling around in the darkness, dousing every available flat surface with water. Kennedy didn't remember all this night-time and rain in the original script. Someone clearly had their artistic filter set to 'MAXIMUM NOIR'. Beware the director seeking short cuts to gravitas.

'KENNEDY!' a voice boomed and suddenly here was the halfwit himself, coming towards them out of the darkness, taking his headset off. 'Who's been up to no good then?! Leading the talent astray, huh?' A bearish arm going round Kennedy's shoulder now. 'Yeah – like Julie needs any prompting? Eh? Amirite? Tell me, you Irish maniac – amirite?'

'Hi, Kevin,' Kennedy said, struggling free from the

madman's grasp. 'Kevin, this is Paige. Paige – Kevin. The director.'

'Pleased to meet you,' Paige said, extending her hand, Kevin taking it between two massive paws.

'Hey, Paige.'

'Wow,' she said, looking around. 'Some set.'

'Yeah, it's a doozy. We build it up then we blow it up.'

'Paige is a writer too,' Kennedy said.

'Well –' she began to protest.

'No kidding? Hey, we could use a polish on this piece of shit. The guy they got in sucks.' He punched Kennedy playfully on the arm. Kennedy managed a polite, rictus grin while quietly wishing a good deal of harm on the man. All around them was noise and activity – banging, hammering and shouting.

'Scott around?'

'He's always around. Probably in his trailer.'

'Boss?' a girl asked, suddenly appearing at Kevin's elbow with a clipboard. 'I really need to know what colour you want that door to be, the props guy can't find that gun you want and we got a problem with Scene 91. I don't think you'll be able to put the camera where you want if you're going to . . .'

She went on. As he often did on movie sets, Kennedy gave heartfelt thanks to the universe that he was not a director.

'Hi, Kennedy.' Michael Curzon coming over now, brooding, insanely, uselessly handsome. 'How's things?'

'Hey, Michael. Grand. Just grand. This is Paige.'

'Hi there.'

'Hello,' Paige said, coy and a little nervy, intimidated.

'Sorry, Kennedy, can I get a minute?'

Never go to the set. Absolutely goddamn right.

'Uh, sure, Michael.' He turned to Paige. 'Will you be OK? I won't be long. There's craft services over there. Food and drink and whatnot.'

'I'll be fine. Hey –' she picked up a shooting script from a chair with the words 'SCOTT SPENGLER' stencilled on the back – 'will it be OK if I read this?'

'Sure. Be back in a minute.'

She settled down in the chair and opened the screenplay, crossing her tanned legs, her skirt short even by her own standards.

'So,' Curzon said when they were a few yards away, 'is that like, uh, your daughter?'

Kennedy ignored it. 'So, Michael, what's on your mind?'

'Oh man,' Curzon began.

Fifteen minutes later, in his trailer – smaller, less well appointed than Teal's – Curzon was *still* talking. Kennedy, meanwhile, was mentally adding the phrase 'Say the words "what's on your mind?" to an actor' to a list he carried around in his head. The list already included stuff like:

'Round off an evening with a chain of Jägerbombs.'

'Agree to sit on the Writers Guild Arbitration Panel.'

And 'Lower your bare nutsack into a meat grinder.'

The list was entitled 'THINGS NEVER TO BE DONE'.

'I mean, it's a nightmare. Every scene, man, every goddamned scene, she's in there, wanting me to do less and less, trying to get dialogue changed, close-ups reduced. Any half-decent line I have, and I mean *any fucking thing*, she wants it given to her character! She has no interest – NO

FUCKING INTEREST – in the integrity of the piece. I am only saying this because I have the utmost respect for you and your work, Kennedy, and it . . . it pains me, man. I know you fucked her and all, man, and these things happen but, you know, it pains me, really fucking pains me to see this happening. The other day, the scene in the CIA office when we're being held and I have that speech about my father's involvement in the Bay of Pigs thing in '61?'

Finally Kennedy's ears pricked up. 'Eh? What fucking "Bay of Pigs" speech?'

'Oh, has that, is that a new . . . we felt it would add another layer if my character had a father who had been in the intelligence agency himself, you know? And it'd made him remote and emotionally unavailable to his children? We improvised some stuff, Kevin wrote some dialogue – you know Kevin's a writer too, right? And anyway we're –'

What the fucking fuck? Oh these actors, with their 'layers' and their 'backstory'. *How many children had Lady Macbeth?* Kennedy thought to himself.

'Anyway, we're blocking the scene out and –'

'Michael?'

'– suddenly she pipes up with –'

'Michael?'

'– "Oh, maybe we don't need that speech because the aud—"'

'MICHAEL!'

'Huh?'

'Why are you telling me all this?'

'Why? Because, like I said, she's wrecking the movie, man. She's damaging your work.'

'She's a Big Fucking Star, Michael. That's what they do. That's all they do. Her job – her raisin de fucking cunting entrée – is to swan around causing untold grief and wrecking everything in her path. Come on – what are you? Five years old? You know this.'

'Not on this scale, man. And I mean – what am I? *What am I?* Chopped fucking liver? I've done Beckett, man. Pinter. I did *Long Day's Journey into Night* Off-Broadway.' Kennedy again had cause to thank the universe he had not been forced to endure any of these performances. The theatre: something middle-class handpumps did to feel cultured. He was firmly with Nabokov on this – one of God's greatest jokes had been making Shakespeare a dramatist. 'Let's see that fucking bitch do that,' Curzon added. 'Bitch. Cunt.' He smacked an empty Diet Coke can with the back of his hand, sending it flying across the room and onto the floor, where it joined several others. The place was a mess. Come to think of it, Curzon was a mess too: red-eyed, blotchy, light stubble. Looked like he'd been hitting it pretty hard.

Kennedy sighed. This, like everything else, was getting closer to being over. 'So why tell me? What the fuck can I do? I only work here same as you. Talk to Kevin. Talk to Scott.'

'They don't care. They'd let her take a fucking shit in my mouth if she thought it'd improve the scene. Come on, man – you and her are . . . close.'

'Don't believe everything you read in the papers, Michael,' Kennedy said, getting up, buttoning his jacket. 'And chin up. You're not down the mines as my old ma would say. You're working, you're getting paid. So, you know, heads down, bully and shove and all that.'

'Huh?'

'Never mind. Look, you're a comer, Michael. If it all goes well in a couple of years you'll be living the dream and doing all the shit she's doing now. OK? See you later.'

'Hey,' Curzon said, 'you busy? Wanna hang out? Do some blow?'

'Really, really not.'

Bay of Pigs speech?' Kennedy said to himself as he came out of the trailer, striding back towards the set. Jesus wept, this was all going tits. He checked his watch – 6 a.m. in Los Angeles. Braden would probably be at the gym. He dialled the number, got voicemail. 'Hi, it's Kennedy. Listen, I'm on the set at Pinewood. They are literally making this thing up as they go along now. Can you officially request a copy of the current shooting script from the production office? We might need to think about getting my name taken off this piece of shit.' He hung up, stepping around some crew who were hoisting up an enormous sheet of sugar glass – a fake window that presumably Teal or Curzon, or more likely a stunt double, would soon be leaping through – and back into the darkened hangar.

You know Kevin's a writer too?

That fat bastard couldn't write a convincing message in a birthday card. Directors. You saw it all the time. Good directors who made decent pictures working from scripts decent writers had spent months, years, sweating over. But it's not enough. That 'Directed by' credit suddenly doesn't look half as appealing as that 'Written and Directed by' credit. So they sit down in an empty room and try and do the thing. And their heads are filling with what? Nothing. With a pair of chimps picking each other's fleas. Because it's *so fucking hard.* There's nobody to yell at, no one's asking you any questions. It's just you. Asking *you* questions. To write clearly is to think clearly. And thinking is hard work. So somehow they manage to come up with maybe half a dozen ideas for scenes they want to shoot then they get some nobody writer in to connect one scene to another – uncredited – and bang, there it is: My Screenplay by Todd Cuntfuck aged 29½. But it gets made – because, hey, the guy's a genius director, right? And the movie tanks – because it's a quarter of a lame idea written on a sanitary towel by a Full Mental Retard who basically hasn't got two thoughts to rub together. And the guy never works again. And now that 'Directed by' credit is starting to look pretty good again. Which is a shame because no one will hire him and if he'd just stuck to that one thing he did well . . .

Kennedy saw Kevin in the middle of the deluged set, surrounded by adoring crew – his DP, the first AD, the continuity girl – as he pointed to something, doing the director thing. Fucking weasel. He came round some scenery and saw Paige – in conversation with Scott Spengler, both of them laughing as he approached.

'Kennedy!' Paige said.

'Hey, maestro,' Spengler began. He was wearing a preppy cashmere pullover over a white silk shirt with tailored jeans. Not a hair out of place. The uniform of the super-rich middle-aged. 'I met your student.'

'Yeah, so I see. Scott – why the fuck is Kevin rewriting my fucking script?'

'He's not.'

'That's strangely at odds with what Michael Curzon just told me.'

'Look, Kevin just straightened out some of the ideas the

kids came up with during the improv and shot a little bit of it. It'll probably all end up on the cutting-room floor, Kennedy. We're making the movie you wrote. The *great* movie you wrote.'

'You see, Paige?' Kennedy said, indicating the grinning Spengler. 'One may smile and smile and be a villain.'

'Scott was just telling me how much he's been enjoying working with you,' Paige said.

'Really?'

'You the man, Kennedy,' Spengler said. 'Hey, you guys gonna stay and have some food?'

'No, we've got to get –' Kennedy began.

'I'm *starving*,' Paige said.

'Yeah, we'll have lunch in my trailer. Freddy's doing the rare roast beef today. It's the best. You English love that shit. Come on – I wanna hear more about this *Bone Collection* thing.'

'*Bone Collectors*,' Paige corrected him.

Oh yeah? Kennedy thought.

'Sure, that's what I said,' Spengler said, placing a hand on the small of her back, directing her towards the square of sunlight in the back wall that led out onto the back lot.

For most people the expression 'lunch in my trailer' would have conjured images of plastic cutlery and paper plates on their laps in a caravan. If Teal's trailer made Curzon's look shabby then Spengler's made both of them look like something you saw people selling burgers out of in motorway lay-bys. It was actually *two* trailers: very large RVs somehow bolted together and knocked through, creating a colossal living area. Interior-decorated to the max, it was basically a five-star hotel suite on wheels. An apartment. Rather than paper plates, there was bone china, Waterford crystal and solid silver flatware on a crisp white tablecloth. A beautiful arrangement of lilies in the centre, a gift, 'from CAA', Spengler said. (What was it with these guys and flowers? Kennedy wondered. Always sending each other fucking flowers.) Paige sat between them and Spengler's chef served rare roast beef and baby vegetables glazed with butter. They split a bottle of Krug as an aperitif and then had an incredibly good St Estèphe with the entrée. Then crème brûlée, blowtorched right at the table and accompanied by a glass of a very acceptable Sauternes and Spengler's spiel. Talk of projected grosses. Of test screenings and opening weekends. Distribution networks and funding partnerships. Tax shelters. Above- and below-the-line costs. Domestic and foreign. Guarantees and completion bonds. Dollar versus Pound. The FTSE and the Dow. Profit participants. Downloads. Cable and airline sales. He was glad she was hearing all this in a way. Hearing all this real movie talk.

Kennedy had eaten worse meals in caravans. Back in Kilkee, the rain drumming on the metal roof and his ma singing something to herself at the wee Baby Belling as she emptied the cans of ravioli into a saucepan. The smell of bread on the edge of burning. Lunch. (To this day, when very hung-over, tinned Heinz food – spaghetti, ravioli, mac and cheese – on toast was his go-to comfort food.) Da trying to listen to the match on the transistor radio. Patrick just a baby in his cot. Him and Gerry playing with Granny. That time, he was maybe seven, Gerry just five. Gerry being naughty. Granny saying something to her, something terrible. Unforgivable. What was it? *'Kennedy's a good boy and . . .'* He realised now that she'd been drunk. Those whisky glasses with the swollen bottoms, the ones they'd won at the bingo. *'Sure and these are greedy wee cups now, aren't they?'* Granny had said, pouring. His first experience of a transferred epithet. Granny, Da and Gerry now just dust and bone. Ma headed the same way.

His name, someone was saying his name.

'Sorry?' Kennedy said, looking up from stirring his espresso.

'Still with us?' Spengler said. They were both looking at him expectantly.

'Yeah, just. Sorry.'

'I was saying, have you read this script of your protégée here?'

'Just the opening. It's good. She can write.'

'You got an agent yet, Paige?' Spengler asked, topping her glass up.

'God, no,' Paige said. 'I haven't even finished it. I'm still studying.'

'Ah fuck all that.' Spengler said. 'You gotta just get out there and do it. Put it on the page. Don't get it right – get it written and all that bullshit. Trust me, no one ever took their girlfriend to see a picture on a Saturday night because the writer came top of their class or whatever. Kennedy – am I right?'

'No.'

'Ah fuck him. What does he know?' Spengler winked at Kennedy and raised his glass. Kennedy returned the gesture, Paige joining in. Kennedy looked at Spengler, gleaming in his silk shirt between all the heavy crystal and silverware, with his perfect teeth and skin and hair, the aura of health and cash that flowed from him. Their glasses suspended in the air, Spengler said, 'A toast. To *Bone Collectors* by Paige . . . what's your second name, honey?'

'Patterson,' she hiccuped, laughed.

'*Bone Collectors* by Paige Patterson. And may all your points be gross.' He clinked his glass to hers and they all drank the sweet, syrupy dessert wine. An underling came in with a stack of papers for Spengler.

'Bihoveth hire a ful long spoon,' Kennedy said, pronouncing it in the full medieval fashion, sounding out all the vowels, 'that shal ete with a feend.'

'What's that now, pal?' Spengler asked.

'"He that would eat with a fiend should have a long spoon." From "The Merchant's Tale",' Kennedy said, looking at Paige.

'Yeah? I didn't see that,' Spengler said, signing.

'Oh, you'd like it,' Kennedy said, smiling at Paige now. 'It's a love story.' Under the table, she ran her toes up his calf. He looked at her. Christ, she was just . . .

Paige went to the bathroom and Kennedy pulled his chair closer to Spengler. 'She's something, huh?' Spengler said. 'You sly old dog. First Julie, and I do want details there, my friend, now –'

'Shurrup, listen, you're a rich American, you're into doctors and stuff, can I ask you something?'

'Fire away, pal.'

'I've got this . . . on my . . . it's . . . feck.' Glancing towards the bathroom, speaking sotto voce, he got it out in the end.

'Christ, get that checked out, you maniac.' Spengler took out his BlackBerry and started scrolling through. 'You

English. Get to sixty before you have a prostate exam. Goddamn suicidal. Here, I'm texting you the number of my guy in Harley Street.'

'Ach, I don't really hold with private medicine.'

'Fine. Why don't you queue up at your socialist utopia clinic for a few months while your prick falls off?'

'Christ. Is he any good this fella?

'Dr Beaufort? He's the best. Fixed me up right after a . . . thing on location a few years back.'

'Yeah, yeah, everything's "the best" with you.'

'I'm telling you, Kennedy. This guy's old school but he's the best dick doctor in London. He ought to be, the sonofabitch costs enough. But I don't want you worrying about that. The bill will come straight to me.'

'Oh no, I can –'

'Enough. My treat. Ease your conscience about betraying your beloved NHS.'

'Some treat.'

Later, that night, in bed, in a room at Dean Street Townhouse, after the drinks and the dinner, basking in the afterglow, he nearly said something to Paige, something he hadn't said in many years. But he didn't, he just said, 'Do you fancy something from room service?'

FORTY–TWO

'I haven't even thought about it really.'

'You'll need to start thinking about it pretty soon, Robin . . .'

'Yeah, I know.'

They were in the main dining room at Le Manoir, discussing Robin's university options. Father and daughter, finally breaking bread. Keith was in the car park, stretched back in the driver's seat of the Mercedes with one of the thrillers he favoured, waiting to take them back up the motorway. ('For Christ's sake,' Millie had said, 'do you really *need* to go to Le bloody Manoir? She'd be just as happy at Pizza Express on Deeping High Street.' '"O reason not the need",' Kennedy countered automatically.)

'You must have some idea of what you want to do?'

'Must I? I'm not the only one. Clarissa and Mattie are talking about . . .'

Right enough, he thought as she talked on. As soon as he'd said the words Kennedy realised what an utter pile of old balls they were. Who the fuck knew what they wanted to do at sixteen or seventeen? Well, Kennedy had, true, but he was, as we have seen, abnormal. He remembered consciously using the word 'suddenly' in a story for the first time, when he was around seven or eight years old. The rush. Like kicking a door open. All Chandler's men coming in, with their guns drawn.

Three kinds of people in the world, Hanif Kureishi said. *Those who didn't know where they were going and never got there, those who didn't know at first but found it along the way, and those who knew from Day One what they were going to do.* This had been Kennedy. And he'd just got on with it, to the exclusion of pretty much everything. 'The house could burn down,' Millie said to him once, long ago, 'and you'd come staggering out with that computer before you thought about me or the baby.'

He realised Robin had finished and was looking to him for some kind of response. 'Uh. Yeah. Fair point,' Kennedy said.

'Christ.' She smiled and shook her head.

'What?' he said, refilling their glasses. One of the great civilised pleasures of Europe this, Kennedy thought. Having a glass of wine with your kid aged between sixteen and twenty-one. You just try that shit back in California and see what happens. (Kennedy *had* tried it. He thought the maître d' was going to call in a SWAT team. An air strike.)

'Dad,' Robin said, 'you ask a question and have no interest in the answer. Why bother?'

Kennedy sighed. 'I've been a terrible father, haven't I?' Robin held her hand out horizontally and wavered it, signifying fifty–fifty. They laughed. 'At the same time, though, you seem OK, Robin. You seem happy enough.'

'Yeah. I suppose so. I mean, compared to some of my friends . . .'

'Me and your mum splitting up doesn't seem to have fucked you up too much.'

Man hands on misery to man, it deepens like a coastal shelf. Get out as early as you can, and don't have any kids yourself. Gerry.

'I don't really remember you being together. It was more,' Robin said, thinking, chewing, 'more, like,' she held a finger up, acknowledging the error, warding off his automatic admonishment for the slack, punctuating use of 'like', 'sometimes when I went to one of my friend's houses and they'd have both their parents there and everyone would be sitting down to dinner together. Sometimes I thought . . . I just thought it would have been nice to have had that.'

'You must have hated me.'

'I never hated you, Dad. I just, you know. I *missed* you.'

It took a few seconds for the potency of these words to break through the excellent Beaujolais and fully penetrate the heart of Kennedy Marr. (The Heart of Kennedy Marr. O frosted chamber! Shamed pump! Terrible ventricle!)

Ach. What had he done here? In breaking love for himself had he dented, *dinged* it, for the person whom, more than any, he should have been demonstrating its primacy to? The pain endemic to the children of the divorcee: the longing to fix the sundering. Would Robin grow up finding it difficult to love? To trust the monster? Or would she love too easily? Or would none of it matter?

Waiters floated silently through the hushed food temple. A cork creaked then popped out of a bottle nearby.

My children are the most important thing in my life.

Well, it was easy to imagine how trying to say this aphorism with a straight face might go for Kennedy: a reel of out-takes. An *It'll Be Alright on the Night* special of corpsing and fluffed lines and 'CUT!' Sitting in a room and making stuff up had been the most important thing for him. (*'Players and painted stage took all my love, and not those things that they were emblems of.'*)

'Oh, don't look so sad,' Robin said. 'It's all right. I didn't miss you *that* much.'

They laughed and he was conscious of how agreeable it was being with Robin, laughing with her. He should have done more of this. Much more. *What can I say? — you missed it, Kennedy.* He sensed the regret queuing up, taking its place in the colossal line in his head, and thought of the old 'Labour's Not Working' poster from the late seventies, of his pain schedule, becoming ever more hectic.

FORTY-THREE

He approached the doors to the ward and realised that once he opened them there would be no going back. A nurse, or Patrick, would see him and hail him and usher him into his mother's presence and that would be that. And, for a moment, the urge to turn on his heel and run was overpowering. Just get the hell out of there, drive back into Dublin and check into the Shelbourne or the Clarence and attack the minibar. Or straight to the airport and back to Heathrow, or even to Shannon and a flight to New York and then on to LA.

If he did not go, she would not die. But here he was. Feel the fear and do it anyway and all that bollocks. He pushed open the doors and went on to the ward.

The hospital smell: death muffled by the anaesthetic fug of disinfectant and drugs. The second time in the last twenty-four hours he'd experienced it. That morning, en route to Heathrow from Soho, he'd stopped off at Harley Street to see Spengler's Dr Beaufort. A ruddy-faced pensioner with hair the colour of ash. An ashtray on the desk too. This *was* old school. He'd copped a feel of Kennedy's johnson, given him a tiny local, and then jabbed a needle in to get a sample of the growth, which had, as its name implied, kept right on growing, moving from petit pois to most definitely pois. 'I wouldn't worry too much if I were you,' Beaufort said. 'Most likely a cyst. I'll give you a call and set up another appointment when I get the results back. Should only be a week or so.'

Kennedy moved on down the ward. 'Palliative care' they called it. Most people took it to mean alleviating, managing and softening the pain of those on a one-way road. Kennedy, a great lover of the dictionary – *'the democratic history of the human mind'* – whose battered red *Chambers* was never far from his side, knew the further layer, the older, obsolete meaning of 'palliate': to cloak, to *disguise*. Walking this long ward, he wondered why that usage had fallen out of favour. For it looked to be snugly apt. The drowsing skeletons lining the walls: pumped full of morphine to cloak, to shield the world – to shield the family members gathered round most of the beds, talking quietly to one another – from the awful, immutable truth. *Lay ya ten to one, lay ya one to five, no one here gets out alive.*

No one. Fuck a thousand women and make a billion quid? Fuck you – die. Live a life of celibacy and charity? Fuck you – die. Conquer the known world? Fuck you. Lie on the sofa eating pizza and bagel chips in front of chat shows for forty years? Die. Help old ladies across the road? Die. Bugger kids? Same door pal. And so on.

Some of the patients just stared straight ahead while their families talked over them. Rheumy eyes, eyes flecked with shards of crimson, looking into the mid-distance, for the tip of the scythe coming over the brow of the hill no doubt, the faceless black cowl beneath it.

Actually, when Kennedy did picture the Reaper, he never thought of him this way. He usually formed the image of a bright and cheerful – but ruthlessly efficient – administrator. 'Ah, hello there. Come this way please.'

'Really? There must have been some mistake.'

'Ha ha. Yes, very good.'

Passing on his right now the most dreadful sight of all: a man completely alone in his bed at peak visiting time. In his seventies maybe, this shallowly breathing cadaver. This guy who had, once upon a time, most likely been everything to someone caught Kennedy's eye. Kennedy nodded, attempting a benevolent smile. The man just stared back, his head turning slowly to watch Kennedy as he passed by, reeking of life. *Oh, you poor bastard*, Kennedy thought. *What have you done?* How strenuously had this fucker offended love? What had he done to it that he was here – teetering on the precipice without so much as a grape, or a bottle of Lucozade, or a chattering pensioner as backup?

Intellectually speaking Kennedy knew that on the one hand he was that most awful, dread cliché: the middle-aged novelist trying to come to terms with his own mortality. The value of all this self-awareness in the face of the grave? Precisely zero. Yeah – because that'd fix it, huh? 'Hey, grave? I am perfectly aware that the cradle rocks over an abyss and all that. So I'm fine. Thanks.'

You heard people saying it. You did hear it here and there. *'Well, we've all got to go sometime.' 'Everybody dies.'* Kennedy generally assumed the people speaking these words were either a) fifteen years old, or b) mentally retarded. Everybody dies? Who the fuck were they talking about? *'Listen,'* he wanted to scream in their faces, *'they weren't kidding. It's real, you fucking idiots. This is a real thing!'* Christ, he wished he'd managed to pound another Scotch on the flight, or grabbed a half-bottle somewhere on the way here.

Approaching the end of the ward now, composing his features into an expression of surprised cheerfulness, he could see Patrick sitting on a chair at the end of a bed, Patrick raising his hand as he saw Kennedy, Kennedy returning the gesture. The point of no return . . .

He stepped around the curtain and there she was, turning to see him, her face already lighting up as she said, 'Son . . .'

His first thought was – *she's no different.* The hair was a little greyer, the face more lined, the cheeks a little more hollow, but really . . .

But no. She was holding a hand out towards him. The arm was a pipe cleaner, a winter twig, the veins and arteries bulging out, blue through white. They'd gone from being wiring to being ropes to being piping. *Ropes. Gerry. Good ropes.* Saying 'Ma . . .' now as he embraced her and very nearly gasped, quickly softening his grip lest she powder to dust in his hand. It was like you'd gone to pick up a set of golf clubs, preparing yourself for the weight, and found the bag empty. 'Jeez, Ma,' trying to recover, going for levity, 'we're needing to get a good dinner in you.' *Oh Christ, the state of her. The guilt, the incredible guilt.*

'Very funny now.'

'Patrick,' he said, coming round the bed, embracing him, Patrick looking older too. No grey in his hair yet, but some in his stubble, those pouches beneath the eyes. 'I'm so sorry,' he whispered in his brother's ear.

'Ach, sure you're here now, aren't you?' Patrick, seeming genuinely pleased to see him, despite everything, as Kennedy pulled a plastic chair up beside the bed. What had he ever done to earn the love of these people, given the way he treated them?

'And how's the wee one?' Ma asked him.

'Robin? She's grand, Ma.'

'Mind – not the wee one any more, eh? She'll be a young woman now.'

'Aye. More like her mother every day.'

'Oh, you're in there too. Don't you worry about that. How's Millie?'

'Grand.'

'You know they came to visit me back in the summer there? They were on their way down to the west coast for a few days.'

'She told me. So then, how are you feeling?'

'Wee bit t—' she went to prop herself up on the pillows and winced.

'Ma?'

'I'm fine. Fine now. Just a wee bit tired.' The noise of the ward, the low rumble of conversation, the comings and goings, the clatter of a Formica tray being dropped somewhere.

'Christ, it can't be easy to sleep in here, Ma.' Kennedy said. 'Can we not get you moved to a private room or something?' He looked at Patrick. 'Or to an—'

'And what would I do in a private room now? Sit and look at the four walls? At least there's a wee bit of life in here. Had a nice lady in that bed across there until last week. Rosie. But that's her away . . .' They let it hang there. 'Anyway now, how've you been? Are you enjoying being back over?'

'Aye, it's fine. Busy, Ma. You know.'

'How's that new film of yours going? The one with that pretty wee thing in it?'

He thought of Julie Teal. Of the cleft apple of her oiled backside glistening below him. 'It's fine, Ma. Well, it's a royal pain in the arse is what it is, but it's fine.'

'Is she hard work then?' Patrick asked.

'You could say that . . .'

'You're getting paid though, son, aren't ye?' Ma.

He laughed. 'Aye, Ma. We're getting paid right enough.'

'Oh good.'

'And how are we enjoying teaching?' Patrick asked with just the trace of a smile.

'It's . . .' Kennedy spread his hands.

FORTY—FOUR

The last time he'd found himself at the foot of a hospital bed like this.

Geraldine.

She'd done it in the flat and – incredibly – a neighbour, Eddie, had found her after only a few minutes. He'd been a customer, come to try and buy some hash. Kennedy had met him later, a stooped, grizzled, yellow-skinned man with a mouth full of broken, discoloured teeth, like a bag of mixed walnuts and raisins. Kennedy had taken him for being around fifty. He'd been shocked when he'd read the man's witness statement later and discovered they were the same age at the time – thirty-four.

Eddie had cut her down and called the ambulance. They'd performed CPR and defibrillation at the scene and managed to restart her heart before taking her to the hospital. Kennedy got the call around 7 a.m., the call part of him had been expecting for nearly twenty years, someone from Brighton A&E, saying, 'It's about Geraldine Marr.'

Oh, Gerry – what have you done now?

He'd collected Ma and Patrick at Heathrow and they'd driven down to Brighton together. Kennedy knew the town well – assignations, weekends. Fucking. He took rooms at the Grand for the three of them. '*In the name of the Lord, Kennedy,*' Patrick said. '*It's lovely and all but is there any need for all this now? Sure, could we not just find a B&B?*' Ma would normally have said something like this too, but she wasn't saying anything then. Wasn't noticing anything. She wouldn't be for a while. But *Unthinkable* was well over the million mark in paperback, his third novel out and doing well too. Film rights optioned for all of them. The Grand it would be.

At the hospital, his mother weeping as she rocked gently back and forth. Gerry was a mess – her arms a latticework of cuts and slashes, tiger stripes all down them from the Stanley knife she just didn't have the courage to press down deeply enough. The crooks of her elbows bruised and mottled with track marks, her hands bruised and cut, the knuckles swollen – forever punching walls, windows, people. The damage she'd wrought on her body in her short life, like it could barely contain the rage within her. Tubes feeding her through these arms and nose and the steady rasp of the ventilator as it breathed for her for three days while tests were run, sent off, analysed.

On the third day, leaving Ma at the bedside, Kennedy and Patrick went into a side room (some kind of family room, a sofa, plastic flowers in a vase, making Kennedy think of that pastel seagull poster, of institutional attempts at kindness) with the head doctor. 'We're intelligent people,' Kennedy had told him. 'Please, be straight with us.'

Gerry's brain had been deprived of oxygen for somewhere between five and fifteen minutes. He produced X-rays, milky white on translucent blue, showing a cross section of their sister's brain. She'd basically succeeded in effecting a massive stroke. The neurologist indicated the affected areas with the tip of a silver pen. All of the upper brain function had been wiped out: memory, speech and mobility, all gone. If she did somehow regain consciousness she'd be a husk. There would simply be nothing left of the person they'd known. It would be blinking and liquidised food. Kennedy and Patrick had looked at each other and almost laughed – it was so like Gerry, to somehow not only fail at the simplest task but to fail in the grandest, most outré manner. To have it conclude in the worst possible way for everyone around her, to cause the maximum amount of grief.

The three of them went for a walk on the pier. It was a freakishly stunning day – windless, the blue of the sky unbroken by a single cloud. Patrick and Kennedy laid it out for Ma on a bench overlooking the sea, the cartoon music and jangle of the arcades incongruous behind them. Ma looked at the water, quietly taking it all in. 'No,' she said finally, shaking her head and saying quietly but fiercely, 'Gerry wouldn't want to live like that.'

The doctor suggested, in the gentlest way possible, that they could turn off the ventilator and see how she managed to breathe on her own. One possible outcome would be that her lungs would fill with fluid and she would be unable to clear them herself. She would basically drown without ever regaining consciousness. However, he warned, this could take days, even weeks or months. They agreed. Signed the necessary forms. *Months?* Kennedy had wondered as they walked towards the cafeteria for coffee, to give the ICU staff a chance to do the things they had to do with the tubes and machinery. He acknowledged within himself that he now wanted his little sister to die and felt no shame about it. He had failed Gerry in life. Not now. In the end they hadn't even got as far as ordering their coffee when one of the nurses came rushing in to get them. 'She started crashing the minute we took her off.' Gerry's lungs – desiccated. Flyblown from nearly two decades of skunk and cheap cigarettes. Mayfair. Kensitas Club. Berkeley.

Gathered round with the curtains drawn, the three of them watched her die. The awful sounds she made as she slowly drowned in her own saliva: great honking, rattling breaths, like the worst snoring you ever heard. Ma held her right hand and Patrick the left. Kennedy stood at the foot of the bed. The pale blue digital numbers giving pulse, heart rate and so forth gradually winding their way down-wards towards zero as the terrible rasping breathing increased in volume and intensity. Patrick cried softly, his head inclined, while Ma spoke to Gerry through her own tears. *'Oh my wee girl,'* she said. *'My poor wee girl.'* And she said, *'What have ye done to yourself now?'* *'You were my beautiful wee girl.'* *'I let you down.'* And, over and over again, Ma said: *'I'm sorry. I'm sorry. I'm sorry.'*

It took quite a while, over twenty minutes by Kennedy's watch, but finally there were no more honking breaths and all the numbers read zero and she was gone. Kennedy walked to the head of the bed and kissed his little sister's forehead for the last time. (*'My big brother'll get ye. Kennedy'll batter ye.'*) It was surprisingly warm, almost sweating. He leaned into her ear and whispered, 'I could have done more for you. Goodbye, Gerry.'

A few minutes later, while his mother and Patrick were hugging each other and crying, Kennedy excused himself and went to the bathroom. Dry-eyed he sat on the toilet with his little black Moleskine notebook and wrote it all up: the angle of the light across the bed from the horizontal window above them. The colour of those digital numbers. The exact words his mother had used. Existence was the job after all.

He only cried once during the whole time, when he had to go to the flat, to retrieve what belongings Gerry had. It struck him how cold the place was. Even though it was daytime and sunlight was streaming through the blinds the place was almost icy. The electricity system seemed to work by some sort of purple plastic key that one preloaded at the newsagent's. Gerry clearly hadn't been in a position to load money onto the key for some time and he found himself wondering if she'd been sleeping fully clothed, wrapped in a sweater and a couple of fleeces in bed. Or on the sofa watching TV. No, wait, no electricity. He saw the stubs of a couple of candles down there by the fireplace. He pictured her reading by candlelight, wrapped up in a duvet on the sofa, fingerless gloves on, her breath misting in front of her. Maybe even reading one of his books.

There, on the little dining table in the living room, had been the heartbreaking pile: the sad drift of brown envelopes with their hellish contents: *'IF YOU DO NOT PAY BY . . .' 'IF YOU ARE UNABLE TO . . .' 'FINAL REMINDER . . .' 'PLEASE CONTACT US IMMEDIATELY'*. The rent arrears, the maxed-out credit cards, the overdraft, the gas and electricity bills.

(And how much of this was archetypal in the tableaux of suicide? he wondered. That drift of mail surely featured. If you were to write it into a scene that would be all you'd need. No dialogue, just a slow pan over those envelopes, a glimpse of their contents, before ending on the person climbing the stepladder, or putting the gun under their chin.) There was nothing nice in his sister's mail, no pleasant surprises. No invitations to openings and launches. No unexpected pale green WGA envelopes with five- and six-figure residuals cheques. No bubble-wrap-encased novels for her consideration. It was simply a one-way torture system. There were the signs of other, less official debts around the flat too. Other signifiers: the scuff marks on her front door, the hole where a boot had clearly gone through it. The blades in her bedside drawer. There had been all of this in her flat back in Limerick too, Kennedy remembered. Gerry – her incredible talent for attracting chaos, finding mayhem. (*Finding Mayhem* would, it occurred to him, make a pretty good title for a certain kind of book.)

He walked through to her bedroom and sat down on the floor. His breath had misted in front of him as he looked up at the ceiling and wondered how many nights she'd lain here, adding up the bills, going over them, wondering if she borrowed X off Kennedy and Y off Ma and whatever off Patrick could she keep the wheels on the wagon for another month? The mad scramble every month to somehow make it work. The bullshit and lies required. The mad plans and schemes and deals, everything half-baked, quarter-baked. Raw. He sat at the table and totted it all up.

She'd taken her life for twelve thousand pounds.

He could have written a cheque there and then for all

of it. He went over the dinners he'd picked up, the cabs, the holidays, the spectacular bar tabs, the clothes, the club fees, the cigars, the drunken impulse buys on eBay, the movies and music downloaded, thirty, fifty quid here and there without thinking. The rounds of complex, expensive cocktails he'd stood near-strangers, the bottles of champagne ordered in bars and restaurants on the flimsiest of pretexts – because it was Friday. Because of the unexpected Turkish translation sale. Because of . . . oh, who gave a fuck? Because he could. He felt like he was going mad for a moment. He felt like Schindler, at the end, crying and stumbling around outside the factory, *'This ring, five lives, this car . . .'*

He covered his face as the tears finally came. 'Oh, Gerry. Oh, you stupid bitch. Why didn't you . . .' Kennedy wept, crumpled up on the cheap laminate flooring in his sister's cheap, rented flat.

It would have to wait, would have to distil down through him before eventually being purified enough for a novel. In much the same way that it took three tons of rose petals to make a litre of rose oil, Kennedy knew that it took a lot of pain, a lot of experience, to make three or four hundred pages of fiction.

FORTY-FIVE

'Go on now, Patrick,' his ma was saying. 'I've seen your face every day. Go and get yourself some coffee or something and give me some time to catch up with your brother here.'

'OK, Ma.' Patrick got up and pulled his overcoat off the back of the chair. 'Are you wanting anything from the shop?'

'Ach, no. I'm grand. Oh – maybe some of those wee sweeties I like. You know the ones.'

They watched him leave. Kennedy said, 'He's a good man, Patrick.'

'He is that. Do anything for you. Unlike some others I could mention,' she added, a hint of a smile on her lips. Kennedy nodded, taking it. 'Here now, pull your chair up here so I don't have to bloody shout.' Kennedy moved up to the head of the bed, beside her. Up close her face was white and crenellated. Like the surface of the moon. Her hair too. She'd stopped dyeing it a few years back. In her youth it had been almost identical to his – a thick, unruly black mop. Her eyes were shining brightly though. (Perhaps the drugs, the morphine. Or something more metaphysical? Dying stars, shining their brightest just at the point of extinction.) He could see the veins in his mother's hollow temples almost as clearly as if they were outside the skin and he thought of the Lloyds building in London. (*Oh, mind – when will you be done with all this? With all your writer-y schtick? When will you just let me be?*)

'You know what I'd really like, Kennedy?' she said once they were settled closer together. 'Now that I can smell those cigarettes on you –'

'Christ, Ma, is this the deathbed scene where you make me promise to stop smoking?'

'Pfft! Like I can make you do anything. Sure you've known it all since you were five years old. No, I quite fancy one myself to tell you the truth.'

'You haven't smoked in twenty years.'

'And you think you know everything I've been up to?'

He laughed and looked along the ward, at the milling groups of nurses, at a doctor reading a chart at the foot of a bed. A cleaner on a stepladder was hanging Christmas decorations, silver tinsel and green and red swathes of crepe paper. 'I think that might be difficult to pull off in the present circumstances, Ma.'

'Ach, what difference would it make now?'

He looked at her, began to say something.

'Wheesht now,' his ma said. 'Let's talk about you. I hear you've been in a bit of bother.'

'Ah . . .'

'Ha! Don't think I don't hear things in here. Gallivanting in the papers with that wee actress? Fighting on a plane?

The temper on you, boy. Just like your father, God rest his soul.'

Like Gerry, Kennedy thought.

He looked up – at the simple wicker cross she had pinned to the wall beside her bed. The wooden rosary beads coiled beside her water jug on the cabinet. He knew his ma believed she would be seeing her husband again soon. Finding him somewhere in that great parkland teeming with every soul that had ever lived and repented. Would Geraldine be there too? Suicides: banned from the kingdom of Heaven. Despite her beliefs would Ma's heart make an amendment to allow this? And would Gerry be strangely altered in this new place? Somehow unscarred? At peace? She caught his gaze and, from it, his train of thought. 'And don't you go starting in about Our Lord now, you hear? Or I'll have you thrown out of here on your ear. I know very well your thoughts on that subject.'

'The stuff in the papers . . . it's all just a bunch of nonsense, Ma.'

'Don't you kid a kidder now.'

'Well, mostly nonsense.'

A pause. His ma rearranging her features, signalling a change to tone, of topic. 'You'll need to be there for your brother now. He's going to take this awful sore.'

'How do you think I'm going to take it?'

'Pfft! Be more meat for the grinder! Something to go in that wee notebook that's in your pocket there.'

'Ma! I –'

'Kennedy, listen to me now.' She reached out and took his hand. He folded both of them over hers, tiny and warm between his palms, a little bird. 'You have many fine qualities, but caring for others is not among them. That was always Patrick's job.'

'I was thinking about Gerry the other day. About Kilkee. Holidays down there, at the caravan park in the summer.'

'Happy times,' she said.

'Ma, do you remember, one time Granny was drunk and there was an argument about something, something Gerry had done. She'd been bad. And Granny said something to us, to me and her, we were in the bedroom. Playing on the bed. She shouted at Gerry. I just can't remember . . .'

His ma closed her eyes and breathed in. 'She said that you were "a good boy", but that Gerry . . . Gerry was "a bad wee stick".' That's right. That had been it. Gerry – barely five and hearing this. 'She was a wicked old devil with drink taken, your father's mother.'

'Ma? Do you think part of Gerry just thought, *Well I'll show you all. I'll be the baddest stick I can be*"?

She was quiet for a long time, looking sadly into the middle distance, looking down the gunsight of the past. 'There isn't a day goes by I don't wonder what happened to my wee girl to make her the way she was. Not a day. I thought I brought you all up just the same. But something . . . something must have happened. I failed her in some way. There was just . . . that much *rage* inside her. "Could start a fight in an empty house," your father used to say. Remember? I failed her. Patrick too. I failed them both . . .'

'How?'

She turned and looked at him. 'By loving you too much, son.'

'Ma, don't s—'

'Shhh now. I'll be dead soon, I get to say what I want. With you, Kennedy, it was . . . the minute they put you in my arms, I looked in your eyes and it was like we knew each other. Really *knew* each other already. Like we . . . like we'd known each other before. I can't explain it. It was the oddest thing. I could see your whole life for you and I knew you were going to do something different, something amazing. The way you used to cry when you were tiny, you used to *howl*. It was like the world wasn't lined up the right way for you and you were just going to scream the place down until you fixed it.'

The world wasn't lined up the right way for you.

It struck Kennedy that this was a pretty good definition of why one wrote. Someone got here before you and made the rules and this would not stand. *Fuck them.* Chaos and insanity could be shaped into narrative and, as the castle of cards became a castle of 'beautiful glass and steel', as the 'disparity between the conscious and unconscious mind' was eased, for a short time, between the covers, from page 1 to wherever, the world could be made to march to your tune. Sometimes it felt like that was what he'd been doing for twenty years – screaming the place down. Howling. But you couldn't fix it. Art might respond to the screaming but life just shrugged and went about its business.

'The world wasn't lined up the right way for Gerry either.' He was saying this through tears now, his head dropping, his shoulders shaking, his hand going to his face, his face wet as his ma pulled his head to her side, gathering him to her like she had done so many times when he was young.

'But she'd nothing to say about it, son. She just wanted to blot it out.'

313

Three pounds forty-four pence.
Sign here.
The crusted saliva on the front of her sweater.
Would she have seen seagulls from the window?
'Bye-bye, stinky Kenny. Bye-bye.'
A bad wee stick.
'There, son, that's OK. You cry now.'

Kennedy clung to his mother as he wept. *The guilt – oh dear God, the incredible, chest-caving guilt.* The things he'd done to this woman who'd borne him. The calls he hadn't answered. The letters he hadn't replied to. The visits he'd put off and then cut to the shortest possible time. Because he was busy, busy, busy. All the hours he didn't spend with her. The way he'd mocked her simple beliefs and expressions as soon as he was old enough to think he knew better. *You wanted me to have all the learning you never had and I used it to put distance between us, running away as soon as I could and never looking back: Glasgow, London, Los Angeles, further, always further away. You filled me with the confidence to think I could do anything I wanted and, Christ, I did all that and more. I did anything I wanted and all the stuff I didn't want to as well. Can't we turn the clock back, just by a few minutes? I'll take you for that wee drive to the seaside. Out to dinner. A weekend away together. Like the time we went up to Dublin for your birthday and I took you on a horse-drawn carriage ride around the Green, like you'd always wanted to. The way you cooed when the waiter in the Clarence gave you the bread with tongs and all I could do was laugh at your innocence. And I was the apple of your eye, your firstborn, and I should have done better by you and now it's all over and, no, you can't turn the clock back, not even by one second. I was everything to you and I turned my back on you so quickly. I'm sorry, I'm so sorry, Mum. I loved you almost as much as you made me love myself. Quite a thing that. How did you manage it?*

Poor selfish Kennedy, unfaithful son. Poor, poor Kennedy.

'You have a good cry,' his ma said, stroking his hair, blissing out on its perfume as only a mother smelling their child's hair for the last time can.

FORTY-SIX

Crying, Kennedy thought – a couple of hours later, as he finished buttering a second roll and began folding a layer of smoked salmon on top – now this was an activity very much underrated. *This was some good shit.*

He was ravenous. Felt like he'd slept for ten hours having had three orgasms. He stopped a passing waiter. 'Excuse me, could we also have an order of the creamed sweetcorn please?'

'*"Also"? "An order of"?*' Patrick said.

'Sorry. Fucking LA.'

They'd said their goodbyes to Ma, Kennedy promising to come back again the following week, meaning it too, and were having late lunch, in Shanahan's on St Stephen's Green. A great table, right up in the picture window of the big Georgian dining room, overlooking the Green. A foul afternoon outside, the dark blue sky seeming to press right against the glass, staining it like the reservoir of a fountain pen washed with Indian ink. She'd said other things to him too, before Patrick came back. Before they left. Final things.

'*Fifty euros for a steak?*' Patrick had gasped, before desperately scanning the menu for something cheaper. Kennedy had overruled – they were both having the 12oz filet mignon. An excellent bottle of burgundy – a 2001 Chassagne-Montrachet – stood in the middle of the table, half of it already in Kennedy's veins. Patrick still had the same three inches he'd been poured twenty minutes ago.

'You have no idea how to *lunch* properly, Patrick,' Kennedy said.

'I never have lunch.'

'What do you mean?'

'I. Don't. Have. Lunch.'

'Jesus.'

'Anyway, this isn't lunch. This is a freak show. This is a fiftieth wedding anniversary. A graduation meal. I mean, who spends two hundred euros on *lunch*, Kennedy?'

Kennedy wiped his mouth and looked at his baby brother, uncomfortable here among the well-heeled Dubliners and wealthy American tourists who'd deigned to wander out of the Shelbourne over on the north side of the Green.

'Living well is the best revenge, Patrick.' Christ, how much he hated death. And how fiercely he ran to embrace its foes: wine, food and company. Love. Life.

The food came – Patrick's steak medium (naturally Kennedy's eyes had tilted upwards to the eighteenth-century cornicing during the ordering of this atrocity), Kennedy's blood rare. Potatoes whipped with butter and flecked with tiny green chives. The emerald spinach in its little copper pot, oozing butter too, studded with nubs of bacon.

'So, how are Anne and the kids?' Kennedy asked.

'They're grand. You should come out and see them.'

'I will, I will. Sorry, I've got to get back tonight though. I'll come to the house next week. Maybe for New Year too. The film will have wrapped by then. The university's gonna be on holiday . . .'

'What are you doing for Christmas?'

'Thought I'd go back home for a couple of weeks.'

'Home?'

'LA.'

'It's home now, is it?'

'I guess so.' Kennedy refilled his glass. Patrick accepted a tiny splash.

'You didn't think about spending it with Millie and Robin? Seeing as you're over and all . . .'

'Ach. They've got their own thing going on. She's nearly seventeen now. We'd probably see her at dinner for a couple of hours and then she'd be off with her mates. So . . .' He tailed off. Patrick nodded. Kennedy swirled his wine in the huge balloon, looking into the ruby vortex. After a moment he asked, 'What's it like, Patrick?'

'Eh?'

'Being with the same person for that long? What is it now – seventeen years you and Anne? Having your family around you all the time?' Patrick laughed. 'What?' Kennedy said.

'Sorry. Just your tone of voice. You'd think you were probing one of mankind's greatest secrets. It's how most people live, Kennedy – they meet someone, they settle down, have kids . . .'

'But how do you make it through all those years together? All the changes, all the –'

'Changes? What changes? You get up, you go to work, pay the bills, and the kids just grow up around you like little plants. You know your problem?' What was it with people and this? Some days it felt like he might open the curtains to see a queue of people stretching round the block, waiting outside the house for their turn to tell him what his problem was. Taking numbers from one of those machines you get at the deli counter. 'Too much time to think about yourself.'

'Well, better an unhappy Socrates than a happy pig and all that, Patrick.'

'Yeah? How's that working out for you?'

Kennedy smiled. 'Touché.'

'I mean, it seems easier to me than the way you live.'

'How do I live?'

Patrick twirled a hand, gesturing around at the restaurant, the meal, the wine. 'Your life just doesn't seem that real, Kennedy. Flying here then there. Got to eat there. It's – do you want me to be honest?'

'Just say what you're going to say.'

'While it looks quite glamorous I imagine it's just a bit . . . empty.'

'Oh yeah. It's empty all right,' Kennedy said, nonchalant, draining his glass, picking up the bottle again. Patrick put a hand over his glass. 'Oh, come on,' Kennedy said. 'How often do we get the chance to sit and have a drink? What kind of fucking Irishman are you?'

'One that's due back at the office.'

'For what?' Kennedy looked at his watch. 'Two hours? Take the rest of the afternoon off. My flight back isn't till eight.'

'I can't, Kennedy. A case I'm working on. I need –'

'Can it be that important? I'm missing a rough assembly screening to be here, you know.'

Patrick smiled and leaned forward, elbows on the table. 'Here's the thing, Kennedy. The other week, it was the day you rang to say you couldn't get over actually, maybe why I was a wee bit short with you, anyway, I had to attend the post-mortem of a lad. He was on the register of kids we were watching but, as it turned out, maybe not as high up as he should have been. What had happened was the boy had run into the living room – just playing, you know? – and booted his daddy's bottle of vodka over. This is eleven o'clock in the morning, mind. Your man sees the bottle go over on its side and empty onto the carpet. So he sets about the lad with the old fists. Smashes his head off the wall until he loses consciousness. The skull was fractured so badly the doctor thought he'd been hit by a car. He died in the ICU later that night.'

Kennedy stared at the tablecloth.

'Now, this was a kid who no one in the department had recommended be taken into care, basically because there just aren't the resources for the amount of visits we'd need to make to say with any authority that we had to intervene. But we'd another surprise still to come. The pathologist turned this lad over – six years old he was now, Kennedy – and his,' Patrick laughed a dreadful, mirthless laugh, 'his backside had been split open. Turned out Daddy had been raping him too.'

Kennedy shut his eyes. He wanted to stuff his fists in his ears.

'Now I've got to go back to the office where we're going

through all the casework for the last couple of years to try and justify why no one picked up on any of the sexual abuse. But, you know, I appreciate the sacrifice of you missing your screening thingy.'

Silence for a moment.

'I'm sorry, Patrick.'

'Ach. No – I'm sorry. I shouldn't have . . . bad day at Black Rock and all that. Anyway, I'd better be going. Thanks for lunch. It was a real treat. Oh – here.' He slid something across the table as he stood up. 'I was going to mail this, but I thought I'd be seeing you sooner . . .'

Kennedy looked at the piece of paper, his vision starting to swim a little. A cheque, printed in Patrick's proud block caps, like their dad's. 'What's this?'

'Five grand. It's about the rest of what I owe you for the loan for the extension.'

'Oh Christ. Just keep it, Patrick.'

'No. We're square now.'

'Patrick, honestly. Have a holiday. Put it towards a new car or something. Take Anne to –'

'I want to pay you back.'

'I don't want it.'

Patrick sighed. 'Look, Kennedy, just take the fucking cheque, OK?'

'Christ, there's no need to, shit, OK.'

He folded the cheque, stuffed it into the breast pocket of his suit, and stood up. The two of them embraced, Kennedy feeling the acrylic rub of Patrick's collar against his cheek. He stood back and looked at his brother, holding him at arm's length. 'Do you think about Gerry much?'

'I do. Often.'

'I keep thinking we could have, I could have . . . ach.'

'She was an alcoholic and a drug addict, Kennedy. The mortality rate pre-forty is off the charts.'

Kennedy nodded, his hands still on his brother's shoulders. He pulled away a loose thread. Brushed off some dandruff. 'You could at least keep the money and buy yourself a decent suit.'

Patrick laughed. 'I've got two suits. What the hell would I do with a third one?'

Kennedy hugged him again. 'See you next week, OK?'

'Sure. Take care of yourself, Kennedy. And good luck with the film. Safe flight back, OK?'

The waiter appeared as Patrick left. 'Would you like to see the dessert menu, sir?'

'Tell you what – could you just bring me a large Armagnac please?'

'Of course.'

He looked out the window as the street lights started to come on, the Green beginning to disappear into the night. St Stephen's Green – in Kennedy's view the single most valuable piece of real estate in twentieth-century literature: twenty-odd acres of city-centre parkland that every novelist now working owed an unknowable debt to.

It had been right there, across the street from where he sat now, on the night of 22 June 1904, that James Joyce had been involved in a 'scuffle'. A rumble. A barney. The old pumpatron – well, not so old then, just twenty-two. Twenty-two on the 22nd. So neat – already after Nora, but not yet having sealed the deal, tried to pull some chick, unaware that her boyfriend was tooling along nearby.

Boyfriend turned out to be a bit handy too and James took his lumps: 'black eye, sprained wrist, sprained ankle, cut hand, cut chin'. A man came to Joyce's aid. A middle-aged Jewish fellow called Albert H. Hunter. (And Kennedy often wondered about the shame his countryman would have felt about this. Battered in public then some auld fella coming in with the handers? Jaysuss.) Hunter saw Joyce home. Along the way Joyce learned that the fellow had an adulterous wife.

Hunter became Leopold Bloom.

He looked down. The Armagnac had been placed noise-lessly at his elbow. He held the glass to his face and let the fumes tear his eyes.

So, out of that scuffle, nearly fifteen years later (a lot of time for experience to distil down through you, all those litres of rose oil), you got *Ulysses*: a 700-page fast-forward button for the novel. And here we were today, still playing catch-up.

Split open.

Her crying too as she'd told him again – *I loved you too much.* What had it done to him, this surfeit, this embarrass-ment of love?

He knew one thing, he did not want to fly back to London, drive up the M40, and sleep alone in the great, empty house tonight. He took his phone out and called Paige. No answer. Voicemail. 'Hey, it's Kennedy. Hope you're well. I'm flying back from Dublin tonight. Probably be home about eleven if you fancied coming over for a bit of late supper or . . . whatever. Gimme a bell. Bye.'

He hung up and signalled for the bill. A few minutes later, as he tapped his PIN into the machine, his phone chirruped. A text message. *Sorry, down at my parents' place. See you in tutorial on Tuesday. P x.*

He sighed and looked out the window.

Right there, on St Stephen's Green, 109 years ago.

FORTY—SEVEN

He'd left the car at Heathrow, in the short stay, costing more for the day than many hotels. Just about sober enough to drive, he was heading around the M25, feeling the sleepy tug of the lunchtime drinking, when he saw Junction 16 coming up, the turn-off for Iver Heath. Pinewood.

Spengler's place.

Come by for a drink sometime.

Suddenly the prospect of hitting his producer's liquor cabinet in fifteen minutes' time seemed much more appealing than spending an hour and a half driving the length of the M40 to an empty house. He checked his watch – just after 9 p.m. Why not? Surprise the old bastard.

He clicked the indicator on and steered the heavy Aston over into the left-hand lane, while, with one hand, he got Spengler's address from his email and tapped it into the satnav.

A little over twenty minutes later he was pulling up the drive. The house was pretty much the Home Counties equivalent of Spengler's Beverly Hills place – huge, sprawling. Over to his left in the dark he could make out the white tramlines of the controversial tennis court. The house itself, however, looked to be in darkness, although Spengler's Range Rover was parked in front, next to an old Polo, probably belonging to one of the staff. Kennedy got out and scrunched across the gravel towards the front of the house. Shit – what if he was in bed? He was American after all. No, *Californian.* A nine thirty bedtime was definitely not out of the question. He walked around to the side of the house and saw light spilling from somewhere towards the back.

He took the path to the rear and could faintly hear music now too. Some kind of R&B. This was more like it. He knew Spengler's wife was back in LA. Maybe he was having a party. Maybe some of the cast and crew? Where was his fucking invite then? He came round onto the back lawn and followed the light and music to a set of French windows. Face at the glass, he peered into a kind of conservatory at the back. No one in there, but an empty bottle of Cristal was upended in an ice bucket on the table. Kennedy knocked on the door a couple of times but no answer. The music sounded louder, coming from somewhere further inside the house.

The door was open so in he went, saying 'Scott? Scott? Hello?' every few steps. He came through a doorway into a big living room, the music loud now. There was a log fire burning in the grate and there, on the floor in front of the fire, her back to him, lying naked on a bath towel . . .

Paige.

He stood there. The song finished. She turned round and

their eyes met. She screamed, then flattened a hand over her mouth. Then, like in a horror film, the door was opening and Spengler was entering, wearing only a bathrobe, a fresh bottle of champagne in his hand. He looked from Paige to Kennedy and said, 'Shit.'

'Kennedy —' Paige began.

He turned round and started walking. Kept walking.

He turned the ignition on and pulled away hard, sending gravel hurtling behind him, costing Spengler a respray on his rented Range Rover in the process.

P.L.A.Y.E.R?

Played.

FORTY-EIGHT

The following evening. The Dean's Dinner Party.

He'd wanted to cancel of course. But, in truth, the old boy had stood by him. Besides, Kennedy reasoned (if 'reasoned' is quite the word we want here, with a couple of 'heroic' Martinis in him by the time he'd finished dressing), you didn't want to sit around wallowing. Get out and in among it. Live, love, ashamed of, etc.

The house was a large, detached Victorian on a leafy street on the edge of Deeping town. Solidly middle class but less grand than Kennedy had been expecting. What had he been expecting? Given the Dean something a touch more Brideshead: footmen in the hall and ironed newspapers with the headline 'ARCHDUKE SHOT!' Kennedy had the place of honour, at the Dean's right. Also gathered around the long dining table were the Dean's wife, Millie, Professor Bell from the F. W. Bingham committee, another lecturer from the English Department whose name escaped Kennedy, an American woman – a visiting friend of the Dean's and a fan of Kennedy's – and Drummond and his wife Karen, who was fairly knocking back the drinks. Drummond, of course, was driving, though they only lived on the other side of town.

'Well – first term nearly over then,' Professor Bell was saying to Kennedy. 'How have you enjoyed it?'

'It's been . . . eventful.'

'Not half,' the Dean said, helping himself to more potatoes. Kennedy refilled his own wine glass with a half-pint of Rioja. 'Between you and me,' he said, leaning in conspiratorially towards them, 'I'd pay to have you stay on for another year. Enquiries are through the roof. Any publicity is good publicity it would seem.'

'Yeah, like they say, Dean, don't read 'em. Weigh 'em.'

'Too true.'

'So, Mr Marr,' this was the American woman, 'what have you made of the standard of creative writing from the students at Deeping?'

Paige. That fuck –

'Ah, some of them can turn a phrase all right,' Kennedy said, aware that the rest of the table was turning to listen to him. He stopped. Rearranged his napkin.

'I sense a "but",' Professor Bell said.

'Well . . . it's just that so few of them seem to have grasped what Fitzgerald called "the price of admission".'

'And what is that?'

Your fucking heart smeared across the page.

'The worst thoughts. The best thoughts. First novels, early work, with very few exceptions, it's all a demented roar in place of technique. Or it should be at any rate.

They've all got little inklings of what technique is, stylistic things they've picked up from other writers. But art created from art just leads to mannerisms. I guess they haven't got anything to say. Which isn't so surprising. Outside of Capote or Mailer, maybe Easton Ellis or Martin Amis, not many people have written a novel worth reading much before the age of twenty-five. But some of the older students, the ones who've been trying to do this for years – Christ, you just want to tell them to give up.' He was aware of that faint smirk playing on Drummond's face as he drained his glass and began refilling it.

'But surely,' the lecturer he didn't know cut in, 'there's a point where you have to encourage them in order to give them confidence, to get the best out of them?'

Kennedy shrugged. 'I don't think "encourage" or "discourage" have anything to do with it. It's cruel to encourage the talentless. Wicked. At the same time it's impossible to discourage a real writer. Can't be done.'

'Mr Marr,' the American lady again, 'what is your view on authorial intent? Dr Drummond here was saying – what was it again?'

Drummond shook his head, not looking at her. 'I was saying that critical theory left the validity of authorial intention behind a long time ago. Of course, notwithstanding Kennedy's touching devotion to his sacred Dead White Males – his Mailers, Fitzgeralds, Hemingways and so on – from a certain point of analysis, you could argue that a text is simply a confluence of socio-political-economic forces.'

'Surely intentionality plays a part,' the American lady said. 'That you have certain ideas you're trying to get across in your books? Things you want people to think?'

'Ach, you just want to delight the reader really,' Kennedy said.

'I must say,' Drummond cut in, 'your loyalty to the church of nineteenth-century literary narrative is touching. You never stop to consider that your holy canon of literature is simply the will of a racist, sexist, imperialist hegemony? That other, questioning, voices are deliberately excluded?'

'What voices?' Kennedy said. He seemed to have finished his wine again. The Dean was topping him up, making a very sly, eyebrows-raised, here-he-goes-again expression at the same time.

'Kathy Acker, say. Or Althusser.'

'Well, these are minor figures. It's doubtful they'll be much discussed, let alone read, in fifty, even twenty years' time.'

'That's my point. Who does the excluding and who governs what is taught? What survives?'

'Time.'

'Time?'

'Yeah, time tends to weed out the chancers. And as for "nineteenth-century narrative", it survives because we *like it*. You get the guys who come along and try and blow it up once in a while, your B. S. Johnsons or whatever, and, you know what? They usually go mad. Then out of print.'

'So,' Drummond said, folding his arms, 'you do very much care about posterity. About what happens to your books in the future.'

'Authorial *intent* is very different from authorial self-regard,' Kennedy said.

'But, when you look back over your work . . .' the American lady started saying.

'Once you've finished the thing. It's over,' Kennedy said. 'You know, *"what cared I that set him on to ride"*?' He tilted his head, his voice ringing softly through the crystal and candlelight.

Here we fucking go . . . Millie thought.

> '*I, starved for the bosom of his faery bride . . .*
> *Players and painted stage took all my love,*
> *And not those things that they were emblems of.*'

That last line, so painful to him now. He leaned forward, lost in it. And who could resist Yeats echoing softly off the oak-panelled walls in Kennedy's musical brogue?

> '*Those masterful images because complete*
> *Grew in pure mind, but out of what began?*
> *A mound of refuse or the sweepings of a street,*
> *Old kettles, old bottles, and a broken can,*
> *Old iron, old bones, old rags, that raving slut*
> *Who keeps the till. Now that my ladder's gone,*
> *I must lie down where all the ladders start*
> *In the foul rag and bone shop of the heart.*'

He finished and looked up, smiling, sweeping his thick black fringe out of his eyes as he reached for his glass and the applause started, Drummond reluctantly joining in. 'Excellent,' the Dean was saying. 'One so rarely hears nowadays . . .' Millie excepted – she'd seen this movie many times – the women at the table were looking at Kennedy and crossing their legs.

'Excuse me,' Kennedy said.

Outside, smoking in the damp December air, he checked his messages. Spengler: 'Look, just call me, OK. I . . .' Dr Beaufort: 'We have your test results. I don't want to worry you but it would best if you came in to discuss the situation at your earliest convenience.' *Oh Christ.* And finally Patrick: 'Kennedy. Call me back.'

He knew. He knew from the flat tone.

'Patrick.'

'Hi. Earlier tonight. She pretty much went to sleep after we left yesterday and that was that.'

'Are you OK?'

'Aye. Yeah. I'll let you know about the arrangements.'

Kennedy hung up and lit a fresh Marlboro with the butt of the last one. Well, there it was. The only woman on the planet who would put up with *anything* Kennedy did. Kennedy felt the rumblings of his usual reaction to death – rage. *Oh, you fucker. You fucking cunt.* Also fear.

'At your earliest convenience . . .'

And with Paige, what was he feeling there? What was going on inside his foul rag-and-bone shop? He'd almost opened the door, hadn't he? He'd almost let it back in again: the primary value. The thing that will survive of us. He'd cracked the door open and an icy blast had pummelled through, knocking him off his feet. Instructive, in a way, to learn that love still had that decimating power, even at his age. He felt all the usual things: useless, rejected, unwanted, empty. And, beneath all that, there simmered an even greater sense of dread. Because, really, at this point in the game, every time could be the last time. God, he wanted to crawl inside a whisky bottle and just inhale as deeply as he could.

He flicked the cigarette away and walked back into the house. Everyone was in the lounge now. Standing around with coffee or brandy. Across the room he saw Millie talking to the Dean's wife. He helped himself to a huge whisky, downed it, and went to make his way across to her.

'Wow,' the American lady said as he went to pass. 'Still smoking, huh?' He had pounded three cigarettes on the trot. He might as well have had smoke coming off him.

Kennedy smiled weakly and went to go around her.

'Have you ever tried to stop?' Drummond asked.

Oh good. Most welcome. *Excellent.*

'Ah, what did you say now?' Kennedy asked, just the edge of that Limerick bar room in his voice. Millie swivelled with a warning glare, the only one who knew Kennedy's conversational tropes well enough to recognise an early warning sign, to know that it had taken an incredible effort of will for the words 'the fuck' not to have been vigorously inserted between 'what' and 'did'.

'Well, I'm just surprised that you're still, you know, on the old fags at your age. Once you've had kids and everything.'

'I see . . .' Kennedy said, nodding, rubbing his chin. 'Tell you what, Dennis, I'll quit if you'll help me. I'll quit on one condition – could you possibly find it in your heart to, say, contract Aids or something?'

334

Heads turning.

'Kennedy!' This was Millie.

'Excuse m—' Drummond went to say.

'Aids. Could you get Aids? Maybe start on the brown and share needles with a squat full of vagrants?'

'*Kennedy*,' Millie, hissing.

'Or just have some crazed, HIV-positive Muscle Mary shunt a diamond-cutting belly hugger up your manhole? Though, admittedly, either of these routes would involve you in the process of becoming vaguely interesting. Yes, a problem that right enough. Maybe just getting some crazy strain of syphilis would be more your speed? The kind of shit that makes your dick look like a fucking foot and then kills you?' The Dean's wife was staring at Kennedy with an expression worthy of someone witnessing a 747 containing their immediate family piling onto the tarmac. 'Because I honestly think,' Kennedy went on, 'that would help me get through the withdrawal period, you know? If I could come to the ward, or hospice, every day and see your smug non-smoking fucking face slowly hollowing and waxing as you died. If I could just set myself the goal of being there at the very end, to whisper a few well-aimed taunts into your ear as your four-and-a-half-stone frame breathed its last. Stuff about how I could maybe start helping Karen here –' he gestured towards Drummond's wife – 'through the grieving process, if you catch my drift.' This brought a couple of gasps, one shriek, and a furious 'KENNEDY!' from Millie, who was tugging at his elbow now. 'So could you do that for me? Get the Big One and help me get off "the old fags"? Eh, Dennis? Me old muck—'

Drummond punched Kennedy very hard right in the middle of the face.

It was a quality punch, the recipient had to admit, even as he wheeled backwards, going down. Fast it was, with a lot of weight behind it and a decent follow-through. Maybe he'd underestimated old Drummond.

FORTY-NINE

He came out and down the steps onto Harley Street. All around him stood the grand Georgian town houses where the great and good had brought their woes and shames for centuries. How many well-shod feet had carried heavy hearts along this pavement? A pub. He very much needed to find a pub. He made a left along to Great Portland Street and went into the George. Wood-panelled, glass, little snugs. Almost empty at three o'clock except for a few BBC types clustered at the bar, Broadcasting House being just round the corner. It was a Samuel Smith's drinker – their own brands of ales and lagers. None of the reassuringly familiar names on the pumps – no Stella or Kronenburg or Amstel. He ordered a pint of the heaviest ABV lager and a large whisky, getting a slight once-over on account of the psychedelic bruising around his eye. The whisky went down in one the second it arrived. He got another and took his drinks to an empty corner table.

Outside of writing Kennedy did not take very much

seriously. He had been told this all his life by a succession of figures: teachers, tutors, the two employers who had been stupid enough to hire him in the brief window between university and literary success, ex-girlfriends, ex-wives. But this would not be taken unseriously. This demanded sober consideration. Clear thinking. (To write clearly is to think clearly. This is why it's so difficult.) He took a long swallow of lager and looked down at his crotch.

The fucker was in there. What was it doing? It was going to kill him. Serious business though this was the writer in him responded strongly to the joke, to the hilarious obscenity of the universe's cruelty: he had lived largely according to the demands of that ridiculous fleshy sack with its bit of tubing. Ministering to its needs he had hurt women variously, wildly and deeply. It was that much-misused term – irony.

Beaufort had not been without compassion – *'Really sorry. I know this must be a terrible blow but I feel I must give you an idea of the bleakest picture'* – before going on to make fast and loose with a stunning array of obscenities: 'oncology', 'malignancy', 'survival rate' and then, finally, inevitably, 'surgery'. He wrote him a prescription for twenty Valium. To 'help him through the nights'.

Boy but they'd had some good times though, hadn't they? Even in here, in this very pub, back in the late nineties, just after publication of *Unthinkable*. He'd been interviewed for Radio 4. (*Front Row*, was it?) After the show a few of them had come here for drink. There was that cute little producer. Started right in the toilets over there, and then a room at the Langham. He remembered his climax. God, what was her name? Kennedy couldn't remember her name, but he could give you chapter and verse on the arc of the ejaculate. No more no more no more.

'Will very much depend on what they find when they go in there. The position is unfortunate, so near the base. The root. Worst-case scenario?'

He drained the pint. Noticed that the whisky glass was empty too. He couldn't remember drinking it. Went to the bar, got the same again. Would there be, could there be, upsides? The unshackling from the madman? The total detachment from the engine of sex. Might there be tranquillity? Even wisdom? Might he be granted the peace to write the books he felt he still had in him? Mildly expansive now with the best part of two pints and five whiskies inside him Kennedy tried to picture this new life. Living quietly, monastically even. Watching with wry amusement the fevers and passions of the humans. Loftily noting their crazed manoeuvrings from his sexless ivory tower, his elephants long slain and in the ground. Had YouPorn, Tube Galore and Red Tube been traded on the stock exchange he could even have watched their tumbling share prices with a measure of smug satisfaction.

'I'm afraid there might only be a couple of inches left. Enough for basic urinary function.'

Unmanned. A peanut. A choad.

Another pint and two more whiskies later and he had come at it from many angles, considered all the strategies and responses, and could see only one possible route. That old question – are your affairs in order? Kennedy, a veteran of affairs, had never kept them in much order. In the legal-specific sense, however, they were actually in remarkably good shape: just last year, at Braden's urging, he'd met with a tax attorney and drafted it all clearly. All property, cash and assets were to be divided two ways – between Robin and Patrick. Robin would be the sole beneficiary of his literary estate, to be administered by Connie.

As to the other matter – the thing of *actually doing it* – well, when? (He already had an idea of the how.) The cliché 'no time like the present' swam into his head. Why not? The Valium prescription nestled in his inside jacket pocket. He had around a hundred thousand pounds' worth of chargeable credit in his wallet. Why not now? Tonight. The Langham! Of course – just round the corner. Take a room. Fuck it – *a suite*. Make a night of it. Astonished at how clearly he was thinking given the amount of booze he was putting away, he checked his watch – four thirty, already dark outside – and made another trip to the bar. How long since he had really taken a walk around London? Over a decade probably. This fine city, where it had all begun for him and which he had so cruelly betrayed for LA, an affair that had grown into a second marriage.

So, it was clear. Clear enough at any rate. He finished his drink and left a fifty-pound note on the bar as a tip.

To the Langham hotel, Portland Place. Just a ten-minute walk even with the stops: first at a chemist to collect his Valium and then at a cashpoint on Mortimer Street, where he used his bank card and then his American Express to withdraw a thousand pounds in cash. He pressed a twenty into the hand of the doorman as he came up the steps and through the revolving doors.

The lobby had changed since he'd last stayed here – the check-in desk now a hard right, up some steps. 'Hi there, bit last minute I'm afraid, but do you have a suite for tonight? Just the one night.'

'A junior suite?'

'No no. Definitely senior.'

'Let me just check for you, sir.' The girl's fingers clacked at her keyboard. She was in her mid-twenties, pretty, dark-haired, East European accent. 'Our Infinity Suite is available. That is a two-bedroom. Our largest.'

'And how much is that fella now?'

'Ah, it, that's ten thousand three hundred pounds per night. Inclusive of tax.'

'Grand.' Kennedy clicked his Amex down onto the marble counter.

'And your luggage . . .'

'No. I . . . we're all good.' She looked at him again. He nearly went to pat his top pocket. Toothbrush. Benjamin Braddock, nervous in the lobby of the Taft hotel. Great scene.

Now this, Kennedy thought, as the porter advanced into the room ahead of him, turning on lights, this is a bit more fucking like it. The whole place, the porter had proudly told him in the lift on the way up, was over two and a half thousand square feet. Some steps in front of them and to the right led down to a living area. To their left: a huge dining table set for eight and a corridor leading to the bedroom (one of the bedrooms) and the bathroom – with basically a small infinity pool in place of a bath. 'Cheers,' Kennedy said, pressing three twenties on the guy.

'Thank *you*, sir. Is there anything else I can do for you?

'No, I'm fine thank you. You work away now.'

The kid left. Kennedy picked up the telephone.

'Hello, room service.'

'Hi there. Could you send up, ah let's see, a dozen oysters, two shrimp cocktails' (*'Shrimp'?* Fucking LA man.) 'a bottle of Dom Perignon and . . . three Martinis?'

'Yes, sir. For the Martinis . . .'

'Gin, Tanqueray if you have it, whatever if you don't, olives, very dry.'

'Very good, sir.'

'Thank you.'

He hung up and walked to the far end of the lounge, passing an antique armoire that contained a fifty-inch flat-screen TV. Kennedy pulled the curtains back, opened the French windows, and stepped out onto a little balcony, his breath misting in the chill December air. He was high up at the corner of the building. Looking right he saw Regent Street snaking away to the south, down towards Piccadilly Circus, the Christmas lights twinkling and sparkling. To his left, just across the street, the great edifice of Broadcasting House, Nash's design, that colossal ship at sea, boldly lit by klieg lights, its masts and antennae jutting into the night sky. Just down the little alleyway opposite was All Souls Place – a narrow dead-end alleyway, where (and why was he only remembering this now?) Kennedy and Millie had rented a tiny room when they first moved to London after graduation. Twenty years ago. Half a lifetime. They –

He remembered her taking the ring off. Placing it on the table between them. Very slow and deliberate it had been. Not angry, not throwing it at him. He wondered how many times she'd rehearsed the gesture in her head.

A bell ringing. He went to the door. Room service –

wheeling a trolley in, piled high with food and drink: plump native oysters on the half-shell, nestling on a sparkling platter of crushed ice, the dark green bottle of Dom in a spun-silver bucket with its napkin collar, fat prawns and shredded lettuce in Marie Rose sauce stuffed into oversized wine balloons. The three Martinis, the glasses frosted and beaded with sweat, little paper lids covering them. Kennedy took one of them and drank deeply. The waiter didn't blink. 'Would you like me to open the champagne, sir?'

'Ach no, I can get it. Here.' He stuffed a brace of notes into the guy's breast pocket. 'Merry Christmas.'

'Thank you, sir.'

'No problem.'

Kennedy finished the Martini, popped a Valium and took his second cocktail back out onto the balcony, pulling his overcoat tightly around him. He lit a cigarette. Really – he felt marvellous. Had Gerry felt this good, towards the end? After the decision had actually been made? What had he been thinking about? Before room service . . . oh yeah – the tiny bedsit, across the road, the summer of 1993. How long had they stayed there? Two years? No – *three*. They moved when Millie's parents gave them some money towards a deposit, on the flat in Maida Vale. Because Millie was –

Yes. Robin. She'd been conceived there. In that little flat tucked in behind the BBC. They hadn't been married at the time, But *'there was good sport at his making, and the whoreson must be acknowledged'*.

Good sport at the making: that demented moment when one of the hundred million maniacal tiny swimmers bust free from the pack, from the scrum, the ruck, and got it across the line. When he exploded into the sun of the egg, setting off the chain reaction, like the uranium being shot into the middle of the nuclear device, but triggering the unspooling, uncoiling DNA. Triggering the opposite of death, Robin's tiny face already encoded in miniature on the splitting, doubling cells. *Oh, baby, I'm sorry. No one asked to be born. Life is unfair, kill yourself or get over it. All that stuff.* Kennedy raised his glass in the general direction of the place and toasted his daughter. He finished the Martini and opened the Dom Perignon, sending the cork sailing across the high-ceilinged room. He poured himself a glass and then wrung half a muslin-clad lemon out over the entire plate of oysters. Dotted Tabasco here and there. By God they were good – he ate five or six on the trot, quickly, bolting them down with swigs of the cold champagne. *Living well is the best revenge.*

'Revenge for what?' Robin had asked him once, a few years ago, when she was twelve or thirteen and over in LA for a visit. He'd said it as they tucked into some sumptuous meal or other. 'For what?' Kennedy had said. 'For the total insult of being born of course.'

He checked the time – six fifteen. Work to be done. Better get a move on.

Kennedy took the bottle of champagne – swigging straight from it now – and one of the prawn cocktails over to the bureau. He got a stack of Langham writing paper out of the drawer – and lovely heavy stuff it was, about 120g – uncapped his pen, and set about writing five letters: Robin, Millie, Vicky, Patrick and Connie. When he looked up from finishing the last one (Connie, just some instructions really, practical stuff and very easy to get down on paper. A contrast to the letter to his daughter: a festival of pain and tears), it was just after seven thirty and the Dom Perignon was finished. He popped another Valium (courage would be needed soon. Obviously it would have to be chemically imported. Kennedy was aware that, technically, this was oblivion rather than courage, but what the hell) and rang room service for another bottle.

A little while later he stacked the letters and the poem on top of the bureau and wandered back out onto the balcony – a little unsteadily it had to be said – where he smoked and watched the throng of people at Oxford Circus, swarming in and out of the Underground's quartet of mouths, their bright winter coats – reds and greens and blues and whites – splashed with the brilliant light from the huge shop windows. *Of course London's a big place. It's a very big place, Mr Shadrack. A man could lose himself in London. Lose himself. Loooooseee himself in LAHNDAHNNNNNN!* Get out and in it just one more time. A sentimental journey or whatever. Live and love. Catch something you might be ashamed of. The doorbell rang. The champagne. *Yeah – let's have a couple more drinks and then get this show on the road.*

Out into the frosted air of Portland Place – another twenty into the hand of the doorman – and a right turn onto Regent Street, heading south. He wrapped his overcoat tighter around him – really very cold now – and walked through the good people of the capital, enveloped in a Ready Brek glow of well-being, an armoured suit of prescription meds and fine wine. *Yeah, London, you're all right by me. You'll do. I shouldn't have left. We could have worked it out. It wasn't you – it was me.*

He made a left on Oxford *('trying to find a friend on Oxford Street')* and crossed the road to take Argyll, avoiding the crowds on the main drag of Regent. (Dropping the 'Street', even in his interior monologue. Fucking LA, man.) Immediately engulfed by the smell of Chinese food and chestnuts, both being cooked at street stalls: MSG and noodles and roasting nuts filling the air. Oh – and there on his right: the Duke of Argyll. A normal human pub, bursting with normal human life, December human life: the office amateurs having a go at being raconteurs and wits among the pumps, optics and Santa hats. Christ, when had he last been in there? Back in the mid-nineties maybe? Back before life became inhuman. Became abnormal. Became members' clubs and account cabs and Michelin stars. Well, a little whisky wouldn't hurt now, would it? *How much we hate death, those of us who write and create. And how fiercely we embrace its foes – drink, company, laughter, life.*

Through the doors and into the crush and the heat and the noise. The Waitresses' 'Christmas Wrapping' playing, everyone roaring, red-faced, sweating, office-party fever. Kennedy got to the bar in one of the central snugs. 'A large . . . oh, what you got – Laphroaig?'

The man shook his head sadly, scanning the optics, and said, 'Glenfiddich?'

Fucking pisswater. 'Yeah. OK. A treble.'

The drink came and Kennedy flattened a twenty on the wet bar. 'Keep the change.'

A cocked eyebrow. 'You sure?'

'Yeah, it's Christmas.'

'Thanks very much, mate. Appreciate it.'

Ah — go on, take it. Pain in the butt. 'I am all you never had of goods and sex' and all that.

He pushed his way back outside to smoke. The little fenced-off area, roped in from the pavement. Crowded. A man caught his eye, smiled and raised his glass. 'Merry Christmas, mate!'

'Yeah, cheers.'

The humans — doing their stuff. Their human thing. He almost felt a part of it. He gazed down Argyll Street, towards the brightly lit black-and-white Tudor revival edifice of Liberty, and a memory came from many, many Christmases ago: him and Millie meeting in front of the shop. Childless, young, in love and penniless, they'd wandered the halls, looking at all the things they couldn't afford. Millie had seen a rug she'd loved, something rare and handmade and priced at five thousand pounds. They'd laughed at the very thought of spending that much on a rug. They'd laughed as they wandered off into Soho, to eat cheap Chinese food somewhere and drink pints of beer in pubs with no door policy and meet some friends who he couldn't even remember now. *Ach — all those people, all those lives, where are they now?* Kennedy knocked the drink back, gagging a little — fucking Glenfiddich — and set off down the street.

In the brightly lit furnishings hall he tapped in his PIN while the salesgirl — flushed, pleased — took down the shipping details. He spelt her name, her maiden name now, and got the address out of his phone. 'Yeah, it's Warwickshire. And it'll definitely arrive before Christmas Day?'

'Oh yes.'

'Great.'

The rug was twelve thousand quid, probably about right allowing for inflation. He even tried to press a twenty on the salesgirl. 'No, really, sir, I can't accept that.'

'Ach, go on now.'

She giggled, reddening. 'I can't. Honestly. Do you want to enclose a note?'

He scribbled the card out, with some difficulty now, his handwriting just a mad, slanting scrawl. *'Millie – you wanted something like this once. Much love, Kennedy xxx'*.

On the way out he bought himself a silk polka-dotted scarf in the menswear department and furled it around his neck – *from feudal serf to spender, this wonderful world of purchase power* – as he emerged onto Great Marlborough Street, turning right, into Carnaby Street, and time for another drink.

The White Horse, busier, rowdier than even the Duke of Argyll had been, the music louder, 'Driving Home for Christmas', people singing along, Kennedy choosing a cold pint of Stella this time, using it to wash down another Valium – whose only effect so far seemed to have been to make him very, very happy. (Not *that* happy of course, there had been no change of plan. It was still down there, that pea of death, nestling near his urethra.)

Carnaby Street. Connie had once had her office just off here, before they got bought up and moved to Haymarket. 1996: she'd taken him to lunch at a little French restaurant round the corner and told him that, after many rejections, they'd finally had two firm offers to publish *Unthinkable*. The advances weren't huge, she'd said, but she'd got a very decent royalty rate so if the book did well, who knew?

Kennedy felt like he'd shot the moon.

He'd rushed home to tell Millie – pregnant with Robin at the time – taking the Bakerloo line to Warwick Avenue, picking up champagne at the little off-licence on Formosa Street on the way, spending about the last thirty pounds in his current account to do so. She'd cried and they'd made love, carefully, on the sofa. They lay there afterwards, him sipping champagne while they joked about what they'd do when he became a best-seller, neither of them able to look down the barrel of their future and know that, just five years down the line, after a million paperback sales in over twenty languages, when Connie's royalties deal had been made to look very far-sighted indeed, Millie would be weeping on the sofa – a different sofa, a bigger sofa, in a different, a bigger house – as she said, *'I wish we were poor again. I wish none of this had ever happened.'*

He drained the lager. Onwards. *Cognac. And fresh horses for the men. Tonight we ride.*

Down Carnaby Street, left and right round Ganton Street and then into Soho proper. The pubs teeming, overflowing now, two policemen standing in front of the Sun & 13 Cantons, talking to a guy in his twenties who was having trouble standing up. *May I suggest you use your nightstick, officer?*

Could it all have been different for them, for him and Millie? *Not without being someone else, no.*

His head was teeming now too, a fuzzbox of Valium and alcohol, overflowing with quotations, swimming with poetry and prose, with song lyrics and lines from movies. It was as if his brain, knowing what lay ahead, was going into overdrive – *clams on the half-shell, feels like prohibition baby give me the hard sell* – throwing everything out there, chucking up every song and film and book and pop-cultural reference he had ever known for the last time as he walked now. To the inevitable.

On to Wardour Street. The Ship! When had he last been in the Ship? A crowd of them used to drink here – summers out on the pavement with lagers. Once again out of the shocking cold and into the light and noise of the pub, forcing his way in at the bar with cocked twenty ready. It had been a premier rock-and-roll boozer, back in the sixties and seventies, when the Marquee was just along the road. The Who, the Stones, all of them propped this bar up. Mick Jones had got the phrase 'complete control' off Bernie Rhodes right there, *right fucking there at the bar.* Went home and wrote the song. Kennedy got a large whiskey – just Jameson's now, beyond caring about the world of malts – and a half of Stella. A 'half and a half' they used to say in Glasgow, a hangover from when spirits were served in half-gill measures, long before Kennedy's time. He could just remember, back in the eighties, when he started at Glasgow University, some of the older pubs in the city's East End still proclaiming themselves 'Quarter Gill Shops'. Serving proud, generous imperial measures in defiance of the tiny, mean metric shots. *Imperial Measures*, it dawned on him, would be quite a good title for a certain kind of book.

He wedged himself in beside the jukebox and sipped the whiskey. Glasgow – he'd liked to have seen the city once again. If he'd thought this through a bit more . . . maybe flown up there. A walk through the West End: the leafy streets, always autumnal in his mind, the Victorian Gothic spires of the university. Where he'd first met Millie.

She'd been eating an apple in the refectory, the Hub, her head dipped, her hair hanging down over her face frowning into a battered copy of *The Rainbow*, as he took his seat opposite with his tray of pie, chips and beans. 'He's an old bastard now, isn't he?' Kennedy had said, grinning as he shook his carton of milk, indicating the book, meaning Lawrence.

She'd looked up at him. 'Do I know you?'

'Kennedy. We're in American Lit together.'

'Mmmm,' she'd said, with moneyed Home Counties confidence. Sweating now in the heat of the Ship, leaning against the jukebox – *'Oh, can't you see me standing here? I've got my back against the record machine', and oh the Aztec Camera version was nice, lugubrious and sad and Roddy Frame had said that when you slowed it down it was just like 'Sweet Jane' and he said when he was singing that line he thought of it as meaning him standing with his back against the record industry, and he must have read that in some interview, in the* NME *or somewhere, nearly thirty years ago, when he was a teenager and oh why would that still cling to your mind when so many other –* Kennedy closed his eyes and held her whole again. He saw her closing the novel and biting again into the green apple, regarding him coolly, sunlight glinting on the Lemonheads badge on the lapel of her brown suede jacket, falling across her pleated black skirt. (Back in the days when female under-graduates dressed like that. When they didn't dress like they were waiting between takes on *Butt Fiends Vol. V.*) She gave his steaming plate of carbs a slow once-over and said, 'Comfort eating, are we?' And she was so confident and beautiful and we were just kids Millie. *Kids kids kids.* 'What are you taking?' she'd asked him, meaning his courses.

'I'm a writer,' Kennedy had replied.

'Really? Where might I have seen your work?'

'You will,' the twenty-one-year-old idiot-retarded-fuckstick Kennedy Marr had replied.

Why had he betrayed her so thoroughly and indiscriminately and repeatedly and, often, for so little pleasure? Hormones, he supposed.

But, no.

That would no longer cover it. No glibness. Not here at the end, in the face of the great, the distinguished thing. Honesty was required of him. Why had he betrayed them? Betrayed even his tiny child as it grew in the womb? The sense that he was owed something more? That as a man of great talent the normal rules did not apply? Ultimately, he'd had no moral code. And, if character is destiny, then here he was, exactly where he was meant to be. The unstable chamber of Kennedy's heart, his foul rag-and-bone shop, reeking of Zyklon B.

And maybe this was a good definition of what writers did: they cleared the human debris from that chamber. They went in there and pulled teeth from the dead and dying, from their own people. They tried to find the gold among all that was ruined and then they threw the corpses on the pyre. Grahame Greene's 'sliver of ice in the heart'? Kennedy wasn't even sure this covered it any more. His heart was a gas chamber and he was his own *Sonderkommando*.

Could it have been any different? Probably not. No. *Not without being* –

The thought drove him to drink, which, thankfully, was close at hand. However, stumbling now, aware of the tranquillising Valium beginning to rubberise his legs, of the effect of the many and varied cocktails, the trip to the bar took a lot longer than expected. It was like crossing the deck of a trawler smashing through the plume and spray of the North Atlantic. He lurched into a guy, a broad-backed office worker with Barbour jacket over cheap suit and tie, spilling his pint. 'Easy, mate, fucking hell.'

'Excuse me, my fault,' Kennedy said, although this seemed to come out faster than he'd intended, and all rammed together – 'Schoosemeemiffault.'

'You all right, mate?' someone said.

'Perfectly all right thanks.' Peffiklyriteshanks.

He turned back to the waiting barman and asked for a half of Stella and a whisky and soda, punctuating his order with a cheerful hiccup.

'Sorry?'

'An harflagerannawhischkyeesewdah . . .'

'How many?'

Kennedy repeated his request.

'A what?'

He made a third attempt.

'Sorry, mate, I know it's Christmas, but Jesus . . .'

'Fucking Paddies,' someone else said. Kennedy made a weary swipe in the direction of the voice before he felt a hand on his shoulder.

'*Stick irrup in yer fooking holes –*'

Moments later, back out on the street, drinkless, Kennedy was suddenly aware of the street lights fizzing, of the traffic noise and the footfall and the babble of the outside smokers and drinkers all merging into one over-riding sensory blur. Oh well – it seemed his time of drinking in pubs tonight was drawing to an end. No matter. Further up the road, at the little Pakistani-operated minimarket on Old Compton Street, the proprietor was much more accommodating. Indeed Kennedy felt fairly sure that if he'd been wheeled into the store in a hospital bed with screeching monitors attached and a chart at the bottom that read 'CRITICAL CIRRHOSIS – ALCOHOL WILL KILL INSTANTLY' he'd still have been cheerfully walking (or wheeling) out with his half-bottle of Bell's and a pack of Marlboro Lights.

Swaying against the lamp post, uncapping the whisky, his phone vibrated again in his pocket and he took it out. A bunch of texts, missed calls. His eyes flickered down towards the bottom of the screen, onto the orangey-white Mivvi-coloured iPod logo. Music. Might be nice to have some music for the last time. There seemed to be two iPod logos, both floating about a half-inch above the screen. A memory popped up and he clicked on one of them. PLAYLISTS. Click again. There it was – 'DAD'S ENGLISH AVENTURE'. The comp Robin had made for him and that he'd, obviously, completely forgotten about. Suddenly he very much needed to hear the music his daughter had put together for him. Headphones. He needed headphones. How to do this? One of those music shops on Denmark Street, surely they'd have . . . but, shit, the time. He checked his watch – it was after ten now. Closed. He looked around; a guy, a teenage boy coming towards him, head-phones dangling from his ears. Kennedy stepped into his path. 'Schoose me.'

The kid frowned, took an earphone out to hear what Kennedy was saying.

'Would you sell me your headphones?'

'Huh?'

'Look, I'll give you fifty quid for them.' Kennedy held out the gleaming pink note.

'Mate,' the guy said, 'these cost like a tenner.'

'Thasss OK.'

'Look, I don't wanna –'

'Take the money. I'm just . . . in a hurry.'

Kennedy scrunched the earphones in as he wandered off, feeling the guy behind looking after him, shaking his head, holding the fifty. He set off along Old Compton Street, carefully avoiding Dean Street – the Groucho, Dean Street Townhouse, Quo Vadis, all undoubtedly rammed with people he knew and now would never see again – and clicked on 'Play' as he walked past the Spice of Life onto Cambridge Circus, and suddenly, deafeningly, 'William, It Was Really Nothing' filled his head. It was a song Kennedy had grown up with but, Christ, the rush! When had he last listened to music like this while walking the streets? When had he last listened to the Smiths? He felt empowered, noble, high. He felt seventeen. Oh, good call, Robin. Excellent. Good opener. He took a swig – crossing Shaftesbury Avenue now, heading south on Charing Cross Road, powdery snowflakes falling softly through the sodium street light while, in his head, the rain fell hard on a humdrum town.

The car park at Limerick train station the first time he ever heard this. Sitting in Stevie Brennan's dad's Vauxhall Nova, watching the trains hurtle by on the way up to Dublin. 1984. He'd been fifteen years old. Younger, even, than Robin was now.

Head, lungs and heart full of Morrissey and Marr's

northern symphony he floated down the Charing Cross Road towards the Strand, beatified, flooded with the deep peace he now knew came from knowing that life was at an end. Here they came, all around him, the humans. See how they joked! How they laughed, the air wreathing silver from their mouths, jetting in twin plumes from their nostrils. These fucking fools. Did they not understand? – they were all going to die. One day soon they would be on that bed, reaching for that final breath and finding it would not come. These people, these idiots, who said smugly, 'Well, of course we all die.' Were they retarded or super-hard? Had they not thought this through at all? *They were going to stop fucking breathing.*

Sometimes, in bed at night, when he was small, Kennedy would imagine what it was like to die by holding his breath. He'd inhale deeply and think 'this is my last breath' and then lie there until his vision started to sparkle and swim and his lungs threatened to break his ribcage. Then – oh the joy! – as he sucked in sweet draughts of fresh air. The realisation that he had more breaths to take – thousands, millions of them. Uncountable.

Except, obviously, they *were* countable. Finite. The tab was running somewhere. If one were inclined to sit there with the stopwatch and the calculator you could probably work out a fair guestimate of exactly how many breaths you had in you.

He cut through the Tube station at Embankment. A woman on her phone, talking to her lover. 'Yeah, hon, just getting on the Tube. Running late. Want me to get anything? . . . OK. See you soon.' You heard them at the supermarket too. 'Hi, it's me. I'm just at the supermarket now. Do we need anything?' Kennedy Marr – a man with no one to call, a man who knew well the sad moment when that number on your phone stopped being 'HOME' and became simply the Christian name of your former partner – raised the bottle in the direction of the woman's back as it vanished away towards the escalator. *Humans – with your endless reservoirs of love and caring – I salute you.* He came out the other side of the station, onto the Embankment. There was a homeless guy sitting there. Young, not much older than Paige. *Ach, Paige – I hope you'll be happy.* He had the cardboard plea: 'HUNGRY, HOMELESS. PLEASE HELP.' Kennedy reached into his overcoat and took out his wallet. Maybe 700-odd quid there. He handed the kid the lot. The kid looked at it – his jaw dangling.

'Mate, this . . .'

'Ach. Work away now.'

'You don't want to . . . you're drunk.'

'That I am. Merry Christmas.'

Kennedy wandered away and took the staircase up onto the bridge, the orange beacons of the taxis hurtling along beneath him, and then, suddenly, there it was, dark and ceaseless, black as oil in the moonlight: the Thames.

Elbows on the rail, bottle in hand, getting his breath back, Kennedy stared down into it. What things this river had seen, what extremities. 'Liquid history', John Burns called it.

The Frost Fairs in winter, as recently as the nineteenth century, the entire breadth of it frozen over a foot thick, thousands skating from north to south, south to north, walking from Putney to Fulham. Chestnuts roasting over fires burning on the ice. Children laughing and playing. The horrors too – the paddle steamer *Princess Alice* being torn in two by the coal ship *Bywell Castle* in 1878: going down in four minutes, nearly seven hundred people dying, right here, right below his feet, the poisoned river itself killing many of them. He looked east – the swollen dome of St Paul's on the north bank, the stone it was built of had travelled the length of the river from Oxfordshire.

And, yes, for centuries they had been coming here for this too. The final thing. A body fished out of the Thames every week. Was that the statistic he had heard? One a week finding themselves saying – *this joke isn't funny any more.* He took a deep slug of whisky, looked left and right, no one coming, and stood up on the bottom rung of the rail. He looked down – a drop of what, thirty or forty feet? Into . . . he checked the temperature on his iPhone. A few degrees above freezing. The water would certainly be a good deal colder than that. A great wave of tiredness poured through him, like his entire body yawning. The Valium. How much had he taken now? The water was rushing around the pillars that supported the bridge, flowing fast down there, tidal, strong currents. You'll go into shock immediately, limbs useless. With the weight of his clothes and shoes, all the booze and pills . . . he imagined his temples going numb, the oily water filling his lungs. Fade out. Two minutes maximum. A tough two minutes mind, but there it was. Would a boat hit his body? Slice him in half? Would he snag under a bridge? Or wash up on the muddy banks where the seabirds would take his eyes? Oh Robin – I'm sorry. I'm so sorry. I was just . . . no good.

I sometimes thought it would be nice to come home to two people like everyone else.

Ach. And they never go away, these things. They're just there. Damn straight, Kingsley. And the best you can hope to do is to coexist with them.

Or not.

He tipped the bottle and drank the last of the foul Bell's. Dropped the bottle and watched it fall, splash and vanish. Green mossy seaweed on the pillars, indicating different water levels. Tidal. He leaned further over. A whoosh of vertigo. Maybe this was . . . excessive. Could it be . . . could he live the cockless life? After all, it had got him into so much trouble. Content and serene with his stump. His choad. Maybe he could . . . let's call the whole thing . . .

But no. Enough of that. *Come, let me be a man to the end.* Final things. Some last words perhaps. Kennedy was fond of last words, something of a collector.

'I go now to the inevitable.' Larkin, for whom so much of life had been about death.

'Nothing but death.' Ballsy old Jane Austen on being asked if she needed anything on her deathbed.

Emily Dickinson's ominous, mystical 'the Fog is rising . . .'

Al Jolson's were frankly terrifying: 'This is it! I'm going. I'm going.' Filled with full knowledge of, and horror at, what was happening.

Marx, fearless and pertinent: 'Go on. Get out. Last words are for fools who haven't said enough already.'

For Kennedy the urge was to say, 'Can I go again?'

He swung a leg over, straddling the fence now. Here it was – the dark backing of Bellow's mirror, roaring beneath him.

He thought of his father, his da the joiner who had worked so hard every day of his life and dropped dead at fifty-nine.

Heart attack when Kennedy was writing *Unthinkable*. Nearly twenty years ago now. His da never lived to see it in print. Kennedy remembered the da smell well – his tobacco-scented cardigans – how strong his hands were, his grip, when he dug his fingers into your leg, or jabbed you playfully in the side. He loved to roughhouse with them, with him and Patrick and Geraldine. (*It'll just be Patrick soon. All on his own. Poor Patrick. I'm sorry, brother.*) On the living-room carpet on Saturday mornings – *Swap Shop* on in the background. Posh Paws – and the three of them climbing all over their da, his body a huge mountain range. Da's hands would always be torn and bruised. Black fingernails and electrical tape over cuts: he took his lumps from hard work.

Here he was about to die and Kennedy had never had a job. A CV even. Imagine that.

School, university, supported by Millie, published at twenty-seven and a millionaire by the time he was thirty. He had owned his own soul all his adult life. With this ownership comes great responsibility. When you made enough money that you didn't have to think about money you had to deal with something pretty interesting. It was called *You*. What did you do with that incredible freedom? It turned out that what Kennedy liked to do was to pinball through Soho. To cartwheel around Manhattan and Hollywood and Berlin, propping up the bar at overpriced hotels and members' clubs, swigging cocktails and laughing and joking and arguing and fighting and fucking. Oh, bad choice! Very bad. He should have had more children, lots of them, and hung out with them a lot more. Been that mountain range on the living-room carpet on a Saturday morning. Because – and obviously he was only realising the truth of this now, at the end, when the information was of no use to him – children are all about the quantity – screw the quality crap. The divorced dad trying to fit the zoo, the aquarium, the museum and three restaurants into one day until everyone's exhausted and hating each other. They just want you lying there reading your paper or whatever until you tickle them on your way to put the kettle on. They just want you *around*. You don't have to *do* much. Witness the parade of wife beaters, kid beaters and alcoholic maniacs proudly toting their World's Greatest Dad mugs the world over. Their kids loved them. *He'd been raping him for months. But the boy had been running into the living room to show his dad something, to tell him something. Excitedly running to Daddy. Who raped you. Who was hitting the off-brand vodka at eleven in the morning. Who smashed your tiny skull to pieces off the living-room wall. Oh, Patrick – how do you do it? Why have you not ripped your ears off? Why aren't you in jail? Or an asylum?*

Every book was the wreck of a great idea, yes. Some lives too. Because he'd gotten it wrong. All wrong. Invested in the wrong stocks. Backed the wrong horses. The faces of his Dead White Males swam around him in the night sky, rotating like a fairground ride – Bellow, Updike, Nabokov, Miller, Mailer, Hemingway, Faulkner, Fitzgerald, Amis. Oh, fellas – you all steered me wrong. I should've been listening to the girls.

Give me another go. I'll get it right this time.

Who'd have thought it, Gerry, eh? Me and you both . . . you know? What's it like through there? On the other side? Well, we're about to find out. Death, where is thy . . . ach, come now, let me be a man to the end. Here, take my hand, brother, sister. *The problems of the third act are the problems of the first ac*— ach, fuck it.

He swung the other leg over and pushed forward into nothingness, cold air streaming by his face, the water rushing up to meet him.

All around him London went on humming.

FIFTY

Come, lover
Feast upon the edge of the abyss
Gorge oblivious while, black leagues below,
Sightless birds turn slowly in awful circles

At our backs, the arid winds
of the choices we have made
That have led us here,
To this last banquet

There, on the far side,
The flowers I sought shine unplucked
Their ice-cream petals intact
To taunt those who will come after me

Oblivious to the quieter blooms around me
Their picking became all my business
Alone at the great wheel I steered the ship
Off the charts when harbour was there all along

Tea, toast, brown bills
The calendar you kept
and photographs on the fridge
Oh, how their mundanity sparkles now they are gone

All for the urge to leap over the side
Diving deep in strange waters
There to stare, lungs bursting,
Into the jewelled eyes of fathomless creatures

FIFTY-ONE

We have, all of us, imagined our own funeral. We've run the songs through our head. Stood at the front and scanned the gathering. I can't believe he came. Where's she? and so forth. We like to picture the faces of those who loved us the most contorted and broken by grief. Who will cry the hardest? Who will truly miss us? Will there be people there who we always wanted to sleep with but it just never happened? Who'll turn up who loathed you but just fancied a day out with free food and drink? We imagine the readings, the eulogies. (The difficulties come when we start to imagine our children at our funeral — how hard it will go for them.) You obviously wonder about the turnout: will there be rows and rows of empty pews? Or standing room only? Best-seller or remaindered? When you die in old age the chances are the turnout will be slimmer. Go young and you have more of a chance of packing them in. And we wonder about the stories people will tell of us, at the bar afterwards. Do you remember that time he said this? Mind when she did that? A day to be talked about. We believe that if we were there then we could see in the faces of the grieving those who truly loved us: the men who delighted in our company, the women who pined for us.

And here, today, in the small, packed church on the outskirts of Dun Laoghaire, here was the stark grief of the front pew – Patrick and his wife Anne and their children, Patrick red-eyed and looking as though he hadn't slept much in the last few days, Anne tenderly holding his hand as he listened sadly to the priest. Connie Blatt, dignified, the English ruling classes. Connie did her crying in private. Then there was Millie: composed, thoughtful. And, next to her, Robin: looking beautiful in a black dress, looking older than her sixteen years. She held a damp tissue in her hands, and her head was hanging down. Her first funeral. The coffin, its contents, so hard to look at. *The Physical Impossibility of Death in the Mind of Someone Living.* Her dad had taken her to see the Hirst shark, in New York, at the Metropolitan Museum, about five years back, a Christmas holiday trip. She'd loved it. The big cow cut in half too. They'd gone to the Oyster Bar at Grand Central Station after. Her first oyster. Her dad could get her to try anything. She looked up at the coffin. *'What's "bury"?' Rosie said. 'Something you do when people are dead,'* a line from a song on a compilation her father had made her once. Something indie, from the eighties. She couldn't quite remember who sang it. As the line came to her Robin felt her shoulders go and a sob escaping her.

Kennedy put his arm around his daughter and squeezed her shoulder. 'There,' he said softly. 'There, there, now.'

'And now to read for us from St Paul's Letter to the

Corinthians,' the priest was saying, 'Kathleen's eldest son, Kennedy Marr.'

He got up and walked to the pulpit. He felt a little self-conscious, with that bloody great plaster still on his forehead, the vivid bruise around his right eye. He looked out at the congregation, a fair old crowd for someone his mother's age. He looked down at the leather-bound Bible on the lectern, already open at the correct page for him.

Good shoes are important, son.

They certainly were. The John Lobb brogues had saved his life. Not without a certain amount of embarrassment though. It had happened like this . . .

As he swung the second leg over and pushed off into thin air he felt the snagging as the loop of the lace of his left shoe caught around the protruding bolt of the railing. He fell forwards, the double-knotted lace proving strong enough to take his entire body weight. (*Goddamn lace probably cost more than the average pair of shoes.* Thank you, Braden.) With a bang his head smacked off the brickwork of the bridge and there he was – dangling upside down, the blood rushing to his head, the black Thames rushing beneath him. He'd been expecting the lace to break any second, but the quality footwear just went on doing what it had been for the English upper classes for centuries: holding things together. Then he heard footsteps, voices, and suddenly someone was saying, 'Jesus Christ, mate, how did you . . . hang on. Let's . . .' and their hands coming over the railing, grabbing his legs, pulling him up: the homeless guy and a friend, laden with cans of drink, just back from spending a chunk of Kennedy's money at some all-night booze hole. (A sound investment indeed, Millie, thank you.) The second he stood up the shock of what had happened combined with the sucker punch of all that Valium and Kennedy passed out. When he came to he was in a hospital bed at St Thomas' on the Southbank, furiously hung-over, his throat raw from the tubing after they'd pumped his stomach.

He looked back down at the Bible, at the nonsense. There was a time, recently, when Kennedy would have refused this. When he would have outraged this Catholic gathering by going off-map and reading some poetry, or something he'd written himself instead. But his ma had believed in the nonsense. And he was done with not playing by the rules for a while. The rules looked pretty good to him right now. 'Brothers and sisters,' he began, his fine, lilting reading voice ringing off the stone walls, 'Knowing that the One who raised the Lord Jesus will raise us also with Jesus . . .'

Fortune's wheel does turn. Indeed. And quickly sometimes. The past week, the week of his convalescence, had been filled with fairly remarkable reversals. St Thomas' had decided to keep him in for observation. He'd mentioned his doomed, cancerous penis to the attending doctor. The doctor had brought a colleague from oncology in to examine Kennedy's troubled organ and, well, to say that old Dr Beaufort in Harley Street was a quack would be putting it mildly. It was possible the last copy of the *Lancet* he'd read might also have carried news of the discovery of penicillin. A feature on leeches. Spengler's input here had almost cost him a lot more than the integrity of his screenplay. There would have to be surgery, yes, but minor. The growth was benign. Kennedy would have a small scar, an ivory welt on the top of his dick, but that would most likely be all. And God bless the NHS.

He rang Spengler, expecting to get no further than a flunky – but still intending to give him or her a piece of his mind to pass on to their boss, and also to warn him that his beloved and ruinously expensive doctor was in fact a sub-Mengele lunatic who shouldn't be allowed near cattle – and got an unexpected response. Spengler took the call. He was very pleased to hear from Kennedy. He apologised about Paige (well, after a fashion: 'Hey, if I'd known you were that into her I'd never have gone there. I mean – you're a bro, right? I thought she was just some fangirl you were banging.'), and brushed the warning about Beaufort aside ('Really? Wow. Whaddya know? Fuckin' Limey doctors.'), before going on to give Kennedy some genuinely surprising news.

The studio's reaction to the rough cut had been incredible. 'Gonna be a smash, buddy. Let's start thinking about the sequel. This piece of shit opens like we all think it's going to then you're looking at a blank fuckin' cheque. Write your own ticket, pal.' The movie business – you had to love it. You could most likely batter the producer unconscious, fuck the star in the ass, give the director a petrol enema and, if the cards were good, you came up smelling of roses. But Kennedy wouldn't be doing that. No more. Let some other schmuck write some God-awful sequel to something that shouldn't have been made in the first place. Let someone else bank that colossal fee and those residuals cheques from the WGA. Let them spend months and years of pain creating something that'd very likely only exist as a Netflix embar-rassment in twenty years.

Kennedy had other plans.

A strange thing had occurred in hospital. On the morning of the third day he'd woken up and felt, strangely, unaccountably, well, *marvellous.* It took him a while to figure it out. It couldn't have been some incredible drug therapy – he wasn't on anything. Finally it came to him. He hadn't had a drink in three days. Not having a hangover. Fuck – *this* was what it was like. It was like Saturday morning when you were fifteen years old.

He'd only had one visitor during that time – Connie. The only person he'd told about what had happened. (Millie, Robin and Patrick – the only people who really cared – thought he was in London for the week going over the rough cut of the film. He'd explained the bandage with a 'drunk, slipped' coverall.) Connie did the super-agent stuff: she sent books and magazines and hampers from Fortnum's. She visited every day and she cried when he told her what he'd very nearly done, the whole story leading up to it. He talked the way he should maybe have been speaking to someone like Dr Brendle for a long time. She'd dabbed her eyes and smiled at him, taken his hand, and said, 'Just write it, darling. All of it. Make me cry.'

He'd started outlining the novel during his last few days at St Thomas'. It came in great chunks, the curtains drawn around his bed late at night, the little reading light on as he filled page after page of an A4 legal pad in longhand. Premise, plot, characters, set pieces. He felt twenty-five years old again. Outlining? He was already nearly ready to begin the great lonely journey. Crossing the Atlantic, in a bathtub. Much angry grey water all around, terrible beasts sliding around in the fathoms beneath you, but knowing that land was out there, somewhere, on the other side. He even had a title in mind – *Straight White Male*. He quite liked that. It was the kind of title that would live on every page and was full of arrogance and delusion, like its creator.

'. . . the word of the Lord,' Kennedy finished and closed the Bible. He looked up into the faces of his loved ones – Patrick, Millie and Robin were all smiling, knowing what the hypocrisy would have cost him.

After the chapel, to the cemetery along the road. A freezing December day, the week before Christmas. A cold wind whipping in from the Irish Sea. The ferries coming and going down at the port. The Martello Towers dotting the coastline in the distance. *Stately plump Buck Mulligan.* Him and Patrick, three of their cousins and Robin were charged with lowering the coffin into the ground. Robin was nervous, terrified she'd drop the cord, even though the thing was absurdly light considering it contained what had once been his mother. Four and a half stone she'd been at the end. What – sixty pounds in American money? Between six people? Ten pounds each. A few bags of sugar. Robin stood opposite him – her eyes watering, streaming in the cold wind, her tongue protruding a tiny bit from between her teeth, as it did at moments of great concentration, as she fed the black cord carefully through her fingers. There she went, to the inevitable, shadows spreading like a stain across the coffin lid as it disappeared down into the earth. The one who started it all, whose gaze had been the first to meet his with love. He would deal with it, the guilt. Like everything else a way would be found to coexist with it. Looking at Robin he knew this now. Suicide, that beautiful luxury. Once you have children, it really was off the menu.

Then the flowers, pale yellow roses thrown by the grand-children, patterning softly onto the pine lid, and the priest was thanking them for coming and inviting everyone to join the family for refreshments at Patrick's house, where there was a fair spread laid on. Buried with ham, as they used to say. Kennedy watched Millie talking to Patrick's wife, her head inclined, nodding sympathetically. He put his arm around Robin's shoulder and said, 'Come with your old daddy for a wee walk now.'

The two of them took a path that led away from the other mourners, who were all following the main avenue of the cemetery back up to where the cars were parked – the great, black hearse, gleaming in the brilliant winter sun. They wandered along, making a left, then a right through the frosted headstones, Kennedy being mildly surprised at how well he remembered the location after such a long time. A decade now. Four, five, six graves along and there it was on the right:

GERALDINE MARR
BELOVED DAUGHTER & SISTER
1971–2003
'In balance with this life, this death.'

'Aunt Gerry,' Robin said quietly.

He'd chosen the quotation, from 'An Irish Airman Foresees His Death'. Ma had left it to him. Kennedy had felt it appropriate – the parallels between the life of Yeats's fighter pilot and the junkie: lonely impulses and cloudy tumults. Yes, the writer too.

'Do you remember her at all?' Kennedy asked.

'Not really. I think . . . we met her that one time. In London?'

'We did. We did.'

On Kensington Park Road, in the winter of 2001, a cold day like today. Lunch at Osteria, Kennedy's treat. Gerry had been just out of prison. Bound for Brighton and a 'fresh start'. Robin had been four at the time and still a nightmare in restaurants. He remembered asking the waiter to bring her some ice cream to have while they ate their entrées – terrible parenting, but the only way you were guaranteed five minutes' peace back then.

'Do you think about her much, Dad?'

For Robin that lunch had been an entire sentient lifetime ago. Just last week for Kennedy. Yesterday morning.

He remembered her wearing her little beige fur-trimmed parka and mittens. Millie in that grey cashmere coat from Agnès B she used to love, one of the first nice things he'd bought her. He remembered how Gerry's coat had been too thin and that she'd looked tired and dark-eyed over the steaming plate of risotto – the ferry from Dun Laoghaire to Holyhead and then some bus, some mad dole cruiser to Victoria. But she'd been filled with optimism, with talk of bar work, overtime and a friend who was making *four hundred euros a week, Kennedy!* He remembered walking up the Portobello Road after lunch, a man pulling a Christmas tree along behind him like a corpse. They'd bumped into his friend Ed near the corner of Lancaster Road and Robin couldn't pronounce his name, she'd called him 'Bed' and they'd laughed. 'Bye, Bed.' He remembered . . . he remembered everything. Existence was still the job.

'Every day, Robin. Every single day.'

He felt something in the small of his back – his daughter's arm going round him, her head resting on his shoulder. Tall now. Nearly as tall as he was. He looked at the crown of her head, smelt her hair. The boundless urge to protect and to nurture. And yet, a few years older, unknown to him, in the right dress, in the right light, the urges all flowing the other way. O cruel wiring.

'Ach, the dead only have one thing to say to us, Robin.'

She looked up at her father and waited.

'Live,' Kennedy said, smiling. '*Live.*'

He'd written that once, in a book.

They stood there, looking at his sister's grave, their breath pluming smoky into the air, and Kennedy, always working, always a bit of him somewhere else, always most fully alive when alone, imagined the camera pulling away from them now, a crane shot, tracking back and up, higher and higher, the platform silent on its metal track, the cemetery beginning to fill the screen as the headstones stretched away for hundreds of yards all around them, silent beneath the cold, clear Irish sky.